AN
EYE
FOR
AN
EYE

ALSO BY CAROL WYER

Detective Natalie Ward series:

The Birthday
Last Lullaby
The Dare
The Sleepover
The Blossom Twins
The Secret Admirer
Somebody's Daughter

Detective Robyn Carter series:

Little Girl Lost
Secrets of the Dead
The Missing Girls
The Silent Children
The Chosen Ones

Comedies:

Life Swap
Take a Chance on Me
What Happens in France
Suddenly Single

AN EYE FOR AN EYE

CAROL WYER

THOMAS & MERCER

Text copyright © 2021 by Carol Wyer
All rights reserved.

Published by Thomas & Mercer, Seattle

www.apub.com

Amazon, the Amazon logo, and Thomas & Mercer are trademarks of Amazon.com, Inc., or its affiliates.

ISBN-13: 9781542020985
ISBN-10: 1542020980

Cover design by Dominic Forbes

Printed in the United States of America

AN
EYE
FOR
AN
EYE

AN
EYE
FOR
AN
EYE

PROLOGUE

MARCH 2021

Kate blamed her clumsiness on the erratic swaying of the outdated train, rather than the wine she'd drunk, or the little white pills she'd taken to help her get through the flesh-pressing, back-slapping event. She preferred to work the investigations rather than be commended for her, or her team's, actions. The pills had been necessary. The wine had not.

In the small train bathroom, Kate rinsed her palms with cold water. She had got through the event and could concentrate again on day-to-day business. Rather than pointlessly networking, she would rather have been wrapping up a recent drugs bust. Her thoughts were interrupted by the buzzing of her mobile phone. She shook her hands dry then slid the device from her pocket, and as she did, the train lurched to the left, sending her phone skidding towards the toilet. With an exasperated click of her tongue she leant forward to retrieve it, but it was trapped behind the cistern. She manoeuvred her body into the space between the toilet and the wall, and slid down to capture it between her long slim fingers. No sooner had she gripped it than the train lurched once more and the bathroom door flew open, smashing against the steel bowl with a clatter.

The noise took her by surprise. The stupid latch hadn't caught properly. Or had she not locked it? The alcohol was to blame. It had impaired her faculties. She probably forgot to lock it. Now, stuck behind the door, she shoved it away with her elbow in annoyance. Aided by the swaying train, it shut, allowing her to back away from the toilet, phone in hand. The screen displayed 'Unknown Caller'.

She edged back into the corridor, turning right towards the doors with 'First Class' etched into the frosted glass, before pausing to gain balance on the swaying train. At first, she didn't register the sound of popping, like a champagne cork, but when it happened a second time she looked up. She blinked.

No.

It isn't possible. Not again.

Her brain scrambled to make sense of the scene in front of her. The fuzziness she'd been experiencing vanished, and the wine she'd drunk transformed into a giant acidic lump in her throat.

Ahead of her, a figure marched through the train car. His arm was raised and in it a weapon swung left and right, systematically shooting passengers.

Pop!

A piercing scream rose only to be wiped out by the train's gears.

Shards of ice travelled through every vein in her body, and for the first time in her life, DI Kate Young was paralysed with fear. Suddenly, the bathroom door swinging open made sense. The man had kicked it in to check no one was inside. The very act of forgetting to lock it might have saved her life.

She had no time to reflect. One part of her brain screamed at her to run and hide and a voice in her head anchored her to the spot.

It's happening again. A gunman was wiping out the train. What if he wasn't acting alone and there were others with him, callously

2

taking the lives of men, women and children? There could be another killer behind her. What should she do?

Pop!

She glanced behind her, towards the shut metal doors separating the carriages. There was nobody. At least, not yet. The man in first class might be a loner. She had to hope he was. Training and instinct finally took over as she pressed herself against the wall of the speeding train, knees knocking and heart smashing against her ribcage. She had to act, and quickly. She inhaled deeply and then reached for the door handle, tugged it downwards, and raced through the gap as the doors parted. The man was ahead. Four paces . . . three paces . . . two paces. She was within striking distance. She extended her arm, ready to surprise him, grab him around the neck, pull him to the floor and disarm him. Somebody leapt up and blocked the aisle.

'Kate!' It was a soft growl. Superintendent John Dickson's face was grim. 'Sit down, Kate.'

The train rattled from side to side, shaking her back to reality. An unlatched window slapped shut. *Pop!* The man she'd almost attacked was unaware of what had happened and continued through the train carriage and out of the far doors. There was no gun in his hand, only a rolled-up copy of the *Metro*. John's warm hand firmly grasped her upper arm, his fingers digging into the soft flesh. Confusion washed over her. She'd been so certain of what she'd seen. She edged back into her seat. John squeezed in beside her.

'John, what just happened?' she whispered

'You almost injured a member of the public, but you caught a lucky break. I was watching out for you. You've been jumping at shadows ever since . . . ever since . . . well, we don't need to discuss the matter. Not here.'

3

His voice drifted over her. She stared ahead, hands gripping the armrest, heart thumping solidly in her chest. What was the matter with her? She never got it wrong.

'Kate . . . I'm saying this as a concerned colleague, rather than your boss. Your reaction was understandable. You've been under an enormous amount of strain recently, but you can't keep pushing yourself. I know you were against taking too much time off in January and you threw yourself back into work against all advice, but this proves we're right to be worried about you. You should *not* be here.'

She stared at him. What did he mean? She'd proven herself competent, hadn't she? The incident two months ago had been traumatic, but she and other officers affected by it had taken some time off and attended the counselling offered at the time.

This was a blip. The pills. It was most likely the pills that had made her jump to conclusions. She cursed herself for mixing them with alcohol. Surely Superintendent Dickson knew this slip-up was uncharacteristic of her?

She focused on his lips. He was still speaking. She tuned back in. His voice was like melted butter. 'I want you to take extended leave, maybe go on holiday, get away for a while in the sunshine. It'd do you good.'

She had been working hard – maybe too hard, but it was understandable, wasn't it? She'd been trying to get to the truth for two months. She couldn't take time off. Not yet.

Dickson's face was pure sincerity, but a voice in her head exactly like her husband Chris's scoffed, *'Time away from the force, so you can't rattle any cages.'*

'I'm fine. Just a little tired . . . the wine.'

'No, Kate. You need to take some proper time off. And that's an order.' He returned his attention to the book lying face down on the table, leaving her with her thoughts.

'He's worried, Kate. And worried men have something to hide.'

CHAPTER ONE

FRIDAY, 4 JUNE 2021 – MORNING

Kate was trying not to scream. Anguished howls reverberated in her head. She scrabbled for sanity and found it hidden in the recesses of her mind. She knew she was dreaming. The same nightmare she'd had almost every night for the last two months. She would wake up. She had to ride it out, control it like Dr Franklin had told her.

'Part of your brain will comprehend you're experiencing a nightmare, no matter how real it feels, and your mind will protect you. Let your consciousness assimilate what is happening to you and, in time, it will learn to influence what ensues in the nightmare. You can control it.'

Stood in the swaying corridor of the four-thirty train from Euston, Kate pressed her back against the wall of the corridor, spread her feet to gain balance and thumbed the mobile. What kept her rooted to her spot was the sight of the shadowy figure beyond the closed doors, head and shoulders turning left and right as it advanced up the aisle, systematically picking off the occupants, one by one.

Dr Franklin was right. This was a lucid dream and no matter how much Kate wanted to influence the outcome, she was powerless to do anything other than observe. The murderer moved slowly, so slowly. Kate's fingers, slick with sweat, slid over the mobile's screen and she pressed the phone to her ear.

The whooshing and clunking of the train's coupling as it stretched and strained in the corridor drowned out the voice at the other end of the line. Kate spoke, but there was no sound. It was as if the soundtrack in her head had been muted. Then came another sound, like the chattering of a thousand excited parrots.

The noise amplified and the parrots transformed into something more recognisable, a regular sound: an alarm. Kate's limbs were incapable of movement. She willed her hand to lift and silence the noise coming from her bedside table, but it refused to cooperate, and too foggy with sleep, Kate remained immobile. There was a grunt behind her and the din ceased.

Kate fought for consciousness, desperate to shake off the horrendous nightmare.

'Bad night?' Chris asked. He asked the same question most mornings, even though most mornings she didn't reply. She didn't need to. The sweat-soaked pillow held the answer to his question.

'Yes. The usual.'

'The doctor explained it would be like this for quite some time. You know, Kate, those pills aren't helping you. Maybe you should lay off them.'

Her lips felt numb as she mumbled, 'I will.'

'I mean it, Kate. You're so . . . well . . . not yourself these days. You should ditch the pills and think about returning to work.'

'What if I have another lapse and actually harm an innocent person this time?'

'You won't.'

'I might. If Dickson hadn't been there—'

His voice was stern. 'Kate, listen to me. We've spoken about this. You slipped up. You were stressed. The guy looked suspicious. You reacted appropriately to what you thought was happening at the time. Hardly a big surprise, given what happened to—'

'Don't. Don't talk about it. Stop right now.' She pulled the duvet over her ears. She didn't want to discuss the matter any further. She'd screwed up and it hurt. She'd valued her reputation, pleased to follow in her father's footsteps, proud of what she'd achieved, and one action had negated everything she'd striven for. The fact she'd slipped up in front of Dickson was even worse.

Chris fell silent for a moment then asked, 'You okay?'

'Yes. Thanks.' Chris had always been there for her. He would never let her down. In that she had supreme confidence. She loved the very bones of this man. *The very bones*. It had been one of her father's expressions. In this case, as eye-rolling as it was, Kate felt it was true.

She'd met Chris at an accident scene in September 2015. She'd been off duty when she witnessed the foreign lorry, oblivious to the BMW overtaking it, swerve from the middle carriageway of the M6 into the fast lane and propel the car into the central reservation. Hit with such force, the BMW had been thrown into the air, then, rolling over and over, it had landed on the opposite carriageway, mangled and torn. The services had arrived promptly, but Kate had been on the scene immediately. The occupant of the car was alive, his face bruised but with broad features and the greenest eyes she'd ever seen. His legs had been trapped by the steering wheel and crumpled metalwork. He didn't appear overwhelmed by what had happened. It was the shock and adrenalin that had protected him and so Kate stayed with him, talking to him the whole time as they waited for help.

He'd been surprisingly articulate, given the situation. 'I know it sounds stupid,' he'd said to her, 'but could you hold my hand? I'd feel better if you did.'

She'd taken his wide hand in her own and held it gently.

'You have lovely soft hands,' he'd said, his eyelids fluttering as he began to drift out of consciousness.

She was losing him. She couldn't let that happen. She squeezed his hand and, when he focused on her, grinned at him. 'It's not the worst chat-up line I've heard.'

'When I get out of here, I'll treat you to some truly awful chat-up lines.'

'I'll look forward to that. But I'm paying. My treat.'

'Bossy.'

'Yes, I am.'

'I like that.'

She'd stayed. Right up to the point the paramedics and firemen asked her to move aside, and then she'd reluctantly done as requested, anxious for the stranger, now unconscious. She'd stood beside the roadside while they cut him free from the wreckage and lifted him into the air ambulance to transport him to hospital, and she'd driven the forty miles to Stoke-on-Trent hospital immediately afterwards, where she'd waited to hear how he was. She'd stayed all night, and the following morning, at five o'clock, when he'd come around from the operation to repair his shattered leg, she'd been his first visitor. The man with the sea-green eyes had somehow smashed through the invisible armour she wore to protect herself from feeling too deeply.

The bedcovers shifted as Chris sat up. The warm, comfortable sensation was replaced by cool air.

Her heart felt easier. The first rays of light were creeping through the gaps in the curtains and a car was starting up outside, its engine chugging into life. People were stirring, getting into their daily routines. Kate would get into hers. She'd go for a run, shower and then . . . Sleep was coming for her again, wrapping its tentacles around her and dragging her back from the surface. This time she relaxed into it, allowing it to pull her into its soft embrace, and she sank into a dreamless, numbing sleep.

◆　◆　◆

When she awoke later it was with a mouth dry and stale, the product of the medication. The bitter taste in her mouth made her grimace. She plodded downstairs, still in her nightwear – one of Chris's old work shirts. No one would see her. What did it matter if she hung about the place dressed for bed? It wasn't as if she had to be anywhere. A stab of shame made her consider pulling on her running gear and going out. She'd let her exercise routine slide badly. It'd been a while since she'd taken the usual route through the park and around the lake, alternating sprints with longer periods of jogging, before stopping beside the gnarled chestnut tree to go through a rigorous exercise and stretch routine that would leave her shiny with sweat and high on endorphins. *Two months, to be exact.* Another day off wouldn't hurt. The pills. Chris was right. She should give them up, but they took the edge off her nerves and helped her through the mind-numbing days. She needed them. Maybe she could cut down. Little by little.

She poured filtered water into a glass, popped two from the silver-foil packet next to the kettle, and downed them. The liquid slipped down her throat, a cool, refreshing trickle. She dropped on to the bar stool next to the trendy island, all thoughts evaporating as she stared with unfocused eyes into space.

A clatter of the letterbox brought her back to her senses. She'd no idea how long she'd been transfixed. She lost a lot of time these days. Anaesthetised was good. She collected the letter – junk mail – and threw it on the kitchen top, her attention drawn to the cereal box standing there. Chris had scrawled on a sticky note and stuck it to the box. She read it and chuckled.

'These are yummy. Please buy some more of them.'

He'd added a smiley face. Chris always ate breakfast, no matter what time he got up. She'd known him settle down with a bowl of cereal at 2 a.m. This variety contained chocolate pieces. She'd buy him some more when she went to the shops. Would she go today? She put on the radio and turned it off almost immediately. The music hurt her ears, making her wince. Who'd have thought auditory senses could be so sensitive? She trudged to the sink and stared into the garden, focusing on a clump of wild poppies with vivid scarlet petals that had chosen to grow in the garden border. Why had they seeded here? Poppies were for remembrance, and she didn't want to remember. She wanted to forget.

A local landscaping company had designed the area for the busy couple who didn't enjoy gardening, and succeeded in producing a garden with low-maintenance plants and shrubs producing all-year-round colour, AstroTurf that looked like real grass, and wooden decking, perfect for entertaining. The decking had been her choice; the fire pit for barbecues, with the semi-circular stone seating, had been Chris's. The first year, they'd hung up palm-tree-shaped fairy lights for a tropical feel, and on the warm summer evenings, they'd snuggled up on plump cushions, replete with feasts of grilled meat, to watch the fire as it glowed crimson reds and deep orange until it finally died away. The second year, the summer hadn't been so kind to them and they'd spent less time outside. The cushions housed in the blue-painted garden house at the bottom of the garden hadn't been out for a long time. *Five years?* Chris had taken on more assignments. He'd received the recognition he deserved, but that success meant longer spells away and she, well, Kate had always been a career woman. They ought to make more time to enjoy the fire pit and romantic seating. She'd drag out the fairy lights and see if they still worked . . .

The figure walks down the carriage, his back to her, gun in his hand.

She blinked hard to dispel the image. The pills were having an effect. A familiar haze was descending, wrapping itself around her like an invisible soft blanket. She wound her arms around herself protectively. *Deep breaths. In. Out. In.* The image of the train carriage swam out of view as she let out a final lengthy breath. With slow movements she made her way to the kettle, filled it. She must unearth the fairy lights. It would be nice to sit outside. It was beginning to feel warmer of an evening. The ring of the doorbell jerked her from her reverie and she ambled into the hall once more.

The person who greeted her was the last she expected to see. DCI William Chase, dressed in jeans and a checked shirt better suited to a cowboy than a fifty-eight-year-old detective, was standing awkwardly, a small bunch of flowers in his meaty hands. His chestnut eyes bore an apologetic look, eyebrows half-raised as if expecting confrontation.

He thrust the flowers towards her. 'From the boys. Their favourites.'

By 'boys', William meant his bees. He was a keen apiarist with several hives on an allotment, and actively promoted the protection of bees. She took the bouquet of freesias, breathing in their perfume and admired the rich golden hues of their delicate petals.

'Come in, William,' she said.

'I'm sorry,' he mumbled. 'Is it a bad time?'

'It's always a bad time.' She left the door open and moved off, leaving him to wipe his feet and follow her into the kitchen. He took a seat without being invited to do so, and watched in silence as she filled a glass vase and dropped in the flowers before placing them on the kitchen table. 'They're beautiful. Tell the boys they have good taste.'

'I shall.' His eyes searched her face. 'Kate, I'm not going to beat about the bush, here.'

Kate had always got on exceptionally well with William. He was more than her DCI; he was a close family friend, somebody who had stood by her throughout her life and career.

'What is it?'

William's jowls had sagged, creating creases in his neck, giving him an appearance of a tortoise, an impression further enhanced as he craned his neck to look in the direction of the garden. Over the years, his once jet-black eyebrows had turned the same grey as his hair, which in turn had thinned to reveal a pate spotted with dark liver patches, but his eyes were still as bright as the day he'd taken over the department.

He cast them on her. 'Superintendent Dickson wants you back. He's asked for you.'

'He has?'

'Yes.'

'I don't think I'm ready,' she said, turning away from him. Outside, a few drops of rain splattered against the window. Maybe today wasn't a good day to fetch the cushions and fairy lights from the shed.

'I know it's been tough for you, and I understand if you want to take more time off, but you have to face up to coming back at some point. You're not a quitter, Kate.'

William had been one of her father's closest friends. If she closed her eyes, she could conjure up an image of the two of them chugging cans of beer, laughing and joking in her dad's kitchen. William was one of the reasons she'd joined the force, and in spite of his relationship with her father, he'd never shown any favouritism when it came to work. He'd treated her as he did all his officers, and that was how she'd wanted it. He wouldn't have come here today to ask her to return to work without good cause. 'Why me?'

'Because you're the best we have.'

'What if I screw up again? I messed up on the train and in front of him. I'm surprised he wants me back.'

William let the ensuing silence hang between them and cast his eyes around the pristine kitchen. It looked like it had been prepared for a photoshoot for a home-and-garden glossy magazine feature – almost too clean, nothing out of place, and no impression of anyone actually living in or using it.

'You're blowing it out of proportion. You'd been under extraordinary pressure and made a mistake. Nothing bad came of it.'

'He saw me, William. The superintendent stopped me from injuring an innocent man and if he hadn't hauled me back in time, heaven knows what would have happened.'

'But nothing happened, and he wouldn't have requested you if he didn't think you were up to the job. Kate, we need you. Look at you. What are you doing with your days? Cleaning? You're wasting your talent here. You need people around you. You need to feel part of a team again. You're holed up here like a hermit.'

She suppressed the urge to reply, 'No, I have Chris.'

When, instead of responding, she studied her feet and wouldn't meet his gaze, he asked quietly, 'Do you want to spend the rest of your life like this? The Kate I know would want to fight back, get back into action and right wrongs. That's what the Kate I know does, and she's bloody good at it.'

Kate swallowed. 'I don't think I am *that* Kate any more.'

'Okay, let me ask you this, then. Would you head a small team, you and two officers of your choosing, for me? It's *me* asking you to come back. I need your expertise on this, Kate. You're still my finest officer.'

'I'm not so sure.' Kate considered the endless ritual of house-cleaning she'd adopted, rubbing away at surfaces as if she could erase the past, the fog-filled days, the lack of meaning to her life and the memories she tried so hard to banish. Would focus on a

13

case help to loosen their grip on her every waking and sleeping moment? She had a lot of time for William. When her father had been moved to the care home, William had visited him every single week without fail, even when her father no longer recognised anybody: not William, not Chris and not Kate. She shrugged off the morbid thoughts.

As if reading her mind, William spoke. 'It will help you find yourself again. I know you, Kate. I know how you operate, and you'll bury yourself in the investigation until you get a result and you'll emerge stronger from it. I've known you since you were a small child. I've watched you grow. I'm asking you to do this for different reasons to Superintendent Dickson. I want you to take it on for *you*. I want the old Kate to resurface. She's only temporarily out of sight. She's still there. She needs to be coaxed out.'

The kindness in his voice brought a lump to her throat. A vision flashed before her, of William, eyes glassy with tears but spine ramrod straight and head held high, as together they'd stood shoulder to shoulder while her father's coffin was lowered into the earth.

'Okay,' she said. 'I'll do it.'

CHAPTER TWO

FRIDAY, 4 JUNE – LATE MORNING

Ervin Saunders, Head of Forensics, showed Kate into the laboratory. Light flooded into the room through high windows from which it was impossible to view the university campus below. A woman with flawless midnight skin looked up from a microscope. She was more suited to a catwalk than the laboratory. Her ebony hair had been twirled artistically into a barrette. Her face was almost perfectly symmetrical; a perfect example of what is called 'the golden ratio'.

'Faith Katakwa, our newest recruit,' said Ervin. 'So eager to join us, she wrote countless begging emails to me. My reputation is fearsome.' He straightened his waistcoat with a flourish.

Ervin was deemed as slightly off the wall by most of his colleagues, giving off an air of mad professor meets nineteenth-century dandy. He'd once confided in Kate that he purchased his clothes in charity shops, or from special boutiques, pandering to others with similar sartorial elegance, and was no stranger to a sewing machine. He'd run up many of his more flamboyant outfits himself. At work he was more restrained, and today was wearing a tweed three-piece ensemble with shiny brogues.

Kate liked Ervin hugely. Whilst some thought him bizarre and pedantic in his ponderings, she found him thorough and dedicated.

Nothing escaped his attention, not the slightest piece of evidence or detail.

Faith shrugged. 'I'd heard he was the greatest.'

'Hush! My ego can't stand so much pampering. I'll be impossible to work with for the rest of the day if you keep up such flattery,' he replied with a twinkle.

Ervin guided Kate to a bench where several photographs and a report were laid out in preparation for her visit.

'Alex Corby,' he said, tapping the first picture. 'It wasn't pretty. Not that murder ever is, but this one can be summed up in three words: clinical, calculating and thorough.'

Kate studied the first picture of Alex Corby, face contorted and bloodied, fat tongue extended. Ervin folded his arms and adapted the stance of a lecturer addressing a small group of students; right foot forward, head to one side.

'I appreciate this is all conjecture on my part, but I know you like to hear my opinion and I think the murderer tortured Alex by widening his mouth with an implement not left behind at the crime scene. There were signs of external and internal bruising around the mouth and lips. We found no fibres in his mouth, but we uncovered microscopic fragments of metal, from which I deduced the object in question was metallic.'

Kate nodded. Ervin unfolded his arms and pointed to the second picture. 'As you can see, his hands and feet were secured with cable ties, the type you can find in any DIY store.' The photograph showed Corby as described, his mouth agape, and with hands tied behind the back of an ornate dining chair. 'And last but not least, one of his eyes was removed, and we have not yet found it.'

'Before or after death?' Kate asked, lifting the picture to study it more closely. Alex's right eye socket was empty and encrusted with rust-coloured blood.

'We can't be certain. Harvey Fuller is the pathologist on this and will undoubtedly have a better idea.'

Kate swallowed. Corby's face was a mess.

'There was a foreign object lodged in his pharynx, which we identified as a tiny piece of apple and that was the likely cause of his death. There were remains of a sliced and diced apple at the crime scene.'

He pointed to yet another photograph, this time of a white china plate containing a red apple chopped in sections, its white flesh browned due to exposure to the air. An antique silver fruit knife with a glistening mother-of-pearl handle had been left on the same plate next to the fruit.

'Let me get this straight,' Kate said. 'The killer removed the metal instrument they used to torture Corby, but left behind the apple, used to choke him, and this knife?'

'Spot on. And here's the surprise: the knife's an antique, a Colen Hewer Cheshire made about 1880, and worth at least sixty pounds. It's one of a set we found in a cutlery drawer in the dining room. The killer either didn't know its value or wasn't interested in taking it.'

Kate rubbed her cheek. The knife bothered her. Would the killer be sufficiently educated to use a fruit knife to chop up an apple? 'Were there other types of knives in the drawer?'

Ervin nodded knowingly. 'Small and large, yet this perpetrator chose the fruit knife.'

'What about the apple? Was it already in the house?'

'There was a fruit bowl in the kitchen, but it only contained a bunch of bananas and, given there were no other apples in the fridge, I can't confirm that with any certainty.'

'Okay. Thanks.'

'Anything you want, just shout out. We're under strict instructions to give you as much assistance as possible.'

Those orders would have come from Superintendent Dickson. She'd discovered during her briefing with William that Dickson and Corby had been roommates at public school and remained good friends ever since. It came as no surprise to Kate that he'd want full cooperation from everybody on this.

'Any chance this was a burglary gone wrong?'

Ervin shook his head. 'Corby was wearing a Rolex and a wedding ring. We found his wallet, containing several credit cards and about a hundred pounds in notes, on the kitchen top. There was nothing obvious missing: televisions, computer, mobile phone, PlayStation, all in situ, and no evidence of any disruption. There were no drawers pulled out or any pictures removed. We discovered a safe in a wardrobe in the master bedroom, but it was locked and no fingerprints on it other than Corby's. In brief, the perpetrator left no evidence. Obviously, we've still got a team conducting a full investigation at the house, and Faith and I are sifting through all the potential evidence we've received, but for the time being it appears somebody entered with the sole intention of murdering Corby, and they took their time doing so.'

'Any idea of time of death?'

'We think yesterday. Mid-morning to mid-afternoon.'

'Thanks, Ervin. And you too, Faith.' She nodded in the direction of the woman who'd been quietly examining slides the entire time Kate had been there.

Faith returned her smile. 'It was nice to finally meet you.'

'I'd better talk to Harvey and see how he's getting on. I'll give you a call later. Am I okay to take these photographs?'

Ervin scooped them up from the table in one movement and placed them into her hands. 'All yours, Kate.' He walked with her to the far end of the laboratory and whispered as they neared the door, 'How are you holding up? Honestly?'

Her heart rate began to gallop and panic threatened to race through her veins, but she controlled it long enough to say, 'I'm okay. Really.'

He stooped a little, rested his hands gently on both her shoulders and gazed directly at her. 'I know you think you can handle everything without any support, but there are some of us who want to help, Kate. Ring me if you need anything. Anything at all.'

She nodded dumbly and left before the shaking became too hard to disguise. *Focus*, she told herself. *Focus on the investigation.* She squeezed her eyelids together and took a deep breath . . .

◆ ◆ ◆

The train pounds the rails like a demented monster, oblivious to the carnage on board. The shadowy figure moves relentlessly through the first-class carriage.

A shout.

The pop of a gun.

Screams.

◆ ◆ ◆

Grey tendrils of mist blurred her vision as she drove away. She fought the rising fear. She could do this. She *could* face her colleagues, even though news of her breakdown would have reached every one of them within an hour of it happening. The fact she'd lost face with them, the day she messed up on the train, pained her deeply. It would be a long, hard climb back up to the elevated position she'd enjoyed before her faux pas.

The clouds, pregnant with water, sucked all colour from the landscape and even the rainbow-hued planters by the bus shelter seemed monochrome. Somebody had spray-painted the word 'scum' on the back wall of the wooden shelter, above the heads of several passengers hunched on a plastic bench. Their eyes seemed to follow her as she passed them, tyres splashing through freshly formed puddles.

It was a mercifully short hop from the university campus, where the forensic laboratory was situated, to the police station, a solid brick-built building with few windows and a wooden faded blue door. It hadn't been modernised in decades and even had the original old police lamp hanging outside. The door required a hefty push, and Kate noticed it made the same comforting groan it had always made. Nobody had oiled the hinges since her absence, which, for some reason, pleased her. She'd practised some deep breathing in her car before entering and her hands had stopped trembling; she would pass for a seasoned, confident detective even if her inner self was waiting for inevitable asides, remarks or put-downs about the incident on the train. Some people got a lot of mileage out of others' mistakes, and although it had happened in March, she was prepared for any sarcastic comments. The entrance was as old-fashioned as the exterior, a waist-high formal desk at the far end of a dowdy room containing waiting-room chairs against cream walls with photographs of missing persons and notices about protecting homes from unwanted intruders. This wasn't the main station, but an annex to the modern, high-tech, purpose-built headquarters, and the place where for the last three years she had headed a specialised crime unit. It might be jaded and smack of a bygone era, but she felt an affinity with the place, not only because it felt so familiar but because it was where her father had worked before her.

She greeted the desk sergeant and made her way through a door to the corridor and narrow wooden staircase behind reception that led to the landing where she'd be working. With each creak of the stairs, she felt more comfortable. She knew this place. It was part of her DNA. On the first landing, she halted. Her old office, adjacent to a busy ops room, was upstairs, but she wouldn't be using it. She'd been assigned a different room on this floor. Heavy footsteps thundered down the stairs and Neil Cousins, one of the other DIs from upstairs, almost collided with her. He took a step backwards when he recognised her, his face a rainbow of emotions from surprise to concern. His voice was hesitant, the tone of somebody talking to a terminally ill relative.

'Kate! I didn't expect to see you back so soon after—'

She shrugged it off. 'Had to come back sometime. I was getting fed up at home, sitting about with my feet up, watching daytime television. You know, there are no good cop dramas on in the afternoon. It's all quiz shows and soap operas. Never been one for soaps.' She clamped her mouth shut to stop the babble, then regretted it as the look she'd been dreading appeared – the look of sympathy.

'I'm sure you know best, but take it easy. You went through a truly awful ordeal—'

'Kate!' Another voice interrupted the conversation. It was Morgan, one of the officers she'd chosen to assist her on the investigation. At over six foot, with a superb physique, DS Morgan Meredith ought to have been an athlete. He'd played football at county level in his youth but instead of pursuing a sporting career had joined the force at eighteen and was one of the department's rising stars. At twenty-four, he stood every chance of reaching the upper echelons before he hit forty. Kate had picked him because they'd worked closely on several tough cases in the past, and she'd been impressed by his dedication and energy. Not only was Morgan wiser than his years but he could pull several all-nighters in a row without any complaint whatsoever, and he was discreet.

She was grateful to the young man who meandered across, a grin playing across his face. 'Got to tear you away, guv. I've been sent to accompany you to the boss's office. As if you've forgotten where it might be.'

Neil moved off with a 'Right, well, no doubt we'll bump into each other.'

Morgan observed the man's departing back and, lowering his voice, said, 'I wasn't asked to fetch you. You had one of those rabbit-caught-in-the-headlights expressions. I figured you could do with someone to deflect any unwanted attention.'

Her shoulders sagged a little. Neil had almost sent her racing back out to her car. Although she was grateful for Morgan's apparent sixth sense, she was ashamed that she had allowed her panic to show. Neil would have seen it, too. She was undoubtedly the laughing stock of the station and needed to sort her shit out quickly if she was to ride this out. 'Cheers. Had a moment of first-day nerves. Crazy, isn't it?'

His face grew serious. 'No. Perfectly understandable.'

She switched to work mode. 'Are we set up and ready to go?'

'Yes. Emma's trying to work out how to set up equipment in what can only be described as a broom cupboard. Bloody budget cuts. You'd have thought they'd have sorted us out a room in the new building.'

She heard the smile in his voice. The floorboards issued creaking protests as Morgan strode beside her. 'DCI Chase has briefed us. That's to say, he told us we're working directly under you, and the whole thing is to be kept hush-hush. He said you'd fill us in when you arrived. Here we are.'

He pushed open the door, a room next to a cupboard of cleaning supplies. He hadn't been far wrong. The space was cramped with two desks pushed together back to back and a third hard against the wall. There was one window, splattered with a Rorschach inkblot of bird mess that resembled an animal-hide rug. Squeezed into one corner was a whiteboard and pen.

She pointed at it, and Morgan shrugged. 'It was the best they could do for us.'

Twenty-three-year-old DS Emma Donaldson, in a white shirt, black trousers and low-heeled boots, was tapping at a computer keyboard. Under the light of the window, her raven-black bobbed hair shimmered a deep shade of blue, emphasising her pale, delicate face. Emma might look frail to some, but appearances were deceiving and the young woman, who lived with her grandmother on a tough housing estate in Stoke-on-Trent, could handle herself in any situation. Emma had not only grown up with six older brothers but was an expert in tae kwon do, training most evenings at her brother Greg's martial arts academy. She was also as ambitious as Morgan, and together they made a formidable team. Kate couldn't have chosen better.

Emma finished her task and stood up to greet her boss. She lifted a handful of pens placed beside notepads. 'Hi, Kate. I *borrowed* some supplies from one of the briefing rooms and I've got the computers up and running, so we're good to go. Oh, and I got us some water from the canteen. I told Iris it was for you and she gave me all these.'

Ten individual bottles of water stood on the far desk. Iris, a sixty-something widow, had always treated Kate well. She would have to make the trip across to the canteen to thank her, but not yet. She wasn't ready for meeting fellow colleagues or any other staff yet.

She smiled at Emma and, placing her bag on one of the chairs, addressed them both. 'First off, thanks for agreeing to be part of this investigation.'

Morgan rested his back against the wall, a giant in the limited space. 'Elite squad. That's what we are – an elite squad.'

'We can't be a squad. A squad is lots of people. We're only three members. We make up a team,' said Emma.

Morgan widened his shoulders and adopted a body-builder pose, fists together, muscles bulging. 'Like *The A-Team*.'

The corners of Kate's mouth twitched. These two always worked well together. 'Whatever we are, it's to remain under wraps. We're dealing with a sensitive issue – the murder of a VIP.'

Morgan threw Emma a look that said, 'I told you so.'

Kate drew out the photographs Ervin had given her and laid them out on the desk in front of her. 'Alex Corby.'

Emma pulled a face. '*The* Alex Corby of Corby International?'

'Corby International?'

'Morgan! You must have heard of Corby International. They're a massive exporter of British food – from breakfast cereals to chilled meals – based in Stafford. Alex Corby was one of the top ten UK entrepreneurs in 2019. He's worth millions. He was voted one of Britain's sexiest men – last year, too,' said Emma. 'He's pretty fit for an older bloke.'

Morgan gave an exaggerated sigh. 'Ah, there it is. *Fit.* That explains why you know so much about him.'

Emma ignored his teasing. 'It'll be all over the media. When did this happen?'

'His body was discovered yesterday afternoon. His secretary, Lisa Handsworth, tried to contact him and when she couldn't reach him went to the house and spotted him through a window. She raised the alarm. No information's been released to the media yet. Superintendent Dickson has insisted on a media blackout for the moment, partly out of respect for his widow and children, and partly to give us a head start before the news hounds get a sniff of it. Just for info – Alex and he went to school together and were good friends.'

'They won't be able to keep this under wraps for long,' said Morgan, who'd shifted his bulk away from the wall and was bent over the photographs.

'I know. Which is why we need to work as fast as we can. So, let me bring you up to speed. Alex Corby's wife, Fiona, and their two children, Hugh and Jacob, were spending the half-term holiday at their villa in the south of France, leaving Alex home alone. At some point, we think between mid-morning and mid-afternoon, when his body was found, Alex Corby opened the security gates to a person or persons unknown and granted them access to his house. They overpowered him, cable-tied him to a dining-room chair, and tortured him.'

'How?' Emma raised one eyebrow quizzically.

'The killer inserted a metal implement into Alex's mouth, prising it open, and force-fed him small pieces of apple, one of which lodged in his throat and caused asphyxiation. Although the remains of the apple were left behind, the instrument used to torture him was removed from the scene – or so we believe. We don't know what it was, but it made cuts and abrasions on the inside of Alex's cheeks, palate and tongue.' She tapped the relevant photographs as she spoke. 'Forensics are still searching the house and grounds.'

Emma lifted the photograph of the knife and discoloured apple and commented with a shake of her head, 'It's been cut into microscopic pieces, almost all identical.'

'Killer's either a chef or got OCD,' said Morgan.

'It's a valid point, and one worth noting. It helps us piece together a profile of this killer. Methodical. Neat. This was a well-planned attack. We don't know if the plate, knife and apple were already out when the killer arrived, or if they searched for them. Bear both in mind for the time being.' She thought for a second; she had already worked out how best to approach the investigation on her way to the station. It was time to action those strategies. 'I'll talk to Harvey Fuller, the pathologist on this investigation, to confirm what I've told you. I'd like you, Emma, to learn more about Alex Corby and his business. Find out if Corby International has shareholders or board members, or even if Alex had a silent partner, and talk to all of them. Also, see if there have been any business dealings that raise cause for concern, or if anyone has threatened the company, or Corby directly.'

Emma scribbled notes on one of the new pads as Kate spoke.

'Because of the remoteness of the Corby mansion, it's unlikely anybody would have spotted any comings and goings. The house is reached via a lane leading off the B5103 – the main road, linking Uttoxeter and Abbots Bromley to Rugeley, which passes over the reservoir.'

Blithfield Reservoir, constructed in a shallow valley once consisting of farmland and the River Blithe, was an 800-acre man-made lake set below rolling hills and divided roughly in half by the causeway. It was also home to an abundance of wildlife and recognised as an important habitat for wildfowl, which meant it was frequented by visitors keen to explore the ancient woods or participate in recreational activities such as sailing and fishing. For Emma, however, it meant only one thing.

'I know it. It's on the Ironman route,' she said.

The Ironman Triathlon, considered one of the most challenging one-day events, was made up of a 1.9-kilometre swim, followed by a 90-kilometre bicycle ride and finishing with a 21.1-kilometre run, and Emma had competed in the Staffordshire event three times.

'Then you know how rural it is out there. Alex Corby's home is at the end of a private road, off Lea Lane near Admaston, and I believe it overlooks the reservoir. The nearest neighbours are almost a mile away. Can you pinpoint it for us?'

Emma pulled up a map on her screen and zoomed in on the area in question.

Kate traced an invisible circle around the residence. 'Because of its location, there'll be few, if any, surveillance cameras in the vicinity. All the same, I'd like you to search for vehicle movement in this area. We're especially interested in anyone who travelled on the B5013 at any time between mid-morning Thursday into early afternoon. I'll also leave that with you, Emma.' Kate could count on her sharp eyes and patience for such a time-consuming task.

Kate continued. 'I want to check out his home as soon as possible. His wife was contacted last night and is currently making her way back from France to her parents' house near Uttoxeter, but we aren't expecting her to reach there until later this afternoon. I'd like to interview her when she does. I also want to talk to Alex's secretary, Lisa Handsworth. Morgan, you'll accompany me.'

'Guv.'

Outside the station, a lorry sounded its horn noisily, making Kate's heart flutter . . .

The train's horn sounds as it whooshes past a station. It isn't slowing. It isn't stopping. Nobody can help them.

She steadied her nerves, eyes on the photographs. 'There's one more thing. As you can see, Alex's right eye was removed. The killer appears to have taken it with them, probably as a trophy.' Kate was fully aware that taking a trophy would help prolong, and even nourish, the perpetrator's fantasy of the crime. Some stole a victim's wallet, their ID, a lock of hair or a piece of jewellery. It was rare they kept hold of a body part, unless it held a significance for the murderer. 'I'm happy to accept that as a theory, but eyes are considered to be the windows to the soul, and there might be a greater reason the perpetrator is hanging on to it. I've nothing else for the moment. Any questions?'

Emma tucked her hair behind her ears, a sign she was ready for action, and responded for both of them. 'No. All clear.'

'Morgan, give me a couple of minutes to check in with the pathologist, and then we'll pay Alex's secretary a visit.'

He flexed his fingers as if preparing to play a piano. 'I'll make a start on surveillance cameras for you, Emma.'

'Cheers, big man.'

Kate left them to it and, heading into the corridor, rang the pathology lab. She was met with an accent that took her back to a trip she and Chris had made to the Norfolk Broads shortly after they'd moved in together. Chris, who'd hired a sedan-style cruiser, the perfect size for a couple, revealed he was actually able to pilot the *Fair Jubilee*. It was the first boat Kate had ever been on and she'd been mesmerised by its luxury, the spacious bedroom and the corner whirlpool bath. Their plan had been to spend evenings on deck, drinking wine and stargazing, but the weather had had other ideas; so, fed up with the persistent rain, they'd abandoned the boat and got drunk at a pub not far from where they'd hired it. She jerked herself away from the memory, concentrating on the strong drawl at the end of the phone as Harvey introduced himself and explained his findings.

'Alex died of violent asphyxiation through choking. The actual foreign body causing the occlusion of the air passage was lodged between the pharynx and the bifurcation of the trachea. There were twelve pieces of apple in total in his stomach. Unlucky thirteen, slightly larger in size than the others, killed him.'

'Is it possible he was force-fed them until he choked to death?'

'Evidence would suggest so. There are small lesions on his scalp, commensurate with a force being executed on the hair follicles, suggesting somebody tugged hard on his hair to force his head into a recumbent position. The abrasions on the roof and inside his cheeks and the microscopic particles are undoubtedly from a metal implement inserted into his mouth to hold it open, thus preventing him from masticating any food. Furthermore, there's evidence of petechiae around and on the surface of his left eye. This haemorrhaging, caused by pressure build-up, suggests he struggled to cough and dislodge the object in his throat. There's also a bluish tint around his lips, which we usually associate with asphyxiation.

'The object didn't fully obstruct his air passage, so he'd have probably been conscious for several minutes. His brain would've died some four to six minutes after the introduction of the segment. It was, to put it in layman's terms, starved of oxygen.'

'What about his eye? Was it extracted while he was alive?'

'Removed post-death.'

'Did you discover it anywhere on or inside his body?'

'No.'

'What time do you think he was killed?'

'Death occurred sometime between eleven thirty in the morning and two o'clock in the afternoon.'

'Were there any signs of a struggle or fight?'

'Nothing. No trace of any other DNA. We've got further blood tests to run to check for drugs and then we'll be through with him, but if anything else comes to light, I'll get in touch immediately.'

'Thank you, Harvey. Will you send the complete report across?'

'Of course, I will. Nice to chat to you. I've heard so many good things about you. You've certainly not had an easy time of it, yet here you are back in the saddle again.'

Chris had warned her that some people would still be angling for information about the incident on the train. Harvey was doing it. She had to get off the phone before he could say anything else. She excused herself and pressed the 'end call' button.

Returning to the office, she recapped the conversation she'd had. 'So, with regards to CCTV or safety camera footage, search for vehicles in the area between ten and two. We'll extend that window if we think we need to. This attack was as methodical as we suspected. Not only did Alex choke on a slightly larger portion than all the others found in his stomach, it was the thirteenth piece.'

'Triskaidekaphobia,' said Morgan. 'Unlucky thirteen. Stephen Ho in the vice squad told me number four is considered unlucky in Chinese culture because it sounds almost exactly the same as their word for death.'

Emma mumbled, 'Good work, Detective, you've established our killer's unlikely to be Chinese.'

'You should reign in that acerbic wit of yours,' said Morgan, his face mock serious. 'I'm keeping an open mind, as is appropriate in these situations. The killer might be superstitious or be pandering to numerical myth.'

Emma rolled her eyes. 'You need to get a life. You spend too much time reading Wikipedia.'

While she was all for morale-boosting banter, Kate steered the conversation back to the investigation. 'The killer pulled hard on Alex's hair to force his head backwards. I'm wondering if we might be looking for two suspects: one who dropped food into his mouth and another who kept his head in position. It's only a thought, but bear it in mind. Okay. Morgan, let's go visit his secretary.'

Morgan froze the image of the B-road passing through the village of Abbots Bromley close to the reservoir, the timeclock in the corner on Thursday at 10.27 a.m. A green tractor and trailer filled the screen. 'Not spotted a great deal up to this point, Emma. Only a couple of vans. I've made a note of the times. Over to you.'

Emma, her mobile phone tucked into her chin, gave a thumbs-up. Kate picked up her bag and moved back into the corridor. Nobody was about and she hoped she could exit the building before anyone she knew stopped to speak to her. The foil packet in her coat pocket scrunched satisfyingly as she wrapped her fingers around it, and hesitated. The urge to pop a couple of pills was strong. She'd taken one of the bottles of water solely for that purpose, but Morgan's solid footsteps behind her made her reconsider. She didn't want Morgan to see her. Somehow it felt shameful to reveal her reliance on them.

She gave them a squeeze for reassurance and tried to focus her attention on what she'd say to Alex's secretary. Pills would only hamper her judgement. She'd take a couple later, when her body screamed for them, and not before.

CHAPTER THREE

FRIDAY, 4 JUNE – AFTERNOON

The weather suited Kate's mood. Dark clouds had descended, compressing the skyline and creating an air of claustrophobia.

'Not far,' said Morgan. 'It's always a nightmare getting about at this time on a Friday. Bloody traffic. I reckon half this lot are trying to get away for the weekend.'

Kate looked at the car in front of her, the rear loaded with three bicycles on a rack. In front of it was a campervan, and behind the squad car, one with a roof box. Morgan was right. People would travel miles for forty-eight hours by the seaside, far away from their homes and stresses of ordinary life. She couldn't remember when she and Chris had last taken a weekend break.

'It's along this road.' Morgan had turned into a street close to the town centre lined with parked cars, and they crawled forward, searching for Lisa Handsworth's house, reading off numbers of the identical Victorian semi-detached residences, all requiring attention and repairs. Number 58 was no different to the other houses in the street, and parking in the only available spot several metres away, they walked to it. The rusty hinges of the front gate protested loudly as Morgan pushed it open and marched up the cracked, weed-filled pathway. The dingy red paint on the door had peeled away in places to reveal flashes of brown and yellow underneath.

The doorbell repeated a mournful wail several times before they heard bolts being drawn sharply back.

Lisa peered myopically through a face-sized gap and, after scrutinising both ID cards, she opened the door fully to reveal a grey tiled floor and dark hallway. A fat ginger cat sitting on a blue rug caught sight of the visitors and fled up the stairs before they'd fully entered the property.

'That's Butterscotch,' Lisa said. 'He doesn't like many people.'

She walked them into the far room: a kitchen, where she busied herself scraping plates into a bin, then piling them into a dishwasher. 'Sorry. The place is a bit of a mess. I've not been able to do much since—'

'I'm so sorry about Mr Corby,' said Kate, smoothly. 'I'm sure it was a terrible shock to discover him.'

Lisa pulled at a dark strand of hair that had escaped her Alice headband. Whilst certain A-list celebrities like Paloma Faith or Rachel Weisz might be able to carry off the eighties look, the plum velvet accessory stuck up on the secretary's head looked vaguely ridiculous. She gave up tidying her hair, pulled a tissue from the sleeve of a baggy cardigan and blew her nose.

Her eyes filled with tears as she spoke. 'It was horrible. I don't think I'll ever forget it.'

'Come and sit down,' said Kate.

Lisa left the washing up and did as instructed, head lowered.

'Do you feel up to talking to us about it?' Kate was met with a nod. She continued, 'We appreciate your cooperation and silence. It helps give us a head start in the investigation. Can you tell us exactly what happened yesterday – why you went to the house, the lead-up to you going there – anything you think might be relevant?'

Lisa's fingers worried the edges of the tissue, her words ponderous. 'Alex rang me first thing yesterday morning to say he wasn't coming into the office and was going to work from home. A

33

contract we'd been waiting for turned up in the morning's post so I phoned him, and he said he'd come in early afternoon to collect it.'

Kate interrupted her with, 'What time did you ring Alex about the contract?'

'I think it was around ten thirty. The post arrives between ten and ten thirty most days, and I checked through it as soon as it was brought up to the office.'

If Lisa was right with her timings, they'd established Alex was alive and well then. 'Thank you. Please continue.'

'He didn't come in as promised and at lunchtime I rang his mobile again, but it went through to the answering service, so I left a message to say I'd drop the contract off at his house in the afternoon, unless I heard back from him before then.' Lisa blinked away some tears. She'd abandoned the tissue and worried a loose thread of cotton on the bottom button of her cardigan. 'I left the office at half one or so. When I got to his house, the electric gates were open, so I figured he was at home and expecting me. I rang the doorbell, but nobody answered and I thought he might be in the orangery, at the back of the house, and hadn't heard the bell. I went through the side gate and past the dining room, which overlooks the garden, and I don't know what made me look inside, but I did . . . and then I wished I hadn't. Alex was tied to a chair and it was . . . horrific . . . his face was covered in blood and . . . I panicked. The attacker could have still been in the house so I ran like crazy, back to my car, got inside, locked all the doors and then dialled emergency services. I drove down the lane to the road, where I waited for the police.'

Her version tallied with what Kate already knew. The call to the emergency services had come in at 2.25 p.m.

'Did you see, or think you saw, anybody else in the house?'

'No. Everything happened so quickly. One minute I was calling out for Alex and then I spotted him, and then . . . I was shit scared. I dashed for my car.'

34

'It's okay. Yours was a normal reaction. You were frightened. It's understandable. I understand how hard this is for you, but can you think of any little detail that might help us, even if it doesn't seem important?'

'No.'

'And nobody came after you when you drove away?'

Lisa shook her head.

'You didn't see anyone drive past you while you waited for the police?'

'Sorry, no,' Lisa whispered. She suddenly leapt to her feet and dry-heaved into the sink. After several attempts she groaned loudly. 'This is awful.'

Kate explained. 'It's most likely delayed shock. Have you eaten today?'

'No.'

'Then you must. We have officers trained for this sort of situation. Would you like me to send one across?'

Lisa rested her hands on her hips, drew several breaths, and replied, 'I'll be okay. My friend Sam will be over later. This is such a shock. I've worked so closely with Alex for two and a half years. He was more than just a boss.'

Kate digested this information. 'Were you ever more than—'

'No.'

'But you've been to his house before? You knew he worked in the orangery.'

'Sometimes, when he was working from home, he'd ask me to join him there.'

'Do you know his wife and children, too?'

'Not as such. I arranged birthday cards, presents, surprises, restaurant bookings, trips to theatres and so on, all on Alex's behalf. I have all the relevant dates in my diary. I can tell you a great deal about Fiona, including her clothes sizes, favourite perfume and taste in music or food.'

'You'd say he was a good employer?'

'He was. I liked him a lot. We got on so well and were . . . friends. I can't imagine what it'll be like without him.' Her mouth turned down and her eyes watered again.

'I expect it's interesting work.'

'When I tell people I'm a secretary, they assume I type letters or emails all day, but they're wrong. Of course, I do some of that and take calls, arrange meetings, Skype calls and other secretarial duties, but there's lots more to the position. I used to travel abroad with him and stayed in some pretty amazing hotels – places I'd never have seen if I hadn't worked for him. We met one client in a casino in Monaco!'

'You spent a lot of time together then, in hotels?'

Lisa shook her head at Morgan's question. 'Not *together*. It was purely work.'

There'd been no sign of any masculine presence in the house, no shoes or coats in the hallway they'd passed through. Morgan spoke again, 'Are you in any serious relationship?'

'I was living with somebody, but we split up about a year ago.'

'Because of the hours you worked?' Kate said, aware of a sudden twitch that had developed in Lisa's left eye.

'Jealousy. He thought I was having an affair with Alex.'

'But you weren't.' Kate observed the fresh tugging on the cardigan button.

'No, but my dumb ex-boyfriend didn't believe me and I couldn't be bothered to try and convince him otherwise. He left. Not heard from him since.'

Kate changed the subject. 'What's your relationship with Alex's wife like?'

'Okay.'

'Did she ever go away on trips with Alex and you, or was she involved in the business in any other way?'

'Why are you asking me about her? I thought you were here to ask me about Alex.'

'We're trying to gather information from everybody who knew Alex, and you were close to him.'

'Excuse me,' said Morgan. 'Would you mind if I used your toilet?'

Lisa shook her head. 'It's upstairs. The door straight in front of you.'

'Thank you.'

He meandered away and Kate resumed the questioning. 'Did Alex ever talk about his wife to you?'

'He didn't discuss his personal life with me.'

'Did he seem anxious about anything recently?'

'Not especially, but Alex was nearly always wound up about something or other – all work-related. Actually, he *was* worried last week about a new start-up venture in India. The lawyers have been struggling to sort out the contract for weeks and he was concerned the company would pull out of the deal. That's how I knew the contract was important and why I took it around to his house.'

'Can you remind me what time you left the office at Corby International yesterday?'

'About one thirty. I can't be sure of the exact time.'

'Did anyone see you leave?' Kate asked.

'Our office is on the top floor and there's a back staircase that leads directly to the staff underground parking area. I used that and I didn't see anyone down there. That's bad, isn't it? It means I can't prove what time I left.'

Kate pulled out her notepad and pen. 'Give me your vehicle registration and we'll run a check on surveillance cameras. I'm sure your alibi will stack up.'

'But there aren't any cameras at the car park.' Lisa's fingers returned to the button on her cardigan, and worry had crept into her voice.

'There'll be cameras along the road you took: speed cameras, automatic number plate recognition cameras. The roads are filled with them.'

'I didn't travel on any main roads. I took the country lanes, via Milford and along the B5013 toward Admaston and the reservoir. I've never seen any cameras along them. You won't be able to verify my story.'

'Camera locations are not usually made public knowledge and there's every chance your car will have been picked up en route, no matter which way you went.'

Lisa's fingers wound the loose thread into a minuscule ball as she gave out her Fiat 500's registration.

Kate jotted it down and asked, 'Do you have any keys to Alex's office? We'd like to look around it.'

Lisa stood up and reached for a fuchsia-pink Ted Baker tote bag with a gold bow affixed to the front, left on the floor under the table. She delved inside and extracted a silver heart-shaped keyring, which she handed to Kate. 'This is the key to my office,' she said, pointing at the smaller of the two brass keys, 'and the other's for Alex's office. Those are filing cabinet keys.' The four other keys were so small they resembled bracelet charms. 'Do you want me to come with you? I can show you where everything is.'

'It'd be better for you to stay here and keep as low a profile as possible for the moment. Take some time to get over this. If anyone from the press tries to contact you, don't divulge anything. I can't stress how important it is to keep this as quiet as possible for as long as we can.'

Lisa's eyelids fluttered and she lowered her head to examine the button she'd been pulling at.

Kate couldn't shake the feeling the woman was hiding something. 'Can you think of anything else at all? Maybe something Alex told you in confidence?'

The 'no' that followed was little more than a puff of air.

'One last thing. What did you do with the contract?'

Lisa's head jerked up and she blinked several times in confusion. 'Contract?'

'Yes, the contract you took to Alex's house.'

Lisa blinked again and produced a rapid, high-pitched yapping that stopped as abruptly as it had begun. 'Shit. I don't remember. I must have dropped it somewhere near the house. I was in such a state, you understand . . . after I saw Alex . . . I can't think what happened to it. Is it that important?'

Kate extracted a business card from a slim plastic box in her back pocket. 'Let me know if and when you find it. I'd like to take a look at it. My mobile number's on this. Call me if anything else comes to mind. We'll return the keys shortly.'

Lisa peered at the name on the card and read, '"Kate Young". I know you. I saw you on the news at the beginning of the year . . . the gunman on the train.'

Her voice rumbled on. Kate's vision began to swim as she battled with the sudden surge of panic. Chris had prepared her for this. He'd told her that people would be naturally curious and want to know all the gory details. His advice had been to say nothing. She followed it and kept quiet while Lisa continued.

'I read about it in the newspaper. All those dead people—'

Morgan's voice interrupted the concerned dialogue. 'Sorry to butt in, ma'am. We're needed back at the station immediately.'

Kate excused herself and left as quickly as her leaden feet would allow her. Her fingers touched the foil packet again and she squeezed it hard.

'That's twice in one day you've rescued me,' she said as Morgan unlocked the car door.

He shrugged. 'DCI Chase told us we were lucky you agreed to work this investigation because you were still "fragile". We were asked to make sure you didn't get hassled.'

Fragile! Is that what they thought she was? Somebody who needed handling with care? Although she was exasperated, she was still grateful for Morgan's interference. 'I'm not as frail as DCI Chase might imagine, but thanks all the same for stepping in. In reality, I've been off for too long.'

'Not a prob . . . guv . . . if you want to talk about any of what happened, I'm a good listener and I don't gossip.'

'Thanks, but I'm actually fine.'

Morgan threw himself into the driving seat. Kate released her grip on the pills. She could get through the day without them if she concentrated on what she'd learnt so far.

She slid into the passenger seat. 'When we get back to the station, would you run a background check on Lisa? I'm under the impression she fancied Alex. Maybe more than fancied. She might even be behind his murder – unrequited love and all that. We can't rule anything out at this stage.'

'Will do. I confess I had a quick snoop about and didn't spot anything to be concerned about, although her shelves are filled from top to bottom with romance novels, and quite possibly every soppy film ever produced on DVD.'

'Quite the romantic, then?'

'Defo. And pink . . . so much pink . . . everywhere. Walls, cushions, teddies . . . even pink toilet paper.' He screwed up his face.

Kate managed a brief smile. 'I want to take a quick look at Alex's office before we meet his wife.'

'Sure.'

They joined another queue of traffic. The town seemed busier than usual and she couldn't fathom why; then it struck her. It was the school half-term holidays. The place was undoubtedly full of families, searching for ways to occupy their children. A pang like a dull firework exploded in her chest. She'd always thought she'd have children by now, but her career had been all-consuming and the time had never seemed right.

She set aside the musings, stabbed out a number and lifted the mobile to her ear. Ervin picked up on the second ring. 'Hi, Ervin. Did any of your team happen across a letter addressed to Alex Corby? It might be an A4-sized envelope, possibly post-marked India. It contains a contract.'

'I'll check with the chaps. I've been working another case this afternoon. I'll get back to you, *tout de suite.*' Kate could imagine him waving his elegant hands like a magician as he spoke with a perfect French accent.

Morgan rested his elbows on the steering wheel and stared at the queue of traffic ahead, indicators all blinking as they waited to turn right into the retail park. 'I think Lisa was lying. It's odd she doesn't recall what happened to the contract.'

'I agree. I'm also suspicious she went out of her way to take it to his house, especially as she knew his wife was abroad. Don't contracts get emailed these days? Or, even if it was posted to the office, she could have scanned it and emailed it across to Alex. It seems fishy to me.'

'I suppose she might have been having an affair with him.'

'I wondered the same thing, even though she denied it.'

'People will say all sorts of shit if they feel cornered. Can't believe half of what they tell you.'

'True.' Morgan was right; people would go to all sorts of lengths to hide the truth.

CHAPTER FOUR

FRIDAY, 4 JUNE – AFTERNOON

Corby International's headquarters were surprisingly modest for such a successful business. Situated on a small business park, with eight other similar buildings, the unprepossessing two-storey brown-brick building, the nerve centre of a multimillion-pound corporation, seemed more suited to an accountancy firm. This was, as Kate knew, not where all the action took place. Corby owned several huge warehouses outside Stafford, where all the packaging and processing of orders were carried out.

Kate paused by the entrance and peered through the glass door into a narrow reception area furnished only with circular leather pouffes or large footstools. The door was locked, and a note below a buzzer informed her she needed to ring for entry.

'Let's try the car park,' she said, making her way around to the side of the building and into a wide tunnel that led down a floor. Their footsteps rang as they marched down the tarmac and into a garage, or car park as Lisa had called it, lit by automatic strip lights and large enough for up to twenty vehicles. There were only two cars parked up; Kate assumed most of the staff had been instructed to take the day off.

The staircase Lisa had mentioned was at the rear of the garage and Kate paused briefly by a space next to the stairs reserved solely for Alex Corby's use before ascending the stone steps and exiting through a heavy door. This opened out on to a carpeted corridor and a six-panel mahogany door, containing no identifying plaque. Beside it was a lift.

Morgan was incredulous. 'A lift! Just for one floor. We could do with one of those at the station, save running up and down those rickety stairs all the time.'

Kate turned the key and the door sprang open to reveal a comfortable office, covered in the same wool-rich Axminster with a tartan yellow and grey pattern as the corridor. It was furnished simply with a half-moon wooden reception desk on which stood three metal document trays and a computer. On the wall was a mural, a map of the world, in which the countries were not drawn out and coloured but created with their names in various font sizes.

Morgan headed for the desk and opened the drawers, one after another. He pulled out a book and held it up so Kate could see the title. It was a well-thumbed Mills & Boon entitled *The Boss's Inexperienced Secretary*. 'See! She's a die-hard romantic. Found this at the back of the bottom drawer.'

'You found anything else?'

'No, the other drawers are empty. I'll take a look at her computer.'

He began typing while Kate looked around the room. The filing cabinets Lisa had mentioned were in the far corner. The drawers were labelled alphabetically and Kate unlocked the top one, riffling through letters A to F and finding only information about food suppliers. Morgan gave a small grunt, indicating he was making progress. Kate left him to it and unlocked the interconnecting door to Alex's office. She drew a breath as she stepped inside, and wrinkled her nose in surprise. It was more sitting room than workspace, with two black leather settees set at right angles to each other and a marble-surfaced coffee table sitting between them. A cabinet

43

in black wood stood against the wall behind one of the settees. She opened it and marvelled at the impressive array of bottles there, including a bottle of Bruichladdich Black Art 1992 whisky and, one of her personal favourites, a Talisker 10.

Box files on the shelf near his desk yielded nothing helpful. Nor was there anything other than stationery in his drawers. Behind the seating area was a plain ebony desk. Kate ambled over and looked at the photograph placed on it. It wasn't of his family but of Alex with a group of five friends, taken in front of a ski chalet, a layer of snow like thick icing sugar on the roof. The men, appropriately clad in thick ski jackets and woollen hats, with teeth on display and arms round each other's shoulders in familiar camaraderie, looked like a group of young students rather than the thirtysomethings they were. The man on Alex's left looked familiar. She lifted the frame and peered more closely. It was her superior, Superintendent John Dickson.

As she studied it, Chris's angry words boomed in her mind: *'John Dickson insisted you take extended leave? I admit you made a bad call on the train, but to be forced to take leave for at least three months is crazy! He has an agenda, Kate. I don't trust him one iota.'*

She believed him. It was almost as though he were beside her at that moment.

'Got something!' Morgan's voice was loud to her ears, making her jump. She'd been lost in thought again.

'What is it?'

'Lisa uses this computer to check her Facebook account.'

Kate replaced the photo, hastened back to Morgan and looked over his shoulder. 'You got into her account? How?'

Morgan grinned. 'She made it easy for me. She did what most people do when setting a password. She used her cat's name, Butterscotch, as her computer password, and the Facebook account is set to be permanently logged in from this terminal. She obviously doesn't worry about anyone using her computer.'

Kate made a *tsk-tsk* noise.

'The email account is also password-protected but under a different password, and I can't crack it,' said Morgan.

'Anything interesting on her Facebook page?'

'Lots of stuff about going off on jollies with her boss, photos of hotel rooms . . . and this,' he said, pointing at one of Lisa's status updates.

Kate read it out loud. '"So lucky to work for one of the best-looking men on the planet and to be spending the weekend with him in a five-star hotel in Thailand. #bestjobintheworld #sexyboss."' She screwed up her face. 'I think she had a crush on him and she was willing to admit it publicly. Alex could easily have found out about it. Still doesn't prove a lot. Have a quick check through and see if you can find anything else.'

She watched as Morgan clicked the mouse repeatedly and navigated the pages.

'It's full of the usual sort of stuff you'd expect to see,' he said.

Kate took in the cat photos, selfies with mates and online quizzes. 'Yes, nothing too weird. She definitely enjoyed her job.'

Morgan continued past updates about choices of outfits for important meetings and business travel with Alex.

'She's got hundreds of friends. Seems to spend loads of time online,' he observed.

'What about these private messages to several friends? Samantha Granger?'

'Might be that friend she mentioned? Sam?'

Kate nodded. 'Could be her. Is there anything in their messages about Alex?'

Morgan scrolled through them so quickly, Kate had no time to pick out any information. He returned to one sent to Sam at 9.30 a.m. on Friday, 28 May. 'Only this one.'

Kate read, '"Alex's in a totally shitty mood. The Bitch has been giving him a hard time about not going on holiday with her and the sprogs again. He's shut himself in the office and told me to take the day off when I've finished with the post, so I'll be free if you fancy going out to town for a coffee. Love these sudden days off. Three in the last two weeks. Might do some shopping. You up for it, babe?"'

'I couldn't spot anything else that rings any alarm bells,' said Morgan.

'That's okay. You've done well. This suggests she doesn't like Alex's wife, in spite of what she told me, and that Alex was in the habit of giving her days off for no good reason. I think we'll leave it here for the time being. Best to talk to Fiona Corby.'

Morgan closed down the computer and stood up. 'Where to next, boss?'

'Blithfield Reservoir. Fiona's staying with her parents, who live on the other side of it, somewhere along the main road towards Uttoxeter, near Bagot's Wood. Place called Pine Trees. We'll drop in at the Corbys' house after we've spoken to them.'

'Do you think Lisa could be involved in this?' Morgan asked, as he selected drive mode and pulled away smoothly.

'We've come across crimes of passion before, yet this seems a truly brutal way to dispatch a lover, or a love interest. I can't marry up the big hearts-and-flowers romantic we assume she is with somebody who'd tie up a lover, torture him and steal his eye.'

'Me neither. It's difficult to associate somebody who likes fluffy kittens and films like *Notting Hill* with stuffing food down somebody's throat until they gag and die.'

Kate mused again over the possibility that Lisa was in love with her boss. Could there be more to the woman than they first thought, and might she have been driven to murdering Alex?

Her mobile buzzed in her pocket. She withdrew it and stared at the screen. Her stomach lurched at the name: Tilly, her stepsister. It was five thirty in the UK so it would be the early hours of the morning in Australia, only half-past three. Tilly was becoming more persistent. This was the second time in the last three days that she'd tried Kate's number. Kate declined the call and rested her head against the seat back. Tilly would have to join the queue of those who claimed to be concerned for her well-being. Kate wasn't ready to talk to any of them.

CHAPTER FIVE

FRIDAY, 4 JUNE – LATE AFTERNOON

Fiona Corby was in her forties, but with her flawless tanned skin and full lips she could easily pass for a woman in her early thirties. She wrapped elegant fingers around a Villeroy & Boch NewWave porcelain mug covered in emerald butterflies. Her engagement ring clanged lightly against the side of it, drawing Kate's eye to the enormous diamond cluster, and she unconsciously felt for her own sapphire band, far more modest in price but extremely precious to her.

Fiona's lips trembled, but there were no tears. Alex's wife was either in deep shock or not as upset by the revelation her husband had been murdered as one might have expected. She perched on the kitchen stool in her parents' farmhouse kitchen in a pair of faded jeans, fashionably ripped at the knees, and a Dolce & Gabbana T-shirt with a heart detail and printed logo in Italian, a look she succeeded in carrying off well. Her mother, Gwen, had taken the two boys to the sitting room. Her father, Bradley, stood propped against the range cooker, his brow low and his head turning left and right pendulously in disbelief.

Morgan sat quietly with his notepad while Kate spoke to Fiona. 'Did your husband tell you he was expecting any visitors?'

Fiona continued to stare at her mug. 'No, he didn't.'

'Have you any idea what his plans were for yesterday?'

Fiona glanced over at her father for help, but his eyes remained fixed on the floor. 'I . . . we . . . I didn't ask . . . things weren't great between us.'

'Were you experiencing marital difficulties?' Kate asked, as kindly as possible.

'Not exactly. We argued before I went away and I was so pissed off with him I didn't phone him all week. I neither knew nor cared what his plans were. I never knew what he was up to anyway. Alex was a businessman. First and foremost, he was a businessman. His family came second to the bloody business.' She stared at the mug, as if it held all the answers to her problems. 'Alex is . . . Alex *was* a kind man, but he wasn't great at emotional stuff. Don't get me wrong. It worked for us. I did my own thing and he did his, and we had some good times together when he broke away from work.'

'Which wasn't often enough.' The gruff voice surprised Kate. Bradley Chapman had been quiet up until that moment. 'He was a cold fish. Didn't appreciate what he had in my Fiona and the lads.'

'Dad!'

'I speak as I find, Fiona. I understand this might not be the right time or place, but that's how it is. You know how I feel about him. I said from the off he wasn't right for you.'

Fiona flinched as if she'd been struck. 'He should have been with us at the villa. If he'd come as planned, he wouldn't have been killed.'

'Was Alex supposed to have been in France yesterday?' Kate asked.

'He didn't always manage to get away for holidays because of the business, but this time I'd persuaded him to join us. We'd had a rocky few months and I wanted us to try harder, for the boys' sake. I thought it would do us all good to spend this holiday together – after all, it was only a week. Alex promised he'd take time off. He even talked about chartering a boat for a couple of days. Then, the day before we were due to leave, he told me he had to pull out because there was a major deal to be sorted. I offered to cancel the travel plans and stay behind with him, but he wouldn't entertain the idea.'

'Did he seem more anxious or worried than usual?'

Fiona shrugged. 'No more than normal. There are always concerns when running a business, especially one like Corby International, but he didn't confide in me because I'm not part of the great Corby Empire. In fact, I have no dealings with it, other than to arrange the occasional soirée or attend a function.'

'Who, other than you and Alex, has keys or access to your house?'

'Our cleaner, Kelly Innes.'

Morgan looked up from his notes. 'How do I write Innes? Is it one or two "n"s?'

Kate waited while Fiona gave him the cleaner's details, then continued, 'And which days does Kelly work?'

'Mondays and Thursdays.'

'Then she would have been at the house yesterday?'

'No. Because we'd planned on being away for half-term, she took the week off too, to visit relatives in Ireland.'

'And she's the only other person with access to your property?'

'Yes. No. Well . . . there's Rory, too, our gardener, but he doesn't have a house key – only the keys to the shed and garage. Rory Winters,' she added, searching for his contact details on her phone. Morgan again took them down.

'How often does Rory visit?' asked Kate.

'Once a week, depending on the weather.' Fiona placed the phone in her lap, shoulders drooping.

Kate would find out when he'd last mown the lawns and visited their house. Having not spoken to her husband all week, Fiona probably wouldn't know if or when Rory had last visited. 'What about your financial situation? Did Alex have any debts or concerns about money?'

'I don't think so. He never divulged exactly what he earnt, but there's no mortgage on our house, or the villa, and he paid for everything: cars, school fees, household expenditures, everything, and gave me a generous monthly allowance.'

'You don't have a joint bank account?'

'No. Separate ones.'

'And do you have any income of your own, other than what you receive from Alex?'

Fiona flushed. 'You make me sound mercenary. No. I don't work. I've been a full-time mother and homemaker for the last ten years.'

'That's a job in itself, and a worthwhile one,' said Bradley.

'I'm certainly not implying otherwise, merely fact-finding. It's important to understand why this has happened to Alex, and I'd be grateful if you'd agree to us accessing his private bank and savings accounts,' said Kate. 'To see if there are any discrepancies, or if he had any debts he didn't tell you about.'

Fiona traced the outlines of a painted butterfly on the side of her mug. 'When can we go home?'

'I'm sorry, but it won't be for a few days yet.'

'But I have to collect the boys' things. They'll need their school uniforms . . . sports kit . . . backpacks and books. They're due back at Gilmore High School on Monday. They'll need everything ready for their return. Matron is strict about that.'

Bradley strode towards her and put a beefy hand on her shoulder. 'The lads don't have to go back to school, sweetheart. They're going to need some time to get their heads around this.'

She looked up in confusion. 'But . . . they'll miss lessons and their friends.'

He squeezed her shoulder. 'Alex is dead, Fiona. You can't pack the boys off to boarding school and expect them to carry on as if nothing's happened. I know this is difficult, love, but you have to be strong.'

Fiona gave a dry sob and rested her head against her father's chest. He stroked her hair, making soothing noises. 'Best if you leave us for a while,' he said.

'I understand. It's a tough time for you all, especially with your son-in-law being as well known as he was. We've been trying to keep it from the media, but they'll soon find out. You might want to unplug your phone, or even go away for a few days.'

Bradley grunted. 'I have no doubt it'll be challenging. We'll look after them. They'll stay with us until the commotion dies down. The dogs will keep any nosey buggers at bay.'

The two German shepherds he referred to had barked wildly at Kate and Morgan when they'd rung the bell and were now shut in a room at the back of the house.

'I have to ask you this, sir. It's standard procedure.' Kate prepared to be shot down by the solid man with wide shoulders whose craggy face was etched with sorrow. 'Can you tell me your movements for yesterday?'

'After breakfast, I took the dogs for their regular hour-long walk, then left for work. My first pupil was in Abbots Bromley at ten.'

Kate had spotted the white Mini with a red, white and blue flash down the left-hand side and logo and company name emblazoned on the bonnet – 'BKC Driving Tuition'.

'Could you give me the name of the pupil, sir?' asked Morgan.

'Sierra Monroe. Lives in Yeatsall Lane.'

'Thank you.'

Bradley continued, 'I took Sierra out for an hour's lesson and then I was free for a while, so I drove to Lichfield and stopped at

Brown's Café for a mug of tea and a read of the newspaper. My next lesson was in Cannock at one thirty, so I left about one to get over there.'

'Who was your pupil?'

'Charles Seagar.' Bradley gave Morgan the address. 'My last pupil, Roberta Bird, had a two-hour intensive lesson that was due to end at five thirty, but I received a call from Staffordshire Police around four fifteen to tell me Alex was dead, so I abandoned it and came home.'

'And what about your wife – was she at home all day?'

'Gwen went to a leisure centre with friends for a couple of classes and lunch. She was at home when I rang her with the terrible news.'

He rubbed his daughter's back gently, as if she were a child. She pulled away from him and faced Kate once more. Two thin ribbons of sooty mascara had stained her cheeks.

'Is there anything else you can think of that would help us, Mrs Corby?'

Fiona swallowed hard and shook her head. 'I've no idea who would want to kill him.'

'Could it have been a burglar?' Bradley looked Kate square in the eye.

'We're still looking into that possibility, although it doesn't appear so. Mr Corby was still wearing his wedding ring and watch, and his wallet was on the kitchen top with credit cards in place. Maybe when Mrs Corby feels able, she'll look to see if anything is missing.'

Fiona ran the tip of her forefinger under her eyes to clean away any smudges. 'The most valuable items were stored in a safety-deposit box at the bank. Alex didn't like to keep the pricey items in the house. There's a safe in our bedroom wardrobe containing some foreign currency and documents. I can give you the combination.'

Morgan once again took note. When he was done, Fiona looked at her father with dewy eyes. He put a hand on her shoulder but spoke to Kate. 'Is there anything else? If not, I think we'd like some time to be alone. The boys haven't yet fully understood the enormity of what's happened and—' His voice faltered.

Kate rose. 'Of course. Please accept my condolences again.'

He nodded mutely and steered Kate and Morgan towards the front door. They passed the sitting room; the door was slightly ajar and Kate could make out the sounds of a television. No doubt the boys were inside with their grandmother. At least they'd be in loving hands and helped through this tragedy.

Bradley opened the door. Kate thanked him again and was about to move away from the step when he edged closer to her. He lowered his voice. 'For what it's worth, I think he was a self-centred man who didn't truly appreciate what he had. He loved his business far more than his family, and if he'd got his priorities right, he'd be here today.' He shook his head. 'She'll never get over this, you know?' He turned away and was swallowed into the dark hallway.

Morgan's mouth turned downwards. 'He was definitely not Alex's biggest fan.'

Kate was about to agree when her phone rang.

It was Emma. 'Ervin says he hasn't come across an envelope or contract.'

'We're about to head over to the house. How are you getting on?'

'It seems Alex ran the business single-handedly, so he's the only director on the books – managing director, to be more precise. He uses external services for his accounts and legal advice: Mark Swinton, an independent accountant, and Digby Poole, a lawyer and partner in his own practice, Babcock & Poole. I spoke to a couple of Alex's salespeople. They're both shocked and appalled by what's happened and neither had a bad word to say about him. To quote them, "He was a great guy."'

Lisa had told them Alex was often wound up. The sales staff either saw a different side to Alex or were being economical with the truth. 'Did their alibis check out?'

'Yes. Both of them were at work all day. I've been assured their fellow colleagues will confirm that, given they share the same open-plan office. I'm still checking through everyone's whereabouts.'

'Alex can't have got where he has in business without ruffling some feathers, so keep digging. Also, can you run a quick check on Bradley Chapman, Alex's father-in-law? And, if you get five minutes, see if anyone at Brown's Café in Lichfield can remember Bradley being there lunchtime yesterday.'

'I'll get on to it. I asked the tech team to go through CCTV and surveillance camera footage to save us some time, and we have a list of registrations for vehicles in the vicinity between 10.30 a.m. and 2.30 p.m. and footage captured by the camera on the B5013. I still need to contact those vehicle owners. And just so you know, Alex's accountant, Mark Swinton, will be coming into the station later.'

'Good work. Any idea what time he'll be there?'

'Once he finishes his appointments, so not for an hour or so.'

'I'd like to have a word with him. Can you ask him to wait there if we're not back by then?'

'Sure.'

Kate rang off and told Morgan what she'd learnt. 'Who do we believe? Any, or all of them?'

The investigation couldn't be reliant on hearsay or people's opinions. What was required was hard evidence and, to date, they had none.

'My gut feeling is that no one we've spoken to so far harbours the sort of deep-seated anger required to murder somebody in this way and to pluck out his eye,' said Morgan. 'Whoever did this was either furious with Alex, or was attempting to extract some important information from him through torture.'

Kate couldn't fault his logic or hunch, but assumptions sometimes led to poor policing, and mistakes could be made. Such as the one she'd made on the train with Dickson. 'I'm with you. However, much as I'd like to eliminate these people, we have to stick to procedure, so we'll have to go through all the motions to make sure they're not involved.'

Morgan cursed as a tractor, filling the entire lane, forced their car hard against thorny branches that raked at the paintwork. Kate gritted her teeth at the shrill rasping, like fingernails down a blackboard. The vehicle rumbled past, its driver perched high above in his cabin, unaware of the dark look Morgan gave him.

Rain pattered on the windscreen, tiny feet dancing a repetitive rhythm against the glass. Ahead, amassed clouds, their burgeoning plumes sweeping across the melancholic canvas of the sky, were reflected in the angry, gunmetal waters of Blithfield Reservoir. The wiper blades swiped stickily at the spray on the screen, each movement accompanied by a squeal.

As they cleared the waters and climbed towards Lea Lane, Emma rang back. 'I've got some info on Bradley Chapman.'

'Go ahead,' said Kate, turning on the speaker.

'He was in the SAS for fourteen years, from 1982 to 1996. His younger brother, Jack Chapman, is currently serving five years in Winson Green prison for GBH. He glassed a barman and caused serious injury to his face. Jack's also got past convictions for car theft and possession of drugs. However, Bradley is squeaky clean. Immediately after leaving the SAS, he became a security guard for ERC construction company in Stafford, and then set up his own driving school ten years ago. Oh, and he's a member at Krav Maga Elite, Stafford.'

'What's Krav Maga?' asked Kate.

'It means "contact combat" in Hebrew. It's a mixture of martial arts, combat techniques and self-defence. It was originally taught to the Israeli army. I've never tried it myself but there's a guy at my brother's gym who teaches it and I've seen them go through their moves. It's hard-core stuff – physically and mentally. All I can say is, Bradley must be tough to be practising it.'

'He'd have no trouble overcoming Alex, then,' said Morgan.

'None whatsoever,' Emma replied.

'That doesn't make him a murderer,' cautioned Kate.

'But Krav Maga! Sounds to me like he was still putting himself through serious paces to stay in shape. Action-fit,' Morgan added.

Kate couldn't disagree, but they couldn't assume he was capable of murder because he was an ex-SAS soldier who was into martial arts.

Emma had more news. 'I also rang and emailed a photo of Bradley to the barista who was on duty at Brown's Café yesterday. He didn't recognise Bradley or remember serving him, but said it had been busy, and he doesn't have a great memory for faces.'

'That's strange. I'd say Bradley looks pretty distinctive,' said Kate. In fact, he stood out with his thick white hair, rugged face and physique. Surely the barista would have noticed him even if it was busy at the café. Or was she reading too much into this?

'Well, either the barista *is* crap at recognising faces, or Bradley was lying,' said Emma.

'Would you ask the tech team to run through the camera footage on the road from Abbots Bromley to Lichfield for us? See what time his car passed any points.'

'Already put in a request.'

'Good work. We'll have to see what they come up with.' A vague prickling in Kate's scalp accompanied her words. Bradley loved his daughter and grandsons and had a clear dislike of his son-in-law. In Kate's experience, love and hate were two powerful reasons for people to commit murder.

CHAPTER SIX

FRIDAY, 4 JUNE – EVENING

No sooner had they turned into Lea Lane than the clouds parted and the sun reappeared, bringing light and colour back into the day. Minute smoke signals of steam lifted from the road as warmth condensed the rainfall. They arrived at Alex's house and passed through the open colossal wooden gates and crunched over yellow stones that sparkled like topaz in the bright light. This was the only way in and out of the property and, with dense leylandii hedging surrounding it, it was unlikely the killer came in any other way. Morgan drew up beside Ervin's Volkswagen Beetle convertible.

The house was a converted eighteenth-century timber-framed barn. To Kate, the whole place resembled a swanky hotel or a spa, with its private laid-to-lawn gardens and immaculate flowerbeds, and views over a paddock in which two horses grazed peacefully, oblivious to what was going on at the house. She half-expected a peacock to strut up to the entrance, or a porter to rush out, demanding to take her luggage. She could never imagine living in such palatial quarters. Morgan must have felt the same. He sniffed loudly as he clambered out of the car and surveyed the grounds before collecting his protective clothing from the boot. Kate joined him and together they suited up, slipping on the obligatory latex gloves, mask and plastic overshoes before showing their ID to the officer on the door and heading inside.

'Hi, Kate.' Ervin was standing inside what Kate could only describe as a magnificent entrance, with richly patterned rugs on a marble floor, bronze statues in every corner and a wide staircase that wouldn't have looked out of place in a BBC period drama. An ornate carved table stood to the left of the hallway, next to a statue of a ballet dancer, her leg lifted at an impossible angle. Navy eyes and a chestnut-brown fringe were all that was visible of the officer on her knees there, dusting for prints.

Kate lifted a hand in greeting before joining Ervin. He spread his arms wide. 'This is going to take far longer than we initially imagined. It's an absolutely humongous house – fifteen rooms in total if you include the bathrooms – and we have to examine them all. Come on, I'll show you where Alex was killed.'

Morgan, momentarily distracted by a gleaming eight-tier chandelier containing rod-shaped LED lights, brought up the rear. 'And they only have one cleaner to work two days a week! I'd have thought you'd need an army of people for this place.'

'I'm sure they don't use all the rooms on a regular basis,' said Ervin. 'Some are purely for entertaining purposes. This way.'

Kate and Morgan followed him into a dining room, where various markers had been set on surfaces, reminders of what had been taken away for further examination. The investigators had finished in here and the apple, knife and plate had disappeared, to be replaced with small flags noting their positions. Alex's body had also been removed, but to Kate's heightened senses the room still smelt of death and terror – stagnant remains of blood and sweat that had permeated the chair in front of her; the one where Alex had been held captive and tortured.

◆ ◆ ◆

Blood sprayed on the doors to the first-class carriage. Muffled plead-
ing and squeals of fear over the rumbling of the train as it races on,
urgently, to its destination. The gunman is passing through the train
carriage, mowing down everyone there, one by one. His body turns to
the left. A businessman, heading home from a meeting, is next to fall.

◆　◆　◆

Kate's fingers curled automatically around the foil packet in her
pocket, but she let go of it quickly and banished the image from her
mind, focusing instead on the room. The person who'd designed
it had gone for a Victorian Gothic look: silver-grey wallpaper and
dark grey velvet curtains that hung at white-framed French windows; candle-holder lights suspended from a cream ceiling; a large
black-and-white painting of a man's face; a deep mahogany table
shining like polished glass on which sat a pair of identical heavy
silver candelabras. Ten chairs, each with black-and-white tapestry
fabric backs and grey cushioned seats, had been placed in perfect
symmetry around the table, apart from one, pulled away to face the
window. The deep reddish-brown stains on the cushions indicated
Alex had been bound to this very chair.

She brought to mind the picture of Alex with his head tilted
back, mouth open. The apple, knife and plate would have been to
his right as he sat here, unable to attract any help or to escape. She
envisaged the murderer's unhurried actions as they released pieces
of fruit into Alex's open mouth, tugging at his hair to ensure he
kept his head back. Maybe they even stood behind Alex as they
pulled, and had looked out at the same scene as their dying victim.
What sort of person would act this way? Was what she could see
relevant? She searched for clues as to why Alex had been positioned
here: a lawn, a flowerbed of tall white lilies; a flower associated with

death. Had Alex's killer wanted him to see them and make that connection? Kate could not be certain. Beyond the garden, the reservoir shimmered in the distance, a gigantic, moody body of water. Maybe that was what they'd wanted him to stare at as he died.

'Why did they move the chair here to face the garden?' she asked.

Ervin looked out. 'I can't help you. All I see is a nice garden and a spectacular view.'

Maybe it was as simple as that. The killer had let Alex observe the beauty of what he was about to lose for ever.

'The killer was well prepared,' she said at last. 'They knew Alex was alone.'

There was something about the entire scenario that niggled at her. Alex had been placed in front of the window, bound hand and foot before being subjected to torture, yet he hadn't resisted. 'Harvey didn't find any defence wounds on Alex's body. He remained submissive throughout, even when he was choking to death, and that surprises me. I can't imagine why he wouldn't fight back.'

Morgan had been listening intently. 'There might have been two assailants. He's more likely to have complied if one of them held a gun to his head or threatened him in some other way.'

'That's a valid point.' Kate gave a thoughtful nod. 'The only other thing I could come up with was that he was drugged and that rendered him unable to react. Otherwise, even if he didn't struggle against his bonds, he would instinctively react when whatever was used to pry open his mouth was inserted, or when he knew he was choking. Ervin, have you any idea what the assailant used for that?'

'We haven't come across anything that fits the bill.'

'Whatever it was, it was used to torture him,' said Kate.

Morgan continued to stare towards the water, an endless sea from where he stood. 'But why?'

Kate shrugged. 'Information? Something to do with his business. Or a code, or password.'

'Safe combination?' suggested Morgan.

Ervin shook his head. 'Nobody's touched the safe other than Alex.'

'Maybe they forced him to open it and then tied him up,' said Morgan.

It was another theory that couldn't be dismissed. 'Morgan, give Ervin the safe combination, will you?' said Kate. 'Fiona said there ought to be only foreign currency and some documents in there, nothing of value.'

'We'll check it out, photograph whatever is in there, and then you can run it past the victim's family on the off-chance they spot something's missing.'

'Thanks. So what else can you tell us?'

Ervin waved his arms like a tour guide pointing out important attractions. 'It's a spotless room. Nothing on the chest of drawers, or on the picture frames. I suspect it's been recently cleaned.'

'By the killer?'

'It wouldn't be the first time a murderer has cleaned up after themselves,' he replied.

'Are there no prints at all?'

'A couple of partials on the backs of chairs and a couple on the door to this room, but I wouldn't get your hopes up. I highly suspect they belong to members of the family.'

'Ervin. We found this.' The officer who'd been dusting in the hall had appeared.

'Thanks, Charlie, where was it?'

'Hall. Stuck behind a radiator.'

'I didn't spot any radiators in the hall,' said Kate.

'There's an antique table in front of it,' said Charlie.

'Ah.'

The envelope was addressed to Alex at Corby International and was postmarked India. Kate took it from Ervin, opened it and read the contents. It was the contract.

'Could you see if any of the prints on this letter and contract match any inside this house?'

'Certainly.'

Kate checked her watch. She'd wanted to talk to Alex's accountant, but this was more important: the find meant that Lisa had come inside the house, despite what she'd said earlier. 'I hate to cut and run, but we need to speak again to the woman who found his body.'

'That's fine. I'll crack on with the safe,' Ervin said, and rolled his eyes at the unintended pun.

'Thanks for all your input.'

He gave her a sharp salute and beetled away. She tramped back outside, where she peeled off her gloves and dropped them into the disposal unit. Morgan mirrored her movements. She tugged at her paper suit, shimmying it over her shoulders and down to the floor, and looked up at him. 'Lisa Handsworth lied to us. She went inside the house.'

'How did the contract end up behind a radiator?'

'No idea, but I can be sure of one thing – she spun us a story. Come on. Let's get to the bottom of this.'

Kate balled her suit, added it to the gloves and overshoes and marched back to the car. They'd made headway and had a suspect in the frame.

The desire to redeem herself burned deep inside, but it was tempered with caution. She'd made a mistake on the train with Dickson, and she wasn't going to make another. She needed to gather the facts and evidence before she could be certain Lisa had anything to do with Alex's murder.

A note she'd written, Dickson's name encircled in red, flashed before her eyes. Superintendent Dickson, the man who wanted her to lead this investigation. It still seemed peculiar he'd asked for her . . .

◆ ◆ ◆

'Sir, why have you passed the Euston train investigation across to a different team? We were first on the scene. This should remain in our patch.'

He gives a long-drawn-out sigh. 'I'd rather you didn't question my decision.'

'It's crazy to pass this over to London. I want to take the lead on this.'

'Kate, I'm sorry. No.'

'Sir!'

'There's no discussion to be had on the matter. Now let it drop.'

'Sir, at least make sure the investigation remains with a team up here in Stoke.'

'That will be all, Kate.'

◆ ◆ ◆

Why insist on her involvement this time? Especially as he was the one who'd forced her to take extended leave? Kate wanted this. She wanted the chance to redeem herself, collar a suspect, be able to tell Dickson she'd succeeded, yet she wasn't going to dive in head first. No matter how much she needed this for herself, she'd lead the investigation the way she had always worked, diligently and carefully so there were no loopholes and they caught the right person.

'You okay, guv?' asked Morgan.

'Sure.'

'You were mumbling to yourself.'

'Just chucking about some ideas. Sometimes it helps to vocalise them.'

'Yeah. Right.' Morgan tore his gaze away from her and fired up the engine.

She needed to be more prudent. She couldn't afford to have her own officers doubting her sanity.

CHAPTER SEVEN

FRIDAY, 4 JUNE – EVENING

Kate hammered on Lisa's door, lips pressed together in a disapproving thin line. It opened wide and Lisa greeted them with, 'Did you find something at the office?'

'Could we come inside, please?' Kate was firm.

Lisa made no attempt to respond but stood aside to let both officers in. The sound of murmuring voices caught Kate unawares for a second until she worked out it was the TV. Lisa shuffled forward, her soft slippers swishing against the bare tiles like skis on powder snow. Kate and Morgan followed her into the sitting room, where she dropped on to a settee overflowing with cushions of all sizes and hugged one tightly to her chest. She didn't offer them a seat.

'Would it be okay if we sat down to chat to you?' asked Kate.

'Yes.'

Kate settled on the edge of a chair next to Lisa and leant in towards her. 'You lied to us, Lisa. You *were* inside Alex's house yesterday. We found the contract.'

'I didn't mean to lie . . . I got so scared. I was inside the house and I knew you'd think . . . but I couldn't. I could never harm Alex.' She clasped the cushion tighter, a shield to combat and deflect the barrage of questions forming on Kate's lips.

'I need you to understand how serious this is.'

'I do.'

'Then tell me what actually happened.'

'I . . . didn't . . . I didn't kill . . . him.' She turned first to Morgan then back to Kate, then squeezed the cushion as if it were an accordion, and spoke. 'It wasn't all made up. I took the contract around to Alex's house at about two. His car was parked outside so I rang the doorbell, but he didn't answer and when I banged on the door, it just . . . opened. I went inside, half-thinking he'd deliberately left it unlocked for me, and called out his name. I dropped the contract on the hall table, along with my handbag.' The picture of the blue-eyed kitten on the cushion was now squashed into a fat ball of fluff. 'I don't know what drew me to the dining room. I think I heard a noise and the door wasn't closed, so I went in and . . . there was Alex. I panicked. I thought the attacker might still be in the house so I ran for it, snatched up my bag and raced to my car. I forgot all about the contract.'

'Why didn't you tell us this before?' asked Kate.

'I really don't know. Scared you'd think I killed him, I suppose, and I was in shock.'

'But by lying to us, Lisa, you were perverting the course of justice, and that is a criminal offence.'

Lisa's mouth flapped open and the kitten grew wider again. 'No! I didn't mean to.'

Kate moved on quickly. 'You said you thought you might have heard a noise. What sort of noise?'

Lisa's mouth hung open for a few seconds. 'It might have been a creak.'

'Did you hear any other noises?'

'No.'

'Or see anyone else?'

'No.'

'Yet you ran away because you thought whoever killed Alex was still in the house?'

'Yes. I was terrified.'

Kate felt it was strange Lisa had gone directly to the dining room and not looked elsewhere for Alex first. She decided to try tripping her up by repeating questions to pick up on any anomalies, but Lisa stuck fast to her story.

'And where exactly did you place the contract?'

'On the hall table. I put it underneath my handbag.'

Kate folded her arms and regarded Lisa closely before asking, 'Why? Why didn't you carry both the contract and handbag around with you? After all, you wanted to hand the contract to Alex. I wouldn't go into somebody's house and put down my bag, especially if I hadn't been invited in.'

'It was a sign to let Alex know I was around. If he'd been outside or upstairs and not heard me, he might have been surprised to see me. If he saw my bag, he'd know I was there.'

'He'd have seen your car.'

She hung her head. 'Sounds so stupid now.'

'The door was locked when the police arrived. Did you shut it after you?'

'I slammed it shut in case I was being chased. It takes time to open a lock. I have a similar self-locking mechanism on my door. A few seconds could have saved me. Look, I'm so sorry I didn't tell you this sooner. I was in a terrible state. I'd found Alex and . . . I wasn't thinking straight at all.'

'I understand. But at this juncture I'm afraid we can't simply take your word for any of this, especially as you've already given us one false version of events. Until we can clear you, you'll have to remain part of our investigation. You will have to provide a full statement at the station, as well as DNA and fingerprints, in order to be eliminated from our enquiries. I'd like you to come by tomorrow, please.'

Lisa's jaw dropped. 'I never meant for this to happen. I was frightened. You believe me, don't you?'

Kate got to her feet. 'We'll see you tomorrow.'

◆ ◆ ◆

The growling coming from Morgan's stomach made Kate aware that none of them had stopped working since lunchtime. It was nearing seven thirty and although she didn't feel hungry, she asked, 'Want to stop and pick up a takeout?'

'Sure. Any preference? There's a fish-and-chip van close by.'

'Whatever you fancy. My treat.'

'If I'd known that, I'd have suggested that smashing Indian place in Stafford.'

They stopped near the van and ordered cod and chips from a man in a brightly coloured headscarf. The food came in cardboard boxes printed with newspaper images.

'When did they stop serving these in actual newspaper?' she asked, slopping vinegar into her box and spearing a fat chip with a green plastic fork.

'I think that might have been back in the noughties,' scoffed Morgan. 'When was the last time you ate fish and chips?'

'Can't remember exactly. When I was a kid, my dad used to treat me every Friday when the fish-and-chip van came to our village.'

She was overcome with sadness at the memory of her father's hand holding on to hers as they waited for the man in a white hat to fry their supper. That was before her stepmother, Ellen, and stepsister, Tilly, arrived on the scene. There'd only been the two of them then – the perfect combination – father and daughter. She surveyed the chip dangling from her fork and stuffed it into her mouth.

She turned away and watched another customer lift the large red bottle and squirt copious amounts of ketchup over his food. The bright red stood out, a large paintball of colour, and without warning the scene began to disassemble, fragments exploding and breaking away, only to re-form until the vehicle became a train carriage.

Kate walked along the length of platform beside the carriage with feet of lead. She passed windows marked 'First Class', desperately trying to keep her focus straight ahead on the backs of fellow colleagues who drew level with the open door and awaited her arrival. In spite of her efforts, her gaze was drawn against her will to the window directly before the door, splattered crimson, a face pressed against the blood.

'Kate? You all right?'

The words shattered the illusion and she coughed a couple of times and bashed a fist against her chest. 'Yeah. I'm fine. A chip went down the wrong way, I was eating too quickly.' She folded the top down on the box. 'I'll grab something for Emma and then we'll head back.' Leaving him by the wall, she strode across to the van, chucked her box in the bin and ordered Emma's food. She'd got away with it this time, but she'd have to exercise caution from hereon in.

The hallucinations could occur at any time, accompanied by terror that usually sent her scurrying for Chris. The medication kept them at bay. She jammed her hands into her jacket pockets, where her fingers sought and retrieved two pills. Keeping her back to Morgan, she dry-swallowed them. She took a couple of paces away from the van so that Morgan couldn't detect her sudden anxiety. She only needed a few minutes to collect herself; the time it would take for Emma's food to be prepared. She busied herself, checked her phone, discovered a text from Chris. She couldn't remember the phone vibrating. The fat fryer sizzled in the background as she read it:

Sorry Babe

Shit signal here.

Speak soon.

Love you.

X

It was a welcome message and, together with the pills, it righted her again. She took the food and hastened back to the car, where Morgan was waiting with news that Alex's accountant, Mark Swinton, was waiting to be interviewed at the station. She slipped back into the passenger seat, her calm restored. She could focus again.

CHAPTER EIGHT

FRIDAY, 4 JUNE – EVENING

Ian Wentworth dismissed the waiter with a haughty wave of his hand. There was no way he was going to leave the incompetent buffoon who worked at the overpriced establishment any tip. The meal had been a total let-down: the wine wasn't sufficiently chilled, his portion of sea bass pathetically small, and the so-called *frites maison* so anaemic he'd questioned if they'd actually come straight from blanching and bypassed the frying stage. Naturally, he'd complained, but in this neck of the woods nobody actually knew who he was or appreciated the influence he had in his capacity as business advisor to the government, and his lofty position wielded no power.

It wasn't only the meal that had been a complete waste of time; his companion for the night hadn't shown up. Ian had waited a full half-hour, squirming in anticipation of what was to come, before realising his escort wasn't going to show. Not wishing to lose face in front of the waiter, Ian pretended to take a call from a fictitious colleague and exclaimed loudly that it was a shame their flight had been delayed and maybe they could reschedule the meeting for the following day.

He wasn't sure the waiter bought his act, but he was past caring by then. He ordered his food and gulped down another glass of the expensive Sancerre he'd chosen. It wasn't as refined as some he'd been privileged to enjoy in his lifetime, but it was palatable.

With his server somewhere out the back, no doubt grumbling to his co-workers about the tight-fistedness of his client, Ian threw his napkin on to the table and eased out of the booth. He'd settled on this restaurant because of the individual booths, each with red leather banquettes. His was at the back of the room, as far away from the entrance as possible, so there'd be no way anybody could have spotted him and his companion. It might be a little-known restaurant close to the Peak District, but Ian knew there was always a possibility of being recognised and, worse still, becoming headline news for all the wrong reasons.

He had no intention of contacting his date to find out why he hadn't turned up. Ian had met Jazz on an exclusive dating site and used an anonymous name during the online chats. No doubt Jazz had, too. It was best to let it drop.

Outside it was breezy but mild. Here in the foothills of the Peak District National Park there was less light pollution than in the city and, looking up, he was rewarded with a clear view of the Plough, the only constellation he could identify. He inhaled deeply. Forget Jazz. He'd return to his holiday cottage and go online instead. He might get lucky and find somebody else who fancied a steamy night of sex.

His car was at the far end of the car park, beyond which was nothing but fields. Ian wasn't a lover of the country. He missed the noise, the buzz and the decent coffee shops. His stone cottage served a purpose. It allowed him to be anonymous for a while and was a hideaway where he could indulge in his fantasies, providing, of course, he had somebody to indulge them with.

The door to his ancient Land Rover opened with a rasping creak. The vehicle was a boneshaker but suited the rural setting and allowed Ian to blend in. Here, he could be mistaken for a local farmer rather than the townie he truly was. It was only a ten-minute drive back to Raven Cottage, a small croft secreted up a winding track and perched on a hillside. Ian had to admit that from the upstairs bedroom the house had spectacular views and, best of all, no neighbours to bother him. He'd bought it dirt cheap from a Welsh woman who'd only used it as a holiday home for decades. With time and age against her, she'd tired of it and had been more than happy to take Ian up on his offer. She'd thrown in the Land Rover for an extra thousand pounds.

He drew up outside the property and dropped gracefully from the car. He prided himself on his fitness. He regularly trained at his local gym and made sure he kept the weight off his lean frame. He hadn't been blessed with height or good looks and had to compensate by ensuring the rest of his body was physically attractive. No one would notice the thin, hooked nose and pale, high forehead with its ever-thinning hair if he sported a flat stomach and firm buttocks. For a sixty-one-year-old, he was in decent shape, and regular shots of Botox helped him maintain his youthful appearance.

He unlocked the front door, clicked on the light and discarded his car keys on a wooden table afflicted by considerable surface patina. There wasn't a sound to be heard – a far cry from his penthouse apartment in Lichfield, built on what had once been hospital grounds. He'd been one of the first to purchase off-plan and had commandeered the entire top floor of a nice three-storey block overlooking a park, filled most weekends with families and joggers.

He caressed the soft leather of his Gucci loafers as he removed them and carried them towards the kitchen. You could tell a lot about a man by his shoes, and Ian had a penchant for expensive footwear. He'd purchased these from a boutique in London and, a year later, they still retained a fresh leather smell he equated with quality shoes.

The kitchen door was a faded cream colour with a cast-iron thumb latch. It opened with a determined click and he shouldered the warped door gently to ease it open, as he always did. He hadn't had it repaired or changed. It was part of the old charm of the cottage.

Ian exchanged his shoes for slippers and examined the under-soles of the loafers for signs of dirt. Satisfied they were clean enough, he placed them on a shoe rack by the back door. He brushed a hand over his midriff and moved through the kitchen towards another door which led to the study, where he kept his laptop. He'd log on to one of the few *exclusive* websites he favoured and get over tonight's let-down with Jazz, because he'd be certain to find a pul-chritudinous young man eager to enjoy a night or two of fine company and exhilarating sexual pleasure.

He was aware something was odd the second he pushed open the door. Yellow light from a table lamp fell softly across his desk. He'd turned off all the lights before leaving to go on his date. He took a tentative step forward and halted immediately, his gaze drawn to the desk on which his laptop normally rested. It was still there; however, he was drawn to the object beside it – a jar, inside which floated a jellylike substance. He approached it step by step until he could see exactly what it was, and then, fumbling for his phone, he dialled the emergency services.

Mark Swinton, dressed in jeans and a sweatshirt, was grey-faced. He sipped the glass of water provided and stared wide-eyed at Kate. 'I still can't believe it. I only spoke to him yesterday morning to let him know I'd submitted the VAT return.'

'We were hoping you'd be able to tell us about Corby International – if it was going through financial difficulties; if Alex had been having trouble with any of his suppliers.'

Mark removed his wire-rimmed glasses and rubbed under his eyes before replying. 'It was in great shape. Alex had acquired rights to operate in several foreign countries this year and each depot was performing well. From a financial perspective, there were no issues or problems and he certainly didn't mention any to me.'

'What exactly does the company do?' asked Morgan, sat next to Kate in the interview room.

'It's a simple formula; the company gets food suppliers in the UK to agree to let Corby International sell their British products abroad. Those products are placed in various shops and supermarkets overseas. It's basically a supply-and-demand model.'

Kate understood. Alex had built up a successful business by acting as a middleman. 'Why the warehouses? If he's acting as a middleman, he doesn't need to store goods, does he?'

'Corby International stores *some* goods, especially for smaller suppliers who don't have an adequate storage facility of their own and otherwise wouldn't be able to meet the high demands for their products. CI charges them for storage and arranges transportation for the goods.'

'And Alex headed the business alone?'

'Not exactly alone. He was the MD, but he employed people to negotiate placements and product purchase. As you know, I handle Corby International's accounts, and Digby Poole deals with legalities, especially overseas contracts. We three would meet regularly to ensure the smooth running of the company.'

Morgan stopped writing and asked, 'When did you all last meet?'

'A couple of weeks ago. I only needed to go through some figures and Alex wanted to talk to Digby about the India contract, so once I was done, I left them to it.'

'How did he seem then?' said Kate.

'He was . . . simply Alex . . . that's to say, professional. He was dedicated to the company. Did everything by the book. He was one of my best clients . . . the best. Nobody else comes close to matching him for thoroughness.'

Kate kept up the line of questioning. 'Have you worked for him for long?'

'Since he started up Corby International.'

'What about his personal finances? Did you handle those too?'

'Yes.'

'And were they healthy?'

'Very.'

'He hadn't run up any debts?'

'None.'

'What time did you ring Alex yesterday?'

'Nine thirty.'

'How did he seem?'

'Okay, but—'

Kate cocked her head. 'But what?'

'Well, he was working from home because he couldn't face going into the office. He was having issues with Lisa.'

Morgan looked up from his notepad. 'His secretary?'

'His *ex*-secretary.'

Kate ignored the look Morgan threw her at this sudden revelation and pressed on. 'He'd fired Lisa?'

'That's correct. Alex dismissed her on Tuesday.'

'This would have been Tuesday the first of June?' said Kate.

'Yes.'

'Why did he sack her?'

'I have no idea. He didn't wish to discuss it with me.'

'Did he mention Lisa yesterday morning, when you spoke to him?'

'Only that he'd spoken to Digby and everything was in hand, but he was taking the morning off while Lisa cleared out her desk.'

'And you know no more than that?'

'Sorry, no.'

Once the interview ended and Mark had left the room, Kate addressed Morgan. 'Lisa again. Why didn't she tell us she'd been fired?'

Morgan shrugged. 'She spoke so highly of him, too.'

'You know, I'm already heartily sick of this woman. Have we got Digby Poole's contact details?'

Morgan rummaged through his paperwork and handed them over. Kate dialled both his mobile and landline and shook her head. 'I can't get hold of him. We'll have to follow this up.'

'Fine by me. I take it you don't want to wait until morning?'

'No, I don't. That's not a problem, is it?'

'Not for me.'

'Okay, bring Emma up to speed and find out everything you can about Lisa Handsworth. I'll ring DCI Chase and then we'll head over to her house.'

'What if she's in bed?'

'We wake her up,' said Kate, rising in one swift movement.

'Fair enough.' Morgan picked up his notebook and scooted off to find Emma, leaving Kate to make her call.

Jazz music was playing in the background, and William laughed when she enquired if she was disturbing a dinner party or get-together. 'No, I'm home alone. There was nothing on the television so I thought I'd put on a CD and read for a while. How can I help you?'

Kate explained where they were in the investigation. She ran through her findings and thoughts about the individuals who were giving her cause for concern – Lisa Handsworth and Alex's father-in-law, Bradley Chapman. 'So, although I intend to follow up on these individuals, I'm not convinced at this stage that either one of them has strong enough motives to commit murder, especially in such a brutal fashion.'

'Listen, Kate, I have complete confidence in you. I know you'll get to the bottom of it. Superintendent Dickson will be delighted you are making as much progress as you are.'

'I'm not sure how much actual progress we're making yet. We have a suspect who has lied and kept information from us and another who disliked the victim. We're a long way off charging anyone.'

'Nevertheless, Kate, you are on track. See where these lines of enquiry lead you and follow your instincts. They've never let you down before.'

She caught sight of her reflection in the blackened window – tall and thin, so thin she was bordering on undernourished. She ran a hand through her limp hair. She looked a mess, and hardly a good example to lead such an important investigation. She needed to pull her socks up. William had been chatting affably and she'd not caught all his words, only the end of a phrase: '. . . and I'll arrange search warrants for Lisa Handsworth.'

She'd always been open with William, never holding back any information, yet something had changed recently. His attitude; the unwarranted false praise. Of course, her instincts had let her down before – the day she almost took out an innocent passenger on the train journey with Superintendent John Dickson. Why was William behaving this way? And why would he be keeping Dickson fully informed when they had nothing concrete to offer him? She thanked him and ended the call. There it was again; anxiety tightening its knot in her stomach. Something about all this didn't feel right. She had to tread carefully. Very carefully indeed.

CHAPTER NINE

FRIDAY, 4 JUNE – LATE EVENING

It was after ten by the time Kate and her officers gained access to Lisa's house and began searching. Her friend Sam, a young woman with a buzz haircut, pierced upper lip and a sour attitude, shot daggers at Morgan as he exited the sitting room with Lisa's laptop under his arm.

'Why are you treating her like a criminal? She's not done anything wrong,' Sam repeated for the umpteenth time. She'd arrived five minutes after Kate and her team, and Lisa had fallen into her arms in floods of tears.

Sam patted her friend's shoulders. 'It'll be okay, hun. Don't let them push you about. I'll stick by you.'

'You can stay in the room if Lisa wants you to, but only if you remain silent.' Kate's eyes glittered. She was in no mood for histrionics from either woman. 'Lisa, I need you to tell us exactly what happened between you and Alex on the afternoon of Tuesday the first of June.'

Lisa blubbed and snuffled even more loudly. She lifted red eyes and shook her head.

Sam spoke up. 'Oh, for goodness' sake. Leave her alone. Can't you see she's upset?'

'I asked you to keep quiet. If you can't, you can leave.'

Sam pulled Lisa into a tighter embrace.

'Lisa, what took place on Tuesday for him to suddenly fire you?'

Lisa blew her nose and sat up straight, shaking off Sam's hand as she did so. She swallowed and began, her voice strained and jerky. 'He didn't fire me. I quit. Alex called me into the office, immediately after lunch. I thought it was to take notes, but he had a tumbler in his hand and invited me to join him in a celebration because he'd had confirmation the India contract was signed and on its way. He invited me to sit down on the settee and poured me a glass of whisky. I'm not used to alcohol, especially early afternoon. I felt woozy. I couldn't finish the glass so I told him I had some emails to send. He insisted I finish my drink and' – her lips began to tremble – 'he sat down next to me, so close his thigh was pressed against mine. He kissed me on the lips. I pushed him off and jumped to my feet and told him I couldn't . . . I wouldn't. I reminded him he was a married man . . . and he flipped. He accused me of being a prick-tease. He grabbed me and forced me back down and—' Her final words were obliterated by soft sobs. Sam was slack-jawed at this admission.

'Are you saying Alex Corby raped you?' Kate asked, her tone appropriate to the situation.

'I couldn't fight him off. I tried. I begged him to stop. He wouldn't. Then it was over and he flipped again – back to the old Alex. He said he was truly sorry, that he'd had too much to drink and he'd misread how I felt about him and he shouldn't have forced himself on me. He kept repeating how sorry he was. I felt . . . dirty and used. I couldn't move. I sat and cried. He went down on his knees and begged me not to tell anyone, and promised it would never happen again. I can't explain how I felt. I didn't know how to act. I didn't know what to do. He suggested I took the rest of the day off, to decide whether I'd want to continue working for him.

I was numb, completely numb. I went home, ran a hot bath and stayed there for over an hour. I had to get clean. I threw away all the clothes I was wearing. I dumped them in the rubbish. I couldn't think straight. I wasn't sure I could face him again.

'He rang me the following morning. He wanted to make it up to me and said if I went into work we could discuss the matter. I went in and he apologised again, but I'd thought about it overnight and I told him I didn't want to talk about what had happened, and it would be best if I looked for another job. He insisted on providing me with compensation and a glowing reference. I said I'd think about it, and then went to town because I felt safer in a crowd. I didn't want to be in the office alone with him ever again.'

'Yet you went into work on Thursday.'

Lisa nodded. 'I rang him to say I'd accept his offer and asked him to stay away from the office so I could collect my belongings. He agreed and said he'd head to the bank while I was there, to arrange a cash sum for me as a *settlement*. He asked for one last favour: if the contract for India arrived, I was to bring it with me when I went to collect my money from him.'

'How much was he going to give you?'

'Fifty thousand pounds.'

Sam shook her head in bewilderment. 'You were willing to keep quiet for money? He raped you! No amount of money is ever going to make that right.'

Lisa's eyes filled again. 'I know, but I can't explain how I felt. It was like I was on autopilot. I wanted it to go away. I just went along with him. It was the easiest thing to do. Who'd believe me? He's so powerful and important. How could I prove he'd done anything to me?'

'If you'd reported him, the police would have helped. We have specialist teams, doctors, staff – all experts in this field, and they could have treated you and gathered evidence to use against him.'

Kate studied Lisa's face, searching for the truth. Her story didn't quite ring true. It was all too convenient: the alleged rape, the pay-off, going to Alex's house to collect the money and finding him dead. There was one question still bothering her. 'You agreed to go to this man's house alone, even after he'd raped you?'

Lisa gulped. 'I know it sounds reckless, but I took precautions: a pepper spray and my mobile in my hand. I was never going to cross the threshold. I was going to take the money from him on the doorstep, give him the contract and walk away.'

'It still sounds reckless to me,' said Kate.

'He owed me the money. It wasn't going to make things better, but he owed me something – the bastard – and I was going to take it!'

'You should have reported him,' Kate insisted.

'And what would the police have done? I'd have been dragged through courts and my version of events challenged. I couldn't face it. I didn't want anyone to know. You can't possibly imagine what it feels like when something like this happens to you. It changes you. You want to hide. I thought the world of Alex and yet he treated me like shit, and did *that* to me. You can never understand how I feel.'

Kate watched as fat tears fell down Lisa's cheeks. The truth was, she did comprehend. She'd met other women who'd had similar experiences.

Her stepsister had been one such victim when she'd been in her teens. Tilly had been in complete denial of what had happened to her. She'd refused to discuss the attack but at night she'd suffered nightmares, waking in tears, and Kate had been the person who'd comforted her. She'd soon understood that, in spite of Tilly's protests, she was struggling mentally to accept what had occurred. Tilly hadn't wanted to be reminded of the incident and was fearful of all men for some time afterwards, so what Kate couldn't grasp was Lisa's willingness to visit her attacker, knowing he was home alone – money or no money.

Emma, who'd been searching the house while Kate interviewed Lisa, rapped lightly against the wooden door jamb. Kate's head jerked up.

'Boss.' Her tone was quiet but urgent. Kate left the women and joined Emma in the hallway so they were out of earshot. 'We found a bag of clothing in the dustbin outside – blouse, skirt and underwear. They're fairly new, show hardly any signs of wear and they smell like they've been laundered.'

Kate groaned. 'If they're the clothes she was wearing when Alex attacked her, we're not likely to find any DNA evidence on them then, are we? Anything else?'

'Nothing unusual.'

'We'll have to treat her claim as serious. Check with Ervin. See if he found fifty thousand pounds in the safe. If not, it might have disappeared with the killer.'

When Kate returned to the sitting room, Sam was still hugging Lisa, who continued to sob.

'Lisa, can you tell me why you washed your clothes and then threw them out?'

The woman lifted her face, blotchy with angry red patches on her round cheeks. 'I wasn't thinking clearly. I wanted to erase the memory of what had happened, but even when they were clean and dry, I knew I'd never wear them again. I shouldn't have washed them, should I?'

'It would have been better if you hadn't.'

'I know. I know. I'm sorry.'

'Don't worry about that now. Let's go back to Thursday. When you were in the house, did you happen to see any money lying about?'

'No. I only saw Alex. I didn't kill him.'

Kate persisted. 'Listen, it's crucial you level with me. Did you spot the money and take it because you felt it was yours?'

'No. Of course not. I wouldn't steal.'

'It would be understandable. After all, he'd treated you badly.'

'I didn't! I'm not a thief.'

'No one is suggesting you are. We're trying to find out who murdered Alex. Did you tell anyone at all about him attacking you?'

Lisa shook her head. 'I was too ashamed to tell anyone.'

'You should have told me, hun,' Sam said. 'I'd have looked after you.'

'I'm sorry, but we're going to have to question you more about this, Lisa.'

'I can't. Please. I'm . . . so . . . tired.'

'All right then, I suggest we do it in the morning. Try and get some rest. Sam, can you stay over?'

'Definitely. I won't leave her. I'll drive her to the station first thing tomorrow.'

Emma was waiting outside for her in the car and spoke as soon as she clambered in. 'Ervin says there was nothing in the safe other than house insurance documents and about a thousand pounds' worth of euros. No other money.'

'Either Lisa made up the whole story, or she saw the money lying around and took it herself, or the killer absconded with it.' Kate glanced at her phone. It was well after eleven. 'We'll call it a day. Has Morgan headed back to the station?'

'Yes, he said he wanted to make a start on Lisa's laptop.'

'It can wait. We all need some time off. We'll run ourselves into the ground at this rate.' She instructed Emma to drop her off at her house, then rang Morgan on the way and ordered him to go home, too.

Emma was quiet the rest of the journey. Kate remained lost in thoughts about the case. She couldn't fit the pieces of the puzzle together. Man's appetite for violence never failed to astound her. She shut her stinging eyes and, for a second, she could once again hear the rattling of the train as it sped along and could make out the outline of the man in the carriage. She shook herself free of the hallucination. It would be back. It would return to haunt her when she was on the verge of slumber and, no matter how much she concentrated on this investigation, she would not prevent it from happening.

◆ ◆ ◆

Back home, she took a couple of pills and headed straight for bed. As she began to doze off, she heard, 'Hi. Where've you been?'

'I went back to work today. John Dickson asked for me.'

'Did he? Did he indeed? That's interesting.'

'I'm investigating the murder of one of his friends.'

There was lengthy pause. She knew he was going to urge caution. 'How far do you trust Dickson?'

'I really don't know. First he ordered me to take extended leave because he thought I couldn't cope and then he specifically asked for me to head this case.'

'Exactly. And who passed over the investigation in January to a London crime unit?'

'He did.'

'You should have been the SIO on it.'

'I know.'

'And why do you think he didn't want you to lead it?'

'We're on unsafe ground here, Chris.'

'Hear me out. He deliberately had the case transferred to London so it was out of your hands and away from your patch so you couldn't find out what was going on. He claimed you weren't up to the task when we both know you were. Then, in March, he took you along to a meeting in Birmingham by train, not only by train but upgraded you to first class. He knew what he was doing. He waited for you to screw up, used it to send you on leave and then insisted you return before the three months was up.'

'He wants me to screw up again, doesn't he?'

'That would be my take on this, and why would he want that?'

'It might be because I tried to get some answers about the Euston incident.'

'Might be?'

'It's most likely because I'd been asking questions, digging into the case.'

'Exactly.'

She felt her pulse rate increase. She didn't want to be reminded again of the carnage that had taken place on the four-thirty train from Euston at the beginning of the year. Kate had been one of the first responders to attend the scene and discover the compartment of passengers who'd been gunned down. It had been little wonder she'd reacted as she had when faced with what she'd believed to be another gunman when travelling home with Dickson. 'I made discreet enquiries.'

'Not discreet enough. He found you out and he set you up, made sure you were left discombobulated by the whole event, and then he forced you to take a leave of absence. He wanted you to stop probing.'

'But how did he manage to stage that fake-gunman situation?'

'It isn't important how – more why, and the answer to that is he wanted you out of his hair.'

'Then why did he request I lead this investigation?'

'Because he thinks you're broken, Kate. He wants somebody he can manipulate, somebody who might make mistakes.'

'Surely he'd want somebody he felt could solve the case?'

'Maybe he's hoping you won't be able to solve it,' came the reply.

Chris fell silent and Kate digested his thoughts. She trusted her husband one hundred per cent. He was astute, with an uncanny ability to home in on and expose wrongdoings; a gift that had earnt him a great deal of respect in his profession. He wouldn't hurl allegations without reason. Maybe this investigation would give her a chance to find out the truth about John Dickson. She would make it her personal mission.

CHAPTER TEN

SATURDAY, 5 JUNE – MORNING

Weak rays of early-morning sunshine filtered through the tree canopies. Kate's footfalls were light as she jogged along the leaf-strewn track through the forest, past oak, sycamore, maple and Scots-pine trees. A burst of soft tapping from a woodpecker drilling for insects came from nearby, followed by a sudden explosion of wings as a pair of pheasants, disturbed by her arrival, hastened for safety elsewhere. It was cool in the shadows, and therapeutic. It gave her time to reflect on the investigation. She was aware of Chris directly behind her. Not pushing her on, merely a running mate.

She hadn't run around Blithfield Reservoir before. It had been a whim to drive out to the car park at 5 a.m. and choose one of the three routes normally used for walking. She bounced along the longest, the Yellow Route, that wound first through the woodland towards a dell and a bird-feeding station. Although she was aware of the fluttering of wings, she had no time to observe the various species that flittered from feeder to feeder, but concentrated instead on her rhythmical breathing and watching out for tree roots or obstacles. A slight strain in her calf muscles indicated the ground was rising and, puffing hard, she and Chris left the forestation behind and traversed a wildflower meadow ablaze with yellow buttercups, into Stansley Wood, where flashes of pale blue caught her eyes – late-flowering bluebells, frail, tattered heads bending and bowing in unison. Her breath came in short, sharp gasps. She was out of condition and cursed her laziness in not getting back into an exercise routine sooner.

'Look . . . bluebells,' she said.

'You remember Hem Heath Woods?'

'Of course I do.'

◆ ◆ ◆

'Stop the car!' Chris unclips the seatbelt, shoves open the door and leaps out in the direction of a five-bar gate. He clambers over it and disappears into the woods.

She stares idly at leaf-rich branches that appear to frame the darkened scene, and the harder she stares, the more she makes out the beauty of delicate fern fronds balancing on a carpet of green moss, and subtle colours in the foliage that carpets the woodland. The sat nav indicates they are at Hem Heath Woods. To Kate it is the stuff of fairy tales and she half-expects a sprite or deer to emerge. There's movement, and it isn't a woodland creature who appears but Chris, a bunch of bright blue bluebells in his hand. He brings their freshness and sweet perfume into the car with him and presents them to her.

'What are these for?' she asks.

'They represent gratitude, but also everlasting love and constancy.' Then he grins wickedly. 'In actual fact, I was bursting for a pee. I spotted these in the woods and I thought I'd earn some brownie points . . . maybe to be cashed in this evening, after a takeaway and a bottle of wine.'

She can't help but mirror his grin. 'Yeah. Okay. Brownie points earnt.'

◆ ◆ ◆

Their feet thudded against the ground, a steady, hypnotic *slap, slap, slap*, and soon they were on the home straight, the car park only five minutes away. The last push was up hilly ground and that was where exhaustion disorientated her.

The forest grew grey and slipped from view, shifting in a blur to transform into the interior of a train carriage, and a figure untangled itself from the bark of an oak tree and moved ahead of her, his gun swinging left and right.

Kate fought the terror that filled her veins with freezing liquid nitrogen and considered all possible actions. There was so little time. She wouldn't be able to save everybody, but she had to act. The gunman would transit through this first-class carriage and into the next, where there were more unsuspecting passengers who'd become his victims. It was too late for the elderly couple visiting their grandchildren, but there were others here who needed help: a fair-haired girl clutching a Paddington Bear, her eyes wide with fear.

Kate pounded up the incline in pursuit of the gunman, then as quickly as it had altered, the landscape re-emerged and she was once again beside tall tree trunks, heart smashing against her ribcage. She bent over, hands on knees, unable to hear Chris's concern for the drumming in her ears. She couldn't tell him what had happened. She couldn't tell anyone about her nightmares. She had to deal with it herself. She needed to regain control, and she would. This had to stop. She gulped in lungfuls of air and forced back angry tears. When would this terror end?

◆　◆　◆

Kate downed the glass of water. Even after the run, her head was still woolly from the lack of sleep, and her mouth dry. How many pills had she taken last night? She remembered popping two before bed, but had she risen during the night to take another two? She couldn't remember.

Chris's words from the night before rang in her ears. John Dickson. Whatever Dickson might think about her state of mind, she'd prove him wrong and, if necessary, bring him down into the bargain. A sudden urge to talk to Chris about this again overcame her, and she rang his number, only to be met with an automated voice informing her that Chris's voicemail box was full. She typed out a text for him:

Hey.

Just wanted to say thanks for coming running with me.

Please ring when you can.

By the way, your voicemail box is full. Best delete some messages.

Love you.

She left the mobile on the shelf above the basin, drew back the shower screen and reached for the shower tap, and halted as thoughts of Lisa popped into her mind. Her actions still puzzled her. Although Lisa had explained why she'd laundered her clothes and then thrown them away, Kate couldn't commit to believing or disbelieving her. There were inconsistencies in her behaviour that Kate wasn't comfortable about: clothing aside, there was the fact Lisa had publicised her feelings for her boss on social media. Had Alex seen those posts and assumed she would want to have sex with him? She blew out her cheeks. Something didn't feel right, but she couldn't put her finger on what exactly was bothering her.

As scalding water cascaded over her shoulders, she considered the possibility that Alex and Lisa had been involved in a relationship. Water raced down the sides of the cubicle like fat, translucent slugs and she wiped it away, clearing a patch from which she could see her own reflection in the mirror – wet hair clinging to her face and one eye staring out. Thoughts shunted into fresh positions and her mind danced away from Lisa to Alex. Why had the killer stolen Alex's eye?

Her mobile rang as she was towelling herself dry. *Chris.* He'd read her message and was ringing her. She snatched up the phone, but it wasn't him.

'Finally. I've been trying you for days. Why haven't you been picking up?' Tilly's nasal voice was peevish, just as Kate remembered it had always been. That was Tilly all over: spoilt and sulky. However, they'd managed to rub along as stepsisters for a while, both surmounting their feelings of jealousy. Kate had loathed the idea of another woman supplanting her dead mother in her father's affections, and Tilly had hated getting a new father. In the end, thrown together by misery and with no other option available, both girls had given up on their rivalry and become friends – good friends even, especially in the wake of Tilly's ordeal. That was until Tilly did the unthinkable – something Kate still could not completely forgive her for. After her recovery, she had run off with Kate's fiancé, Jordan.

It had only been six months since Tilly had come back into Kate's life, full of remorse and wanting to put the past behind them. She'd contacted Kate by email, saying life was too short to bear grudges. Ellen, her mother, had died. Kate's father was dead. They only had each other, and there was also Daniel to consider – Kate's four-year-old nephew, who needed his auntie. Tilly wanted a fresh start with her stepsister even though she now lived thousands of miles away in Australia. Kate talked it over with Chris, who told her family was everything, and even if Tilly wasn't her real sister, she was still part of Kate's life. Tilly had suffered too, he argued. Ellen's tragic death in a freak motorbike accident, only a month after Kate's father had passed away, had left a gaping hole in her life.

Thanks to Chris, Kate had eventually rung Tilly, who had wept gratefully and repeated that she wished she could turn back the clock and had not absconded with Jordan. Kate had acknowledged that Jordan had been supplanted by Chris and no longer held any place in her heart. Those particular scars had healed and so Kate had loosened the knot of animosity and forgiven Tilly.

'So, why haven't you been picking up?' Tilly asked again.

'Work,' Kate mumbled. 'I'm in the middle of an investigation.'

'Kate! Do you think you should be at work?'

'My boss thought I was ready to return.'

Tilly let out a snort of derision. 'Short-staffed, more likely. Surely he can tell you're not ready for all that pressure and responsibility again. You should take some proper time off – a year or six months at least; come and stay here. I keep offering—' Once Tilly got on her high horse, there was no stopping her.

'It's not full time. I'm working on a small case with a couple of officers from my old team.'

She heard Tilly sucking in air through her teeth. 'Kate, I'm not sure. Are you still seeing Dr Franklin?'

Kate winced at the question. She'd cancelled the last few appointments with the clinical psychologist. She'd get through it all in her own good time, with Chris by her side, not by talking about the horrific event in January with some man who looked perpetually saddened by life.

She prided herself on being honest, as her father had always encouraged her to be. 'No. I didn't go to a couple of sessions.'

The hiatus grew longer this time and, for a second, Kate imagined that Tilly had hung up. The sigh at the other end of the line was drawn out. 'You should go back to him. You can't do this on your own.'

Kate wanted to say she wasn't on her own; she had Chris. But that would start an argument and she didn't have the energy to bicker. She changed the subject to one she knew would be raw for Tilly, even after all this time, but having helped run a centre for abused women over the last ten years, she was probably the only person Kate could question on the subject.

'Tilly, I need your input. I interviewed a woman who claims her boss raped her. After the event, she went home, took a bath, washed her clothes and then threw them out into the rubbish. Have you come across similar behaviour with any of the victims you've spoken to?'

She could hear Tilly wetting her lips to answer. It had been almost twenty years since she'd been raped. Tilly had tried to bury the incident in the recesses of her mind, pretending everything was fine when it clearly wasn't. Ellen had seemed happy to accept her daughter was coping. Kate had not, and had been there for Tilly when she'd finally crumbled.

'I know women who've burned their undergarments, washed them repeatedly until no colour was left, and who scrubbed themselves so hard to get rid of the smell of the man who attacked them they made themselves bleed. I would assume she wanted first to wash away all trace of the rape and then throw away the clothes because they'd only serve to remind her of what had happened – clean or otherwise. The poor woman. I hope you're looking after her.'

Tilly's words burned into her. Maybe she shouldn't doubt Lisa's motives for dumping her clothing. 'I am, sort of. The rape isn't the case I'm working on. It's a murder enquiry. The victim's the man she's accused.'

'Ah.' Tilly let unsaid words hang in the air.

'I'm having difficulty understanding her actions. She's eradicated any trace of her assailant, leaving the police with nothing to go on – no DNA, nothing. Why, Tilly? It defies reason.'

'If you weren't a detective, aware of protocol or how the system works, what would you do if you found yourself in the same situation? Would you think logically and present yourself at the station, or would you act on instinct, race to a safe haven, like home, and dispose of anything and everything that reminded you of what had happened to you? In these situations, reason and thoughts of catching the person often fly out of the window. A victim doesn't want to discuss it with family and friends, let alone the police. They might, like me, feel self-loathing, disgust and shame – so much shame. I know exactly how that feels, Kate. You don't think anyone will believe you. You wonder what you've done to deserve it. You hate the person who's done it to you and, most of all, you hate yourself. Reason doesn't come into it – self-preservation does. You act without thought to protect your mind. You pretend it hasn't happened, and if that means burning your clothes or washing them and then throwing them away, you'll do it. Treat this woman with respect and compassion. She's probably horribly confused by what's happened. She might even doubt it actually took place. Be kind. I know you will be. You were to me. You helped me even though I pushed you away. You were patient and caring when I needed it most, even though I didn't understand I needed it. Remember that and it'll help you understand what this woman is going through.'

Kate exhaled softly. 'I will, Tilly.'

'And promise me you'll make another appointment to see Dr Franklin. By the way, Daniel sends his love. He thinks you're the bravest auntie in the world and he wants to be a policeman when he grows up.'

'Tell him to choose a different career. This one will eat into his soul.' Kate was serious.

'We're so proud of you, Kate. Don't forget it. Have you thought any more about coming to visit us?'

Despite having met Chris, Kate still wasn't sure she could face seeing Tilly and Jordan together. 'I'll let you know. I'm still considering it.'

'Good. Please do. We'd all love to see you. I have to go. I just wanted to check up on my big sister.'

'I'm fine, Tilly.'

'Next time, text me, or pick up the phone when I call you. I worry about you, Kate. Love you.'

'Love you too, Tilly.' Kate knew she meant the words. Much had happened between them both, but Chris had been right. She and Tilly had been close and shared many experiences; it would have been stupid to harbour a grudge any longer. She hung up and glanced at the clock. It was 8 a.m. Time to go to work.

CHAPTER ELEVEN

SATURDAY, 5 JUNE – MORNING

Kate was surprised to see Morgan at his desk when she clattered into the office half an hour later. She didn't get the chance to pass comment on his punctuality because he spoke first. 'Lisa Handsworth is strange.'

'What do you mean by "strange"?'

'She removed several document files and deleted some of her browsing history from her laptop, but she didn't bank on my technological skills. Here's what I've retrieved so far.'

Kate looked at the extensive list, her eyes widening at some of the searches: '"Seduction techniques for a woman", "How to flirt with your boss", "Make your boss fall in love with you", "Seven ways to make your boss fall in love with you" . . . This complicates things even further. However, if she is telling the truth, we have to handle her sensitively.'

'I agree, but here's another snippet of information that might help you work out who's telling the truth. Her mother, Anne, is currently undergoing treatment at an NHS alcohol-and-drug rehab clinic in Shropshire. This is the fifth time she's been admitted to the same establishment. Anne's got a record for possession of class-A drugs and two shoplifting convictions. Lisa was put into care in 2007, when she was twelve, but ran away, claiming the foster parents abused her.'

'What happened about that?'

'The claims were unfounded and quashed. Lisa was rehomed and returned to live with her mother eighteen months later, in 2009. She took a part-time secretarial course and qualified in 2013 and temped at an agency for three years before becoming Alex's personal assistant in September 2016.'

Kate picked up her car keys again. 'That's useful to know. I'm going to visit Fiona Corby and see if I can find out anything further about Alex's relationship with his secretary. What time is Digby Poole coming in for interview?'

'As soon as his plane from Frankfurt lands and his secretary can reach him. She assured me she'd inform him of Alex's death and urgent need to talk to us. I'll carry on rooting about on Lisa's laptop for the moment and see if I can come up with anything else while I'm waiting to hear from him.'

'Good stuff. Catch you later.'

She retraced the route she'd taken that morning to the reservoir and followed the causeway across the water. Tiny white waves skittered across the surface and a flock of gulls bobbed like plastic ducks at a fairground. A silver bus obscured the view ahead, and as she drew closer to its rear she could easily read the name – First Class Travel – and her heart thudded ominously as the words blurred, only to reappear etched on a frosted-glass door that slid open. She hesitated a second before walking into the first-class carriage of the four-thirty train from Euston. Each movement was awkward, marionette-like. Left foot. Right foot. Into the aisle. The smell of death hit her immediately. She'd known what to expect here, but had yet to experience the full horror.

Too close! The bus filled her windscreen. *Stop!* She stabbed her brake pedal and immediately fell back from the vehicle. Mercifully, there was nobody behind her. *Shit!* She inhaled deeply and blew out through pursed lips and repeated the action twice more, regaining control. It had been a close shave.

She turned at the top of the hill, wiped sweaty palms on her trousers, and composed herself. Within minutes she'd pulled up to the Chapmans' house and was pressing the intercom on the gatepost for access. The dogs barked furiously, eager to see off the intruder. A piercing whistle sent them scurrying back towards the house and then there was a tired groan and whirring as the gates opened for her to enter.

Bradley, in dark jogging bottoms and a tight-fitting T-shirt revealing muscular biceps and a thick-set neck, let her into the house. 'You found Alex's killer already?'

'Not yet, sir. I'd like a few words with Fiona again, please.'

He gave a quiet grunt and left her standing in the hallway while he went to fetch his daughter. Kate turned at a tinkling behind her. Gwen Chapman, in a cotton dressing gown that swamped her slight frame, was stirring a mug with a spoon.

'It's been such a terrible shock to the boys, and to us all,' she said, her voice so faint Kate struggled to catch her words. Gwen must have been at least a decade older than her husband and at one stage a striking woman. She still had plump, soft lips, which Fiona had inherited, and similar eyes, the colour of a clear sky on a perfect summer day. However, unlike Fiona, her cheeks had sunk with age, emphasising razor-sharp bones and lengthening her face.

Kate had no comfort to offer. It would take a long while for the scars of such a loss to heal.

'They were considering splitting up,' said Gwen, absent-mindedly. 'I told Fiona to think long and hard before making such a decision, because it would be difficult for the boys without a father around. I've seen what a messy divorce can do to families and I didn't want them to have to go through such an ordeal. Now look what's happened.'

'What's happened?' Bradley was at the bottom of the stairs, moving swiftly towards his wife.

'Nothing.'

'You feeling better?' he asked, putting an arm around her shoulder.

She shrugged it off. 'No, not especially, but it isn't about me, is it?' With that, she wandered back into the kitchen.

'Fiona's on her way down,' he said, and trailed after his wife, shutting the door behind him. Kate glanced about the hallway, eyes falling on the rustic console table near the door and a photograph of the Chapmans: Bradley in military dress and Gwen resplendent in a russet silk dress that clung to her frame and with blonde hair piled high on her head. There were two other photos: one of the entire family, including the children, and one of Fiona and Alex's wedding, taken on a beach. They stood under an archway of brilliant orange and yellow flowers with an impossibly aquamarine sea glistening behind them; Alex in a white morning suit and Fiona in a divine pearl-covered strapless dress beamed at each other and held hands. Kate thought their love was almost tangible.

'Made for each other,' said a voice behind her.

Kate turned slowly. Lilac semicircles hung below Fiona's eyes and she sighed heavily as she tugged the silk tie of the ill-fitting dressing gown more tightly around her narrow waist.

Fiona nodded in the direction of the first photograph. 'They'll be celebrating their forty-third wedding anniversary in September. My mum's,' she said of the garment, tying the belt into a knot to prevent it from slipping.

'I'm sorry to disturb you so early.'

'S'okay. Couldn't sleep anyway. The boys were restless all night and Dad keeps checking in on me every five minutes to see if I'm all right.'

'I need to ask some personal questions about you and Alex.' Kate's eyebrows rose in apology.

Fiona didn't flinch. She moved towards the nearest door, opened it and gestured for Kate to join her. 'Best go in here.'

The room was simply furnished but had a homely familiar scent: a mixture of leather and polish. The smell was reminiscent of her father's study – a converted dining room they'd never used for eating where Kate had spent many an occasion curled up reading in one of the battered leather chairs while he worked at his desk.

'What do you want to ask me?'

'I'm afraid a serious allegation has been lodged against your husband. He's been accused of rape.'

Fiona's lips twitched and she let out a noise: a combination of a laugh and a snort.

'As I said, it's a serious allegation and we're looking to see if it's linked to his death.'

Fiona folded her arms, the diamond engagement ring on display. 'Impossible.'

'It's natural you'd want to defend him, but we have to take it seriously.'

'Who? Who told you my husband assaulted her?'

Kate shook her head. 'We can't divulge that information at present.'

'Well, you tell whoever it is they're a lying, twisted fuck-up.' Fiona's cheeks flushed pink in anger.

'The person concerned is insistent that her version of events is true.'

'Bitch! Fancy doing this to him, to *us*. He's dead and she's making wild claims like this. It's impossible. A month after he turned sixty, Alex stopped getting erections. The doctor explained it was age-related: testosterone levels can drop dramatically in older men when they reach a certain age, which affects not only sexual performance but also mood. At first we persisted, but it became such an issue for him he preferred not to try. I suggested Viagra, but he wasn't willing to take drugs. Alex wouldn't even take pills for headaches or flu. He claimed nature had a way of dealing with everything. He was completely anti-medication. Alex had erectile dysfunction. He *couldn't* have raped her.'

'And you're sure this problem couldn't have been . . .' Kate hesitated. 'Particular to you? To your relationship?'

'Definitely not. He wanted to . . . He couldn't. And anyway, he wouldn't cheat on me and he'd never assault anyone.'

'I appreciate you being so forthright about this.'

'I won't have some heartless cow bandying such utter bullshit. I'll give you the contact details of our doctor. I'll even ring him and tell him he can break patient confidentiality or whatever it is to talk to you. He'll confirm what I've told you. Alex couldn't get it up, no matter what he tried.'

'Your mother said you were thinking of splitting up. Was that because of the sexual problems?'

The words came out slowly. 'I was struggling. We hadn't had a physical relationship for over eighteen months and it was business, business, business with Alex. So, yes, I mentioned to Mum I was thinking of leaving him. If only he'd come to France, we might have saved our marriage. More importantly, he'd be here today and my boys would still have their father.' She excused herself and, pulling a tissue from the pocket in the gown, blew her nose. She blinked away tears before resuming. 'Whatever's been said about Alex is untrue. He was a good man.'

'Thank you.' Kate had all the information she required for the moment. Fiona's parting words were earnest. 'Please find out who murdered my husband, and don't let this woman ruin his reputation. He prided himself on his reputation.'

CHAPTER TWELVE

SATURDAY, 5 JUNE – MORNING

Morgan was waiting for Kate and caught her as soon as she appeared in the office.

'I found this on Lisa's laptop.'

Kate stared at the photograph before releasing a hiss of irritation. Lisa had used an application to alter it, removing Fiona from the picture and superimposing a picture of herself, dressed in white with a matching white headband, on to the image instead. Now it looked like Alex was reaching out for Lisa's hand as both stood under the floral arch in the very wedding photo Kate had seen in Fiona's parents' house.

'There are other photos of him – lots of photos. She must have been stalking him for quite some time. There are pictures of him in his car, on his phone, outside the building, talking to other people. She was obsessed with him.'

'So the bloody woman's been lying to us again! The more we dig into this, the less convinced I am about this rape accusation, although he might still have assaulted her. Fiona Corby is positive Alex couldn't have done it because he suffered from erectile dysfunction. Find out who Lisa was last living with – the guy who got jealous about Alex being her boss – and see if he can give us any more insight into her. Chat with her friend Sam, too. I don't want us to get too sidelined here, but we ought to work out if she could have been involved in his murder.'

Emma chose that moment to bustle into the office. 'I had no joy speaking to all the vehicle owners who were in the area between 10.30 a.m. and 2 p.m. on Thursday, so I went through the footage from the camera at the bottom of the B5013 on the off-chance I'd spy something, and I did. I picked out a cyclist wearing a Bramshall Cycling Club custom-made top who was on that stretch of road, so I contacted the club and got his name – Kyle Jameson. I actually know him. We met at an Ironman event. He's downstairs in interview room B, and he's got something you might want to see – actual photos of a vehicle – a white Mini – turning into Lea Lane Thursday morning.'

'I'd definitely like to talk to him.'

Kate shadowed Emma down the stairs and into the room. Kyle was like every keen cyclist she'd ever seen – lean, thin-faced and long-legged.

He jumped to his feet when she entered. 'Kyle Jameson,' he said, pumping her hand.

'DI Young. I understand you have some photographs we might find useful.' She motioned for him to be seated and he folded on to the chair.

'That's right. I was aware there'd been a car behind me for a while and I waved it past, but it didn't overtake so I glanced around and saw it turn into Lea Lane. I always ride with a GoPro camera on my helmet so I can upload videos to my YouTube channel. Emma asked if I could download any photographs of the car from the footage, and I have. Here they are.'

He spread out three slightly blurred photographs of the side of the vehicle in question. He'd only managed to capture the back left-hand side of the car and no number plate or driver were visible, but there was a distinctive red, white and blue flash exactly like the one she'd seen on the Mini belonging to Bradley Chapman's driving school – BKC Driving Tuition. The date and time were stamped in the top-left-hand corner – *3 June 11.30 a.m.*

'The footage drags on because I filmed the entire route, but I emailed it over to Emma anyway.'

'Thank you. Did you happen to see the driver at all?'

'No. Sorry.'

'No matter. This is most helpful, and there might be something on the footage we've missed.'

'My pleasure. Is that everything?'

'For the moment, and thank you.' Kate stood up, and he bounced to his feet.

'You not doing the Ironman this year, Emma?' he asked.

'Not had a chance to train seriously,' she replied.

He gave her a wink. 'If ever you need a cycling buddy—'

'I'll be sure to give you a ring.'

Back in the office, the team studied the pictures together. Morgan pulled out his notebook and ran through Bradley's movements for Thursday morning. 'He walked the dogs, then took out his first pupil, Sierra Monroe, at ten for an hour's lesson. After that, he went to Brown's Café in Lichfield, and left at one o'clock to reach Cannock in time to pick up Charles Seagar for his lesson at one thirty. We confirmed pick-up and drop-off times with all of his pupils.'

'Remind me where Sierra Monroe lives,' said Kate.

'Yeatsall Road, Abbots Bromley. It's the road that skirts around the back of Abbots Bromley and is literally two minutes away from the reservoir.'

Kate scratched at her cheek. Bradley had been very close indeed to Alex's home. It was unlikely he'd have finished the lesson bang on eleven o'clock and raced off immediately. He might have wanted to discuss the session with his pupil, maybe arrange another, and then he had to switch seats again before departing. The timing worked. There was only one thing for it. 'We'll talk to him again.'

'Just for information, I couldn't find Lisa's car anywhere on surveillance footage to corroborate her claims,' said Emma.

'Lisa said she took back lanes and there aren't any cameras on those, as we know,' said Morgan.

Emma pulled a face. 'I know, but I'd have thought her car would have been caught on camera along the B5013, where I spotted Kyle. She can't have avoided it, unless she went a circuitous route, and that makes no sense. Why not go the more direct way?'

Kate appreciated her officers' diligence. 'I agree. Keep hunting.' The discussion was interrupted by her mobile, and a sonorous voice that would be perfect for a late-night radio show announced he was Digby Poole. He apologised for being unavailable sooner, and arranged to meet Kate at his office in Stone within the hour.

Digby Poole undid the top button of his shirt and tugged at the knot in his mauve tie, loosening it with podgy fingers. Once his neck freed, he stretched it from side to side before resting his forearms on the desk and looking Kate in the eye. An angry rash rising up his throat accentuated his florid complexion, and the yellow sclera of his eyes hinted at a man with underlying health problems. 'I won't beat about the bush. The fact is, Alex's secretary Lisa was threatening to ruin his reputation by claiming he'd raped her. Naturally, Alex denied the allegation, and I totally believed him. In my opinion, the woman is clearly unhinged.'

Kate wasn't going to accept the opinion of a work colleague who only knew the man in a business sense. 'How can you be so certain?'

He pressed his fingers together so hard their tips turned white. His voice was soothing, melodic, and his gaze never left Kate's. 'He wasn't remotely interested in Lisa, or any other woman, for that matter. Alex had one love and one mistress in his life – Fiona and the business. There was no room for another, and absolutely no way on this planet would he ruin his reputation, certainly not by forcing an employee to have sex with him.'

'You said he and Fiona were happily married, but Fiona suggested they had a few problems.'

'None I knew about.'

'Did Alex never mention the possibility Fiona might leave him?'

He shook his head slowly. 'Fiona adored Alex and she loved the lifestyle that came with being Mrs Corby. Besides, she signed a prenuptial agreement, relinquishing all monies and any claim to Corby International in the event of a divorce, so I think it was highly unlikely she'd have upped and left.'

'What did Alex tell you happened between him and Lisa?'

'Early Tuesday afternoon, Alex received the phone call he'd been waiting for regarding the India contract. He was told it was ready and would be with him the next day or two. Shortly afterwards, Lisa appeared with a bottle of wine. She seemed eager to toast the success and he didn't want to be standoffish with her, so he uncorked it and offered her a glass. She accepted and raised a glass to the new contract. Alex said she seemed unusually verbose and rabbited on about a brother in New Zealand and her mother's guest house in Cornwall, and then, out of the blue, she said she knew the real reason he'd invited her to drink with him, and she was more than happy to oblige. She unbuttoned her blouse and made a move to kiss him.

'He blocked the move and told her to do up her blouse. He suspected she'd already had a few drinks, because this was way out of character for her. She turned on him and accused him of leading her on.' He rolled his eyes at the thought. 'Anyway, Alex told her it was all in her imagination and suggested it'd be a good idea if she transferred to a different department. Apparently, all hell broke loose at that point and she threatened to tell the papers he'd raped her, to sully his name and make sure everyone knew what a cheat and liar he was.'

'What advice did you give him?'

'Firstly, I told him not to worry – after all, she couldn't harm him with empty threats. If she'd actually gone to the police or the newspapers shouting the odds, she'd have needed substantial proof – DNA, evidence of having been attacked – and she had absolutely nothing. Alex hadn't laid a finger on her other than to push her away from him. I suggested he arrange a meeting with her and myself, to discuss the matter and come to some arrangement with her. She was blowing hot air. She'd never have carried it out, but if she had, I was prepared to battle it out and clear Alex's name. I convinced him he had little to worry about and suggested he stay out of her way for a day or two and let her calm down.'

'Were you surprised by what happened?'

He cocked his head to one side. 'I suspected she had a crush on Alex. During our meetings, she'd invariably have her eye on him, and she always give him a fawning look whenever he asked her to do anything. No. I'm not surprised, only about the fact she screwed up the courage to throw herself at him.'

His secretary rang through to say his first appointment had arrived, and he excused himself with a final protestation. 'Alex did not rape or harm or even touch Lisa. I can promise you that. I hope you find his killer. He was an honest man.'

Kate retreated from the office, her mind exploding with unanswered questions. Overshadowing most of them was one major concern: if Digby's version of events was correct and Lisa had threatened Alex, and then lied not once, but twice to Kate, what else was the woman capable of? Was she unstable or angry enough at his rejection to have killed Alex? Then again, there was Tilly's gentle advice to be kind to Lisa. Both these successful men had been in positions of power over her. They could have deliberately concocted their own version of events so it would be their word against hers. There was still a chance Lisa was telling the truth.

The office was empty. Kate slumped into her seat and drank in the silence. She'd never been good left to her own devices; she worked better when she was part of a team and could bounce ideas off others. Alone in the cramped quarters, she was overcome with an irrational panic. Her palms began to sweat and, in spite of her efforts to focus on the investigation, she couldn't. A vision of the train carriage began to materialise in front of her eyes. She needed Chris. She rang his mobile and once again got the answering message telling her his voicemail box was full. She tossed the phone on to the desk and forced back the swelling dread. She couldn't run to her husband every time she had an attack. She had to learn to handle it.

She wiped her hands up and down on her thighs and attempted her breathing exercises. In for five counts . . . hold for six . . . out for seven.

Pop!

A body slumps forward, head resting on the table.

She shook herself free of the scene. Her forehead was clammy. The pills. She needed her pills. She delved into her bag, hunting for the foil packets, only to be halted abruptly by the door being thrown open with force. Emma marched into the room, accompanied by Morgan.

'We've interviewed Bradley's pupils, and all the times check out. We also tried Brown's Café. The barista still doesn't recall seeing him. To be fair, the lad isn't the sharpest tool in the box. All of which means, between 11.00 a.m. and 1 p.m. we don't have any clear idea of Bradley's whereabouts.'

'We need to establish if the Mini was his. Bring Bradley in. Emma, you can interview him.'

'Don't you want to, boss?'

'You can take the lead on this. I'll handle Lisa.'

'Is she still in the frame?' Morgan asked.

Kate screwed up her face in uncertainty. 'Could be.'

Morgan crossed the room and turned on his computer. 'There was something niggling me about her Facebook photos, the ones she supposedly took when she was abroad with Alex. They're all too *professional* and she didn't take a single selfie in any hotel. For somebody who snapped endless photos of herself, you'd have thought she'd have posed for a few in a swanky hotel. I most certainly would. Piccies of myself in the posh bathroom, or helping myself to the minibar, or sunbathing by the pool. Anyway, I searched online for images of the hotels she claimed she visited and came across the exact same photos, taken from the same angle – they were all official photos, copied from the hotel websites. If she did accompany Alex to the Burj Al Arab in Dubai and the Mandarin Oriental in Hong Kong, she definitely didn't take those photographs. So, not only did she doctor photos of her with her boss, and apparently stalk him, she made up all this shit too.'

Emma snorted. 'She's a female Walter Mitty.'

Morgan shook his head. 'Lisa's more than a daydreamer or somebody who fantasises about escaping her mundane life. She's a pathological liar. I think she would lie through her teeth about anything.'

Emma leant over Morgan's shoulder and stared at the Facebook page. 'You think she could have killed Alex?'

'I think it's possible anybody willing to live in such a fantasy world might be capable of more than just lying.'

'Maybe so, but we can't speculate. We work facts. Come on, Morgan, we'd better round up Bradley and bring him in for questioning,' said Emma.

Morgan vacated his seat and followed Emma. Kate rooted once again for her pills, took them with a large swig of water and waited for the jack-hammering in her chest to desist. Lisa wasn't the only person living a lie.

CHAPTER THIRTEEN

SATURDAY, 5 JUNE – AFTERNOON

Ian Wentworth was dozing in his La-Z-Boy chair when the whispering voice brought him to his senses with a jolt. He heard his name being called in an eerie, hissed sing-song way that made his flesh crawl. 'Ia-an.' With eyes now wide open, he remained immobile, trying to get a handle on what was happening. He'd turned off the radio to better concentrate on an interesting article about stenting frontal sinus mucoceles in the *British Medical Journal*, so the sound wasn't coming from that. There was someone in the room with him.

This thought filled him with such dread he wanted to curl into a tight ball, as he had done most nights, many years before, when as a child terrified of the dark he would hide from monsters lurking in his wardrobe or under his bed.

There was no wardrobe in this room. It was an open-plan space, incorporating the living, eating and kitchen areas in the apartment. Ian had paid a top designer to imbue it with maximum wow factor. It had style in abundance: a white floating staircase that seemed to hover in front of floor-to-ceiling white bookcases, a huge living space dominated by a grand Steinway piano; white Italian-designed round chairs with kingfisher-blue cushions, and a mock log fire inset a third of the way up the wall. The living space was separated from the kitchen with its bespoke fittings by a black marble T-shaped breakfast bar, against which were eight leather-padded stools. There was nowhere for anyone to hide.

He strained to hear any noise. There was nothing. He must have imagined the sound as he drifted out of consciousness. He was tense because of the jar at the cottage. The police had responded quickly to his phone call. His concerns about being broken into had been duly noted, but since nothing had been stolen, and he had no idea why somebody would have left a jar containing an eyeball on his desk, there was little for the police to go on. An officer with a lived-in face had thought it most likely to have been the work of pranksters who'd discovered he was an ENT specialist, and suggested the eye had come from an animal. Ian had patiently explained he wasn't an eye surgeon, but his words were wasted on the policeman, certain this was no more than a practical joke played on Ian because of his profession.

He stilled his pounding heart. His mind was playing tricks. The front door had a self-locking mechanism and nobody could get in without a key. In spite of his reasoning, he had a sudden urge to draw the little-used bolts across the top and bottom, just for peace of mind. He stood up and spun around, and then let out a half-hearted laugh. There was nobody in sight. The papers he'd been reading were on the floor. They'd tumbled from his lap. He collected them and placed them on the table, his hands trembling slightly. Goodness, he was jittery.

The room was immense. He'd chosen the apartment for that very reason. He needed space around him. On warmer days, he'd open the door from the master bedroom to a private terrace on the roof and sit up there, hidden from view behind an ornate stone wall, listening to the sounds below him. It was perfect up there for sunbathing, enjoying a quiet meal or an aperitif, although Ian never invited anyone here: not business colleagues or even friends. He always arranged to meet elsewhere, in cafés, restaurants, hotels or other public places. This place was sacrosanct, and he would never consider sharing any part of it, which was why he'd purchased the house near the Peak District National Park. Raven Cottage was for entertaining his boyfriends, although given what had happened, he might have to consider moving it on. If the locals were going to hound him, he might be better off cutting his losses and looking for another place, sooner rather than later. Who knew what tricks they'd get up to next?

He walked towards the front door, past Alexandre Cabanel's painting *Fallen Angel*. It was an authentic reproduction of the original and one of Ian's most precious pieces of art. He loved the naked male's angry mien and dark gaze. He paused briefly to gaze at it, and froze to the spot. From the corner of his eye, he spotted the front door was slightly agape. He had not pushed it firmly to, as usual.

The drumming in his chest began again. He edged towards the door and slammed the palm of his hand against it. It shut with a click, just like he was sure it had when he came in earlier. He'd been carrying a plastic bag of groceries as well as his briefcase, and he'd shoved the door with his foot. Had it clicked shut? He couldn't remember. His head had been filled with Raven Cottage and he'd been cross Jazz hadn't contacted him, not even to apologise for standing him up. Ian had been frustrated and tired. Maybe he hadn't thrust hard enough. He lurched forward and slid the bolts into position for good measure. Nobody could enter.

He turned back round, eyes flitting from one corner of the space to the other, before approaching the kitchen area to pour himself a drink. He needed to unwind. He pulled out a bottle of Montrachet from the wine cooler and uncorked it. Searching for a glass in a cupboard above him, he halted once more, arm upstretched. There was a white plastic card, the size of a credit card, on the breakfast bar. It wasn't his. He withdrew, one step at a time, edging back towards the door he'd locked. His brain scrabbled to get leverage on the situation. Someone had broken into his apartment, using the plastic card. He had to get out – escape immediately. He wasn't going to confront the intruder. Instinct told him he was in danger. He took another step backwards, almost level with the painting of the fallen angel, when his mind fired up in wild panic as he registered the cloakroom behind him, to his right. It only housed a few of his coats and an umbrella, but it was still large enough for a person to hide in.

For a second, he was a small boy again, under his covers, afraid of what was behind his wardrobe door. This time, he was alone with his fears. His mother wouldn't come into the room and tell him not to be scared. She wouldn't open the door and show him there was nothing lurking behind the clothes. She wouldn't hug him and tell him it was all going to be all right. Ian was on his own.

He felt the presence rather than heard it – a warmth behind him. The bogey man was coming to get him after all. He opened his mouth to yell, only to have all sound cut off by a quiet voice that hissed in his ear.

'Boo!'

CHAPTER FOURTEEN

SATURDAY, 5 JUNE – AFTERNOON

Bradley Chapman sat stiffly in the chair, arms folded, and glared fiercely at Emma, who was conducting the interview.

Unperturbed by his hostility, she began. 'Mr Chapman, would you please go back through your version of events for Thursday morning?'

'I already told you my movements.'

'Yes, and I have a note here in front of me of what you told us, but I'd like you to go over them again, bearing in mind we have evidence pointing to you being near your daughter's house.'

'I wasn't. I left Yeatsall Lane in Abbots Bromley at about eleven and drove directly to Lichfield.'

'Which route did you take?'

'The most direct one, passing through the centre of Abbots Bromley – the B5014.'

'How long did it take you to get there?'

Bradley's head moved from side to side as he weighed up the question. 'I suppose it was about twenty-five minutes.'

'Where did you park?'

'On a side street near Stowe Pool.'

'What was the name of the street?'

His face scrunched up. 'For heaven's sake! Is it an important detail?'

'Yes, sir.'

'I don't recall its name.'

'I'd have imagined, as a driving instructor, you'd remember street names.'

'Generally, I do, but I don't have many students who come from the Lichfield area, on account of there being numerous other driving schools in the city. I tend to attract clients who live in the country, so I don't often visit Lichfield.'

'But you must drive there to give them practice of city driving,' Emma said.

Bradley thumped the desk with his fist. 'Look, this is irrelevant. I don't remember the name of the fucking road, okay? If you come with me, I'll be able to show you the exact spot I manoeuvred into, but I genuinely don't know what it was called.'

Emma backed down. 'According to a witness, you turned into Lea Lane at eleven thirty on Thursday morning.'

'Bollocks.'

'Are you denying that, following your lesson with Sierra Monroe, you travelled from Yeatsall Lane, over the reservoir and turned into Lea Lane?'

'Damn right I am. Your witness is mistaken,' he said evenly.

Morgan slid the three photographs one after another across the table, lining them up under Bradley's nose. He studied them without a word.

'Is this your driving-school vehicle?'

He rubbed his lips together before speaking. 'No comment.'

'Did you go to your son-in-law's house on Thursday morning?'

'No comment.'

'You realise by answering "no comment" we have little option but to suspect you had some involvement in Alex's murder?'

'No comment.'

'I'm afraid we'll have to hold you for further questioning, Mr Chapman. It might be advisable for you to seek legal advice. My colleague will show you to a telephone.' Emma scraped back her chair and left, head held high. Outside in the corridor, she kicked the wall hard before stomping towards the office, where she found Kate glued to her screen.

'The bastard won't talk.'

Kate cocked her head. 'Won't talk at all?'

'He was sticking to his story of going to the café, but the second we showed him the photographs of his Mini turning into Lea Lane, he clammed up.'

'How did he seem when you brought him in? Keen to help or reluctant, or argumentative?'

'He seemed okay, although he wasn't thrilled about it and said if we were going to try and pin Alex's murder on him, he'd request a lawyer and complain about us.'

'Did he ask for legal representation as soon as he arrived?' Kate asked.

'No, he didn't.'

'How did he behave before you showed him the photos? Reluctant to answer?'

'No. He insisted he'd driven directly to Lichfield and, although he couldn't remember the name of the road, he volunteered to show me the exact spot where he'd parked up. He became uptight after we suggested he drove from Sierra's house to Lea Lane. He categorically denied it until we showed him the photos, then he wouldn't make further comment.'

Kate lifted a finger and waved it as she spoke. 'Let me get this straight. After he saw the picture, he refused to answer any more questions, or even any accusations?'

'Uh-huh.'

'The photos prove he was lying, so my best guess is he doesn't know how to answer without incriminating himself because you caught him off-guard. He'd have had no idea his car would be photographed, especially at the Lea Lane turning, and hadn't prepared for that possibility. Let him cool his heels for a while. We'll tackle him later.'

'Okay, but I'm pissed off all the same.'

'He'll talk. Give it time. Time usually breaks them down.'

'Superintendent Dickson was keen for us to get results quickly.'

'I know he is, but we don't want to make mistakes. We'll talk to Bradley later. In the meantime, why don't you check out the Corbys' gardener, Rory Winters? We haven't spoken to him yet. We've no idea when he last attended to the Corbys' garden.'

'Yes, sure. I'll get on to it.'

Kate went back to her work, one eye on Emma. Emma was a good officer, keen to do her duty, but Kate wouldn't allow her, or any of them, to be pushed along. Dickson might demand rapid results, but working too quickly sometimes resulted in mistakes, and she wasn't going to make any. She paused, her pen in mid-air as a thousand imaginary ants marched up her forearms, raising the gooseflesh on them. *Mistakes.* Was Dickson hoping she'd slip up? The answer was obvious; absolutely, he was.

CHAPTER FIFTEEN

SATURDAY, 5 JUNE – AFTERNOON

Although she was convinced Lisa was lying about the assault, Kate followed her usual pattern of conducting exhaustive research on her suspects before questioning them further. It had served her well in the past and, as much as she wished to quickly solve this case, she couldn't waver from her punctilious methods.

Kate had always been a planner. It had come from her childhood spent alone with her policeman father, one in which she ran the house and their lives because his job gave him little time to handle housework or cooking, and what time they had he wanted to spend with his daughter. As an adult, she'd still write out shopping lists on a magnetic pad affixed to the fridge, adding to the list daily to ensure nothing would be forgotten. Before the advent of GPS, she would plan a journey or trip in a notebook with military precision, working out arrival times or stops along the way, and when it came to work, no one was more methodical than Kate Young. Chris was the yin to her yang, with a devil-may-care attitude and a zest for spontaneity. They balanced each other: he lifting her from too solemn an outlook on life, and she grounding him whenever he had a wild whim to do something so utterly crazy it bordered on foolhardy.

Her world was full of order. Some found her too serious-minded and were irritated by her attitude. Others, like William Chase, praised her for it. It got results.

In this instance, her exhaustive efforts had paid off. She'd uncovered an important piece of evidence from a CCTV camera outside a pub opposite Rugeley Trent Valley station, only four miles away from where Alex lived. Lisa's car was plainly visible parked outside the pub, at the time she claimed to have been at work on Thursday. Kate made a note of the times it arrived and departed, and then, using the UK electoral-roll website, discovered the name and address of Lisa's ex-boyfriend, Robbie Davenport, a postman who also ran a mobile-disco business.

She dialled his number and introduced herself before explaining the reason for her call.

Robbie let out a snort of derision at the mention of Lisa's name. 'That woman is off her nut,' he said.

'Could you elaborate, sir?'

'She's deluded. Lives in cloud cuckoo land.'

'I'd appreciate more details if possible.'

'I first met her when I was DJing at a birthday party in a local sports centre in August 2018. She hung back after the event and helped me clear up, and we chatted. She was thinking of having a disco for her forthcoming birthday party and asked if I'd DJ for it. She'd already booked a venue and invited a hundred people. She was really excited about it. Said it was the first party she'd had since she was a little kid.

'Anyway, she rang again later that month to ask if we could meet up at a local bar. She was like a different person – in tears because she'd had her identity stolen. She couldn't access any of her bank accounts, which meant she couldn't pay bills, and that included the party. She was going to have to cancel my services. I felt very sorry for her at the time and I didn't expect to hear from her, but she rang the next day with a proposition. During our brief chats, she'd found out I was living at home with my parents and was saving up to find a place of my own. She suggested I move into the spare room in her house. I'd pay her rent in cash, which would allow her to pay bills until she sorted out the whole identity-theft thing, and she'd be able to put the party back on. It seemed a win-win situation.'

Kate recalled the tears Lisa had shed when talking about being attacked by Alex, and questioned whether she was able to switch her waterworks on and off at will. It was a callous assumption, but Kate was finding it difficult to believe anything the woman said. She might have felt more inclined to had it not been for all the false Facebook posts.

Robbie continued. 'She was bubbly and friendly and I figured it wouldn't hurt to move in with her, so I agreed. We got on fine for the first few weeks, then not only did she start getting flirty with me, but she told people we were a couple. Once I heard about it, I was pretty pissed off, cos I'd been trying to get it on with a girl I liked from work. I had it out with Lisa and she got all teary and said she hadn't meant any harm, but she was being teased by the women at work for still being single, so she thought it wouldn't hurt to tell them she had a boyfriend.'

Kate pressed the receiver closer to her ear. Tears again, and lies. Lisa seemed to make a habit of both.

'I won't go into all the details, but a couple of months later I found out she was posting stuff on Facebook about us going out for meals we hadn't eaten, holidays we hadn't been on, and there were photos of me she'd taken when I was asleep in the chair with stupid bloody comments like, "Isn't he sweet when he's asleep?" That sort of shit.'

This struck a chord with Kate. Lisa had been conducting a similar scenario with Alex, claiming they'd been on trips abroad together and suggesting they had a close connection. She didn't want to twist Robbie's story to fit her own suspicions but, so far, what she'd heard supported them.

'I wasn't standing for it. By then, I'd started going out with Stephanie and I didn't need Lisa behaving like that, so I announced I'd be moving out at the end of the month. She had a total freak, made threats.'

'What sort of threats?'

'Crazy ones. She picked up a knife, said she was going to cut herself, then ring the police and say I'd attacked her. Luckily, my mate Gav turned up unexpectedly and helped me pack up, so I moved out there and then. Heaven knows what she'd have done if he hadn't. I never heard from her again. Thank goodness.'

Kate doodled a large question mark on her notepad. All of this was corroborating what she'd learnt about Lisa from others. Evidence against her was mounting fast, and Kate was feeling increasingly angered by the woman who had wasted valuable time and, if this proved to be true, extracted unwarranted sympathy. There were others, like Tilly, who had truly suffered; Lisa's lies made a mockery of them and what they had endured.

'Did she say anything about her boss, Alex Corby?'

He gave a low groan. 'She never shut up about the man.'

'What sort of things did she tell you?'

'It was all "Alex invited me to go to Kuala Lumpur with him to clinch a deal," "Alex is going to take me to London next month to a charity ball," "Alex bought me this bracelet as a thank-you for all my hard work." At first, I thought the man must be mad if he fancied her, then I realised it was all made up. She never once went abroad with or without him, and one day she came home with a Pandora charm bracelet she claimed was a present from him, but I found a credit-card receipt for it in the kitchen bin, lying on top of the rubbish. She'd bought it herself.'

Kate could barely keep the irritation out of her voice at the bold cheek of the woman. 'Would you say she had a fixation on her boss?'

'Without a doubt. She even had a photograph of him on her dressing table.'

Kate thanked Robbie for his input and suggested she might need him to come to the station and be officially interviewed. He didn't seem to mind.

'Has she done something mental?' he asked.

'I'm not at liberty to divulge any information, sir, but thank you for talking to me.'

'Sure. I understand.'

Kate ended the call and sat back in her chair. She'd read up about it: compulsive lying disorder, also known as pseudologia fantastica or mythomania, a condition where the liar lies so compulsively they can no longer differentiate between the truth and the fiction they've created. It was difficult to recognise, but Kate had enough information to determine that Lisa definitely had it. She just had to work out if Lisa was also a murderer.

CHAPTER SIXTEEN

SATURDAY, 5 JUNE – AFTERNOON

Lisa was hunched over on her stool like a dejected pigeon, her eyes so glassy that Kate could see her own reflection in them. Sam stood over her, a guardian angel in black, with one hand protectively on her friend's shoulder. Overt threats and harsh voices wouldn't work here and coaxing the information from Lisa was going to be tricky, but the evidence spoke for itself and Kate had confidence it would work in her favour.

'Lisa, I want to help you, but I can't unless you are honest with me.'

'I understand.'

Kate wasn't convinced. She had no intentions of coaxing the information out of Lisa. The woman couldn't deny hard facts. She pulled out a still taken from the CCTV footage outside the pub on the road to Alex's house. 'This is your car, isn't it?'

Lisa glanced at the photograph and sagged further.

'Can you explain why you were at the pub car park the morning Alex was killed and not at the office, where you told us you were? Can you explain what you were doing there?'

Sam was quick to respond. 'She didn't kill him.'

Kate silenced her with a look. 'I understand this is all frightening and confusing for you, Lisa. You thought a great deal of your boss, didn't you?'

Lisa snuffled.

'You wanted him to notice and respect you, didn't you?'

Kate was rewarded with a small grunt.

'And I'm sure he did. You were dedicated.' She paused.

Lisa gave another soft grunt. Kate was gradually drawing her out.

'Alex was a good boss and he needed a secretary like you, somebody who would go the extra mile if needed. He valued you, Lisa.'

Lisa ran the tissue she'd been clutching under her nose and seemed to unfurl a little.

'You'd say he was a good boss, wouldn't you?'

The answer was a barely audible 'yes'.

'He was a good boss. A family man.' She let her words sink in. 'Lisa, Alex didn't rape you, did he?'

The dewy eyes clouded further, but Lisa didn't speak.

Kate didn't rush on. 'He didn't offer to pay you off with fifty thousand pounds, either, did he?'

Silence.

'Lisa, I know what actually happened on Tuesday at the office. I know *you* tried to seduce *him*. And I know about him sacking you because of it.'

Sam released her hand from Lisa's shoulder. 'Is this true, babe?'

Lisa's head appeared to retreat into her shoulders once more, and Sam stepped backwards, studying her friend with narrowed eyes.

Kate waved the photo captured at the car park. 'You were at Alex's house much earlier than you claimed. This proves you were only four miles away from the Corbys' house. The camera footage shows you arrived at the pub at eleven twenty and left fifteen minutes later, at eleven thirty-five. This picture shows your car turning right, heading towards Admaston, where Alex lived. This time you need to tell me the truth about what happened. Do you understand how serious this is?' The words hung like invisible clouds, and Sam shook her head.

'Fuck, Lisa. What did you do?'

Kate held her breath. There was still a chance that Lisa was telling the truth. And if she was, Kate had dealt a cruel blow. She'd been more certain of the woman's culpability when she'd begun questioning her, but now, looking at Lisa's distraught face, she had a horrible feeling she might have made another bad call.

Lisa leapt from the stool, arms out. 'Sam, I didn't kill him. He *did* rape me. You believe me, don't you? She's making this up to accuse me of murder.'

Sam took another step away from her and shook her head. 'I want to believe you, babe, but—'

'But nothing! You're my best friend. You know me better than anybody. You know I couldn't kill anyone.'

'Why did you lie about the rape?' asked Sam.

Lisa screamed. 'Shit! You're actually listening to her and you really think I'd be capable of killing Alex.'

'No—'

The fury was real and Lisa's voice loud. 'Get the fuck out! A real friend would stick by her mate, not doubt her. Go on, get out, you bitch!'

Sam's mouth flapped open and she started to protest, but instead snatched up her car keys from the kitchen top and marched towards the door.

'Sam, would you wait outside for me, please?' Kate asked.

Once Sam had left, Kate sat on the stool next to Lisa, who'd flopped back down. 'I can't stress enough how serious this looks for you. I don't believe you killed Alex, but I can't help you if you persist in lying to me – I'll be forced to charge you, if not with his murder, certainly for perverting the course of justice, which will carry a prison sentence.'

Lisa dropped her head in her hands and groaned.

'No more make-believe scenarios to cover your back. Alex spurned you, and you were hurt. You said things you didn't mean. It got out of hand. I'm not concerned about any of that. I only want to find his killer. Don't you? You cared about him, Lisa. Help me find the person responsible.'

'I want to help.'

'Thank you.'

'You're right. He didn't attack me.'

Kate struggled to control her involuntary reaction to Lisa's confession. As much as she'd doubted her, part of her had been willing to protect the woman and side with her version of events. How could she be prepared to slander somebody she professed to care about? She squashed the rising anger. 'Tell me exactly what happened on Thursday.'

'I thought him sacking me was a spur-of-the-moment thing, and I went to work on Wednesday as usual to try and patch things up between us. I intended apologising for my outburst . . .

Lisa has spent all day waiting for the right moment to say sorry and to explain why she has come to work in spite of being told not to.

She's managed to hold it together, but she doesn't know how much longer she can keep it up. Ought she to knock on the door or wait for him to come out?

She'd misread and mishandled the entire situation. She'd been certain his marriage was on the rocks and had believed Alex had felt something for her. She'd been wrong. Big time. She shudders at the memory of his face, disgusted by her clumsy attempt to kiss him. Yet in spite of that, she still can't bear the thought of not working for him, or not being near him.

Such is her emotional distress, she has to sit on her hands to stop them from trembling. It's half-past four and she can't bear the tension any longer. She'll knock on his door, tell him how dreadfully sorry she is and beg for a second chance with promises she'll never behave in such an unseemly fashion again. He'll forgive her. He can't do without her. They've worked together for too long for him to dismiss her. She stands up, smooths down her knee-length skirt, checks her top button is done up, the picture of a demure secretary. The door to his office opens suddenly, surprising her, and Alex comes out, eyebrows low on his forehead. He smells of woody aftershave and her knees weaken at the sight of this Adonis she dreams about, night after night. She is struck dumb and her apology can't escape her lips.

His voice drips ice. 'I don't know what you're playing at, but I don't expect to see you here tomorrow. As far as I'm concerned, you are suspended, pending a disciplinary hearing.'

She can't catch her breath for shock. 'But . . . I . . .'

He ignores her stammering. 'I expect you to remove your personal belongings and leave your keys at reception. You will receive a letter inviting you to discuss the matter with myself and the company lawyer, Mr Poole, and we'll proceed from there.'

She can't believe her ears, nor does she recognise the man in front of her. He's never spoken to her like this before.

Hot tears pour down her face. 'Tomorrow,' she says, hoping she'll have one last opportunity to explain herself and be exonerated. She doesn't want to leave the company. 'Can I clear my desk tomorrow?'

He gives a sharp nod and marches from the room. She falls to her knees on the carpet. How can she turn this around?

◆ ◆ ◆

Lisa spoke earnestly. 'He didn't come to work on Thursday morning. I knew he was waiting for the physical copy of the contract so I assumed he was avoiding the office until I'd cleared out. I believed if I could somehow talk to him face to face, he'd reconsider firing me. I checked with the front-desk receptionist to see if Alex had requested his calls be redirected and she confirmed they were being put through to his house, so when the contract arrived in the post, I used it as an excuse to visit him at home, late morning. I stopped outside the pub to go over exactly what I wanted to say to him. It was my last chance to redeem myself, you see? As soon as I'd built up enough courage I left and drove directly to his house.'

'And after you arrived at the house, what happened?'

'The gate was open and I was about to turn on to his driveway when I spotted another car outside – a white Mini. I drove off in a panic. When you build yourself up to say something and then you aren't able to, it knocks the wind out of you. I returned to the office and sat in a complete state. I still couldn't put any of it behind me. I had to speak to him and so I left again just before two in the afternoon, and this time, when I reached his house the gates were still open but the Mini had disappeared. I parked up and went to ring the doorbell, but the front door was ajar, so I pushed it open and called out his name.'

Lisa inhaled noisily and squeezed her eyes shut. When she opened them again, they were moist with tears. She stuttered, 'I wish . . . I hadn't gone in!'

'Take your time. Tell me exactly what you saw, everything you can remember.'

'He didn't answer so I left my handbag and the contract on the hall table and decided to find him. I called out again. The kitchen door was wide open, and he wasn't in there, but the door next to it was shut, so I knocked on it. When he didn't answer, I opened it. Alex was directly in front of the window, his head back, like he was

131

looking at the ceiling, and the blood . . . I ran. I grabbed my bag and I raced out, slamming the front door shut behind me. I drove away as quickly as I could and, as I drove, I rang the police. I swear I'm telling you the truth this time.'

'What made you go in, even though he didn't answer?'

Lisa looked Kate straight in the eye. 'A sixth sense. It didn't feel right – the open door, him not answering. I went with my gut.'

'But weren't you afraid you were disturbing something – even an intruder?'

'It didn't cross my mind. I had only one thought – to find Alex and get my job back. I wish I hadn't gone inside. I wish I'd never tried to seduce him. If I hadn't, he wouldn't have been avoiding me by staying at home and he'd be here today. And I wish we hadn't fallen out. I loved him.'

Many killed because of passion and rejection, and Lisa had admitted to both, and although Kate had a feeling she could not have tortured the man she loved, she couldn't take this woman, who'd proven herself an accomplished liar, at her word. For the time being, they'd maintain an open mind, but unless evidence proving Lisa's involvement surfaced, they had no grounds to further pursue this line of enquiry.

'What time did you arrive at Alex's house?'

'I don't know for sure, but it's a ten-minute drive from the pub. That road's narrow and winds a bit. You can't drive quickly along it.'

Kate made a quick mental calculation of the arrival time. 'Can you tell me anything else about the white car parked outside the house at around quarter to twelve? Number plate? Any further details?'

'No, sorry. As soon as I spotted it, I turned around and left.'

'You didn't notice anybody inside or near the vehicle?'

'No.'

'But it was definitely a Mini?'

'Without doubt.'

If only she'd seen stripes or flashes of colour, or remembered any part of the car's registration. 'I'll need you to accompany me to the station to make an official statement.'

'Yes.' Lisa stood on shaky legs and walked to the sink, knuckles whitening as she gripped the sides with both hands. 'I can't face anyone. I've fucked up so badly. Sam . . . she's the only proper friend I've ever had.'

Kate had no words of comfort to offer. It would surely only be a matter of time before Lisa recovered, moved away and probably began fabricating a whole new life.

'I need a minute to wash my face. I look a mess.'

'I want a quick word with Sam, so I'll wait for you outside.'

Lisa's friend was leaning against her car, arms folded, a lit cigarette in her hand. 'Stupid cow. Why on earth did she make up all that shit? I believed her, and now I feel so . . . rubbish.'

'Panic can make people behave in irrational ways.' Kate's words belied the ire that smouldered in the pit of her stomach. Not only had Lisa wasted time in a serious investigation, she'd not cared about the consequences of her accusation – the damage to her boss's reputation and the effect on his family – nor had she given a second thought to those real victims of rape, some of whom could never live normal lives again. Kate's nostrils quivered, but she didn't voice her thoughts.

Sam flicked ash from her cigarette testily. 'I'm not sure I trust her enough any more. She's a total screwball. Anyway, why did you ask me to stay behind?'

'To ask for your discretion. Will you please keep everything you've heard to yourself? If anything gets out, it might compromise our investigation.'

'I understand. I won't say a word.'

'Thank you. Lisa's coming with me to make a statement.'

'Right.'

On cue, Lisa plodded down the path towards them. She drew level with Sam and placed a hand on her friend's arm. Sam shrugged it off angrily.

'I'm so sorry, babe. I've been a fucking idiot. It all . . . got out of hand. I never meant for it to, and I shouldn't have lied to you – not you. Whatever you think of me, I had absolutely nothing to do with Alex's death.'

Sam tossed the cigarette on to the pavement and ground her heel into it.

'I loved Alex so much it messed with my head. But I love you too, Sam. You're my best friend. Don't give up on me.'

As they pulled away, Kate reflected that they now had a second witness who'd spotted the white Mini. Bradley Chapman had better come up with some answers if he didn't want to find himself behind bars.

CHAPTER SEVENTEEN

SATURDAY, 5 JUNE – LATE AFTERNOON

'Lisa spotted a Mini outside Alex's house on Thursday morning,' said Kate.

Morgan looked up. 'And we've come across this.'

Kate tossed her car keys on to her desk and went to look over his shoulder. Morgan brought up a website, the Cindi Kaufer Escort Agency, and pointed out a photograph.

'I haven't been able to get hold of him yet, but the Corbys' gardener, Rory Winters, is also a part-time male escort.'

Kate leant in to read the biography. 'Ok-ay. Speaks Russian and French and likes art and literature. Who's this Cindi Kaufer that runs the agency?'

'Not sure yet, guv, but we're looking into it.'

'Good. Got anything else for me?'

Emma lifted her notepad. 'I have. I spoke to the Corbys' cleaner, Kelly Innes. She recalls overhearing Fiona and Alex arguing the Thursday before half-term. More importantly, Kelly is sure Fiona Corby is having an affair. Apparently, Fiona was behaving furtively – hushed phone calls, text messages that made her blush, dressing "provocatively" to go out shopping, and there were several deliveries of flowers.'

'None of that points at her actually having an affair. Could all have been from Alex.'

'Kelly was certain. She said Fiona hid the cards that came with the flowers.'

'Still not watertight, but we'll keep that in mind. Lisa's in interview room B, waiting to make a statement. Which one of you feels like taking it?'

'I'll do it.' Morgan leapt up.

'Cheers, Morgan. You'll need to arrange for somebody to run her back to her house afterwards.'

'She not a suspect any more?'

'She's changed her story so many times, I'm not completely ruling her out, but in light of what she told me I want to interview Bradley again. I'm also wondering if we shouldn't question Fiona as well. Establish if she is having an affair and, if so, with whom.' She tapped a forefinger against her chin, trying to decide which way to turn. 'We'll interview Bradley first. If he persists in remaining silent, we'll charge him.'

'What with?'

'Being a pain in the arse,' Kate replied.

The door opened and DCI William Chase stood in the doorway. 'I thought I saw you in the corridor, Kate. I'm afraid the news about Alex has leaked. Dickson's asked me to speak to the press. I thought I'd give you fair warning that we're making an announcement in an hour.'

'Oh, shit! What are you planning on telling them?'

'That Alex Corby was found dead on Thursday afternoon in suspicious circumstances, and we're currently investigating his death. I'll keep it as brief and ambiguous as possible. It was only to be expected. Anybody passing his house will have spotted the forensic unit vans outside.'

'He lives at the end of a lane. Nobody would go past.'

William gave a light shrug.

'And we could do with more time without being put under the spotlight.'

'You made any progress?'

'Bradley's car was spotted turning into Lea Lane at eleven thirty, and a quarter of an hour later another witness saw it parked outside the house. But he's not talking and I don't think, at this stage, we have enough evidence to charge him.'

'Okay. I'll leave you to it.' William turned to leave.

Her voice stopped him in his tracks. 'William, keep my name out of the statement to the press.'

'You know I will.'

No sooner had he shut the door than Kate's hands began to shake. Although she'd expected the media to become involved, the realisation they'd now be following the investigation rattled her. She clenched her fists, fingernails digging deep into her palms.

'Everything okay, boss?' Morgan asked, cautiously.

'Fine. I'm just pissed off about this getting out. Let's crack on. Morgan, go on and take Lisa's statement. Emma and I will interview Bradley again.'

She hightailed it towards the door, hoping to make it down the corridor without anyone talking to her. She needed those valuable minutes to calm down and work out what to say to Bradley. She thrust her hands into her pockets and rubbed the foil pack of tablets. In spite of the temptation, she didn't take any. She needed her wits about her, and not purely for this investigation. She had to work out what John Dickson was up to. If he was deliberately trying to sabotage her, it could only be for one reason – the incident in January.

CHAPTER EIGHTEEN

SATURDAY, 5 JUNE – LATE AFTERNOON

Bradley Chapman stared straight ahead, eyes focused on a spot above Kate's head. His lawyer, a sturdy man in his early fifties, combed fingers through his silver-grey hair, then unhurriedly unclipped the lid from a jet-black fountain pen in readiness and, only after clearing his throat, began to speak in a droning voice.

'My client wishes it to be made clear he did not visit Alex Corby at any point on Thursday the third of June.'

Kate replied with, 'We have a witness who filmed Mr Chapman's car as it turned into Lea Lane at 11.30 a.m., and another who claims to have seen a white Mini parked outside Alex Corby's house at approximately 11.45 a.m.'

'Mr Chapman denies being at the Corby residence at those times, and I would like to point out that the Mini is a popular make of car.'

'I am aware of that fact. However, this car had a unique red, white and blue flash along the side panels, exactly like those on Mr Chapman's driving-school Mini.'

The lawyer replied, 'Unique? That's debatable.'

'Mr Chapman, I would like to ask you, rather than your lawyer, the question. Was your car parked outside Alex Corby's house on Thursday morning?'

Bradley didn't reply, and his lawyer blinked lazily before asking, 'Did either of your witnesses recall or note the registration of the vehicle?'

'No.' Kate balled her fists tightly. She had a feeling she knew where he was heading with this.

'Did either of your witnesses observe Mr Chapman driving, or even getting out of the car?'

'No.'

'Then I don't think we need to pursue this line of enquiry any further.'

Kate held his gaze. 'There is insufficient proof Mr Chapman headed to Lichfield along the B5014, as he claimed. His car did not pass the safety camera along the route at any time between eleven and twelve on Thursday morning.'

'Then maybe the camera is or was faulty. Have you checked to see if it was operating correctly?'

'We have no reason to believe it is faulty. Furthermore, nobody at Brown's Café recalls seeing him during the period he claims he was there. Given that information and the fact Mr Chapman can't recall where he parked, thus further preventing us from determining whether his car was actually in Lichfield at the time he says, we have to consider the possibility he did not drive to Lichfield but instead drove from Yeatsall Road in Abbots Bromley to his daughter and son-in-law's house on Lea Lane.'

The lawyer rested his pen on a pad and lifted the photograph. He grunted in agreement before continuing, 'These photographs show a vehicle turning into Lea Lane. You say the markings are unique, but decal stickers identical to these can be purchased from any auto-parts store, or online, and attached to vehicles. There's no photograph of the actual number plate or any proof my client was driving this car, therefore you have no grounds to charge him and little reason to question him further.'

Kate caught the fierce glare that Emma directed at the man, who didn't appear fazed by it.

'Have you anything other than conjecture? Have you any forensic evidence to place Mr Chapman at the scene of the crime?' He took her silence for the answer he expected. 'In which case, DI Young, I request this interview be terminated. Mr Chapman's wife, daughter and grandchildren need his moral support during this difficult and distressing time.'

'We could retain Mr Chapman for further questioning or charge him with perverting the course of justice,' Kate replied. She hated smug lawyers, and they didn't come much smugger than this one.

'I don't think so, DI Young. Mr Chapman has been open with you and told you everything he knows. He wasn't at the scene of the crime.'

Kate couldn't argue any more. The confounded lawyer would drag up some obscure section of the law and insist on his client being allowed to leave the station. It would be better to release him and concentrate on the facts again. Facts and evidence would lead her to the killer, and if it turned out to be Bradley, no lawyer on this planet would get him off, not by the time Kate had finished preparing her case against him.

She ended the interview and scraped back her chair. 'Okay. But Mr Chapman, by keeping silent you are assisting whoever killed your son-in-law and, moreover, impeding our investigation.'

'My client understands,' said the lawyer. He replaced the lid on his pen and, signalling to Bradley they could leave, got to his feet.

Kate had no time to waste. She'd speak to Fiona. If Alex's wife was indeed having an extra-marital relationship, there was cause to probe further. With a prenuptial agreement in place denying her any right to Corby International or his fortune in the case of divorce, she had a motive for having her husband murdered.

Emma followed Kate into the office, a scowl on her face. 'Slippery bastard.'

'Leave it for now, Emma. We'll speak to Fiona.'

'I'm going to have the camera on the B5014 checked out. That fucker definitely headed up Lea Lane and not into Lichfield. He went to Alex's house.' Emma slammed her paperwork on to the desk with a hefty thud.

Kate knew how it felt to be so sure of something you wanted it to be right. 'It might be a long shot, but show Lisa Handsworth a photo of the driving-school Mini and ask her if it was the car she saw on the driveway. Maybe it'll trigger a memory.'

Emma looked up briefly. 'He's lying, Kate. I'm going to prove it.'

Kate looked at her watch. It was coming up to four o'clock and William would soon be talking to the press. She needed to slip away before that happened. She stole down the emergency staircase to avoid the reporters who'd gathered outside the building and made the call to Fiona.

Fiona's voice was angry. 'Where's my father?'

'I believe he's on his way home.'

'Mum's having a meltdown. Why did you take him to the station? He hasn't done anything wrong.' Her voice reminded Kate of Tilly's – whiny and high-pitched.

'He was assisting us with our investigation. Fiona, I'd like to talk to you, too. Something has been brought to our attention and we need to discuss it.'

'What? What are you talking about?'

'I need to speak to you in person about it.'

Fiona sighed. 'Mum's in a bad enough state, so it'd be better if you didn't come here, and I don't want to come to the station. How about we meet at the Truly Scrumptious Café in Abbots Bromley? Do you know where it is?'

'Yes. I know it. Is half an hour too soon to meet?'

'No, that's fine. I'll be there.'

Kate raced to the Audi and jumped into the driver's seat without glancing in the direction of William Chase, who was addressing a pack of journalists. She slammed the door shut and gasped. 'Oh! You surprised me. What are you doing in here?'

'I wanted to see if Dickson would make the statement, but he hasn't,' said Chris.

'You think he should be talking to the press instead?'

'Definitely. He couldn't wait to talk to them about the Euston train incident, could he?'

A vision of a sombre-faced Dickson in full regalia, offering condolences to families. It was true. He was invariably the representative who faced the cameras.

'He's left it to his lieutenant to do his dirty work. Pity you can't lip-read,' said Chris.

'Dirty work? What are you on about? William's only giving out bare details.'

'Look closely. For somebody handing out scant details, he's doing a lot of talking and he's answering questions.'

She screwed up her eyes. It looked like he was responding to the eager journalists.

'Bet he mentions you.'

'He wouldn't.'

'He would if he'd been ordered to.'

'Dickson wouldn't do that, would he?'

'It'd put pressure on the investigation, hurl you into the spotlight, and if the press discover you are SIO on this, imagine the fallout. We journalists love a juicy story and it would give them an excuse to drag up the Euston train massacre.'

Kate swallowed hard. It was the last thing she wanted.

'Remind me, Kate, what did you uncover about the incident?'

'You know full well. Nothing.'

'And why not?'

'You know why not.'

'Humour me.'

'Because I was denied access to the investigation and case notes.'

'On whose authority?'

'Dickson's.'

She placed cool hands on heated cheeks. Dickson had ensured she wasn't granted access to any files, even speaking to the investigating officer personally to ensure she would be kept out of the investigation, a fact she'd uncovered thanks to an old colleague working in the same building as the crime unit on the Euston train case.

'Kate, think about what I'm saying. This could be part of Dickson's plan to keep the pressure on you. If you feel hounded by the press, you're more likely to crumble or make mistakes.'

'I can't do this at the moment, Chris. I've got to interview a suspect.'

'If Dickson had requested a gag order or a media blackout on this, none of those journalists would be stood there, and you'd have the time you need to investigate Alex Corby's death.'

She watched as William shook his head and held up his hand to signal the end of the brief conference.

Chris continued talking. 'Have you considered the possibility that Dickson is involved somehow in Alex's death and is deliberately steering you in the wrong direction?'

'For crying out loud, Chris! That's one step too far.'

'Is it, though? As the old saying goes, there's no smoke without fire. Dickson should be making that statement, not William. He's distancing himself from the investigation for a reason. Answer me this – has he contacted you directly to ask how you are getting along?'

'No.'

'Doesn't it strike you as odd that a man who specifically requested you lead the investigation is staying in the shadows?'

'Look, I can't deal with this. I need to go.'

'Do I have to spell this out for you, or can you work it out yourself?'

Kate ignored him, fixed her eyes ahead and waited for Chris to leave her so she could get on with her job, then drove away without looking back. Chris had gone.

A bell tinkled merrily over the door of the Truly Scrumptious Café, which was devoid of customers when Kate arrived. She took in the bright room and chalkboard next to the counter announcing the cakes of the day, each with tempting descriptions: salted caramel and fresh cream, pistachio with fresh lemon-yoghurt topping, and banana and butterscotch cream cake. A name was swirled at the bottom of the board – Annette-Hannah – the proud owner of the café.

A woman in her mid-thirties wearing an apron covered in cartoon cats appeared – no doubt Annette-Hannah herself. Kate ordered a black coffee.

'Can't tempt you to a piece of today's special – devilishly chocolate cake? I've got one slice left over from lunchtime and it's extremely moreish.'

'No, thanks.' Seeing the look of disappointment spread across the woman's face, Kate realised she might have sounded unfriendly. 'I've not got a sweet tooth. My husband, however, would have definitely chosen it. He's crazy about chocolate.' *Why had she mentioned Chris?*

'Take it then – on the house – for him. It'll only dry out overnight. Besides, I'm confident he'll enjoy it so much he'll send you back for more.' Annette-Hannah ignored Kate's protests and bundled the slice into a paper bag before passing it over.

The doorbell chimed again, announcing the arrival of another customer, and Fiona walked in. Kate slid the cake into her large handbag absent-mindedly.

'Just a tea, please,' said Fiona to the café owner, before facing Kate and asking, 'Where do you want to sit?'

'I'll bring the drinks over to you,' said Annette-Hannah, leaving the women to select a table.

Kate chose the one the furthest away from the counter and door and sat down. Fiona slung her bag over the back of the chair opposite and faced her.

'Thank you for meeting me, especially at such a difficult time,' said Kate.

Fiona rested her elbows on the table and leant in closer to speak, her voice low. 'You have no idea how difficult it is. You haven't helped matters by taking Dad into the station. Mum's been out of her mind today. I can't cope with her. It's bad enough having to deal with everything else; the boys don't understand what's going on and are moping about the house, and we can't go back home or return to normality because it's never going to be normal again! It's like somebody's tipped my life upside down. And, on top of it all, I can't get my head around what's happened. I go through stages where I think none of this is real, and I have to remind myself why I'm staying at my parents' house and why my youngest is sobbing in his bedroom, and then I remember my life is one huge, shitty, fucked-up mess.'

Annette-Hannah arrived with a tray of drinks, interrupting the monologue, and set the cups up on the table.

After she'd moved out of earshot, Kate spoke again. 'You'll need time to adjust, but you have support – a family who cares about you – and it will get easier.'

'You think so, in time?'

Kate slipped a hand into her pocket, felt for the pills and caressed the foil packet.

Not waiting for a response to her question, Fiona picked up her cup and stared miserably at it. 'What did you want to talk to me about?'

There was no need to beat about the bush. 'I wanted to ask you about the affair you've been having.'

Fiona swallowed hard at this revelation. Her response was fast, but not quick enough to hide the unsettled look that crossed her features. Kate knew instantly she was lying when she said, 'I'm not having an affair.'

'Come on, Fiona. Don't mess me about. It won't take the tech department long to search through your mobile devices and establish you've been seeing somebody. We can access phone records, online activity, almost anything – even deleted stuff – and it won't be long before we identify this person and then have to take you both in for questioning.'

'How does me having an affair have any bearing on Alex's murder?'

Kate watched the steam rise from her coffee and let Fiona tie herself up in knots.

'I wasn't even in the country when Alex was killed, so why would you think I was involved?'

'Fiona, it's up to you to help me out here. I can only work on facts, and I know you signed a prenuptial agreement, so in the case of divorce you would receive nothing from Alex's estate. However, in the case of Alex's *death*, you stand to inherit his worldly possessions, which is a pretty strong motive for murder. At least, that's how it would look to some people.'

Fiona put down her cup and clamped her hands under her armpits. 'I couldn't. I didn't.'

Kate gave a light shrug. She didn't need to push hard. Fiona was already cracking.

The words came, hushed and breathy. 'I *was* seeing somebody, but it wasn't serious. What I told you about Alex not being able to get an erection was true. I got frustrated. It's only natural. I'm not a dried-up old woman yet. I had some fun. Nothing more.'

'Did you break up with this person?'

'I fully intended to when I got back from France, then this happened.'

'So the relationship isn't over yet?'

'It is for me.'

'Who have you been seeing?'

'Do I have to tell you? It's so embarrassing. If anyone were to find out—' She looked about again, but there was no sign of Annette-Hannah, who had disappeared into the kitchen. Music, a disco number from the seventies, was playing in the background. Nevertheless, Fiona dropped her voice. 'I swear I didn't have anything to do with Alex's death.'

Kate repeated her question. 'Who were you seeing?'

She counted to fifteen before Fiona answered. 'Rory Winters.'

Kate wasn't surprised. Rory was a striking young man with smouldering good looks and a superb physique. If he was as charming as his escort profile claimed, he'd be a suitable love interest for Fiona.

'Please don't breathe a word of this to my parents. I couldn't bear them to find out. They'd be so disappointed in me. And my boys – what if they find out?' It was the whiny, pleading voice again.

'I'm going to have to speak to Rory.'

'I suppose you must. Is that everything?'

'For the moment. We removed the computer from your house. Forensics are examining it. I'd like your mobile, please, and permission to access your emails, social media accounts and texts. I'm going to examine the conversation history between you and Rory.'

'And if I refuse?'

'I can make you a suspect and seize it anyway. I'd rather do it the civilised way.'

Fiona slid her smartphone across the table. 'When can I have it back?'

'As soon as we finish with it.'

'I'm letting you have this information to help prove I had nothing whatsoever to do with Alex's death.' She pulled out a diary, ripped out a back page and scribbled down some passwords. 'That's the security code to my phone and those are the passwords to my social media and email accounts, although, once activated, the phone is set to automatically log in to them.'

'Weren't you worried Alex might look at your phone and find out about Rory?'

Fiona shook her head. 'He either trusted me or didn't mind me seeing someone else. He never challenged me. I wish he had. It might have proved he cared more about me than I suspect he did.' Tears began to well. She pushed the teacup aside, the milky liquid undrunk, then pulled out a ten-pound note and left it on the table. 'The drinks are on me. I must go. The children will be asking where I've got to.'

Kate accompanied her outside, where she noticed the white Mini parked behind her own car. It had a red, white and blue flash down the side.

'You came in the driving-school car?'

'One of them. This one's not used for business any more.'

'Your father owns two identical Minis?'

Fiona picked up the keys. 'He bought a new one last year to replace this because it had begun to throw up a few problems. He was going to sell it but couldn't get the price he wanted, so he repaired it himself and kept it as a runaround for Mum.'

'I thought your mother drove a Range Rover?' Kate had seen it parked outside the garage on her last visit.

'It glugs fuel. The Mini is more economical for shorter runs. Mum prefers driving the Range Rover so this car doesn't often leave the garage.'

Kate made a mental note of the number plate as Fiona pulled away. She rang Emma to tell her the latest development and was answered by an excited voice.

'I've been checking through footage from the safety camera on the B5014 to make sure it wasn't faulty, and guess what I spotted at twelve thirty, one hour later than we thought.'

'Go on.'

'Bradley's car, travelling along the road towards Lichfield. I ran a check on the DVLA database to make sure it was his vehicle and found out there are two white Minis registered in his name.'

'If Bradley left Yeatsall Road in Abbots Bromley at around eleven, as both he and his pupil Sierra claim, why didn't his car pass through the camera point sooner? He still has to account for one hour.'

'One hour in which he would have time to murder Alex, then drive to Lichfield.'

'Granted, but I just had an interesting conversation with Fiona. Apparently, one of those cars is no longer used for business purposes and Gwen uses it from time to time. Can you double-check Gwen Chapman's whereabouts for Thursday? She was supposedly out with friends. It might be an idea to see if she was actually with them. Good work, by the way.'

Kate found herself on the causeway and deafened by a vast flock of Canada geese that rose from the silvery waters honking triumphantly in unison as they traversed the reservoir. As she pushed on below the scores of flapping wings, she pondered the relevance of the second Mini.

Instinct told her it was important, but she did not dare allow herself to believe the answer would lead her to Alex's killer. 'Facts, Kate. The facts never let you down.' Chris's mantra. She'd keep following the trail. What else could she do?

CHAPTER NINETEEN

SATURDAY, 5 JUNE – LATE AFTERNOON

Rory Winters lived six miles away from Abbots Bromley in a modern semi-detached house on an estate in Rugeley.

Number 14 Bay Road wasn't especially remarkable or distinctive. In truth, it was no more than a brick box with plastic window frames and brown roof tiles. However, unlike most other properties, the front lawn had been replaced with dark red block paving on which stood three pots containing cone-shaped topiary *Buxus*. Kate, walking around a midnight-blue pickup truck parked on the driveway, trailed fingers across the nearest of the trio, the tiny waxy leaves leaving her fingers slightly sticky. The bushes would look lovely in her and Chris's garden.

Her arrival had been observed from behind slatted blinds, and Rory answered the door before she had a chance to knock. She lifted the ID hanging on a lanyard around her neck.

'DI Young. Would it be okay to come in and ask a few questions?'

The young man glanced at the card and flashed perfectly white teeth at her. 'What about?'

'Alex Corby.'

The smile vanished. 'He hasn't complained about me, has he?'

'Can we go inside, sir?'

She found herself ushered into a sitting room – a small but functional space. A remote-control unit lay on the pale-blue settee and a picture was frozen in time on the flat-screen television screwed to the wall.

'Binge-watching,' he said, flicking off the television. '*Better Call Saul*. You seen it?'

Kate shook her head.

'It's better than *Breaking Bad*. I've been glued to it all day.' He stretched languidly. 'What's this about? What's Alex been saying?'

'You haven't heard?'

'Heard what?'

If he knew about Alex's death, he was doing a good job of pretending otherwise.

'Mr Corby was found dead at his home on Thursday.' Kate waited for a typical response – an 'Oh no,' or 'How awful!' or even 'How did he die?' – but Rory said nothing. Instead he dropped on to the settee and gave her a measured look.

Eventually, he spoke. 'And what do you want from me?'

'I'd like to ask you about Fiona Corby.'

'What about her?'

'You've been having an affair with her.'

'You say "affair", I say "liaison".'

'The difference being?'

'A liaison is a romantic tryst, an illicit sexual relationship that's sensual and amorous in nature. "Affair" is a colder word. It doesn't quite explain our relationship.'

Kate was unprepared for Rory's eloquent response. She tried never to prejudge a person or form a biased opinion of them, but she was surprised by his words and his cut-glass tones, far removed from the local accent, suggesting a wealthy upbringing or a public-school education.

'How long have you been in a relationship with Fiona Corby?'

The corners of his mouth turned up. 'Almost three months. Since March the tenth.'

'Is it serious?' Kate asked.

'Yes, it is.'

'How serious?'

'I asked her to move in with me.'

'And did she agree?'

'She wanted time to think about it while she was away in France.'

'When was the last time you spoke to her?'

'The day before she went to France.'

'Friday the twenty-eighth of May?'

'If you say so. It was definitely Friday. She was leaving the following morning.'

'Has she contacted you at all this last week?'

'No, and I didn't expect her to. She wanted some space and time to think through what she really wanted to do. She was sick of Alex's moods and she was fed up with her life, but she was anxious about the children. I didn't pester her. She had to figure it out for herself.'

'Did you do any work at the Corby house while she was away?'

'No. I was pretty busy all week because I got a sudden request to clear a large plot for a house sale. I decided the lawns at Lea Lane could wait another week.'

'So you didn't visit Alex Corby any day last week?'

'Why would I?'

'When I introduced myself to you and explained I wanted to talk about Alex, you immediately asked if he'd complained about you. Why would you ask me that?'

'I thought he might have found out about Fiona and me.'

'It's unlikely he'd have phoned the police about such a matter,' Kate said.

Rory chuckled softly and broke eye contact with her. 'Okay, you caught me out. In actual fact, I borrowed his sit-on mower to work on another job. I thought he might have launched a complaint.'

'And why wouldn't he have confronted you directly about that? You're not very good at lying, Mr Winters.'

His brows furrowed momentarily. 'Seriously, it's the truth. He did speak to me about it, but I stupidly lied to him because I didn't want to lose the contract at his place. You must excuse me. My mind's a bit fuzzy after watching telly all day, and when you told me you were a detective, I automatically jumped to the wrong conclusion and imagined he'd involved the police.'

Kate had heard some feeble excuses in her time but, to date, this was one of the worst she'd come across. 'I'd like to know your movements last Thursday.'

'All day?'

'Why not?' Kate was tiring of the cocky arrogance.

'I was working in the garden I mentioned.'

'Whereabouts?'

'Holly Bush Road, Newborough. I was at one of the converted barns there – The Stables.'

'And who were you working for?'

He sighed. 'Mrs Lancaster. She's an elderly widow. She'll vouch for me.'

'What time did you arrive there?'

'Eight o'clock on the dot, and I was there all day. I cleared the whole garden. It was choked with weeds. I had to cut everything back with a strimmer before I could use the lawnmower. Then I weeded the borders and cut the paddock. I finished about seven.'

'You didn't go to the Corbys' house at any point?'

'As I said, I was at Mrs Lancaster's house all day.'

'Tell me, what did you think of Alex Corby?'

Rory's lips twitched briefly. 'I didn't like or dislike him. He was an okay bloke. I can't say a lot else about him – after all, I'm involved with his wife.'

'Did you know Fiona signed a prenuptial agreement which meant if she divorced Alex, she'd walk away with nothing – no money, no rights to the house – nothing?'

His lips twitched again. 'I didn't know, but it wouldn't have mattered either way. I'm not a gold-digger. I have a house and I earn enough to support a family.'

'About that. How did she feel knowing you are a male escort?'

Unperturbed by the change of tack, Rory continued, 'She didn't object to it.'

'She didn't mind you going out with other women?'

'There's nothing seedy about what I do. I provide companionship for people who otherwise would feel ill at ease or be unable to attend social engagements. Fiona understood.'

'People? Don't you mean women?'

'Occasionally a gentleman might require a companion. I don't discriminate. I offer a service and I'm a professional. I've accompanied people to celebrity galas, operas and even been to a political function where I met the prime minister. Fiona was fascinated by some of the people I've rubbed shoulders with. I'm an escort, not a prostitute, DI Young.'

'It seems at odds with your choice of career.'

'You mean gardening? I'm my own boss. I can earn decent money at it. It keeps me fit and in shape, and I can work the hours I want to suit both my social life and my other occupation, *and* it pays for the mortgage on this house.' He shifted his legs into a figure-four position and, resting a hand on an ankle, stared openly at her.

It was interesting body language, reflecting confidence and youth but also revealing an aggressive or competitive nature. Rory to a T, Kate thought. 'Did you speak to Alex about your relationship with Fiona?'

'Of course I didn't! As far as I know, he had no idea what was going on.'

'He didn't confront you about it?'

'Do you imagine I'd still be working for them if he had?'

Kate had to concede it was unlikely Alex knew about the affair. 'Thank you. If you don't mind, I'd like to take a DNA sample and your fingerprints for elimination purposes.' She removed the necessary kits from her bag.

'I guess I don't have a great deal of choice in the matter.'

'Not really.' She set about the tasks, keeping the conversation to a series of instructions.

'That'll be all for now. I'll leave you my number and if you can think of anything else, call me.'

She placed a business card on the coffee table and followed him to the front door. He saw her out without speaking. The door shut behind her with a firm click.

Although he had an alibi, she'd check it out and talk to Mrs Lancaster. Rory certainly seemed sure she'd back him up, but that didn't mean he couldn't have arranged the murder. But then there was the torture. Kate frowned. Rory didn't seem the type.

She stepped back from the pavement to avoid a toddler pedalling a bike, pursued by an older child on a scooter. Their mother yelled at them to slow down and threw Kate an apologetic look as she scurried past. A few doors down, a motorbike fired up and backed out of a driveway, revving all the while before it sped off. The estate was quiet enough, but the constant hum of traffic on the main road from Rugeley to Stafford was audible and the properties here were nothing like the swanky mansions Fiona was used to living in. It seemed doubtful she would have swapped lifestyles to move here.

The Audi's sidelights flashed as the car unlocked and she slipped into the driver's seat. Of course, there was a chance that Fiona and Rory had arranged Alex's death together but, if so, it left a question mark hanging over the second Mini and where it fitted in all this.

She glanced at her phone before starting the engine. She'd missed a call from Ervin, but he'd left a message.

His voice sounded urgent. 'Kate, could you drop by the lab as soon as you get this? There's something I need to discuss with you.'

The car burst into life. Hopefully, Ervin had some evidence that would give her the breakthrough she needed.

◆ ◆ ◆

Kate jogged up the steps up to the forensic laboratory. The security guard on the desk checked her ID and buzzed her through into the restricted area. Her footsteps rang out as she marched briskly down the corridor and stopped in front of the intercom.

It was Ervin's new assistant who opened the door and greeted her. 'Sorry. You missed Ervin. He got a phone call and raced off.'

'I had to drop these off anyway,' she said, passing over Rory's buccal swab and fingerprint card. 'He wanted to discuss something. Do you happen to know what it was?'

Faith glided towards a desk and lifted a thin manila file. 'It was about this. We received the toxicology report on Alex Corby.'

Kate took the folder and opened it. 'That was quick.'

'Ervin persuaded them to prioritise the case, and I believe orders came from higher up, too.'

It could take days or weeks to get a report. Kate wondered if Dickson had been involved in the process. It seemed logical, especially given his friendship with Alex.

Kate read through it. 'Traces of gamma hydroxybutyrate, GHB, or date-rape drug . . . ?' She looked up at Faith.

'That's right.'

'But Alex wasn't raped, was he?'

'No. There was nothing to suggest so at the scene of the crime, although we haven't seen the pathologist's report yet.'

'How did the GHB get into his system?' Kate asked.

'That's what Ervin wanted to discuss with you. We don't know. We found no traces of GHB at the house, so the attacker either removed whatever they used, or cleaned it thoroughly and replaced it.'

'But you believe Alex was drugged with it?'

'Yes.'

'It certainly explains why he had no defence wounds and didn't try to fight off his assailant.'

'That's what we thought. Sorry we couldn't give you any more than this.'

'No, this is useful. Thank you.'

'How are you getting on? Any suspects yet?'

'We're chasing some leads at the moment. How about you?'

Faith blew out her cheeks and swept a hand in the direction of the table tops, which were covered in plastic evidence bags. 'Ploughing through this lot. We've still got a team at the crime scene, but we've found nothing helpful yet. Killer's a ghost. Left no trace.'

'They must have left something. There must be a hair or DNA or something.'

The young woman shrugged slim shoulders. 'Not so far, Kate. We'll keep working on it, though.'

'It's tough when it's a case like this – no time to yourself. You got family here?'

Faith shook her head. 'My parents are both dead. I have a sister back in Zimbabwe, but we don't get along too well.'

'There's a coincidence.'

'You too?'

'Yeah. Lost my mum when I was five years old. My dad died in 2017. I've got a stepsister, but she lives in Sydney. We talk now and again.'

'You don't visit her?'

Kate looked at the toxicology report again and tried to keep her voice light. 'We had a major fallout. We're only just getting over it.'

'I understand that. Family, eh? Good thing we have our careers to keep us focused.'

Kate warmed to the woman perched on her stool, who exuded an air of sadness yet also empathy. 'Yes, it is, and you are so serious about yours that you travelled all this way just to work in Stoke-on Trent with the great Ervin Saunders.'

She was rewarded with a beaming smile. 'He's a cool guy.'

'Yes, he's one of the best. Okay, I'd better get off. It's late and I have to sort out some stuff before I go home.'

'Look, I don't want to be presumptuous, but if ever you feel like a chat, you only have to shout out.'

'Sure. Thanks.'

Kate meandered back along the corridor. She got along well with Emma, but they had little other than work in common, and Emma spent a great deal of her free time training at her brother's gym. Even when they did go out for a drink it was always in a group with other officers. Kate's life had been predominantly male-orientated, so it was a pleasant change to connect with another woman who'd gone through similar experiences to herself.

She said goodnight to the security guard and headed outside.

She barely noticed the late-evening traffic on the road or the drunk slumped against a wall, and she was so engrossed in a theory that Alex had entertained somebody who drugged him that she didn't notice the man in jeans and blue shirt who was waiting by the entrance to the station.

He homed in on her as she started towards the door. 'DI Kate Young?'

She paused, caught off-guard by his pleasant manner before a sixth sense kicked in. 'No comment,' she said, heaving the door open and marching through it.

'Kate. Give me a break. I worked with Chris—'

His words faded behind her as she stomped past the front desk, which was manned by a female officer.

'Any more journos about?' Kate asked, gesturing in the direction of the man.

'I thought they'd all gone after DCI Chase spoke to them. Sorry. I didn't spot that one.'

Kate grunted a response and headed once more to her office. Her heart had begun the familiar jack-hammering she associated with a panic attack, but she wasn't going to succumb to the white pills. She was getting closer to the answer. The evidence was jumbled, but she'd unravel it thread by thread.

William Chase called out to her as she passed his door. 'Kate. In here, please.'

She drew to a halt. William's voice was heavy. Had he decided to remove her from the case after all? She sidled into his office, a small room for such an important man. With boxes of files on shelves and a desk offset in front of a window, there wasn't much space for the man himself.

He stood up to face her and rested the palms of his hands against his desk. 'I want you to know it didn't come from me. I don't know who passed on the information.'

'What information?'

'That you're heading up the investigation into Corby's death.'

The hairs on her arms lifted. Chris had taught her to look past lies, and suddenly she wasn't sure if she believed William. She couldn't challenge him. To do so would be to give the game away. Instead she reacted as he'd expect. 'Oh shit, William! I can't work if I have a pack of newshounds breathing down my neck. I hate the sodding spotlight. I can't do it. You'll have to find someone else. Get one of the DIs from Stafford to handle the investigation.'

'Kate. We've been through this. Don't quit. What's the alternative? You can't hide in your house for ever. Your father would never forgive me if I turned my back on you now and let you walk away.'

Kate's father had loved William like a brother. William had been there when Kate's mother had died, and again when her stepmother, Ellen, had upped and left to join Tilly and Jordan in Australia. Surely, William would only ever have her best interests at heart.

'Don't run away from this.'

His words stung. She'd never run away from anything, had she . . . ?

She staggers from the train, incapable of thought or speech. William's hand is firmly around her upper arm, guiding her away from the horror in the compartment. She has no conscious awareness of the ground beneath her, and they drift along the platform like two spectres. She feels nothing but his grip, fingers digging into her flesh, and when she turns to look into his eyes, she sees nothing there but blackness.

Was William toying with her emotions, also determined to break her? What would Chris tell her? His journalistic cynicism was second to none and he wouldn't hesitate to claim William was playing her. Who did she believe? Chris or William? The answer was her husband. He was the only person she could truly trust. She had to play the game.

She took a second to make her decision. 'Okay. But I'm going to need you to help smooth the ride.'

'Always, Kate. Always.'

CHAPTER TWENTY

SATURDAY, 5 JUNE – LATE EVENING

When Kate reached her own makeshift office, she paused by the door. Both Morgan and Emma had their backs to her and weren't aware of her arrival.

'I overheard her muttering to herself in the corridor earlier.'

'What was she saying?'

'I don't know, but I'm sure she mentioned Chris.'

'Oh shit! I thought she was over that.'

'Maybe she isn't. We thought she was managing fine until she had that breakdown on the train when she almost attacked a civilian.'

Emma shook her head. 'Nah. She's not having another meltdown. She's fully focused on this investigation, I'm sure of it. She's worked all day, non-stop. She's heading a high-priority case. She's going to be stressed. I talk to myself sometimes when I'm trying to reason things out. You might have misheard.'

'No, he's right about muttering aloud,' said Kate. 'I've been preoccupied with the case and not had much sleep. Sometimes, things make more sense when you actually voice them. I didn't mention Chris, though.'

'Shit! Sorry, Kate. I wasn't trying to suggest—'

'Forget it. We're all under pressure. But don't worry. I'm perfectly fine. No more breakdowns, meltdowns or bad calls.'

Emma stood up, cheeks bright red. 'We're concerned. That's all. Both of us.'

'You have no need to be. Right, let's get back to this investigation. Where are we on it?'

Emma cleared her throat. 'Fiona's mother, Gwen, met her friends, Barbara Jones and Wendy Barrington, at Palm Leisure Centre on the outskirts of Uttoxeter, where they'd booked a "bums and tums" workout class and were then going to take an aqua-aerobics session in the pool. The class finished at ten thirty, but Gwen couldn't face the second. She claimed to have a bad headache and said she'd go into the sauna instead, possibly follow it up with a massage, and meet her friends at the restaurant on site for lunch. Gwen didn't show up at twelve, and at twelve fifteen Barbara received a text from her saying her headache had turned into a migraine, so she'd gone home to sleep it off.'

'Did she book in for a massage?' asked Kate.

'I don't know, because the club's shut until tomorrow morning. Shall I pull her in for questioning?'

It was late, and Bradley would undoubtedly protest loudly to her superiors about hounding the grieving family. She weighed up the repercussions against what they'd uncovered. With Dickson watching her every move, she had to be careful how she responded. If Bradley complained about her, Dickson would have grounds to remove her from the investigation.

At last she agreed. 'We definitely should talk to her, but go gently. She's in turmoil and she might have a perfectly innocent explanation. Tread cautiously. We don't know for certain what time she actually left the leisure club or if she was driving the Mini.'

Morgan let out a derisory snort. 'If it wasn't her behind the wheel, then I'm . . . Jack Sparrow.'

'Jack Sparrow? Is that the best you could come up with?' said Emma in disbelief.

'He's a cool guy. What's wrong with being Jack Sparrow?'

'Whatever. Are you coming? I might have to fight off those dogs. I could do with your peg leg to feed them, Sparrow.'

'Jack Sparrow doesn't have a peg leg,' said Morgan, following her out.

Kate heard drifts of conversation and a laugh. They were, for all their tomfoolery, a conscientious and positive pair of officers. She trusted them to make the right call.

Ignoring the noises coming from her stomach trying to remind her she hadn't eaten for most of the day, she fired up the computer. Gwen might have some answers for them, but the possibility that she'd strapped Alex to his dining-room chair and murdered him didn't seem plausible. They had to dig deeper. With that in mind, she typed Rory's name into the escort website and began reading through the testimonials.

CHAPTER TWENTY-ONE

SATURDAY, 5 JUNE – LATE EVENING

The contents of Ian's stomach swirled in protest as he battled his way back to consciousness once more. It was no longer light outside, so he'd been out of it for hours. The angel of death floated before him, merging with the white bookcase and hovering in front of him. Death, he mused, didn't wear black. It wore white. A giggle attempted to force its way up his throat but stuck in his gullet, confusing him. His mouth was wide open and his throat dry. His efforts to close his lips together were in vain. His mouth remained agape like a flip-top-bin lid. The muscles in his jaw ached dully and as the drowsiness drained from him, the white angel stooped over him, nothing of his face visible other than a pair of dark, furious eyes, so like the eyes of the fallen angel in Ian's favourite painting.

There was an obstruction in his mouth – a metallic-tasting sharp object that stretched against the roof and simultaneously pressed his tongue down so low in his jaw it hurt in places he'd never experienced pain before. He made a gargling noise. The divine being swooped towards him.

Ian blinked away tears of pain as whatever had been inserted into his mouth dug further into the soft palate and caused trickles of moisture to run down the inside of his cheeks and his throat. It wasn't moisture. It was blood. Ian's eyes widened in terror. The angel of death placed a white finger against an invisible mouth.

'Shush! Calm down. Take gentle breaths, or you'll choke on your own blood.'

Ian could barely hear the whispered words. He stared at the angel and pleaded silently for mercy. He was lying back in the La-Z-Boy, but his hands were fastened behind him so tightly that whatever was holding them together had cut into his flesh. He'd never break free. His feet were similarly tied.

The seraph floated away from view and Ian was left staring up at the top of his wonderful staircase. The cantilever stairs with no support between the treads created an illusion of floating steps. *Steps to heaven.* His mind fought to make sense of the situation. Was this a nightmare?

'Alex Corby struggled.' The angel was still close by. It hadn't disappeared at all. 'Try to remain still.'

Fuck! This was no nightmare. This was happening. Ian's heart hammered wildly against his ribs.

'I'm afraid Alex died a slow and agonising death, but not before he told me what I needed to know. He held out for quite some time, but I can be persuasive. He told me everything.'

The seraph shot back into view and held up an apple. 'I hope you're hungry.'

'Why?' The word Ian tried desperately to articulate came out as an angry caw that amused the angel.

'Did you like my present?'

Ian blinked in confusion. His jaw ached badly and the back of his throat was so dry he thought he'd gag.

'I left you a gift in your cottage – a little taster of what is to come.'

The eyeball in the jar. Ian made another noise, this time akin to a pig's squeal, and blinked repeatedly. This creature wouldn't . . . it wouldn't torture him the same way, would it?

'Ah, I see you remember. Yes, it was Alex's eye. I thought it only fitting to send it to one of his dear friends he shared so much with.'

The pounding in Ian's chest intensified. The angel disappeared for a moment, only to pop up again in front of his face, this time holding a sharp knife, which it wielded in front of Ian's eyes.

Ian fought back another scream and squeezed his eyes tightly shut.

Muffled laughter mocked him. 'I'm not going to dig out *your* eye, Ian. I'm going to feed you some supper. I've cut you up some nice juicy apple. Ideal for your poor dry throat. Come on, open your eyes. Pronto! Or I will gouge them out.'

The being was offering him a plate – one of his own pristine white china plates. On it were microscopic pieces of food. He frowned in confusion.

'Count them, Ian.'

There were twelve pieces. A slightly larger piece dropped on to the plate.

'Now, how many are there?'

Ian's heart juddered in his chest. He hoped it would give out soon. Anything would be better than the torture about to be inflicted on him. The angel glided in and out of view and finally settled above him.

'Time for supper. Open wide. Oh, you already have.'

CHAPTER TWENTY-TWO

SUNDAY, 6 JUNE – EARLY MORNING

The door to the carriage begins to slide open and Kate slips through the gap, mind focused on what she has to do. The hiss of the door opening is masked by the pop of the gun and muffled sobbing. She mustn't look at anybody. She has to concentrate fully on the task in hand. It feels like a lifetime since she saw the blood splatter against the glass door but, in reality, it's been less than a minute.

The man wielding the gun is only a metre or so ahead, his broad back to her. His long hair is black and slick. His dark blue jacket hangs loosely on his lithe frame as he moves forward with intent.

The train rattles onwards and the sobbing intensifies. The gunman is drawing level with a woman with blonde hair. Kate steals forward but encounters an obstacle – the body of an elderly man is obstructing the aisle and she has to climb over his torso.

Hurry, hurry, hurry, the train urges. Kate avoids the look in the dead man's eyes that seems to say, 'You are too late.'

◆ ◆ ◆

Kate woke to the sound of her alarm, set for 6 a.m. Chris's side of the bed was empty so she traipsed downstairs and stood by the kitchen sink, where she ran a glass of water and stared out across their back garden. The sky seemed to be on fire, a vibrant crimson orange that, according to her father, heralded bad weather. Kate had never adopted his superstitions.

She headed to what they laughingly called Chris's den: a windowless cupboard under the stairs large enough to house a small desk and a filing cabinet. It was a mess of paperwork. Kate had once attempted to tidy the sheets for him, only to be admonished.

'I like it this way. I know where everything is,' he'd retorted crossly, on the only occasion she'd relocated important documents to the filing cabinet. It was his space, and the one room in the house Kate rarely visited. She'd learnt Chris had his own way of working and it was best if she didn't interfere.

The door was ajar. She didn't open it fully, but spoke through the crack.

'Chris?'

'Yes.'

'William's somehow involved too in all of this. He told me someone had leaked my name to the press. I think it was him.'

'Tell me why you think that.'

Chris had a nose for these things. He'd understand her reasoning. 'It's more a hunch rather than facts. I've been studying his facial expressions and, although he pretends to be concerned, I sometimes see signs that say otherwise. I saw them yesterday.'

'You have excellent perception, Kate. Trust in it. You know, if you're right, and I believe you are, he and Dickson are both going to mess with your head and prevent you from uncovering the truth in this case.'

'I'm stronger than they think.'

'I know you are.' He fell silent.

Kate opened her mouth. Shut it again, then changed her mind and spoke. 'There was a guy outside the station . . . Said he knew you . . . that you used to work together.'

'Ignore him. You've got bigger fish to fry.' He sounded irritated, no doubt because she was disturbing his train of thought. He had deadlines to work to and she was disturbing him.

Their conversation was cut short by the ringing of her mobile and she raced upstairs to answer it.

The woman was softly spoken. 'Good morning, I hope this isn't too early for you. I had a message to call this number and ask for DI Kate Young. I'm Dora Lancaster. You wanted to ask me about my gardener.'

'Good morning, Mrs Lancaster. This is DI Young. Thank you for getting back to me so promptly.'

'I'm afraid I missed your call last night. I usually turn in no later than nine and read for a while, and I always switch my mobile to silent.'

'I understand. I wanted to discuss Rory Winters. He did some work in your garden last Thursday, didn't he?'

'That's right. He did.'

'Can you confirm he was with you all day?'

'Oh, yes. There was such a lot to do. I'd let it go – my arthritis, you see – and it needed proper attention. Rory arrived at around eight in the morning and stayed until about seven. *Emmerdale* was about to start when he tapped on the door to let me know he'd packed up and was ready to leave.'

'You were there all day as well?'

'Oh, yes. I don't go far these days.'

'And, just to confirm . . . he was in your garden the whole time?'

'Apart from around lunchtime, when he disappeared to collect a sit-on mower. I asked him mid-morning if he would cut the paddock field as well, but he couldn't manage it with the mower he'd brought along. Fortunately, he had a friend who lived nearby who lent him a machine better suited to the job. He was gone about forty minutes.'

'What time did he leave to collect the mower?'

'I'm not too sure about that, but it was definitely before I had my lunch and I always eat at midday.'

In that instant, the questions began mounting up. Rory had been working no more than ten minutes away from Alex's house and had disappeared around the time of the murder. He'd already told Kate that he'd borrowed Alex's sit-on for a job, so why not admit it was for Mrs Lancaster's paddock? She was suddenly eager to talk to the man again.

'Did Rory seem at all worried about anything?'

'Not that I picked up on . . . although . . . there was something . . . when I took him some tea and biscuits. He had his back to me and was on his mobile. He seemed . . . angry. I'm not nosey so I didn't eavesdrop. I put the tea down on the bench and left him to it. He hasn't come to any harm, has he?'

'No, I can assure you he's fine. I'm only checking on some facts in relation to the death of Alex Corby. Did you know him?'

'Alex Corby,' she repeated slowly. 'The name rings a bell, but I can't think how I know him.'

'Not to worry.'

'Well, I hope I've been of some assistance.'

'You most definitely have. If you can think of anything else, please give me another call.'

Kate hung up and mused over the facts. The more she thought about it, the more she was convinced Rory had gone to Alex's house on Thursday to collect the ride-on mower.

She rang Ervin, who sounded bright and breezy. 'Morning, Kate. How's it going?'

'I might have a lead.'

'Excellent! Sorry I missed you last night. I had to check on the team at the Corby house. We're almost done there so I'm pulling them out later today.'

'Okay. I have a quick question for you – did you or any of your team notice a sit-on mower in the Corbys' garage?'

'There's no mower. Only a Porsche GTR.'

'Okay. Cheers.'

'Oh, by the way. You made quite an impression on Faith last night.'

'Did I?'

'Without doubt. She told me you two had a nice little chat. I'm glad. She's not got any friends here and I'm worried she's too work-driven.'

'Must be hard for her living and working so far away from family and friends back home. How come she left Africa to come here? It's quite a dramatic change.'

'Well, that's quite interesting, because she studied at the Department of Forensic Science and Crime Investigations at Zimbabwe Institute of Legal Studies, but completed a finishing programme at University College London to certify her qualification. She graduated top of her year and was invited to stay on to take up the MSc programme. Afterwards, she was offered the chance to return to her alma mater to lecture, but she felt she needed some "global exposure" to forensics, had heard about what we do here at Stoke and wanted to join us. She's actually over-qualified for this position by a mile, but she wanted to start at the bottom and work her way up and see how differently we handle investigations, what methods we employ and so on. It won't be long before she's running this place.'

'That won't happen, will it? You've no plans to leave us?' asked Kate. She'd miss Ervin if he moved on.

He laughed. 'No . . . no. She's only staying for a year or so and then she'll return to Zimbabwe. She's incredibly diligent and we're lucky to have her. I do worry, though, that she's too insular.'

'Maybe you should invite her out with some of your friends. She'd love them.'

'Honey, my wacky friends would scare her witless and send her racing back home on the next plane to Africa.'

As he chatted, Kate cast about for her bag. She needed to get going, but she'd always had time for Ervin, who was more than a work colleague; and his friends were truly crazy, but fun. It had been ages since she'd gone out with them. She located the bag lying on the floor by the unmade bed, scooped it up and headed downstairs, spotting her car keys in a pottery dish on the ornate console table by the front door. 'I adore your friends and so does Chris,' she said, as she slipped on her shoes.

There was an awkward pause before Kate grabbed her jacket from the peg and unlocked the door. She needed to check out Rory's movements for Thursday. His words passed over her head. 'Okay. Thanks again.'

Rory must have taken the sit-on mower. Did he kill Alex while he was there? It was a fresh line of enquiry and one she needed to run past the team. This was going to be done by the book. There was no way she was going to slip up, not with Dickson and the whole of the media watching her.

There was a sense of calm in the station and only one officer on reception when she arrived at half past seven. The door to her office was wide open and Morgan was working at his desk. He looked up immediately. 'Morning, guv.'

'Morning. How did it go last night with Gwen?'

'She maintains she was at Palm Leisure Centre, had such a bad headache she tried to book a massage instead of taking the aqua-aerobics class and, when she couldn't get an appointment, went for a sauna instead. After she came out, she couldn't face lunch so she went home. Claims she drove the Range Rover, but we don't believe her. Her body language was all wrong. Emma's already gone to the centre to examine their CCTV footage. We didn't bring her in for further questioning because we didn't have any concrete evidence to contradict her story, and we didn't want to make waves. Her husband wasn't pleased to see us again.'

'Fair enough. I've got some fresh info on Rory.'

She dragged out the file of information she'd amassed on Rory the day before and gave Morgan a quick rundown on what she'd discovered.

'We have a suspect who has motive and opportunity, but I can't see anything in this file that raises any flags. He's not in any debt, although he has a mortgage on a £250,000 house, and, according to his company details, he earns over 60K per annum. Although money is a powerful motivator and so is passion, I'm concerned about the killer's MO. I can't imagine why Rory, if this was a crime of passion, would feel the need to torture Alex or, indeed, how he would have sufficient time to carry out the whole plan: get into the house, overcome his victim, torture him, then clear up, collect the sit-on mower and head back to Mrs Lancaster's house. What do you think?'

'It sounds a little far-fetched to me, unless he had an accomplice. It doesn't feel right, does it?'

'No, it doesn't.' She rubbed the back of her neck. Whatever she and Morgan believed, they still had to adhere to procedure. She let out a heavy sigh. 'We've no other option. We have to quiz him and we have to find the sit-on mower.' She reached for her car keys again. This investigation was a tangled web of deceit, and perplexing, but good policing would get the results they needed, provided she didn't make any wrong moves. She felt for the pills in her pocket. It wouldn't hurt to take them before they left the building, to keep the bad memories, the faces of those on the train, at bay.

'You okay?'

'Why do you keep asking me that?' she snapped.

'You mumbled something about ghosts.'

'I was simply saying the killer is like a ghost; leaves no evidence. I'll meet you by the car in two minutes.' Heat rose up her throat and she departed before he spotted her discomfort or quizzed her further. There was nothing wrong. She was fine.

CHAPTER TWENTY-THREE

SUNDAY, 6 JUNE – MORNING

Rory opened the door wearing only boxer shorts. He ran a hand through his tousled hair and blinked in surprise at the sight on his doorstep.

'What's going on?' he asked, looking towards Morgan, who towered over him by a good six inches.

'We'd like to look inside your garage, and if you wouldn't mind putting some clothes on, we'd like to talk to you again,' said Kate.

Without a word, Rory signalled for them to enter. He pointed ahead. 'You can reach it through a side door in the kitchen.'

Rory headed upstairs, leaving them to find their own way. Morgan took the lead, stepped inside a space sufficient for a small car but filled with cardboard boxes, large plastic bags, tools, paint and what looked like wooden garden furniture, folded and stacked against a wall.

'Bit of a tight squeeze,' said Morgan, breathing in as he shuffled between a set of drawers and something hidden under a dust sheet. He lifted a corner to reveal a John Deere sit-on.

'It's got to be Alex's,' he said.

'Looks that way. Come on, we'll talk to him about it.' Kate returned to the kitchen, leaving Morgan to edge his way back out. He brushed down his trousers.

'No sign of him?'

'Not yet. Look. There are thirteen jars,' said Kate, pointing out a spice rack containing glass bottles, each with corks and filled with a variety of coloured spices.

'Interesting. You don't think—'

They were interrupted by Rory, who'd changed into jeans and a polo shirt but still had bare feet. Kate noticed his manicured toenails and smooth heels. Her own feet were in a far worse state and her nails in dire need of trimming.

'I'm going to cut to the chase. Tell us about the John Deere in your garage,' she said.

He dropped on to a stool, feet on a metal rung, and stared at them through a length of fringe yet to be styled into place. 'It's Alex's. I borrowed it last Thursday to cut Mrs Lancaster's paddock. I hadn't planned on cutting it – I'd taken my Honda mower, but it wasn't powerful enough to tackle such a big job, so rather than let her down, I decided to nip down the road, borrow Alex's sit-on and return it after I'd finished.'

'Why didn't you tell me that when I last spoke to you?' said Kate. 'You lied to me.'

He shrugged. 'I really didn't want to find myself in this situation, with you thinking I murdered Alex. It's as simple as that. It wasn't clever to lie to you, but I knew if I told you about the sit-on, it would only lead to further questioning, at the very best.'

'Well, like it or not, it's come to that, and you could have saved me time and inconvenience,' said Kate.

He made no apology, instead keeping a steady gaze on Kate who asked, 'How long does it take to drive from Mrs Lancaster's house to Alex's?'

'I'm not sure.'

Morgan clicked his tongue in annoyance. 'Don't play hardball with us. It takes seven minutes door to door, doesn't it? We tested it out before we came here.'

Rory's shoulders sagged. 'Yes. Seven or eight minutes.'

Kate continued with, 'Let's say it took eight minutes to get to Alex's house, another eight to return to Mrs Lancaster's place and about the same to load the sit-on. It can't have taken you any longer than twenty-five minutes in total, yet you were gone forty minutes. How can you explain that?'

A muscle flexed in his jaw.

'I'm waiting.' Kate stared unblinkingly at the man, but there was no reply. 'Alex wasn't at work when you went around to collect the sit-on mower, was he?'

Rory dropped his gaze, forcing Kate to push harder. 'Come on, Rory. Help us out here. Tell us what happened or we'll have to do this at the station, which will only take up more time and delay our enquiries further. Unless, of course, you'd like to confess to murdering Alex.' She sat back in her chair with a straight face and folded her arms. Her tactic worked.

'You're right. I'd expected him to be at work, but his car was on the drive, and as soon as I saw it I swung around and headed back to Newborough, but halfway back I changed my mind. I'd already agreed to cut the paddock and I was committed. Besides, financially, it was worth my while and I like to keep Mrs L sweet. She recommends me to her friends. I turned back again, this time with the intention of asking Alex if I could borrow his sit-on. I rang the doorbell, but he didn't answer. When he didn't respond, I figured he'd gone out and left his car at home, so I decided to collect the machine as planned. The bloody thing wouldn't start because it had run out of fuel, so I wasted time hunting down a can of petrol and then I had difficulty loading it on to the truck. It took a good thirty minutes to sort it all out.'

Kate kept her arms folded and the questions coming. 'Why didn't you return the machine after you'd finished with it?'

He sighed and shook his head. 'I was going to. In fact, I was on my way back with it, but as I was approaching the house, I spotted flashing blue lights and I . . . freaked.'

'Why?'

'I got the idea into my head Alex had discovered it was missing and rung the police. I did a quick one hundred and eighty and buggered off.'

Morgan's eyes narrowed. 'You could have explained to them why you took it. Nobody would have charged you.'

'That's exactly what I *should* have done, but I was completely knackered from the day's work and I wasn't thinking clearly. I decided to return the machine the following day when he was at work, and hope he'd let it drop.'

'I'd say that was rather naïve thinking on your part. Mr Corby would certainly have deduced you'd taken it. You do have the keys to both his shed and his garage, don't you?'

'Yes.'

'Then he'd guess it was you.' Morgan wasn't going to make it easy for Rory. Kate let him have his say.

'I'll level with you. When I discovered the police were at his house, all sorts of crazy shit ran through my head, including the stupid notion that Alex was using the situation to his advantage . . . to discredit me and make my life difficult.'

'Why?' asked Morgan.

Rory cleared his throat. 'He knew about my relationship with Fiona.'

'How can you be sure he did?' Kate asked.

'He'd already warned me off.'

'Did he threaten you?'

'Not exactly. He told me to back off and stay away from Fiona or he'd ensure I'd lose everything I've worked for. He fired me on the spot.'

'When did this happen?'

'Friday morning. The day before Fiona went away.'

'Am I right in saying, when you returned the following Thursday to borrow the mower, you were no longer working for him?' asked Kate.

He sighed again. 'No, I wasn't.'

'And yet you still had the keys to the shed and the garage?'

'Yes.'

'In effect, you had no right to enter his property.'

'In hindsight, probably not. Look, I turned back to ask his permission. I wasn't going to steal it, only borrow it.' His voice had become indignant.

'You stole his machine, Rory,' Kate insisted.

'I *borrowed* it.'

'Why didn't you leave your keys to the garage after the confrontation with Alex?'

'I forgot, and he didn't ask for them.'

'How convenient,' muttered Morgan.

'I *forgot*,' Rory repeated.

Morgan snorted lightly then said, 'So, this encounter with Alex last Friday – what happened?'

'Yes. Alex was on his way out when I turned up. He got out of his car and confronted me. As soon as he'd said his piece, he climbed back into his car and drove off.'

'Did you mention this to anyone?' said Kate.

'No.'

'Not even to Fiona?'

Kate wasn't fooled by the wide-eyed look that accompanied his denial. 'You didn't tell Fiona Alex had dispensed with your gardening services?'

'She had enough on her plate, preparing for the trip, and she already had plenty on her mind. Besides, I was convinced she'd decide to leave the stupid bastard so I really didn't give a stuff whether or not I worked for him. Alex might have believed money would keep Fiona manacled to him, but the truth was, she didn't want him. She wanted me.'

'Did you attack Alex Corby?'

'No. I didn't.'

'Did you threaten him in any way?'

'Absolutely not. He didn't answer the door when I knocked. I swear, I didn't set eyes on him the entire time I was there. I didn't kill Alex. I had no reason to kill him. I already had his wife.'

'Thank you, Mr Winters. That will be all for the moment. We'll most certainly wish to speak to you again. In the meantime, please don't make any plans to leave the area.'

On the way back to the station, Morgan was agitated. 'I'm not entirely convinced he's innocent. What if the argument he and Alex had was more heated than he suggested, and Alex threatened to ruin Rory and his business?' Kate had already considered those possibilities, but it was good to hear Morgan's reasoning. 'Rory would then have motive, not to mention a shitload of money when Fiona inherited Alex's estate. He knew the family was on holiday.'

Kate shook her head. 'There's only one flaw in that argument. Rory didn't expect Alex to be at home when he went around to collect the sit-on mower.'

Morgan persisted. 'What if he contacted Alex, demanding to meet him at the house? What if the whole thing had been planned to give him an alibi?'

'He had no way of knowing Mrs Lancaster would ask him to cut the field that day. He went with the sole intention of clearing her overgrown garden.'

'He might have suggested it himself. Or dropped hints, or subliminal messages that she picked up on.'

'That's a huge amount of supposition, Morgan.'

'What else do we have? Most murders are committed by a spouse or by somebody who knew the victim.'

'That's true, and you're correct. I can't put my finger on exactly what's wrong with this scenario, but if Rory's elaborate plan was to do away with his lover's husband, it hinged on too many coincidences. And why not give himself a more concrete alibi, not some wishy-washy one about borrowing a sit-on mower?'

Morgan pumped the accelerator pedal. 'I don't like him.'

'You know we can't be prejudiced in this line of work, Morgan. We can't judge people and decide whether or not we like them. We stick to facts – plain and simple facts.'

'Understood,' he muttered.

She sensed the fight drain from him. He was young and zealous. It was only natural he'd be feeling some frustration, especially since Kate insisted on a more softly, softly approach than he might have preferred. She let it drop and allowed the silence to wash over them.

Emma drew up in the staff car park at exactly the same time as them, bounded from her vehicle and made a beeline for Kate. 'Security CCTV footage at Palm Leisure Centre clearly shows the white Mini registered to Bradley Chapman parked in the leisure centre car park at ten o'clock Thursday morning. The camera alters position every ten minutes, moving from left to right and back again. Every time it returns to its original position it focuses on the Mini, which remains in situ until 11.10 a.m., after which it disappears and is not seen at 11.20 a.m., when the camera next returns to that spot. There's no sign of Gwen crossing the car park, or the Mini driving away. I also checked with reception to see if she had a massage and they said she didn't, nor did she attempt to book one. Furthermore, there were slots available, so she fibbed.'

'How long would it take for her to drive to Lea Lane from the leisure centre?'

Emma gave her a smug look. 'It took me twelve minutes.'

Kate nodded her approval. The timings would place Gwen's Mini at the turning to Lea Lane around the time the cyclist went past. They trooped through the front entrance and into reception, where the desk officer stopped Kate.

'You've got a visitor in interview room D. She wouldn't give a name but insisted she wait for you. Said it was very important. Refused to discuss it with anyone but you.'

Kate shouted over to Emma and Morgan, 'I'll be up in a minute.'

She dashed to the room and opened the door, only to come to a surprised halt. The woman standing by the window was none other than Gwen Chapman.

CHAPTER TWENTY-FOUR

SUNDAY, 6 JUNE – AFTERNOON

Gwen's puffy eyelids were so swollen they almost obliterated her bloodshot eyes. Her lipstick had smudged, leaving a crimson slash below her bottom lip and, together with the sooty mascara streaks, the appearance of a sad clown.

'My family don't know I've come here.'

The woman shuffled from one foot to the other.

'Would you like a cup of tea or anything?' Kate asked.

She shook her head. 'No. I just want to get this over with.'

'You've been under considerable stress the last few days. None of it has been easy for you.' Kate kept her voice calm and soothing while Gwen remained standing by the window, twisting the handles of her shoulder bag around her knuckles. Kate pulled out a seat, dropped on to it. 'Why don't you join me?'

Gwen shuffled forward and took the chair facing Kate, hugging the bag on her lap. She spoke in a breathy whisper. 'I visited Alex on Thursday and I spoke to him. But I certainly didn't kill him.'

'Take your time. You can stop whenever you need to.' Kate shifted to a more relaxed pose. In the past, this had worked for her, with witnesses and even suspects, who unconsciously emulated her stance. Gwen, however, let go of her bag, dropped her face into her hands and sobbed. Kate waited. She had time. Time was fluid. It seemed to last a second or an hour, depending on the circumstances.

Eventually Gwen ferreted in her bag for a tissue, blew her nose and then spoke, her words laboured and thick. 'Fiona rang me on Wednesday evening. She was terribly upset because Alex hadn't joined them in France . . .'

◆ ◆ ◆

'Don't cry, sweetheart. This isn't like you.'

'I've made such a horrible mess of things. I needed to feel loved. I felt so . . . empty.'

'What have you done, Fiona?'

'I got involved with another man.'

'Oh, Fiona!'

'I know. I know. It was a huge mistake. He was attentive and we got on well, and he made me feel desired and wanted, and he also made me appreciate how much I love Alex. I was going to end it. I just didn't seem to find the right time to tell him and then, last Thursday, I stupidly left my mobile on the bed while I took a shower. When I came back to the bedroom, Alex was in bed, and the look on his face gave him away – he knew. There'd been a message while I'd been in the bathroom. Alex hadn't opened it, but he'd undoubtedly read the first few words when it flashed up on the screen and seen who sent it.'

'Oh goodness! What happened?'

'He didn't say a word. He put down his book, turned over and went to sleep. He didn't bring it up the following morning either, but he was distant and only answered me in monosyllables. I didn't know how to tackle the subject and so I begged him to come to France again. I thought it would be easier to talk to him away from home and the

business, and tell him how much he means to me. He refused. Said he
was too busy. I've been waiting all week for him to ring and say he's
changed his mind and has booked a flight here, or even surprise us with
a visit, but there's been nothing. He hasn't even called the boys to ask
how they are. I've screwed up completely. He'll be getting divorce papers
ready while I'm here and, when I go home, it'll be over.'

'Shh! It won't be as bad as you think.'

'It'll be worse. This is all my fault. What about Hugh and Jacob?
They adore their father. They'll hate me for ever.'

'No, they won't. There's still time for Alex to ring you. It's only
Wednesday. Maybe he'll come out for the weekend.'

'You think so?'

'He won't want to lose you, Fiona. Trust me. I'm your mother.'

◆　◆　◆

Gwen looked Kate in the eyes. 'Do you have any children?'

'No, I don't.' Kate had to consciously dispel the cloud she was
sure flitted across her features.

Gwen appeared not to notice. 'Fiona was premature and spent
the first six weeks battling for her life in an incubator, fed by tubes.
She was so tiny and helpless, I was convinced we'd lose her. But
we didn't. She proved to be a fighter and she survived and grew
into a beautiful woman with babies of her own. Her happiness is
paramount. I can't express how important she is to me, and I'd do
anything for her and my grandchildren. After our conversation,
I couldn't sleep for worry. If she was right and Alex was planning
to divorce her, I don't know how she'd have coped. It would have
shattered her, and there were those precious children of hers to
consider too.

'I made up my mind to interfere. Bradley had little time for
Alex, but I always respected him. He was good to my Fiona over

the years, and I know he cared hugely for her and the boys, but I didn't dare tell Bradley what I intended to do. He'd have stopped me because . . . well, nothing would have pleased him more than to see Fiona and Alex break up.'

'I take it he didn't approve of their relationship?'

Gwen heaved a sigh. 'He made it clear from the start he disapproved of Alex, but quite honestly, he disliked all Fiona's boyfriends, and frightened most of them off. Alex was the exception. He wasn't discouraged by Bradley's sour temperament or caustic comments and rose above the snide remarks. He stood up to him, and I respected him for loving Fiona enough to take on her father, treat him with respect and put up with him. Bradley didn't dislike Alex, he hated anyone who had the audacity to replace him in Fiona's affections. You see, Fiona is the most important person in his life, too.'

Kate understood what she meant. Bradley had been jealous of his son-in-law.

'I went to Palm Leisure Centre as planned on Thursday morning, but on the way there I rang Alex and asked if I could visit him at his office. He told me he wasn't there and was working from home, and suggested I drop by around eleven thirty, when he'd be free to talk. I'm afraid I couldn't concentrate on the exercise class and I didn't want to tell my friends what was going on, so I fabricated a headache and told them I'd catch up with them later.

'Alex was expecting me, and I didn't waste time getting to the point. I relayed the conversation I'd had with Fiona and begged him to go to France, talk to her and resolve the problem.' She wetted her lips. 'He promised he'd book a seat on the evening flight for later the same day to patch things up, and the last I saw of him, he was waving me off.'

'Did either he or Fiona tell you who she was having an affair with?'

'No, and to be honest, it didn't matter who it was. My only concern was to get them back together again.'

'How long were you at the house?'

Gwen hesitated. 'Fifteen . . . twenty minutes, tops.'

'What did you do afterwards?'

'I drove to the butcher's shop in Uttoxeter – Reynolds and Sons. I got there around quarter past twelve. Archie Reynolds, who we've known for years, was annoyed because the delivery was late, and he commented it was no use pies arriving in the afternoon when he needed them for the morning rush. He'll most likely remember me being in the shop around that time.'

'Why didn't you come forward before? You could have saved us a lot of trouble.'

'I didn't want Bradley to find out I'd interfered. He . . . doesn't like it when I meddle, especially in Fiona's life. And Alex . . . well, as I said. He didn't like Alex. He'd have been . . . cross.' She stared at her hands and Kate understood in a flash: Gwen was afraid of upsetting or angering her husband.

'I should tell you we have a witness, a cyclist who unintentionally filmed your car turning into Lea Lane on his helmet camera. We believed it was Bradley's car and spoke to him about it. At the time, we were unaware there was a second identical car, and he refused to comment.'

She let out a small groan. 'I remember the bike. The cyclist waved me past but there seemed little point when I intended turning a few metres down the road.'

'Bradley will surely have worked out it was you behind the wheel. Has he not challenged you about it?'

Gwen clamped her hands between her legs. There it was again, thought Kate: acute anxiety. 'No. I only came here because your officers found a hole in my alibi. Why didn't he explain that I sometimes drive it?'

'I can't answer that. He'll have to tell you himself. I can only assume he was protecting you.'

'Protecting me from what? He can't possibly imagine I had anything to do with Alex's death!'

'We'll need to speak to him again about it, because he refused to tell us anything earlier.' Kate had made a mental calculation and, if Gwen's version of events held true, she would have had no time to murder Alex. Kate had one more question to ask. 'Your husband told us he headed from Abbots Bromley to Lichfield just after eleven o'clock, but his car wasn't picked up by a safety camera until an hour later on the B5014 outside Hamstell Ridware, half-way to Lichfield. Have you any idea why that might be the case?'

Gwen's face turned white.

Kate continued smoothly, 'There were several discrepancies in his story, but he refused to cooperate. He might not have liked Alex, but he loves you all. Surely he'd want us to get to the bottom of the investigation, so why do you think he wouldn't open up to us?'

Gwen blinked back tears. 'I can only think of one possible explanation – Alex wasn't the only one being betrayed.'

'You think your husband is having an affair?'

'He's had them in the past. He vowed that sort of behaviour was behind him, but I can't think why else he'd have disappeared for a whole hour and refused to tell you where he was.'

'Have you any idea who he might be seeing?'

'If he's gone back to his old habits, it'll be a pupil. His past lovers were driving-school students.' She chewed at her lip. Tears brimmed again. 'It would certainly explain his recent behaviour – he's been more . . . aloof than usual, and then there are the phone calls he always takes alone. Sometimes he'll go out after one of them, without any explanation as to where he's going or for how long. Now I understand . . . He's seeing somebody, for certain.'

'Why didn't you confront him about any of this?'

A tear broke free of her eyelashes and trickled down her cheek. 'I didn't pick up on the signs. I was preoccupied with other mundane matters and, more importantly, I trusted him. He swore it would never happen again.' She wiped away the tear and lifted her head high. 'I've told you everything I know about Alex. I can't tell you anything more about my husband's whereabouts on Thursday morning. You'll have to question him yourself.'

Kate gave a sympathetic nod. 'Thank you for coming in and clarifying things for us. I hope you don't mind, but I will require an official statement from you about the last time you saw Alex. It won't take long.'

'And then can I leave?'

'Certainly.'

Kate asked the police officer in the corridor to arrange for a statement to be taken and was halfway up the stairs when Emma came bounding down.

Her voice was urgent. 'Kate, there's been a fresh development.'

'What is it?'

'Derbyshire Forensics have been in touch. They've got Alex's eye.'

'What?' Kate pounded up the rest of the stairs and strode along the corridor with Emma, who talked rapidly as she kept pace with her.

'It was recovered from a cottage near the Peak District on Friday evening. The local police received a phone call from the householder, claiming the place had been broken into. When they got to the scene, they found nothing had been stolen but a jam jar filled with formaldehyde and containing the eye had been left on a desk. They suspected it was a practical joke and assumed at first it was an animal's eye. The jar was sent to Derbyshire Forensics, where some cock-up over weekend cover meant it didn't get examined until today. DNA testing proved it to be Alex's. They contacted us as soon as they identified it. The senior officer apologised and has launched an enquiry as to why this happened.'

'Bloody hell! We can do without these sorts of setbacks. Okay, who's the house owner?'

'I only spoke to Forensics. You need to talk to DI Terry Robinson about it. He's expecting your call.'

Morgan handed Kate a piece of paper.

'Gwen is giving a statement in interview room D,' said Kate. 'Can one of you collect it when she's done? It accounts for her movements on Thursday morning.'

'I need to go to the men's room. I'll pick it up on my way back,' said Morgan, and headed out of the office.

Kate punched out the number on the paper and then grabbed a pen to make notes. DI Terry Robinson sounded flustered and overworked, and even though he was expecting her to ring him, it took several minutes for him to locate the correct paperwork and give Kate the information she required.

He read out the statement in a pedestrian fashion, pausing heavily at the end of every sentence. 'A call came in at eight thirty on Friday the fourth of June, from Mr Ian Wentworth of Raven Cottage, Ashbourne. He'd gone home to find his house had been broken into and was afraid the intruder or intruders were still on the premises. Officers were immediately dispatched to the premises but, on their arrival, there was no sign of any trespassers. Mr Wentworth said nothing of value seemed to have been stolen but a jar containing an eye had been left behind on a desk in his study. He instructed the officers to remove the container but did not wish Forensics to attend the scene, nor for any further action be taken.'

'Didn't he want to know who had left the jar?'

'No. The officers mentioned he appeared jumpy, which was understandable, given the circumstances, and asked them to take the jar away immediately. Believing it to be some practical joke, they brought it back to the station, where it was duly dispatched to the forensic laboratory at Derby University for closer examination. I'm afraid there was a problem regarding weekend cover and it got overlooked.'

'Yes, so I hear. It could have helped us hugely if we'd known about this sooner.'

'Obviously, but as I said, it was one of those unfortunate things.'

Kate bit back more angry words. They would serve no purpose other than to alienate a fellow officer in the next county. 'Do you know anything about Ian Wentworth?'

'We're short-staffed here at the moment. I only received this information a short while ago and as soon as we'd established the identity of the eye, I contacted you, so I haven't had a chance to look into his background. I believe he's an ENT surgeon, but that's as far as my knowledge stretches.'

'Does he have any connection to Alex Corby?'

'Again, I haven't had any opportunities to establish if he has.'

'How long has Mr Wentworth lived at Raven Cottage?'

'I don't seem to have that information to hand. I can tell you it's his holiday cottage. His primary residence is on your patch, which is why I alerted you as soon as I could.' There was further rustling of papers as he searched for the address. 'Here it is. Festival House, Lichfield.'

'Have you got a telephone number for him?'

He read it out for her. 'I hope he can help you with your investigation. Have you any further questions?'

'No, thank you. We'll look into it.'

'If anything else comes to light, I'll let you know.'

Suddenly, they had several directions and leads. Kate gave Emma the news. 'Alex's eye turned up at a holiday cottage belonging to Ian Wentworth, a Lichfield resident.'

Emma raised a balled fist, punching the air. 'A new lead. Do you want me to track him down?'

'No. I'd like you to talk to Sierra Monroe again. Gwen believes her husband is having an affair with one of his pupils, and since he taught Sierra from ten until eleven and we can't establish his whereabouts for the ensuing hour, she's the most likely candidate.'

'He's having an affair?' Emma's face scrunched up in surprise.

Kate fiddled with her pen, clicking the top several times as she tried to make sense of the eye turning up in a jar.

'You think Bradley is having an affair with a twenty-year-old?' Emma repeated, dragging Kate away from her thoughts

Kate put down the pen. 'It doesn't matter what we think – we have to investigate Gwen's claim. Start with Sierra, then speak to all his other pupils.'

Emma pulled a face. 'I can't believe he'd be shagging a girl younger than his own daughter.'

'Just follow it up, Emma. If nothing else, it might clear him from the investigation,' said Kate.

Morgan turned up at that moment. 'Clear who?' he asked, placing Gwen's statement on Kate's desk.

'Clear *whom*?' said Emma. 'It's whom, not who.'

'What?'

'Never mind,' she replied with a wry grin. 'Bradley might have an alibi for Thursday.' She scooted across to her desk and tapped at the keyboard.

Kate turned her attention to Morgan. 'Find out what you can about an ear, nose and throat specialist, Ian Wentworth. He lives in Festival House, Lichfield. There must be some reason he received Alex's eye.'

Morgan logged on to the general database and said, 'He has a website.' He twisted his screen around so Kate could see the unsmiling portrait of a large-nosed man who looked to be in his fifties, with jet-black hair. There was something familiar about his face, as if she knew him, yet she'd never heard of him before today.

'You read through the information on the website and I'll root around on the general database.'

Ian had attended school in Sutton Coldfield and from there had gone to London University to study medicine. Alex hadn't gone to either educational establishment. If Ian had known Alex, it wasn't through studying together, so maybe they'd met socially or Alex had been one of his patients. Kate was certain Chris would have another theory. He'd undoubtedly bet there was a connection between Wentworth and Dickson.

Emma gave a small cough. 'I've found out something interesting. Sierra's father, Cooper Monroe, is also an ex-SAS member who not only happens to work part time as a security guard at Corby International's warehouses but was in the same squadron as Bradley Chapman. Do you still want me to question Sierra?'

Kate pondered the question. There was no reason not to speak to the girl. The fact that her father and Bradley served together in the forces didn't negate the possibility she was having an affair. 'Yes, stick to the plan, and Morgan, you tackle Cooper. Establish his movements for Thursday. I'll speak to the surgeon.'

With both officers deployed, Kate rang Ian, only to listen to a recorded message informing her he was unable to take her call. She left a message for him to call her back.

No sooner had she hung up than William rested a hand against the door frame and peered in. 'Hi, Kate. Superintendent Dickson has been asking me how you're getting on. It's been three days and he'd like an update.'

'As you said, it's been three days,' she replied.

'How far along are you?'

This wasn't like him. He was always more approachable than this, and was a cajoler, not a pusher.

'William, that's like asking about the length of a piece of string. What's up?'

'Nothing, merely trying to establish where you are in the investigation. Last time we spoke you were looking into Lisa Handsworth and Bradley Chapman. Any updates?'

'Lisa looks like a dead end and we're still working on Bradley's whereabouts,' she replied.

'Any other suspects?'

'We've been looking into Rory Winters and Fiona Corby. It appears they've been having an affair.'

'Any cracks in their alibis?'

'None so far. Gwen Chapman was at Alex's house the day he died, but I don't believe she killed him.'

'Believe? What about facts, Kate?'

'She wasn't there long enough to murder Alex, and as soon as she'd finished her conversation with him she went to the butcher's in Uttoxeter.'

'And you've checked out this story, have you?'

'Not yet.'

His eyes locked on to hers, point made.

'She didn't kill him.'

'I'm sure you'll detail all that in your report. Make sure you let me know as soon as you find out anything new.' He patted the door frame and vanished, leaving her feeling slightly perplexed. Why had he been so sharp with her? His behaviour had seemed out of character recently. Because of that, along with an increasing suspicion that both he and Dickson were out to topple her, she'd held back about Ian Wentworth. She wanted to keep it under wraps until she could speak to the man. She couldn't trust William, and with that realisation came a rising sense of panic. She had to get out of the station and away from everyone.

She snatched up her bag and car keys and clattered down the back staircase and into the car park, where she inhaled deeply. The scene was shifting again, the car park transforming into a station platform, the line of parked cars morphing into a ten-carriage silver train. *No! Not now.* She made it to the Audi, avoiding the stares of pleading faces – the faces of ghosts she couldn't help. She slid into the driving seat and pressed out a single white pill from the foil pack in her bag and dry-swallowed it, resting against the cool headrest until the present returned and the past was banished once more.

Once she felt able, she started up the engine, keen to escape. Out of the corner of her eye she caught sight of the man who'd stopped her the night before – the journalist – and floored the accelerator pedal. He raised a hand in her direction, but she ignored him and hurtled out of the car park, putting distance between them both as quickly as possible.

CHAPTER TWENTY-FIVE

SUNDAY, 6 JUNE – AFTERNOON

Festival House, named after the gardens opposite Lichfield's famous clock tower, overlooked one of the many expanses of green especially created for city-dwelling individuals within the estate. Although still considered to be one of the smallest English cathedral cities, Lichfield had grown over time to a population of approximately 104,000, and an entire estate of several thousand people lived on land where once a hospital had stood. Kate pulled into the general car park and made the short distance to the block where Ian lived on foot.

The entire area had been, Kate mused, tastefully designed. It was verdant and neatly maintained, with tidy hedgerows and clipped green lawns: a haven of pedestrianised tranquillity. Two swans swam gracefully on the pond adjacent to Festival House, approaching her as she neared them, in the hope of being fed.

Festival House resembled a three-storey mews complex rather than a block of flats. The façade was cream-coloured with fake arches that disguised the three separate entrances, giving the impression each led into one individual house. She found the bell for the penthouse next to the middle door, and rang it. No one responded. She took a pace back and looked up at the top floor but could see nothing of the apartment as it was set back slightly and concealed by a concrete balustrade.

'You looking for somebody?'

The voice surprised her. It had come from a woman wheeling a buggy in which sat a contented chubby baby chewing on a plastic ring.

'I was hoping to catch Ian Wentworth. He appears to be out.'

'His car's here. I just parked next to it. He might have walked into town, though. It's easier than trying to find a space to park.'

'Do you live in this block?'

'Bottom floor. Ian's on the top.'

'I don't suppose you can let me in so I can knock on his door?' Kate showed her ID.

The woman pulled a face. 'He done anything wrong?'

'Just want to ask him some questions about a break-in.'

'What, here?'

'No. In Derbyshire.'

The woman let out a sigh of relief. 'Thank goodness. Not being funny or anything, but I've been a bit edgy today. I went into the kitchen in the early hours to fetch the baby's milk, and I was sure there was somebody hanging about over there in the alleyway. My husband went outside to check but didn't see anyone.'

'Can you describe the person?'

'No. It was too dark to see anything other than vague shapes and movement.'

'What time was this?'

'Two in the morning. You don't think they were casing the place, intending to break in, do you?'

'It might have been a drunk or somebody on their way home who stopped for a piss. I wouldn't worry about it. As I said, this isn't about a break-in here.'

'Yes, I guess you're right. I've been overtired recently, what with this little one getting me up at all hours.'

'What's your name?'

'Hayley. Hayley King.'

'Well, Hayley, if you see anyone lurking about in the early hours again, let the police know.'

'I shall.'

'Could you let me into the block?'

'Yes, sure.' Hayley pulled a key out of her pocket and slotted it into the lock. The door swung back to reveal a tiled hallway and a metal staircase. 'My apartment's here,' she said, pointing to the left.

Kate held the door open while Hayley dragged the pram inside, then climbed the stairs to the top landing and stood in front of a white door that was partly open.

She shouted, 'Mr Wentworth?'

There was no sound.

'Mr Wentworth, it's the police. I'm coming in,' she called.

When there was no answer, she extracted a pair of disposable gloves from her jacket pocket and pulled them on. She pushed the door open and stepped inside, senses alert in case an intruder was on the premises. The smell, akin to rotting fruit, hit her olfactory senses immediately, causing her to catch her breath and pause. She recognised the first whiffs of a decomposing body. The apartment was a vast open-plan space of entrance room, dining and kitchen area and sitting room all in one. Her gaze fell to the far end, where a grand piano was standing in front of white floating stairs, then was drawn to the chair in front of the bookcases. She approached with caution, each step drawing her closer to the grisly scene.

A man was resting in the chair, mouth wide open. She'd already known what to expect. The open door had prepared her and the splashes of crimson on the cream carpet beneath the La-Z-Boy hinted at it. His right eye had been plucked from its socket. The crime scene had to be preserved but she needed to check for signs of life – for her own peace of mind – and was sideswiped by a vision so vivid it froze her to the spot . . .

◆ ◆ ◆

An elderly man's body has fallen into the aisle; his torso is blocking her path. The gunman is unaware of her presence. She raises a foot, clambers over the man without looking at his face, and clears his body.

Pop!

A blonde-haired woman is lying face down on the table, her friend hunched over in the corner, crimson stains on the headrest.

Pop!

Kate can't breathe. The smell of death is everywhere.

She takes another step. Ever closer to the assailant.

Then she catches sight of a child's shoe.

◆ ◆ ◆

Kate's fingers trembled as they searched in vain for a pulse from the carotid artery. Ian had been dead for hours. The plate on the coffee table beside his body contained eleven microscopic pieces of chopped fruit. The remainder of the apple stood next to them. Ian hadn't made it to the thirteenth piece. He'd choked far sooner.

She rang Ervin, told him to meet her at the apartment straight away, and then called DCI William Chase.

'William, the killer's struck again.'

'Where are you?'

'The penthouse at Festival House in Lichfield. It belongs to Ian Wentworth.'

'Is he the victim?'

'Yes.'

She imagined she could hear him sucking in breath.

'Do you know him?' she asked.

His response was quick. A little too quick. 'No. Have you notified Forensics?'

'I rang Ervin before I called you.'

'Good. Okay. We'll need to keep a lid on this. Contain the scene and I'll meet you there as soon as I can.'

As she studied the ruined face in front of her, she couldn't set aside the feeling she knew the man, or had seen him somewhere before – just as she'd thought when she'd seen his portrait photograph on his website.

There was little time to consider it further. She had a duty to perform: secure and record the scene and ensure it remained uncontaminated before Forensics and the pathologist arrived.

First, however, she rang Morgan, whose voice kept breaking up. 'Hi, Kate. I'm on . . . way back. I can't . . . locate Cooper . . . house . . . Sierra doesn't have a clue where he might be.'

'Okay. Leave him for the moment. We've got another victim and I need you and Emma to join me in Lichfield as soon as possible.'

'I'll tell Emma. Where are you?'

Once she'd given details to Morgan, she hastened downstairs, knocking at doors to ask the occupants to vacate the building. No one was at home. Even Hayley King didn't answer her door.

Kate wondered if the woman had actually seen somebody in the shadows in the early hours of the morning – if so, that person might have been the killer. She stepped outside, ensuring the front door was left open, and stood in front of the building to keep folk away until an official cordon had been put in place. There wasn't a soul in sight. A plane rumbled overhead, a departure from Birmingham airport, and she watched it travel across the azure sky.

She checked her phone for new messages and Chris's voice made her look up in surprise.

'Kate.'

'What are you doing here?'

'Making sure you're okay. You look troubled.'

'I am a little. It's William.'

'What about him?'

'He recognised the victim's name, Ian Wentworth. I could hear it in his voice. He was . . . guarded. I needed to find out if Ian knew Alex . . . and Dickson. And now I can't ask him. It's . . . frustrating.'

'But maybe convenient for somebody else – the killer. Ian can't tell you what you need to know. You'll have to get the info some other way.'

'His face . . . seems familiar.'

'In what way? Have you met him before?'

'No. I felt something similar when I saw his photo on his website.'

'Photo. Think, Kate. Think.'

She shut her eyes for a moment. Of course! She'd seen Ian before. He hadn't aged as much as the others, but it was definitely the same person. Ian Wentworth was in the photograph of Alex Corby and John Dickson taken on the ski slopes. Dickson knew both men!

'Dickson . . . photograph.'

The sound of distant sirens alerted her to the arrival of the team.

'Be careful, Kate.'

'I shall,' she said absent-mindedly, staring up once more at the shining silver speck and the vapour trail it had left behind.

Corby, Wentworth and Dickson. What had she got herself involved in?

CHAPTER TWENTY-SIX

SUNDAY, 6 JUNE – EVENING

Festival House was quickly cordoned off and a forensic team led by Ervin set up inside the penthouse apartment. Kate and her officers, in full protective clothing, caught up on the investigation in the hallway of the building, away from the activity taking place on the estate. Uniformed officers kept curious observers at bay, but word was getting out fast. It had been impossible to ignore the forensic team with their paper suits and white metal cases, streaming from the car park, or the police officers who were at present conducting door-to-door enquiries.

Emma kept her voice low. 'Sierra swears she caught the bus to Uttoxeter, where she works at the Cinebowl Entertainment Centre, at eleven fifteen on Thursday morning. She last saw Bradley in his car parked outside her house, on the phone to somebody. She lifted a hand and waved goodbye and he returned the gesture, but she didn't notice him pull away. She's got a rock-solid alibi, because not only is there CCTV on the buses, which will undoubtedly support her story, but she sat next to a friend and work colleague, Donna Croft, who was on the same shift as her. I can follow this up to confirm it, but I'm convinced she wasn't having sex with her dad's friend.'

Emma's perspicacity was not to be ignored. If she was sure there was nothing going on between Bradley and Sierra, it was good enough for Kate.

'We should question Bradley about his missing friend and query his whereabouts for Thursday again,' said Morgan.

Kate nodded. 'We're going to have to, because I'm uncomfortable about Cooper's sudden vanishing act.'

'Kate! You can come up.' Ervin's voice travelled the three floors without having to be raised.

'On our way,' she called back, leading the ascent.

Several white-suited officers were performing practised choreographed actions throughout the apartment, some on their knees searching through drawers, others bent over furniture dusting for prints, while more still padded from area to area and ascended or descended the floating staircase.

The pathologist, Harvey Fuller, was still examining Ian's body. He glanced up at the trio's arrival. 'It looks as if the same implement, or a similar one, has been used.' He shone a tiny torch towards the roof of Ian's mouth, the beam revealing red-raw ridges where an object had cut into the soft palate. Using a spatula, Harvey pointed out gouges inside the man's cheeks. 'The marks look identical to those I found inside Alex Corby's mouth.'

'And again, there's no sign of the object that caused this?' Kate was perplexed by this fact.

'No sign at all,' said Ervin, who'd joined them. 'That's to say, we haven't come across it.'

Harvey continued, 'As you can tell, the body's in what we call the rigid stage. The victim's muscles are stiff and his body core is at room temperature, and has probably been so for some time.' Kate was aware that a body, normally thirty-seven degrees Celsius, would lose one point five degrees of heat every hour after the heart stopped beating until it reached room temperature. Harvey continued, 'My best guess is he died late last night, approximately eight to twelve hours ago. I might be able to give you a better idea after I've run the post-mortem.'

'Anything else you can tell us?' Kate asked.

'I need to run further tests, but there are well-marked asphyxial changes in his throat and remaining eye, suggesting he choked to death.'

'Like Alex.'

'Yes, I would say so.'

'Thanks, Harvey.' Kate turned away from the gruesome spectacle and searched for William. She didn't spot him, but she did glimpse Faith, checking the kitchen top.

'Once again, this has been meticulously executed,' said Ervin. His face was covered with a mask so only his eyes, heavy-lidded from lack of sleep, were visible.

Kate agreed. Whoever had done this had been well prepared. There was no sense of haste, which was something she'd discuss further with her team later, during the debrief. They needed to draw up a profile of the person, or persons, involved in this.

'I don't suppose you've found anything useful yet?' she asked.

'I know you're only asking me because you have extraordinary confidence in my abilities to unearth clues and evidence but, seriously, have you seen the size of this place? Can't you find me some victims who live in normal-sized houses or one-bedroomed bijou apartments, like mine?' The corners of his eyes crinkled warmly as he spoke.

'I'll make a note for next time,' she replied, and earnt a chuckle. 'I see you brought Faith along.'

'I thought she'd enjoy working an actual crime scene. She's been stuck on lab work ever since she arrived, and has been pestering me to get some hands-on experience. I also thought it would be useful to have a fresh-faced enthusiastic forensic scientist at the scene, to help offset this jaded one.' He turned and raised his voice. 'Faith, how are you getting on?'

Her head snapped up at the mention of her name. She lifted a blue-gloved hand in greeting. 'Fine. Everything's pristine, though. Ian must have had OCD. I've never seen such a clean place.'

'Maybe the killer cleaned up after themselves,' said Morgan, who had wandered across to join her.

Faith shook her head. 'No, it's far more likely Ian or whoever he employed to clean kept it this way. The fridge shelves are immaculate and everywhere smacks of excellent housekeeping rather than a clean-up job.'

Kate wandered over to the kitchen island and stared at a jet-black bowl where oranges, apples and even cherries had been layered according to size and colour. 'Who on earth organises a fruit bowl like that?'

'Somebody with OCD,' Faith replied before making her way up the staircase.

Kate studied the fruit. The apples were bright red and shone like large glass balls. The apple on the plate beside Ian was a different variety and colour.

'Are there any other apples in the apartment?' she asked Ervin.

'Don't think so.' He checked the fridge. 'None in there.'

'Can you find out what variety it is, please?' she asked, indicating the pieces on the plate.

Ervin opened his eyes in surprise. 'They come in varieties? I thought they came in red, green or yellow.' The glib comment produced a chuckle from Morgan, who gave Ervin a thumbs-up. Ervin gave a small bow. 'Sure, I'll check it out for you. Right, I'd better get on. I swear the killer is a ghost. There's not a bloody trace so far.'

Kate spotted a Hewlett Packard laptop in an evidence bag next to a similarly bagged mobile, propped beside the bookshelves.

'Can we take his phone and laptop?'

'I think Faith intended to examine them.' Ervin looked around for her, and seeing she was no longer downstairs, waved airily at the objects and said, 'Go ahead, they've been listed as evidence and dusted for prints, so take them. She's got plenty to keep her busy anyway.'

'Thanks. I'll send them to the lab once we've taken a look at them.'

'There's no hurry. We're up to our eyeballs in work. Oh dear, not the best choice of words, was it?' he added, wincing.

'Emma, Morgan . . . time to go. One of you bring the laptop and phone with you, will you?'

They headed to the hallway and started removing their protective clothing.

'Initial thoughts on this?' asked Kate, tugging off her overalls.

'We're definitely looking for the same killer,' said Morgan. 'The whole torturing element leads me to think they're either trying to extract information from the victims, or punishing them.'

'But how could the victim give information with their mouth stretched open? They wouldn't be able to speak,' said Kate.

'They could make noises or gestures to yes-or-no questions,' Morgan suggested.

'True. We'll consider it. I won't discount any theory at this stage.'

Emma yanked off her plastic overshoes, balled them and threw them in the bin. 'I'm worried about the whole eyeball business. We initially believed whoever murdered Alex removed and kept his eye as a trophy, but they didn't. It was left in a jar at Ian's holiday cottage as a warning. This MO – the apples, torture, choking the victims to death and then stealing one of their eyes is . . . unusual.

207

I don't know who we're looking for here, but I can't help but think the perp will send Ian's eye to another victim.'

'I agree the MO is highly unusual, but we can't automatically assume there'll be another victim,' said Morgan. 'This could be it. The killer has targeted these two men for a reason and is done. We don't often come across serial killers and you're suggesting that's what we have here.'

'We don't want to jump to conclusions, but there could well be another intended victim,' said Kate. 'We need to establish what connects Alex and Ian because that might lead us to them and/ or the killer.' She already had one connection – Dickson. She balanced on one leg to remove her shoe protector, but a wave of nausea and dizziness made her place her foot back down on the ground.

'You okay?' asked Emma.

'Loss of concentration for a second,' Kate replied, waiting for the black spots in front of her eyes to disappear. She didn't want to mention Dickson's involvement or his relationship to the dead men. She had to keep it to herself for the time being, not simply because she didn't want him to know she was suspicious, but because she had unfinished business with him. He'd blocked any efforts she'd made to become involved or learn more about the incident on the Euston train and she had yet to establish why. At this point, she wanted to keep him on side. It was always best to keep your enemies close.

She regained her balance and removed the final overshoe. 'I'd intended asking Ian what he knew about Alex, but now that opportunity's gone we can only go back to Alex's family and ask them about Ian. Keeping the lid on the murder of a businessman was one thing, but if the media gets wind of this and makes any connection between the two men or finds out about the eye in the jar, it could blow up in our faces and we'll have mega problems containing it. Morgan, get hold of Bradley. Emma and I will meet you back at the station. I have to talk to DCI Chase about how best to handle this.

Emma, drag up everything you can from databases, phone records and Ian's laptop. I'm looking for links between him and Alex.'

'On it.' Morgan pushed open the door and they exited the building.

A small group of reporters was lying in wait for them. Kate heard her name being called and shielded her face from the cameras, then froze . . .

◆ ◆ ◆

'Kate, can you confirm this was a one-off attack?'

'Have you any idea as to why the gunman opened fire?'

'Have you spoken to any of the other victims' families?'

'Kate, could you tell us—'

All the shouts blur into one cacophony of noise. She no longer shuts her eyes against the camera flashes. She is frozen in time. Completely numb. William, by her side, has his hand on her shoulder. The weight is comforting. She allows him to steer her through the sea of faces, shouting at them to back off. A car is waiting outside the station, its rear door open. William helps her inside, shielding her all the while from the baying crowd, then turns to yell at an insistent photographer, attempting to snap the overwhelmed detective.

Kate shrinks into the seat and stares ahead. William clambers in next to her and they're whisked away, leaving bedlam behind. The interior of the car is comfortable and Kate wants to sink into it and disappear for ever.

'It'll get easier. They'll stop asking questions eventually,' says William, after a few moments.

She nods but inside she knows they have to keep asking questions. It's the only way she'll ever discover the truth.

◆ ◆ ◆

The hacks were firing questions at her. Incapable of ungluing her feet from the spot, Kate stood and gawped.

'Is it true one of the residents has been found dead?' shouted a female voice.

'No comment,' yelled Morgan. His voice wrenched Kate from her trance-like state.

'Can you confirm somebody has died under suspicious circumstances?'

'As my officer just told you, no comment.' Kate shouldered her way forwards, flanked by Emma and Morgan.

It was only when she reached her Audi and was once again behind the wheel that she crumbled. Emma and Morgan hurtled off in different directions, sirens blaring, and Kate, key in the ignition, could not turn it. Flashes of memory hit her repeatedly: faces, blood, more faces, all of them staring at her.

She squeezed her eyes tightly shut, but still the faces on the train came: the elderly man, the businessman with his tie slightly undone, the woman face down in a pool of blood. She thumped the steering wheel hard with both hands. 'Stop!'

The hallucination retreated as quickly as it had arrived and she drew a shuddering breath. She reached for her bag, popped two pills and downed them with a sip from a bottle of water, then fired the engine and pulled away into the traffic.

CHAPTER TWENTY-SEVEN

SUNDAY, 6 JUNE – EVENING

William Chase was concern personified. He marched towards Kate and swept her to his office and offered her a seat.

'You didn't come to the crime scene,' she said.

'I had something urgent to attend to. Fill me in.'

'Exactly the same MO as with Alex. The victim choked to death on a piece of apple, and, given there were eleven pieces remaining on the plate, my money is on there being two pieces of apple inside Ian Wentworth's throat or stomach.'

'Do you think there's any relevance to that number, apart from the fact it is considered unlucky?'

'There might be, but I'm not fixating on it.' She watched for any tell or giveaway to indicate William was trying to push her in a certain direction, but his questions were quick-fire.

'Which eye was missing?'

'Right eye. Same as Alex's.'

William pursed his lips. 'What else?'

'We believe the implement used to force open Alex's mouth was also used on this victim.'

'Any idea what it was?'

'None at all.'

'What's your plan of action?'

'We're trying to establish a link between the two men.'

William cleared his throat. 'We already have one. Superintendent Dickson was friends with both of them. I spoke to him immediately after you rang me, which is why I was unable to attend the crime scene. It's obviously of great concern to him.'

Dickson would have had no choice but to reveal his connection to both men. He knew she would have found out about it eventually, so he was pre-empting that by ensuring the news came from William, 'his lieutenant', as Chris had called him, so as not to arouse suspicion.

She maintained a poker face. 'I know he was at school with Alex, but what's his connection to Ian?'

'They met on a skiing holiday in the French Alps years ago and formed a loose friendship, saw each other a few times in the early years, less in latter ones.'

'The superintendent told you this?'

'He did. In the strictest confidence.'

'Do you think I should interview him?'

William shook his head. 'I doubt he can tell you any more than he has me. While he and Alex were in regular contact and even met up for the occasional drink, he rarely saw Ian – "once in a blue moon".'

It was no more than she expected. Dickson had used William to relay sufficient information to keep her off his back. 'We're concerned the killer will send Ian's eye to another intended victim and then attack again. Obviously, we can't be sure, but the modus operandi is so unusual we can't rule out the possibility we're dealing with – I hate using this term – a serial killer.'

'You only have two murders at the moment, Kate.'

'Which is why I'm loath to jump to such a conclusion at this stage. However, it would be irresponsible not to consider this possibility and I'd like to know what information we should release to the press. They'll soon put two and two together and realise the cases are related in some way.'

William strode to the window and clasped his hands behind his back. He stared out for a moment then said, 'John wants us to keep all of this as low-key as possible. We're only going to release essential information to the press and all details of the investigation are to remain strictly within the team. You know how people jump to conclusions, and if the words "serial killer" get bandied around, there'll be a major shitstorm. Make sure your team stays tight-lipped, and the press office will handle media requests. You're okay with that, aren't you?' The question was deliberately fashioned for agreement and accompanied by a steely gaze.

'Yes.'

'Good. Thanks, Kate. I knew you'd understand. We can't have any information leaks. It will only lead to alarm.'

Dismissed, Kate stood in the corridor. She was baffled as to why her superiors were so insistent on keeping everything under wraps. If this was the work of a serial killer, it would require more than a small investigative team, who in turn would require the support of the media to help track down the person or persons responsible. The answer was out of reach.

Bang! A door slammed, and the corridor swam out of focus. A frosted glass door marked 'First Class' materialised before her. She blinked away the mirage. The gunman on the train, William, Dickson and her. They were linked in some way, just as Ian and Alex were.

Downstairs, Emma was in the office, hunched over Ian's laptop.

'You got past the security?'

'For some weird reason, it wasn't password protected. I'm surprised, especially as he was into porn . . . Look what else I've found.'

Kate traversed the small space and studied the page advertising the Cindi Kaufer Escort Agency website.

'He visited the website yesterday morning,' said Emma.

'That's a coincidence we can't ignore. Talk to the people who run this agency and get hold of Ian's profile. I want to know if he ever went out with Rory.'

'Will do. Oh, and for the record, he had no cleaner, so he either had OCD, as Faith suggested, or the killer cleaned up the apartment.'

'Right. One of Ian's neighbours, Hayley King, thought she saw somebody hanging around in the early hours, around 2 a.m. Might want to talk to her. She lives on the ground floor.'

'I think she gave a statement to one of the officers. I'll double-check.'

'Cheers.'

Kate heard Morgan way before he appeared as he thundered up the stairs and along the corridor.

'Someone's in a bad mood,' remarked Emma, as the floor shook in time to his footsteps.

Morgan halted by the door, face set in a scowl. 'Bradley refuses to let me question him. Bastard says he'll only talk to the boss.'

Kate got to her feet. 'Then let's hear what he has to say for himself.'

◆ ◆ ◆

Bradley remained motionless on his seat, arms folded, legs apart and feet planted firmly on the floor. He didn't acknowledge Kate when she and Morgan entered the interview room. She greeted him regardless and slid on to the chair opposite him. Morgan sat down beside her.

'I don't want him here,' said Bradley.

'By "him", I take it you are referring to DS Meredith, and he'll be staying here during this interview.'

'Then I don't have anything to say.'

Kate pushed back her chair and rose in one swift movement. 'Fine. I won't waste my time. DS Meredith, will you caution Mr Chapman, please, and have him removed to the cells?'

Bradley extended his arms. 'Whoa! Hang fire. I only wanted to talk to you in private. I don't need cautioning.'

She paused. 'I take it you wish to continue this interview?'

'Yes.'

'Then DS Meredith will remain present. Are we clear?'

'Yes, all right.'

Kate resumed her position. 'Do you know why you're here, Mr Chapman?'

'Yes.'

'Do you wish to contact a lawyer?'

'It won't be necessary.'

'Then I'd like to remind you this interview is being recorded.' She pointed to the camera in the corner of the room. Bradley grunted. 'Let's begin, then. I'd like to discuss your whereabouts on Thursday the third of June between 11.00 a.m., when you left Sierra Monroe, and 1.30 p.m., when you picked up Charles Seagar for his driving lesson. Your wife believes you were with a lover for some of that time.' Kate let her words sink in.

Bradley wasn't thrown by this accusation. His response was a quiet 'I know she does. She had it out with me earlier.'

'Were you?'

'No. I wouldn't hurt Gwen.'

'She said you have had affairs in the past, all of them with driving-school students.'

He shook his head. 'They were a few meaningless flings, not affairs, and they happened a long time ago, shortly after I left the army. I confessed to them and we put them behind us. I've not cheated on her since.'

'Did you tell your wife where you were between 11.00 a.m. and 1.30 p.m.?'

'No.'

'Why not?'

'I made a promise to somebody.'

'Mr Chapman, I don't need to remind you this *promise* is likely to land you in deep water. Is it worth going to jail over? Is it so important you'd be prepared to abandon your wife, daughter and grandchildren and do time? Tell me, who you are protecting?'

He stared at her with eyes the colour of an ice fjord, and answered, 'I was with Cooper between eleven and twelve o'clock. After I left him, I drove to Brown's Café, as I told you, and then on to Cannock for the lesson.'

'Where were you both?'

'At his place. After her driving lesson, I dropped Sierra outside her house, took a phone call and, soon after she'd left for work, I spotted Cooper in the garden, so I got out and talked to him.'

'I was led to believe he works on Thursdays.'

'He took the day off because he was feeling under the weather.'

'What was wrong with him?'

'Depression. He's been suffering from it for a while. He was having a bad day.'

'Where is Mr Monroe at present?'

'I honestly don't know.'

'You're making this difficult for us.'

'That's not my intention. I have no idea where he is. The fact remains, I *was* with Cooper Thursday morning and nowhere near Alex's house at the time he was killed. I did *not* visit him that morning and . . . I don't think you have any evidence to prove to the contrary. I know you won't have found any DNA or my fingerprints, purely and simply because I . . . wasn't . . . there.' The ex-military man was back, eyes glittering dangerously. He'd told her what she wanted to know and was currently on the defensive.

Kate changed tack. 'Do you know Ian Wentworth?'

'No.'

'Have you heard his name? Maybe Alex mentioned him.'

He shook his head. 'Never come across him.'

Kate pushed forward a photograph of the surgeon taken from the Little Aston hospital website. 'Are you sure?'

Bradley studied it for a whole minute. 'I've never seen this man before.'

'You looked at the photograph for a long time.'

'I was trying to work out if he'd booked me for a driving lesson, but I've not met him, and his face isn't familiar.'

Kate drew the photograph back across the table and set it aside. 'Where were you last night, Mr Chapman?'

He blew out his cheeks then gave a resigned sigh. 'I was with Cooper.'

'Mr Monroe again!' She deliberately paused, weighing him up, like a cat with a mouse. 'You were with Mr Monroe last night, yet today you have no clue as to his whereabouts.'

Bradley didn't blink, eyes trained on hers. 'I don't know . . . where . . . he . . . is. Fact.'

'Okay, let's assume you don't know. Did he drop any hint or tell you he was planning to go away?'

'Yes. He said a few days away might help clear his head.'

'He didn't tell you where he intended going?'

'No.'

'Has he vanished before?'

'Not vanished. He often takes time out for a few days. We've even gone off together, fell walking or trekking around Snowdonia National Park. It harks back to our training days. Guys like us sometimes need to get away from ordinary life and be at one with nature. Cooper was in a bad place mentally and needed to sort himself out. He'll be back in a day or two.'

'Do you happen to know why he was feeling so low?'

'I'm not a shrink. I didn't delve into his mind. We all get down at times, don't we?' He stretched his beefy neck to the left and then right until it cracked. Kate could imagine him and Cooper fighting together, comrades in arms. There was undoubtedly a lot he was hiding and, moreover, would never divulge.

Morgan piped up. 'You said you were on the phone before spotting Mr Monroe in his garden. Who were you speaking to?'

'A client. He rang to rearrange a driving lesson because he had the flu.'

'If we check your phone records, will I be able to establish that fact?' Morgan's unexpected and aggressive question clearly raised Bradley's hackles. He pulled the mobile from his pocket and slid it across the table top towards Morgan with such force that it landed in his lap.

'I'll give you his name and number and you can speak to him yourself, or you could simply check my phone. Phil Johnson.'

Kate, prepared to step in to diffuse the situation, was relieved when Morgan calmly lifted the mobile, checked the call log, and having satisfied himself Bradley was telling the truth, placed two fingers on top of the phone and pushed it gently across the table, back to its owner.

'Are you sure you don't want to ring Phil?' asked Bradley, goading Morgan further.

Kate spoke before Morgan could react. 'There'll be no need.'

Bradley tore his gaze away from Morgan's face and back to Kate, who asked, 'You talked to Cooper for almost an hour on Thursday morning. What did you discuss?'

'I'm not prepared to divulge that information. It's irrelevant.'

'It must have been quite a deep and meaningful conversation to last an entire hour, or were you simply shooting the breeze?'

'It's none of your business what we talked about.'

'It can't have been idle chit-chat. You wouldn't be so defensive if it were. Why won't you share any of it with us?'

'No comment.'

'This isn't a press conference.'

'You wanted to know where I was on Thursday morning and I've told you, and I'd like to reconfirm I was also with Cooper last night. I have no idea where he might be and I don't wish to tell you what we talked about. It has no bearing on your investigation.'

Kate resisted the urge to sigh heavily. 'Fair enough. Just so we can be absolutely certain about this, can you tell us where you met up with Mr Monroe last night?'

'At his house.'

'Was anyone else there who can confirm your whereabouts?'

'No. Sierra was at work and stayed with a friend overnight.'

'How long were you there?'

'A few hours. I arrived at eightish and left in the early hours, around 2 to 2.30 a.m.'

'And what did you and Mr Monroe do for all that time?'

'Talked.'

'Talked again?'

'Yes.'

'What did you talk about?'

'Things that don't concern you, or this investigation.'

'And after you'd *talked*, you went home?'

'Yes.'

Kate weighed up his responses and came to the only conclusion she could. 'I'm sorry, but until Mr Monroe reappears and confirms your story, we can't take your word for it.'

'That's your prerogative. Once you locate him, you'll find out I've been nothing but honest. You have an explanation for my movements last Thursday. As far as I understand it, I'm free to leave at any time unless you charge me.'

Kate bit her lip. With no reason to charge him or detain him further, she had to let him go. An officer escorted him out and she stayed behind in the interview room with Morgan, who chewed at a thumbnail and let out a heavy sigh. 'Sorry, I shouldn't have butted in.'

'It's fine.'

'He was pissing me off. The fucker's trained in psychological tactics so he probably knew how to push my buttons.'

'We all mess up from time to time. You pulled it back, didn't rise to the bait when he practically threw his phone at you.' It was nothing compared to the cock-up she had made on the train journey with Dickson.

'We're dealing with a pro, aren't we? He could be bluffing about not knowing Ian Wentworth.'

'My gut says he's telling the truth about Ian. He gave us what we asked for – an alibi and a name – Cooper Monroe.'

'Then we'd better locate Cooper.'

'Can I put you on his tail?'

'Sure thing. I'd really like to find out if Bradley is telling us the truth and why the hell Cooper's conveniently gone AWOL.'

'Over to you.'

Morgan loped off in the direction of the office, leaving Kate to ponder her next move. Superintendent John Dickson had known Ian and Alex, but there was another person who might also have known them both – Rory Winters, the gardener. She scraped back the chair with fresh determination. With luck, Emma might have found out if Rory had escorted Ian to any functions, and if he had, she was going after him.

CHAPTER TWENTY-EIGHT

SUNDAY, 6 JUNE – LATE EVENING

Kate burst into the office. 'How are you getting on?' she asked Emma.

'I feel like I've completed a crash course in otolaryngology.'

'If I had any idea what that meant, I'd applaud you.'

'All Ian's documents are work related. Websites visited are fifty-fifty work and pleasure. He prefers older films – *North by Northwest*, *Maltese Falcon*, *Sunset Boulevard*. He's downloaded quite a collection. It seems he's not interested in any sport, subscribes to and reads *The Times* online, plays sudoku, gets his jollies looking at gay porn, and . . . went out with Rory Winters four times this year.' Emma passed over the notebook in which she'd written the dates she'd got from Cindi Kaufer at the escort agency. 'How do you want to play this?'

'Talk to Rory.'

'I'll hand the laptop to the tech boys. There's stuff I can't access.'

'What do you think would be his motive for killing them both?' asked Morgan.

'I don't think we can get ahead of ourselves just yet,' said Kate as she rummaged in her large shoulder bag. She screwed up her face. 'Bugger, where are they?' She pulled out the paper bag Annette from the Truly Scrumptious Café had given her the day before, and rested it on the desk while she continued searching. At last, she retrieved her car keys and jangled them at Emma. 'We'll take my car.' She picked up the bag and headed for the door.

'Don't forget this,' said Emma, picking up the bag and frowning at a patch of brown coming through the paper. 'I think it's got crushed. What is it?'

Kate spoke absent-mindedly. 'Oh, it's for Chris – chocolate cake.'

She took the bag and dropped it back inside her shoulder bag.

Rory's pickup truck stood outside his house, the open cargo area filled with square hessian sacks. Emma stood on tiptoe and peered into the first sack.

'Grass clippings,' she said to Kate, who was on the doorstep, finger on the doorbell.

'What were you hoping for? A body?'

Emma spun in the direction of the voice behind her. Rory had materialised from nowhere. His grubby T-shirt was damp with perspiration and clung to his defined pectoral muscles.

Emma recovered her composure quickly. 'Stranger things have happened.'

'Not around here, they haven't,' said Rory, his white teeth on display.

Kate spoke up. 'We'd like a word with you.'

'I could do with a quick wash first.'

'It won't take long,' said Kate.

He shrugged. 'Then you'd better come inside.'

He led the way to a homely kitchen with an armchair in one corner, over which was a tartan blanket in grey and yellow that harmonised with the pale grey decor. A shabby-chic retro wall clock in yellow hung on the wall over a wooden table, adding to the overall cottagey feel.

Kate perched on a yellow-cushioned chair next to the table and began the questioning. 'We believe you know Ian Wentworth.'

Rory remained poker-faced. 'What if I do? What's it got to do with Alex's death?'

'How well did you know him?'

'Why's that important?'

'Rory, I haven't got time to play games with you.'

'I can assure you, I don't play games.'

Kate shot him a cold look. He was deflecting. 'Just answer the question and tell me what you know about Ian Wentworth, or you know the alternative – a trip to the station. We've spoken to Cindi Kaufer, who confirmed you escorted Ian on four occasions this year.'

Rory rolled his eyes, then acquiesced. 'Oh, what does it matter? Yes, I escorted Ian earlier this year.'

'Which events did you attend and when?' Kate asked.

'I don't recall the exact dates, but I'll have them somewhere on my phone. He wanted somebody to accompany him to the cinema.' He thumbed his phone for his calendar as he spoke and held it up so Kate could see the screen. They were the same dates Cindi had given them: 12 February, 19 March, 23 April and 21 May.

Kate's brow furrowed. 'He invited you to the cinema? It seems an odd choice of venue to me. Don't you usually escort people to social engagements and soirées?'

'He was different. He wanted someone to take to the cinema.'

'That's all?'

He threw his hands up in the air. 'That's it.'

'Which cinemas did you visit and what did you watch?'

'We only ever went to the multiplex in Tamworth. There are several screens there. We watched *Green Book*, which was about jazz pianist Don Shirley and a bouncer as they tour across the Deep South of America in the 1960s, *At Eternity's Gate* about the artist Vincent van Gogh, *The White Crow* about Rudolf Nureyev and a film inspired by the music of Bruce Springsteen called *Thunder Road*.'

Emma spoke up. 'Your memory's good.'

'I store a lot of information. People generally like to chat about films, theatre, news, books and music. I make sure I have something interesting to say to them. It's part of the job of being a good companion. I usually brush up on the latest film releases.'

'Did Ian talk much?'

'No. He wasn't my favourite client.'

'Why not?'

Rory deliberated for a moment. 'This is in confidence, isn't it?' Kate nodded.

'He propositioned me.'

'A sexual proposition?'

Rory jerked his head in discomfort. 'Yes, although not until the fourth outing. After the film we went for a drink in a nearby bar. We discussed the film we'd seen and he reminisced about movies from years ago, then he went off on a tangent, mentioned how difficult it was to find somebody who enjoyed the same things as him. He thought I looked like the sort of bloke who'd enjoy some serious "fun and games" and wanted to know if I'd be up for having sex with him. I told him I was a genuine companion-type escort and didn't offer extras. He didn't flinch. Just kept staring at me, and tutting, like I'd suddenly change my mind. I laid it on the line and told him he'd have to find somebody else to go to the cinema with him. I drank up and left.'

'And this conversation took place on Friday the twenty-first of May?'

'Yes.'

'And that was the last time you saw him?'

'Yes. Why are you asking me about Ian? Has something happened to him?'

'I'm afraid we found his body at his apartment earlier today.'

'Shit! How did he die?'

'I can't divulge any information at the moment, but I would like to know your whereabouts last evening.'

He rubbed at his chin. 'Wow! Dead. Erm, yes. I was here at home and I have a witness who can testify to that.'

'Who?'

'Fiona Corby. She came over last night at nine and stayed until just after midnight.'

Emma's head whipped up in surprise. 'Are you and Mrs Corby still in a relationship?'

His shoulders sagged and he shook his head. 'No. She came over yesterday evening to end it.'

'Fiona was with you quite some time, considering she came to tell you the relationship was over,' said Kate.

'I tried to convince her to reconsider. It was . . . emotional. Actually, one of my neighbours was walking his dog at the time she left and stopped to have a quick word with me about his garden. You can confirm it with Rufus – Rufus Grimm. He lives three doors down. House with a red door.' He pointed to the right.

Emma made a note of the name. It had to be verified.

'Did Ian talk to you about anything else at all, or say anything that set alarm bells ringing?'

'Not at the time. To be honest, I was taken aback when he propositioned me. I hadn't seen it coming. I'd even felt sorry for the guy because on our first trip to the cinema he confessed he was terrified of the dark, which was why he'd hired me. He adored films but needed somebody with him so he wouldn't panic, so he completely floored me with the whole "fun and games" thing. Oh, yes, he said I looked like a man who "liked it rough". I was gobsmacked at that. I hadn't pegged him as a lover of S&M. Shows you how wrong you can be about some people. I totally misread him.' He rolled his eyes and shook his head simultaneously.

Kate signalled to Emma, who put away her notepad. 'If you think of anything else Ian told you during any of your trips to the cinema, let us know. You have my number.'

◆ ◆ ◆

It was coming up to eight thirty when they left Rory's house. The sun was slipping slowly below the horizon. Kate observed it for a few moments, then clambered into the Audi.

Emma eventually joined her and dropped on to the passenger seat with a heavy thump and yawned. 'Well, the neighbour definitely saw Rory with a woman matching Fiona's description, who got into a white Mini at around midnight. He talked to Rory about some sickly bushes in his garden. They were in conversation for quite some time, according to him. Looks like we've slammed into another dead end.'

'There's an outside chance Rory visited Ian after Fiona left his house. We can't completely discount him. We'll get Fiona to verify his story tomorrow and see if there are any discrepancies.'

'He doesn't have a motive for killing Ian, though, does he? Alex, maybe, if he wanted Fiona and Alex's money, but Ian? I feel like we're going around and around in circles,' said Emma.

Kate started up the car and pulled away. 'You'll feel more optimistic after a night's sleep.'

'I wish. A night's sleep would be a luxury. My brain won't let me rest. It keeps going over and over stuff, even though I know it serves no purpose, and I can't sleep.'

'Insomnia goes hand in hand with this line of work. You'll be fine once we've cracked it.'

'What about you?'

'What do you mean?'

'How do you cope with . . . everything?'

'Simple answer is, I don't. I focus on one thing at a time and hope it overrules all the other shit going on in my head.'

Emma opened her mouth then immediately closed it again, but Kate spotted it. 'Something else you want to ask, Emma?'

'I wasn't talking about the investigation. I—'

'Like I said. I focus on one thing at a time.'

Emma gave a quiet 'Uh-huh' in response and Kate focused on the road, discussion dropped.

CHAPTER TWENTY-NINE

SUNDAY, 6 JUNE – LATE EVENING

Kate had only been home ten minutes when the doorbell chimed. She opened up to find Faith on her doorstep. The yellow loose-fitting top and tight jeans she wore suited her far better than the laboratory coat or protective clothing Kate had only ever seen her in.

Faith thrust a bottle of wine in her direction. 'I know it's late on a Sunday night, but I was in the area and Ervin keeps suggesting I drop by to say hi to you, so . . . here I am. You do drink wine, don't you? It's chilled.'

Kate hadn't had a visitor for so long she'd almost forgotten how to react. Unusually flustered, she invited the woman into her home. 'Come in.'

'No. I don't want to disturb you. I only came by to give you the wine – a sort of thank-you. It was nice chatting to you the other day . . . and I haven't met many other friendly faces.'

'Come *in*. I can't drink this alone.'

'Only if you're sure.'

Kate opened the door wide. 'I'm sure.'

Faith followed her into the kitchen and took in the room, turning a full 360 degrees. 'Wow! You have a lovely house.'

Kate looked up from a drawer where she was rooting about for a corkscrew. 'Thanks.'

'Did you do it up yourself?' Faith ran a hand over the ruby-red ceramic backsplash tiles behind the Belfast sink. Kate and Chris had argued over them. She'd wanted ordinary cream tiles, but he'd chosen wildly overpriced ones fired in a kiln in some provincial town in Italy, insisting they would brighten up the clinical-looking kitchen. She'd acquiesced, and red cookware had also been brought in to harmonise with the tiles, followed by matching picture frames and red stools, and eventually she'd been forced to agree he'd been right all along. The place had benefitted from the splashes of colour.

'It took us twenty-three months to get it to this standard – almost two years of living in dust and disarray and cooking on a camping gas stove. I thought we'd never get there. It was a bloody nightmare.'

'But worth it. It's beautiful.' Faith picked up a gleaming stoneware bowl, carefully perched on cream shelves beside the cooker. Kate winced. She hated people moving or touching her prized possessions. The red-glazed ripple bowl had been a present from Chris, and was the most expensive bowl she'd ever owned . . .

'It's beautiful,' she says.

'It's French, hand-made and, well . . . I know it can't replace yours, but it comes with love.'

She feels the undulations and strokes the cool porcelain. 'It didn't matter.'

'Well, we both know it did.'

He'd accidentally knocked the bowl in question off the sink and it had shattered into fragments on the floor. It had been a plain green bowl with a faded rose on the side and nothing special to look at, but it had belonged to her mother and had only been on the draining board because it had got dusty and Kate had washed it. She'd felt a pain when it had shattered – a real pain of loss. She had so few reminders of her mother but, seeing Chris's face, she hadn't made a fuss. Crying or getting angry with him wouldn't mend the bowl. It was, like her mother, gone for ever. She lifts up the new bowl, catches the earnest look in his eyes. He is eager to please and to make her happy.

'Sometimes, it's better to leave the past behind and make new memories,' she says.

She places the bowl on the shelf. It already means the world to her.

◆ ◆ ◆

Kate passed a glass to Faith, who lifted it high. 'Cheers. Thank you for making me feel welcome.'

'I haven't done anything.'

'For one thing, you invited me into your home . . . on a Sunday night, when you are probably tired and only want to put your feet up. I hope you don't mind me landing on you like this.'

'No, it's nice to have company. You settling in okay? How long have you been here?'

'Almost a month. I was in Coventry before that.'

'I thought you came straight from UCL to Stoke?'

'I wanted to, but there weren't any openings, so I took up a position at Coventry until one came free with Ervin. It was worth the wait. That man knows so much. I feel like I'm learning a huge amount every day.'

'So, what did you do in Coventry?'

'Digital forensics. It was . . . dull! It's so time-consuming and laborious and lonely. I worked in a lab on my own and hardly ever left it. I didn't know Coventry had a cathedral until last week!' Her laugh was light and filled the room. It had been a long time since the house had heard laughter.

Kate sipped her wine and listened to Faith's account of the cybercrime unit and her time there. 'And you know nothing about Stoke, because Ervin keeps you locked away in his lab,' she said eventually.

'No . . . but I'm far happier here. Ervin is great. I was elated when he finally offered me an assistant's position.'

She beamed, and Kate found herself emulating the smile. Tension eased from her shoulder muscles and she realised for once she was feeling relaxed – all thanks to Faith and her easy manner. 'Have you had the chance to get out and about much? Stoke's full of history and some interesting places to visit. Trentham Gardens. You should go there, and to the Wedgwood Museum.'

'I've spent so much time in the laboratory I haven't had much opportunity to see what's available. I haven't even had time to visit the main shopping centre. You'd think I'd have found time for some retail therapy.' She chuckled. 'It's all quite different to home.'

'Where's home?' Kate was genuinely interested.

'I come from a town called Juliasdale, but I lived and studied in Harare for three years, so it became *home*, and then London, although I was ready to leave. Too big and noisy for me.'

'Do you miss Zimbabwe?'

Faith shrugged. 'Of course, but I wanted to see something of the world, find out how other departments in other countries conduct investigations, and when I finally get fed up of travelling and learning, I'll take all the knowledge I've accumulated back with me and take up a lecturing post at the university.'

Kate took another sip and became aware that it had been a while since she'd shared a glass of wine with a friend. 'What about the other UCL students? Do you stay in touch with any of them?'

'Gosh, no. I was too busy studying.'

'Didn't you take time off?'

'Not really. My goals were to get certified and then get on to an MSc course. I wasn't interested in socialising. Sure, I had the odd night out, but those friends have all moved on since then.'

Kate could understand. She'd been equally determined to advance her own career, and until she'd met Chris hadn't had much of a social life either. 'What about your family? Do you ever Skype or FaceTime them?'

The mood suddenly shifted and Faith dropped her gaze. 'No. As I told you – I don't stay in touch with my sister and I have no other relations. At present, it suits me to be here. It's quite liberating to leave everyone and everything you've ever known behind.'

Kate wondered if Tilly had felt the same way when she'd boarded the plane to Australia. Faith's voice sounded like it was at the end of a tunnel, and the edges of Kate's world were taking on a familiar fuzziness, brought about by the wine and the pills, which had rustled enticingly in her pocket as she'd walked through the door.

'And then, I got this awesome opportunity to come and work with Ervin.' Faith took another sip of wine and, looking around the kitchen, her eyes fell on a photograph of Kate and Chris in a red wooden frame. It had been taken during one of Ervin's famous Christmas parties, when both had consumed too much alcohol and were pulling faces at the camera.

'Your husband?'

'Yes. Chris.'

'Is he a policeman too?'

'Journalist.'

232

Faith nodded approvingly. 'Good-looking guy.'

Kate glanced at the picture again. Chris had strong features and a wide smile that made him look permanently content with life, and earnest, almost hypnotic eyes. 'What about you?' she asked Faith. 'You got anybody special in your life?'

'I was married for a brief while, to a professor. Crazy, really. It didn't work out. I was too young for such a commitment. Besides, my work is my first love.'

'I was engaged to somebody else before I met Chris.' Kate wondered why she was opening up to a complete stranger. *The pills . . . the wine.* She ought to shut up before she said too much, but still she mumbled, 'He dumped me and broke my heart. I wasn't interested in looking for love again after that and buried myself in work, a bit like you have, and then I met Chris. Got the best of both worlds. I've been lucky.'

Faith raised her glass. 'So there's still a chance I'll find happiness, like you have.'

'I'll drink to that.'

'Tell me,' said Faith, changing the subject. 'Did you find anything useful on Ian Wentworth's laptop?'

'A lot of it had been deleted, but we discovered he was into porn, young men, possibly even S&M.'

Faith didn't seem fazed by the information. 'It takes all sorts, I suppose. I wonder if that's what led to his death – angry boyfriend. Who knows? People can behave in a number of strange ways. I take it the cases are related?'

'We're pretty certain we're looking for the same killer or killers, but, to be honest, we're struggling at the moment.'

'Is there nothing the forensic team can do to speed things up?'

'Magic up some evidence so we know where to look next.' Kate drained her glass, pushed it away from her and decided she couldn't face another. She needed to eat something and then try to sleep.

Faith must have picked up her vibe because she also finished her drink in one gulp and then gathered up her bag. 'I don't want to outstay my welcome. It's late and I've got a bus to catch. Thank you again for inviting me in.'

'No, thank *you*.'

'Let me know if there's anything I can do. Anything at all.'

Kate accompanied her to the door and waved her off, watching her tread lightly down the path in the direction of the bus stop at the end of the road. She shut the door. If she hadn't drunk the wine, she'd have offered to give Faith a lift home. It was nice of her to come out of her way to visit.

She opened the fridge door and realised she'd forgotten to shop. It was almost empty apart from some cheese and a few tomatoes. She sniffed at the Brie, then shoved it back on the shelf. She couldn't face it. The wine churned in her stomach. She helped herself to a couple of rice cakes instead and, chewing as she went, headed towards the stairs. She hesitated by Chris's office door before tapping lightly on it. 'You in there, Chris? I'm going to bed.'

There was no reply.

CHAPTER THIRTY

MONDAY, 7 JUNE – MORNING

Slap, slap, slap.

Kate jogged in the half-light at a steady pace. There were only a handful of other early-morning runners and dog walkers in Queen's Park, a place where she had regularly trained before the life-changing incident on the train in January. Since then the rhythm of her life had been so severely disrupted she'd barely managed to maintain any fitness regime.

She'd woken early after a restless night and decided to run off some of the effects of the alcohol and pills from the night before. Queen's Park was one of the city's heritage parks and housed several characterful buildings, once lodges, as well as ample recreational facilities. It was well known for its winding pathways lined with striking copper beech trees, its horticulture and its lakes, one of which she ran beside, accompanied by a cacophony of beating wings, honks and squawks from the awakening wildfowl.

A man bounded past her, head down, earphones jammed in. Kate preferred to run without music. She liked to hear what was going on around her, her senses on permanent alert. She pressed on towards the avenue of trees that led to the elaborate stone clock tower, her mind on Ian Wentworth. Had he also been drugged? A small terrier darted from the bushes by the tower and snapped at her heels, causing her to look down momentarily and lose her footing. She stumbled and crashed to the ground, winded and disorientated . . .

◆ ◆ ◆

Kate takes huge, gulping breaths. The assailant is crumpled on the floor at her feet, features obscured by a crimson mask. The side of his head is caved in; a pulpy hole in his temple.

Kate makes low, guttural noises, sounds she can't control. The buzzing in her head is coming from the blood coursing through her veins. A woman with auburn hair has her back to her. The gunman shot her twice, once in the head and again in the back.

They'll never find out why this man performed such an atrocious, callous act. Her eyes are filled with hot tears that stream down her face. She can't bring herself to look at the body of the child at her mother's feet. It would be her undoing.

◆ ◆ ◆

A voice brought her back. 'Are you all right?' It was the runner she'd spotted earlier.

She staggered to her feet. 'I'm okay. Thanks. A dog—' She turned to hunt for the animal, but it had vanished.

'A little terrier?'

'Yes.'

'It was racing about the bowling green earlier. I think it's a stray.'

'I'm fine. A bit winded, but nothing's broken.'

'Well, if you're sure.'

'Yes. Thanks for stopping.'

The man slipped his earbuds back in and ran off. Kate checked for cuts and, finding none, began a slow jog back to her car. The thought she'd had before the hallucination was still anchored in her mind, and she needed to act on it.

She phoned Harvey Fuller from her car. He answered after several rings.

'Morning, Harvey. Sorry to ring you so early. I wondered if you'd completed the post-mortem on Ian Wentworth?'

Harvey's voice was thick with sleep. 'Morning, Kate. As it happens, I finished it in the early hours and emailed you the report before I left the lab.' Kate glanced at the dashboard. The digital display showed it was only six thirty. Harvey would only have had about four hours sleep, at best.

'Did you check Ian's blood for drugs?'

'In light of the toxicology report for Alex Corby, we checked for GHB and, before you ask, yes, he tested positive. There were, in fact, greater traces of GHB in his system than in Alex's.'

'Ingested?'

'Surprisingly not. It was most likely administered by injection, which is a more unusual method of getting it into a person's blood system. It's a drug that's easily absorbed, hence it's used to spike drinks, but we found slight scratches and what looks like a pinprick entry point on his neck, and believe the attacker administered it directly into the jugular vein.'

'That suggests the killer surprised Ian and injected him with GHB rather than waiting for him to imbibe it.' It must have been impossible to get Ian to sit down and drink.

Harvey was still talking. 'When GHB is absorbed through the stomach, it can take between five and ten minutes, even longer, before the victim begins to feel the results of it. By shooting the drug directly into both the victims' veins, these effects – drowsiness, relaxation, dizziness, motor control loss – would be experienced far sooner.'

Kate's pulse increased. 'Both of them?'

'Following the discovery on Ian's body, I checked Alex and found a similar entry point, again on the neck, overlooked during the first examination. It was microscopic and had become swollen. Consequently, it had been mistaken for acne, but now I think it was where he also was injected with GHB.'

'Do you have any further thoughts about the scratches on the palate and inside the cheeks?'

'They're almost identical abrasions produced by the same metal implement, or one quite similar. Forensics swabbed Ian's mouth for alien DNA and came up with nothing. If there'd been traces of Alex's DNA on whatever was used on him, it ought to have been transferred to Ian's mouth. The killer either cleaned the device thoroughly before reusing it on Ian or had a replacement one.'

'Have you ever come across marks like these before?'

'I can't say I have. If you trace the lines of the abrasions, they appear to form the shape of a leaf – that's the only way I can describe them.'

'Could you do me a quick sketch of what you mean and email it across?'

'Sure. I'll do it immediately.'

'Thank you, Harvey. I appreciate your speedy work on this, and apologies again for troubling you so early.'

'It's okay. I had to get up soon anyway to take my daughters to school, and as for being speedy, I was under orders to work quickly.'

'From John Dickson?'

'If it wasn't him, it was somebody else high up. William told me I was to pull out all the stops.'

'Did you email the superintendent a copy of the report?'

'No. William asked for a copy, though. I sent it to him when I sent yours.'

'Okay. Thanks again.'

Kate ended her call. It was strange that William had requested a copy of the post-mortem. She was in charge of the investigation. He had no need to get involved. Was he ensuring there was nothing in the files to incriminate Dickson, or was she reading too much into the situation?

She made the ten-minute journey home, where she poured a bowl of cereal. Leaning against the sink to eat it, she picked up the remote control and turned on the television set fixed to the wall. Chris had insisted on having a TV in the kitchen, and when he was home and not engrossed in work, it was never off. He caught every news bulletin. She lifted the spoon to her mouth. As was to be expected, the lead story was about Alex. A female reporter in a blue dress and white jacket stared mournfully at the camera and commented on the lack of progress being made in the Alex Corby investigation. A piece of crime scene cordon, broken free in the recent winds, had become entangled in the hedge above her head and flapped exhaustedly, a reminder of the horror that had taken place behind the firmly closed gates of the Corbys' home.

'Fiona Corby, Alex's wife, was unavailable for comment. She and their two children are staying with relatives during this terribly upsetting time. Police are still searching for the intruder believed to have murdered Alex Corby last Thursday lunchtime, and are appealing for any witnesses. This is Theresa Dulwich for ITV News, Hoar Cross, Staffordshire.'

Kate snapped off the set. At least her own name hadn't cropped up. She dropped her spoon into the empty bowl and stared at the blank television screen. She needed to get going and rouse her team. Both victims had been injected with GHB. They had another piece to this puzzle.

Harvey's sketch was in her inbox, as was the post-mortem report on Ian Wentworth. She read through the latter then printed out the picture. Harvey had drawn an outline definitely resembling the shape of a spoon, a pear or a leaf. She deduced that whatever it was, it needed to be strong to force open the jaw and keep it that way for the length of time it took the killer to torture and dispatch their victims. She put the drawing to one side and concentrated on something else – Ian's holiday cottage near the Peaks.

Morgan and Emma arrived together, voices loud as they marched into the office.

'For fuck's sake, Emma. I'm going to say something. We need to tackle her about it—'

'You're going about it all wrong,' Emma said.

'Going about what?' Kate asked. Morgan looked equally puzzled.

'Hunting for Cooper. You should start with his mobile and find out where it was last used.'

'You did check out his mobile, didn't you?' asked Kate.

'Er, no,' said Morgan.

'Best get on to it straight away. We've heard back from Harvey and it appears both our victims were injected with GHB. There were injection marks on the necks of both bodies.'

'What the fuck!' Emma's eyes widened.

'According to Harvey, the drug acts more quickly if it is injected.'

'Then the killer must have had some knowledge of the drug, its effects and the most effective way to administer it,' said Morgan.

'Or they couldn't administer it via a drink,' said Kate. 'Either way, we know both victims were drugged. The second piece of information is this.' She held up the sketch. 'What does this look like to you?'

Morgan answered first. 'A pear.'

'It looks like an ovoid leaf to me,' said Emma.

Morgan pulled a face. 'What the hell is an ovoid leaf?'

'It's sort of oval, with a pointed end. Nan used to work at a garden centre. I spent loads of weekends there helping her out, and learnt all sorts of stuff.'

Kate glanced at the sketch again. 'What sort of leaf could it be?'

'There are quite a few that resemble the drawing: birch, hornbeam, alder, beech – there are literally loads. Why?'

'Harvey said whatever was used to keep the victims' mouths open looked like this.'

'Can't be a real leaf then.' Emma peered more closely at the sketch. 'Buggered if I know what it is.'

'That makes two of us,' said Morgan.

Kate put the drawing to one side. It was a clue but, until they identified the object, not a useful one. 'I think we need to dig even deeper into Ian Wentworth's life. I'd like one of you to search his holiday cottage near Ashbourne.'

'The Derbyshire boys won't be happy,' said Morgan.

'This is our investigation, and Ian was murdered on our patch, so we'll check out his cottage. Emma, will you do that?'

'What am I looking for?'

'Anything suspicious.'

'I'd also like to go through his phone records,' added Kate.

Morgan ran a hand over his chin. 'I thought the tech team were handling those?'

'Are they? I'll check with them, then. Any questions or anything you want to add?'

Met with shakes of heads, Kate departed to talk to the tech team. No sooner had she left the office than she heard angry voices behind her. Her officers were not in the best of moods. The investigation was taking its toll on them. She palmed the pill sitting in the bottom pocket of her jacket and absent-mindedly dry-swallowed it, and drifted towards the lab.

CHAPTER THIRTY-ONE

MONDAY, 7 JUNE – MORNING

The technical department was housed in a separate building adjacent to where Kate worked, and accessed via a coded door. Kate punched in the correct numbers and entered the room, which contained a table and two benches that reminded her of school science lessons and a glass-fronted office where the person she was seeking sat in front of a computer screen. Geeks came in all shapes, sizes and sexes, and Felicity Jolly was the least geeky person imaginable. At fifty-seven and with steely grey hair, she had an air of authority normally associated with a headmistress or a barrister.

She looked over the top of fashionable Cath Kidston orange-framed spectacles and sighed. 'Look who it is! I suppose you've only come back to hassle me.'

'Nice to see you too, Felicity. How's Bev?'

Bev was Felicity's partner of thirty years, a comic-book illustrator obsessed with manga who had more recently got into designing characters for a popular computer game.

Felicity chuckled deeply. 'Too busy. Spends all her time huddled over her boards. I told her she'll grow into a female Quasimodo if she doesn't watch out.' She stood up suddenly and folded Kate into a warm embrace. Kate was lost in her sizeable frame, and it felt strangely comforting. Felicity then held Kate at arm's length and studied her up and down. 'It's good to see you. You look fine. Bit skinny. Still look fierce. I guess inside you're still shot to pieces. Tough times, eh?'

Kate was saved from having to continue the conversation as Felicity pulled away just as quickly and picked up some manila files. 'Are you here about Ian Wentworth?'

'His phone records. You finished with them?'

'We are, and there's nothing unusual to report. There were calls made to work, hospitals, colleagues, secretaries, restaurants, private clubs and his dentist. I suppose the only curious thing I picked up on was he seemed to be completely friendless. I don't think I've analysed a call log before that hasn't contained any relatives or friends.'

'None?'

'Not one. We went back to the beginning of this year and every call he made was to a business or was work related. Saddest guy I've come across.'

'He must have some friends. Was he using anything else? An app, or social media?'

'The guy was a reputable surgeon. I shouldn't think he had many occasions to hang out on social media liking photos of people's pets.'

'You on social media?'

'I am, but I'm incredibly sociable and nothing cheers me up more than a photo of a cute cat or a daft meme.' Felicity gave another wry grin and pushed her glasses back on to her nose. 'We discovered a couple of dating site apps on it. You can chat and message people from these. He was on Grindr, for one. We're still working on that encrypted file on his laptop. I'll get in touch as soon as we get into it. For now, here's a list of the deleted sites we recovered from both his phone and laptop.'

'He deleted them?'

'He dumped a load of sites, mostly porn related, the day he died.'

'I wonder why he chose to delete them that day.'

'Maybe he was concerned somebody would get hold of his phone and laptop.'

'And why did he delete some sites and not others?'

'I can't help you there. Could be he hadn't got around to deleting them all, or he left some of his browsing history visible purely to throw someone off the scent, away from these deleted sites. They contain highly explicit material.'

Kate accepted it was possible. Ian was an intelligent man, and if he was as tech-savvy as Felicity thought he was, he could easily have hidden every site he visited. 'How far back do these phone records go?'

'A year. You want more?'

'No, these'll do, thanks. While I'm here, what about Alex Corby?'

'We couldn't find any unusual activity on his phone. We tracked all his calls, and again they were mostly work associated. The process has taken longer than usual because he made so many overseas calls and we had difficulty tracing all the locations. Hang on. I'll see if we're finished with the list. Oh, by the way, we sent Fiona Corby's phone back to her. I've got the transcript of all her messages to her lover, Rory. It's like reading a Mills & Boon novel – no, make that *Fifty Shades of Grey*.'

Felicity disappeared into a back office, giving Kate little time to assimilate what she'd learnt before reappearing with two manila files. 'You're in luck. Lance just this second finished with Alex's. A couple of numbers have been flagged: this one is a Derby number we couldn't identify, and the other is to a club near Stafford called the Maddox Club. Only reason we red-flagged it is because

Ian Wentworth rang the same number around the same time in December last year.'

'Do you know anything about the club?'

'Me? Never heard of it. You have to remember, my clubbing days are over. I'm more a cup-of-cocoa-while-watching-a-documentary person these days.' She gave a wink. 'Besides, Bev's got me on a health kick: early to bed, disgusting vegetable smoothies for breakfast and no fucking alcohol! God knows what I see in her.'

Kate knew she was kidding. Felicity adored Bev. 'I'll grab these and scoot.'

'Good luck, and don't be a stranger.'

With the files in her hands, Kate returned to the now-empty office where she flicked through the transcripts of the conversations between Rory and Fiona, and after ascertaining they only contained X-rated dialogue about their sex lives, turned her attention to the telephone numbers Ian had rung. Felicity had colour-coded those that had been repeatedly dialled, and the number for the Maddox Club was highlighted in green. Kate ran the name through her search engine and determined it was a private members' club, founded and run by Raymond Maddox in 2005.

Kate knew little about such organisations, other than they'd originally been set up for middle-and upper-class gentlemen. To her, they conjured mental images of old fossils dozing in wing-back chairs, although, she reasoned, her thoughts might have been swayed by television period dramas. She rang the number and spoke to the manager, Xavier Durand, who informed her Mr Maddox would be returning to the club within the hour and, if she wished to come and visit, she'd be more than welcome. She took him up on his offer.

◆ ◆ ◆

The Maddox Club was located near the village of Lower Loxley, set on a small hill overlooking the meandering River Blithe as it cut a swathe through vast green countryside. It had once been a seventeenth-century dower house – built for the widow of the estate – then had been refurbished and enlarged to become the magnificent three-gabled Elizabethan structure it was today.

Inside was impressive. An ornate stone fireplace graced the reception, manned by an elegant man in a blue suit who held out a hand and introduced himself as Xavier.

His French accent was silky smooth; his handshake firm. 'Mr Maddox should return shortly. Maybe you'd like me to show you around first?'

Curious to know what went on in a private members' club, Kate followed the lithe man as he sprang from behind the reception desk and escorted her to a nearby room. The club resembled a five-star hotel, with elegant furnishings and carpets so thick her feet sank in the rich pile. Xavier guided her first to the library, not typical of any she'd visited, with bookcases containing hardback books and racks of magazines and newspapers downstairs and a wide spiral staircase leading to a galleried landing where a couple of men sat reading on plush settees.

'Here our members can enjoy freshly brewed coffee or possibly an alcoholic beverage. We also offer a butler service.' Xavier pointed to a vintage-style black-and-bronze telephone with a rotary dial and a brass handle on the desk by the door. He lifted a hand in greeting to one of the men, who'd looked up from his paper querulously, and steered her back outside.

Xavier bounced lightly along the corridor, pointing out various rooms. 'We offer rest, relaxation and complete privacy. Members may also stay overnight in one of our five suites, or hold a meeting in our private function room. In brief, we cater for all our members' requirements. Our chef is excellent. He's from the same town as me in France – Albertville, you know it?'

Kate shook her head.

'It's in the Savoie. So beautiful.'

The tour lasted some fifteen minutes and terminated at the reception area, where Xavier left her to see if Raymond Maddox had returned. He had, and Kate was ushered into his office.

Raymond was approximately five foot eight, weighed little more than eight stone and looked like he'd benefit from a long holiday. His eyes rested in dark hollows, the sclera off yellow, and his weak chin was covered with day-old growth. He drank from a bottle of Evian water, wiped his mouth with the back of his hand and asked her what she wanted.

'Does the name Alex Corby mean anything to you?'

'I know Alex. He's a member here.'

'And Ian Wentworth?'

'Also a member. Why?'

'Have you not read or seen the news recently?'

'No. I've been incredibly busy.'

'Then I'm very sorry to tell you both men are dead.'

Raymond tightened the top on his bottle of water, his eyes focused on a point behind Kate. 'I see.'

His reaction was measured and there was no outward sign of distress. Either Raymond didn't know the men well, didn't much care for them or wasn't surprised by the news.

'How well did you know both men?'

'Back in the early days we were friends. They helped me realise my dream of owning a genuine private members' club. They were both investors in this project and provided the funding after the bank refused to lend me the money. In the days when this club was in its infancy, we saw a fair bit of each other. Since then, they've been amply repaid for their belief in me.'

'Did they come here a lot?'

'They used to visit at least once a month, then both became more embroiled in their work. I'd say, over the last five years, I've only seen them on four or five occasions.'

'You wouldn't say you were close friends, then?'

He shook his head. 'No.' His answer was definitive.

'Did you fall out?' Kate was curious why men who'd invested money in the place had not maintained the friendship.

'We were never what you'd call "close". We rubbed along well enough. We had a business relationship rather than a friendship. Part of their payment was lifetime membership of the club, although, to my knowledge, they've not taken advantage of their perks in a long while. I'm not always on site. I've been project managing another site towards Nottingham.'

'Another club like this one?'

He nodded.

'There's demand for such a place? I thought there was a movement towards couples retreats and spa days, not exclusive clubs for men only.'

Raymond's thin lips resembled a slit rather than a mouth. He thought carefully before responding. 'Many women enjoy pamper days with their female friends, while many men enjoy other male companionship, sharing interests and having a place they can retreat to. There are women-only spas, gyms and even women-only clubs; why not a men-only club? Do you have a problem with that?'

'Me? No. I'm trying to understand what it is and who'd come to a private, male members-only club.'

'It's more than a coffee shop or a restaurant, or a library. There's a sense of being part of a small community. A member can dine here, spend a night in one of our rooms or simply pop in for an hour or two, read the newspaper and enjoy a brandy or coffee in the drawing room. It's a "home from home", where he will be waited upon and treated with respect.'

'You don't hold special events or entertainment evenings?'

'We do not need to hold events, and if by "entertainment" you're hinting at strippers and the like, we do not invite them on to the premises.' His face remained impassive.

'Who's in charge when you are not around?'

'Xavier is the manager. He's been with us since we opened.'

'And to recap, you haven't seen either Alex or Ian for months?'

'I can't remember when they last came here.'

'We believe they phoned the club to make reservations – both in December last year: Ian on the thirtieth and Alex on the thirty-first.'

'I don't recall seeing them here.'

'You say both men invested in this business. Tell me how that came about.'

'It was years ago. I don't remember exactly – a party, I think. At the time, I was managing a hotel in Stafford. We got chatting and they began dropping in to the hotel for a drink after work or a meal and the idea of a members-only club was born – a place where men could relax after work or a business trip or a meeting.'

Kate couldn't think what else to ask, so she thanked him and withdrew from the office back to the reception, where Xavier was taking a phone message. He acknowledged her presence by raising a finger to indicate he'd only be a minute. When he'd finished, he turned his eyes on to her and gave a small bow.

'Xavier, how well did you know Alex Corby?'

'As well as I know any of the clients. I knew him by name and would occasionally exchange pleasantries.' He kept his eyes trained on Kate in an almost challenging fashion she found rather strange.

'And Ian Wentworth?'

Xavier pouted slightly and his cheeks expanded before he released the air. '*Pouf!* The same.'

'How often did you see either man?'

He put a finger to his chin, then replied, 'I'd have to check to see how many times exactly, but it wasn't often at all.' He offered a Gallic shrug.

His attitude was perplexing – one minute subservient, the next slightly aggressive, and all his gestures seemed exaggerated to Kate. 'When did you last see either man?'

He sucked in air between his teeth. 'I can't answer without checking the system.'

'Do members have to sign in?'

'The system isn't that antiquated. Each member has a club credit card he swipes on arrival.' Xavier pointed to the box adjacent to the desk. 'We then know when a member is present, and if he requires any extras, such as dinner or a massage, those are automatically added to his bill. Let me check for you.' His fingers danced across the keys.

Kate continued with her questions. 'Do you have many members?'

He kept his head bowed and answered, 'About two hundred but, obviously, they don't all attend at the same time or it would be chaotic.'

'Do you have any big shots here?'

He looked up and his dark eyebrows furrowed. 'Big shots? Do you mean eminent people? I'm afraid we can't disclose any names or professions. Some are certainly distinguished individuals, but we offer discretion here at Maddox. We can't allow such privacy to be compromised.' He lowered his head again and said, 'Ah, here we are. Both men signed in on the second of January.'

'Did they have any extras?'

'Dinner, and they booked a suite each. They stayed overnight.'

'And was Mr Maddox on the premises that night?'

'If I remember correctly, he was on holiday in the Maldives. Maybe you should check with him.'

'I shall. Thank you, Xavier.'

Kate made her way to her Audi at the far side of the car park. She climbed in and stared across the gravelled drive, her brow wrinkled. Xavier was lying. She had nothing other than a gut feeling to support her suspicions. Xavier's reactions to her questions had been distinctly odd. Maybe it was simply his nature, but Kate was sure there was something else behind the fake smile – something shifty. He was withholding something, and Raymond's reaction to the fates of two of his investors had been strangely calm. Kate wasn't sure if her judgement was off kilter or whether she was on to something. She hoped it was the latter.

CHAPTER THIRTY-TWO

MONDAY, 7 JUNE – AFTERNOON

As soon as Kate returned to the office she contacted someone she hadn't spoken to for many years: Lionel Gupping, a retired dentist living in the Yorkshire Dales.

'Good heavens above!' he exclaimed when she told him who she was. 'Haven't seen you since you were fifteen years old. Strongest bite I ever came across.'

Her lips twitched at the memory. As a young teenager, she'd accidentally wounded Lionel's finger when, after repairing a tooth broken during a game of hockey, he'd told her to bite down firmly on a dental roll. He'd issued instructions before removing his hand, and obedient Kate had pressed hard on what she believed to be the cotton roll, only to watch his face crumple in agony. His finger had survived, but Kate had nipped it well and truly, leaving a mark, and thereafter he'd always joked about her famous bite.

'I was extremely sorry to hear about your father. I found out some time after he'd passed away. Had I known sooner, I'd have come and paid my respects. The trouble with living in the middle of absolutely nowhere is that news travels at a snail's pace. How are you doing?'

'I'm doing okay, thanks.'

'And what are you up to – married? Children?'

'Married, no kids, and I'm a DI at Stoke-on-Trent.'

He sounded delighted. 'You were always so curious and, as I recall, bright. I'm not surprised you followed in your father's footsteps.'

She couldn't play catch-up any longer, and as lovely as Lionel was, she had to get to the reason for the call. 'Can you help me out with something? As I recall, you had a load of weird and wonderful implements to help with dentistry. You told me about some of them, remember?'

'Sure, I do. Like I said, you were curious and bright. You were the only youngster I treated who wanted to know all about the tools of the trade. I wondered if you'd gone into dentistry yourself.'

'Mouths are too small a space for me to work in. I'd be worried somebody would bite my finger off.' She enjoyed his hearty guffaw for a minute before she continued. 'Actually, I'm after your expert help.'

'Certainly. Go ahead.'

'Is there a type of device in dentistry used to force open a patient's mouth . . . and keep it open?'

'Are you thinking of a Jennings mouth gag? We sometimes use those to work on a cavity. You can ratchet the mouth open to the desired degree.'

'The device I'm looking for produces a leaf-shaped imprint on the inside cheeks.'

'Leaf-shaped. That doesn't sound like it then. Want me to send you the technical information on the mouth gag?'

'Would you?'

'Certainly.'

'I'd appreciate that.'

'My pleasure. Lovely to hear from you again.'

'Nice to speak to you, too.'

'If you and your husband are ever up in this neck of the woods, come and look me up.'

'Will do. Bye, Lionel.'

True to his word, the image arrived in her inbox only moments after she'd spoken to him, but it didn't appear to be the implement she was searching for. The shape was nothing like the one Harvey had drawn for her. She sent an email and Harvey's sketch to the school of medicine at Keele University, asking if they'd come across anything like it, and turned her attention back to the Maddox Club.

Kate had begun research on Xavier Durand and typed his name into the general database. Born in Albertville in the Savoie region of France, he'd moved to the UK in 2006 and begun working at the Maddox Club the same year. She was scrolling down the page for more results when she was interrupted by a call from Emma, who was at Raven Cottage.

'Did you get the photo I messaged across to you?' Emma asked.

'I haven't checked my phone. I was looking into something else.'

'Take a look and see what you think.'

She waited while Kate examined the image of a trio of paintings, each depicting apples – red, yellow and green – and framed in matching wooden surrounds of the same colours.

'Are these in his house?' Kate asked.

'On the kitchen wall. I don't know if they're significant, but since the killer is using apples to murder the victims, I thought it worth flagging.'

'I agree, although I can't see their relevance at the moment. There are no pictures like these in Alex's house.'

'They might not be anything important, but after I sent it I uncovered something else that definitely is. There's a fully equipped bondage room upstairs, complete with padded table and restraints, and a travel chest containing S&M equipment: various ropes and mitts, hoods, anal hooks, ball locks. He has a selection of gags, too, including a head harness and ball gag and several pacifiers. There's no doubt in my mind he used this cottage for sexual gratification. It's an unremarkable place from the outside, and shabby and uncared for on the inside: peeling paint, threadbare carpets, dingy even. Hardly a "holiday cottage". It's the polar opposite of his apartment in Lichfield and, most importantly, it's alone at the end of an anonymous lane, well away from prying eyes.'

'No wonder he didn't want Derbyshire police crawling all over the place when he reported the supposed break-in.'

'Do you want me to bring back any of this gear?'

'Leave it in situ. Ring Ervin and ask if he can send somebody over to test for fingerprints and see if there are any matches to people we've already interviewed. Have a word with the locals. Find out if any of them spotted Ian with another person the night the jar containing Alex's eye was left in his house.'

'Will do.' Emma hesitated. 'Have you heard from Morgan?'

'No news yet.'

'Just curious to know if he'd called in.'

'No. He'll ring when he finds out something or locates Cooper.' Kate preferred to give her officers free rein to follow up leads without pestering them every five minutes. She trusted them enough to know they'd be pursuing their enquiries, not skiving off. If either was out of contact, it was for a good reason.

Kate didn't think anything of Emma's question until she was reading back through Xavier's history, then she recalled the note of caution in her voice. Something was up between Emma and Morgan: whispers, looks and arguments. She hadn't the energy to fathom what was bugging the pair and then, in an instant, all thoughts of them drained away. It had been so obvious she'd almost missed it. He'd even given her a clue. Xavier had been a waiter for several years, working throughout the Savoie region of France, including the fashionable ski resort of Courchevel. Her mind flipped back to the photograph she'd seen on Alex's desk of him with his friends at a skiing resort, and William's words – Alex had been on holiday with John Dickson when they'd met Ian at a hotel. Could they have also known Xavier from there? Dickson again. How involved was her superior in all this? This could be the opportunity she needed to talk to him face to face. He could tell her if Xavier was working at the hotel at the time he, Alex and Ian had been on holiday. How should she play it?

'Treat it as you would if you believed Dickson was innocent. He undoubtedly thinks he's outwitted you and is above suspicion. Play it cool and be wary how much information you give out,' said Chris.

'You reckon?'

'Definitely.'

She rang William. 'I need to ask the superintendent a few questions regarding the investigation. Do you think he'd see me?'

'I'm afraid he's at a conference in London. Can it wait until he gets back, or would you like me to try and get a message to him?'

What should she do? William would expect her to update him on her progress. She couldn't hide facts from him. She had no option other than to come clean.

'No, Kate! You don't want Dickson getting the heads-up.' Chris's words were urgent.

'It can wait until he gets back,' she said.

'What's it about? Maybe I could help?'

'I doubt it. I'm following up some leads on a couple of individuals who might have known both Ian and Alex. I thought the superintendent might be able to identify them.'

'Who are these people?'

Chris groaned. 'Shit! Don't tell him!'

'Possible business colleagues.' She was spurred on by Chris's voice, and the lie came easily. It was best if she kept William in the dark in case he spoke to Dickson, forewarning the man. She wanted to see Dickson's reactions herself and judge if he was telling the truth when she questioned him.

'I'll try and arrange for you to talk to him when he returns.'

'Thanks, William.'

Kate rang off, her head thrumming. The effect of the pills was already wearing off, but she didn't fish for more. Instead, she shut her eyes and thought about Xavier. If he knew Ian and Alex better than he claimed to, he was hiding something, something that might be relevant to the investigation. Her mind wandered. Her father had believed in cop's instinct and taught Kate to follow suit. On the whole, it had worked for her, and at the moment her instinct was telling her to play her cards close to her chest – very close indeed.

CHAPTER THIRTY-THREE

MONDAY, 7 JUNE – LATE AFTERNOON

It was late Monday afternoon when the call came through from the University of Keele. The medical school hadn't been able to identify any instrument that might have been used to force open a mouth or left abrasions such as those found in the victims' mouths, but one of the team there had passed over the picture to the history department, where Professor Adam Chalmers, a specialist in medieval history, was willing to talk to Kate.

Adam sounded pleased with himself. 'I believe I've uncovered the object you're searching for. There was a device used to torture people during medieval times called the Pope's pear, otherwise known as the pear of anguish or a choke-pear.'

'A choke-pear?'

'It was a fiendish device consisting of three or more leaf- or petal-like parts. The whole thing resembled a pear when closed, but when it was inserted into the mouth, or other bodily apertures such as the vagina or anus, and opened slowly using a handle attached to a long central screw, it would force the orifice wide open. Some choke-pears were believed to contain leaves with razor-like edges to mutilate the flesh, for added anguish.'

'Have you any pictures of this choke-pear?'

'I can do better than that – I can direct you to a collector called Stefan Gaul who lives in Stoke-on-Trent and has one in his collection.'

'Thank you. Tell me, Adam, is it easy to get your hands on one of these items?'

'You might get lucky and find one for sale on the Internet, but most of them will be found in museums or private collections. There's considerable interest in instruments of torture. I'll email across Stefan's contact details straight away and you can talk to him directly. He might know where you can get your hands on one.'

She gave him the email address and before she'd rung off, the details and a photograph of the choke-pear landed in her inbox with a loud ping.

'It's arrived,' she said.

'Great. Let me know if I can be of any further help.'

The instrument of torture was exactly as described, the leaves corresponding to the markings Harvey had sketched. She wasted no time in ringing Stefan and arranged to visit him immediately. In the stairwell, she bumped into Emma, back from Derbyshire.

'We've found out what was used to torture the victims,' Kate told her. 'It's a medieval instrument of torture – a choke-pear. I've left information about it out on my desk, so take a look. I'm off to talk to a collector and see if I can learn more. I shouldn't be long. How did you get on?'

'Forensics are short-staffed, but they'll send somebody across to Ian's cottage tomorrow morning to check for prints.'

'Will you go back and meet up with them?'

'Yeah, I'll do that. I need to talk to a few more locals. Those I've spoken to didn't see Ian or any strangers on Friday night. I've also found out he ate alone at the Duck Inn – a smart bistro about twenty minutes away from the cottage. Apparently, he booked a table for two, but his guest didn't show. The waiter overheard him speaking to somebody on the phone. Something about a missed flight. He remarked that Ian fell into a foul mood after the call and complained about the food.'

'Anyone else in the restaurant at the time?'

'Only two other couples. I tracked them down. They vaguely remembered seeing Ian.'

'Okay, try asking around the village again tomorrow. Oh yes, will you also ask whoever turns up from Forensics to check for fingerprints belonging to Rory Winters while they're at it?'

'But Rory claimed he rebuffed Ian's advances. He's unlikely to have gone to the cottage.'

'Best to double-check. People have a habit of lying to get themselves out of trouble.'

Emma nodded, then hesitated and asked, 'Has Morgan come back?'

'No. He rang earlier to update me on his lack of progress. Cooper is being elusive. What is it with you and Morgan?'

'He's being a jerk at the moment.'

'Sort it out, Emma. I don't want any office politics or fallouts. We've bigger issues to deal with.'

'I know.'

Kate let it drop. They'd resolve whatever it was.

It took Kate twenty minutes to find her way to Stefan's house. The evening traffic was building up and she'd caught every red traffic light between the station and Hadley Street. She stared out at the tail lights in front of her and wondered what her next move would be.

'You need to interview Dickson,' said Chris.

'I know I do, but he's already wary of me and I have to be careful what I say.'

'Trip him up.'

'How the fuck do I trip up my senior officer?'

'Calm down, Kate. Think about it logically. Xavier was in Courcheval at the same time as Ian, Alex and Dickson. They were all mates. Consequently, Dickson must surely know about Ian and Alex's involvement in the Maddox Club and he must know Xavier. If he claims otherwise, then you know he's lying. Use that information.'

'But how? What am I supposed to be trying to pin on Dickson?'

Chris fell silent and all she could hear was the thudding of her own heart. She thumped the steering wheel with balled fists. A car blasted her from behind. The lights had changed from red to green and she hadn't advanced. She lifted a hand in apology and edged forward.

Hadley Street was lined with red-brick houses fronted by matching brick walls in various states of dilapidation and front gardens mostly tarmacked over or covered in gravel. Passing a line of run-down garages, she noticed a group of teenagers vaping by the paint-peeled frontages. They ignored her as she drove by. There were no children where she lived. Her house was on an estate populated only by upwardly mobile couples, a term that had made her laugh when she'd first encountered it. This place reminded her of her roots and the terraced house she and her father had lived in. She slowed down. She was almost at the address, number 167, an end-of-terrace property with white window frames and a blue door. She found a parking space on the street right outside the house and got out of the car.

Stefan Gaul opened the door before she knocked. An infant was crying in the background. 'Teething troubles,' he said, as the cries increased in volume.

Stefan was in his late thirties and Viking-like with his full blond beard, large frame and rubicund cheeks. He was an emergency medical technician for the West Midlands Ambulance Service and, although large in stature, quietly spoken. His handshake was hearty. 'Come in. I keep everything out of the kiddies' way. Don't want them to get their sticky little paws on it.'

They moved directly through the kitchen to the garage via a locked door. It wasn't filled with the usual paraphernalia no longer required inside the house. Instead, it had been converted into a gym with a well-used punch bag suspended from a metal beam, a pile of weights stacked in order of size beside a workout bench, and a mat on the floor. In the far corner stood a metal storage cupboard. 'This is my "man shed",' he explained. 'The car's too big to fit in it, so I use it for my hobbies – keep-fit, boxing and collecting.'

'How did you get into collecting instruments of medieval torture?'

'My father was an escape artist who travelled all over Europe. I didn't acquire his flexibility or skill, but when he passed away a couple of years ago, I inherited his collection. Escapology was his passion and he became intrigued by contraptions throughout the ages used to restrain prisoners. He began collecting all manner of devices. My wife wasn't happy about me keeping them, even though some are quite valuable, and not just historically speaking, so I've already sold quite a number of the larger items.' He unlocked and opened the door to the cupboard.

A range of strange articles stood on each shelf of the locker. Kate recognised thumbscrews and a cat o' nine tails, but nothing else.

'What's that?' she asked, pointing at what appeared to be a pair of rusting scissors with a length of screw fitted to one end.

'It's called a tongue-tearer. The torturer would grab the tongue with it and then tighten the screw, and it literally tore the tongue from the mouth. It was mostly used on heretics.'

'Nice,' she replied with a grimace.

'This is what you're asking about,' he said, lifting an ornate device from the top shelf. 'The pear of anguish, or choke-pear. It also would have been inserted into a prisoner's mouth and then this screw wound up so it opened the mouth wide. It couldn't be removed unless it was unlocked.'

Kate held out her hand and studied the metal object. It most definitely looked like a metal pear. The top resembled an ornate key, bearing a design of two goat-like humans facing each other and playing trumpets or pipes. The key was attached to a length of thick screw that ran through the pear and was joined to one of three engraved petals by a spring. It would be, Kate mused, an attractive piece of work, if its purpose weren't so sinister.

'Want to see how it works?'

Kate watched as Stefan screwed the key and the petals lifted wide. She could well imagine how uncomfortable it would feel inside her mouth.

'What's the significance of the engravings on the key?' she asked.

'I believe they were to differentiate the pear from others – there were different pears for different orifices,' he said.

'Any idea where somebody might get one of these?'

'I saw one for sale on an antiques website a year ago for about £400. If you wanted one, you'd have to know a collector like me, or ask an antiques house if they had any coming up for sale. This one is destined for a museum in Germany – the Medieval Torture Museum – the Mittelälterliches Foltermuseum in Rüdesheim am

Rhein. My father would be happy to know it was going to his homeland.'

'It's not something you can easily get your hands on, then?'

'Not easy, but not impossible. They pop up from time to time on medieval-torture websites.'

'Has anyone tried to approach you for yours in recent months?'

He shook his head. 'Nobody, which is why I contacted the museum and asked if they'd like to purchase it from me.'

'And nobody could have gained access to yours?'

'No way!'

'Do you know anyone else who owns a choke-pear?'

He shook his head. 'Nobody. Is there anything else I can help you with?' He replaced the pear on the shelf and locked the cupboard back up as he spoke.

'No, thank you. You've been most helpful. I'll leave my card in case you hear of anyone who might have one. I'd like to speak to them.' She passed him the card, which he pocketed carefully.

'I'll ask about.'

'I'd appreciate that. Thank you.'

It had been a long day and Kate stopped off at the supermarket for much-needed provisions. As she pondered the possibility that ex-SAS soldiers Bradley and Cooper, who were trained in the art of interrogation, might have a choke-pear in their possession, she filled the wire basket absent-mindedly. It need not be the genuine article. The one used on Alex and Ian could be a replica.

There were few customers in the over-bright shop and she trundled down the aisles, reaching for fruit and tins and packets. The ambient music playing throughout the store changed and she recognised Eric Clapton's 'Wonderful Tonight', the first song she and Chris had danced to at their wedding reception. She slowed down, then reminded herself that retailers used music to influence shopping habits and the slow tempo would make her walk at a more leisurely pace around the store. She sped up, ignored the smell of freshly baked bread being piped from the bakery counter, and headed directly to the checkout, where a bored-looking girl took her basket and began scanning items. As each purchase passed through with a blip, Kate shoved them into the plastic bag she'd brought along with her.

'Twelve pounds fifty-two,' said the girl, passing Kate the last item.

Kate reached for the extra-large box of cereal containing chocolate pieces, eyes fixed on a note with a smiley face stuck to the box. 'These are yummy. Please buy some more of them.' She blinked hard to dispel the image and was overcome with a pain in her chest so intense it doubled her over and took her breath away.

The checkout girl leapt to her feet. 'You okay?'

Kate fought for recovery. 'Fine. Just not eaten today.' She thrust her contactless card against the machine then scooped up the box.

'Don't forget your receipt,' shouted the girl, but too late, as Kate hastened outside, where she sucked at the air, face lifted to the sky, and battled the anger and fear coiling around her heart.

CHAPTER THIRTY-FOUR

MONDAY, 7 JUNE – EVENING

Morgan had spent all day attempting to track down Cooper Monroe. It had been a fruitless effort and by evening he only had one more stop to make, at Corby International warehouse, where Cooper worked. He shoved his mobile back in his pocket. There was another missed call from Emma. No doubt she was worried he'd speak to William about Kate. He didn't feel like talking to her and, if he was honest, he was annoyed that she refused to accept Kate was clearly having problems or even some sort of breakdown.

The problem was hero worship. Emma wanted to be like Kate and wouldn't have a bad word said against the woman. Up until recently, Morgan would have agreed wholeheartedly. Kate Young was one heck of a detective and, because of that, he'd say nothing for the moment, but if he saw Kate taking any more medication, or acting bizarrely, he was going to bring the matter to William's attention, regardless of what Emma thought.

He arrived at the warehouses belonging to Corby International and pulled up in front of a barrier, where a camera read his car's number plate before lifting to allow him access. He drew up beside a hut only a few metres inside the yard. There, a figure in a peaked cap was expecting him.

Jack Pollock, in his early fifties, with heavy eyebrows and a pockmarked face, invited the officer inside. Morgan glanced around the space, big enough for two men, with two chairs in front of a lengthy table over which hung fifteen monitors, each displaying black-and-white images of the yard and warehouses. A mug of tea steamed on the table in front of them.

'Fancy a cup of tea?'

'No, I'm fine, thanks.'

'Fair enough. Take a seat.' Jack dropped down on to his chair and lifted his mug to his lips. Morgan sat beside him.

'I'm looking for Cooper. I don't suppose you have any idea where he might be, do you?'

'I haven't seen him since last Monday.'

'We need to talk to him. He might be able to throw light on our investigation.'

'Into Alex Corby's death?'

'Yes.'

Jack sipped his tea. 'You know, the boss has never once come here in all the years I've worked here. I doubt Cooper will be able to help you any more than I can.'

'What can you tell me about Cooper?'

'What do you mean?'

'Well, what do you talk to each other about when you're on shift together? There are two chairs in this room, so I guess you normally work in pairs?'

'Yes, we usually work in twos. I'm supposed to be with him tonight, but the warehouse manager couldn't find last-minute cover for him, so I'm on my own until he gets back. Pity I don't get double pay for doing the job of two men.'

'What do you both talk about when you're stuck in here all night?' Morgan repeated.

Jack thought for a minute. 'Mostly about the past. He was in the Special Forces. Was in for twenty years. Lifetime, isn't it? Me, I was in the Paras – fourteen years in total, which was more than enough for me, I can tell you.'

'Did he discuss his time in the SAS?'

Jack shrugged. 'Guys like us don't need to reminisce over some of the shit we've seen and done. He said something, though, that resonated with me – he said sometimes he feels like he can't hack his life now. He actually prefers war to civvy life. I understand what he meant. Some ex-servicemen change so much, when we leave the army with its close-knit community and friendships we can't adapt to civilian life. Cooper's one of those men.'

'So he's still a military man at heart?'

'Uh-huh. Through and through. He'd never have left the army if it hadn't been for his wife. His daughter, Sierra, was about thirteen at the time, and she was going through a tough patch, if you get my drift – hanging out with the wrong sort, drugs – you can guess the rest. Cooper's wife told him she couldn't cope with the girl any more and walked out on them both. Pissed off to Canada. Cooper had no choice but to quit and look after Sierra himself. Credit to him, she tidied up her act, got back on track and not only is she holding down a job but doing a part-time course at college, and he's dead proud of her. In fact, he's bloody daft about her. I think sometimes she's the only reason he keeps going.'

'Did he tell you he was going to take time off?'

'Nah, but I'm not surprised. He's been feeling low the last few weeks. I kept asking him what was wrong, but he wouldn't tell me. When he didn't show up for work, I figured it was because of depression again.'

'Again?'

'Yeah. He's up and down like a yo-yo.'

'Has he disappeared before?'

'Yeah. A couple of times when it all gets too much for him. He usually buggers off to the Peak District or somewhere in the open and walks it off.'

'Can you think of anyone he might stay with?'

Jack shook his head. 'No. He doesn't talk about his friends, but I expect he knows lots of ex-soldiers. Brothers in arms for life, you know?'

'Might he be staying with one of them?'

'Could be.' He gave a light shrug.

Morgan scribbled his personal number on a page of his notebook, ripped it out and passed it to Jack. 'If he gets in contact, would you ask him to ring me immediately?'

Jack finished his tea in one gulp and slapped the mug down on the table. 'Sure. However, if he's disappeared, it'll be for a reason, and I'm pretty sure if Cooper doesn't want to be found, then he won't be.'

Back home, Kate flicked through the television channels, settling on a cookery programme. She wasn't a great cook but watching others baking cakes was cathartic. She thought back to the café where she'd met Fiona. She ought to talk to the woman again. She'd deal with it first thing in the morning.

She watched as a contestant attempted to squirt icing on to their offering, her mind elsewhere. Some days she felt she was floating out of reach of the real world. Her mind was working but her body was lying dormant and sluggish, her eyes seeing but not registering what was happening.

The jolt of reality actually made her jump. The pills. It was the bloody pills. How many had she taken? She forced herself up from the settee, holding on to the coffee table for support, and stumbled into the kitchen, where she'd left her handbag and shopping. She hadn't put the milk in the fridge. It stood next to the cereal. What had happened when she'd got home?

She lurched towards her bag and rummaged for the box of pills she'd taken to work. Clumsy fingers located it and she hunted for the foil interior. She let out a groan. She'd taken the lot – an entire strip gone in a day. It was a miracle she could walk and talk. She clambered up the stairs, clinging to the handrail, and made it to the bathroom, where she washed her face under a running tap, letting the cold water rouse her from her stupor.

Several minutes later, she dried off and studied her reflection. She had let herself go. She looked haunted and drawn. Why hadn't she noticed how ill and old she looked? And little wonder people kept asking how she was. She had to take charge. The pills weren't assisting; if anything, they were making matters worse. She opened the medicine cabinet. One box remained. She dropped on her knees in front of the toilet and popped the pills, one by one, into the toilet bowl and flushed them away. She had to break free from their grip – go cold turkey. It was the only way.

CHAPTER THIRTY-FIVE

MONDAY, 7 JUNE – NIGHT

Xavier Durand listened to the solid ticking of the grandfather clock in reception – a timepiece restored to its former glory at a substantial cost to owner Raymond Maddox – and considered his options. He'd withheld information from the police, but to tell the truth would implicate him. He had a wife and three children to support. He couldn't tell the cops anything or he'd not only lose this position, he'd face charges.

How had he managed to get involved in such a mess? Loyalty. Fucking loyalty. He should have ratted them out and to hell with the consequences. They were nothing but a bunch of snotty-nosed bastards anyway. They all treated him like a minion, not like the manager of a top private members' club at all. He snorted at that last thought. How naïve he'd been when Raymond had brought him over to help run the place, promising him he'd be dealing with English gentry. Being the stupid sod he was, and fascinated by his own misinformed ideas of British upper-class culture, he'd agreed and today had a demanding wife, argumentative children and a whopping mortgage. He was like the mythological Titan, Atlas, who was burdened with the weight of the heavens on his shoulders:

Xavier Durand – the man who carried the problems of the fucking world. At least, it felt like he did.

The clock's ticking was getting on his nerves. He'd not slept since he'd learnt both Alex and Ian had died in suspicious circumstances, but finding out what those exact circumstances had been had proved impossible. None of his contacts knew or were willing to talk about the men's deaths. So much for being a confidant to most of these clients. The problem was, of course, he was not 'one of them'. He didn't drive a supercar, hadn't ever owned a holiday cottage in the Cotswolds or Spain, or enjoyed a private education. He was an ordinary man from a small village in France. They'd never consider him an equal. Fuck them! Fuck them all!

It was after eleven o'clock and none of the members intended staying the night. There'd been a huge drop-off in overnighters since January. If it had been up to him, he'd have continued with the operation, but Raymond had panicked big time, and these days the members had to settle for an *ordinary* private members' club with excellent facilities but no extras.

The last two members exited the drawing room, where they'd been nursing a whisky each for the last hour. Xavier rose to his feet and wished them both a pleasant evening. As their voices receded, a hush fell over the place. The rest of the staff had long since left for the night. Raymond rarely set foot in the place any more, so it was up to Xavier to lock up. He ambled to the entrance, listened to the throaty rumble of the Jaguar as it pulled out of the car park. He watched as it turned on to the main road and roared furiously into the distance, and then pushed the heavy door to before locking it. He was going to search for a new position – jump rather than be pushed. It was clear Raymond's heart had gone out of the business, and now the Gold Service was no longer being offered, Xavier wasn't earning the tips or bonuses he'd once been raking in.

He headed to the drawing room to tidy up after the men and return their empty glasses to the bar. The room was oak-panelled, with Louis XIV-style furniture, bureaux and period mirrors with ornate gold frames, and rigid-back chairs with golden armrests and rich red seats. Reproductions of Henri de Toulouse-Lautrec's famous cancan dancers from Le Moulin Rouge adorned the walls, lending the whole room a sense of Parisian chic. It was, by far, Xavier's favourite part of the entire building.

He glanced around to ensure everything was shipshape, even though he knew the cleaners would arrive first thing in the morning. He pulled at his tie, loosening it, and resting his elbows on the bar, exhaled noisily. At last, he could return to his family. He wasn't on duty again until 2 p.m.

He stared at his reflection in the mirror behind the bar – a worn face with heavy eyes and a five o'clock shadow. He needed to move on and find a new appointment. He was done with this place. His reflection vanished as the room plunged into darkness, and before he could move, the door shut to, extinguishing the light from reception and leaving Xavier blinking into the blackness. He remained stock-still, unable to grasp what was happening. The sharp pricking sensation came out of the blue. At first, he thought he'd been stung by a wasp, or a bee, and slapped a hand on to his neck to flatten the creature, then realised there was an obstruction – a thin metal one that was instantly withdrawn. It was only then that he grasped the seriousness of the situation. Somebody was here with him.

His reflexes were slow and when he spun to strike back, it was already too late. His attacker had melted into the darkness.

'What do you want?' he shouted.

He was met with a wall of silence. His mobile. He could use the light to find his way out. He patted his pocket for it, then remembered it was in the back office. *Shit!* He dropped to the floor on all fours to fool the assailant, who'd expect him to fumble about in the dark. He would scurry across to the door. He knew where the furniture was positioned. He'd been in the room enough times to know his way out blindfolded. To his left was a chair. He traced the rigid straight leg with trembling fingertips. If he scrabbled across to the right of it, he'd dodge the large table at the front of the room and should be able to reach the door before whoever was in here got wind of what he was doing.

No sooner had these thoughts entered his head than they began to muddy. Xavier couldn't remember if his fingers had grazed against the front or back leg of the chair, and as he began to sway, he heard laughter.

Galvanised into action by the sound, he scuttled across the thick carpet towards freedom, the pile grazing his palms and causing friction burns as he slid across it, but he didn't care. He powered on, desperate to reach the far end of the room, seemingly miles away rather than the few metres it actually was. He brushed against one of the six turned legs of the library table, each with a slight bulge in the middle and reminiscent of a Greek column. There was only a short distance left to travel.

A kick knocked him off balance and forced him sideways on to the floor. He wasn't going to be caught by the maniac. He pushed back on to his knees and stood up, ready to fight. His hands found the library table and he fumbled for the object he knew was on it.

'Found you.'

The whispered voice surprised him. He gripped the bronze Sphinx paperweight – one of a pair – and held it out to the side, trying to locate the attacker. His mind began to cloud, and then, without warning, his arm clutching the paperweight was wrenched backwards so forcefully he thought his shoulder socket would pop. He attempted to hold on to the Sphinx, but it slipped from his hand. The person cursed and relaxed their grip for a second. Xavier attempted to bolt, but his limbs wouldn't work and both hands were grasped and yanked behind him. He had no energy to fight. His body refused to cooperate and an abrupt wave of disregard for his safety washed over him, numbing his senses to his predicament.

'Why?' The word sounded as if somebody else had spoken it.

'You really need me to tell you why?' The voice was sharp and filled with hate.

Hands grabbed his shoulders, whereupon he stumbled and lurched drunkenly beside his attacker, who guided and dropped him on to a padded seat. Euphoria replaced the fear. He knew this chair; he rubbed his hands on the gilt lion's-paw armrest and was transported back to an era he never knew other than from pictures and television. He was sitting on a red-and-gold throne like Louis XIV himself. The lights in the drawing room were switched on. He chortled at a new thought: Xavier was the Sun King.

He drifted back and forth, crossing the bridge between reality and make-believe, and didn't scream until he saw what his attacker held in front of his face – a terrifying metal device that was undoubtedly going to cause him considerable pain.

CHAPTER THIRTY-SIX

TUESDAY, 8 JUNE – MORNING

The door to the first-class carriage opens unexpectedly and she flinches. The young officer who moves through the doorway releases a soft groan at the sight. Behind him comes another white-suited officer, followed by another. She feels tugging at her elbow. She can't move. She isn't ready to leave yet.

'Kate, come on.'

She shakes her head.

William's hand tightens its grip. 'You've seen enough.'

◆ ◆ ◆

Kate was unable to concentrate on the television. The faces of the morning presenters, sitting on a red sofa chatting pleasantly to guests, had gradually morphed into those of the victims of the gun attack on the train in January. A woman wearing a pale pink lace top, blonde hair in finger waves, transformed into one of the two friends who'd been on a day trip in London together and never made it home. The male presenter changed into the businessman, and an elderly interviewee became another victim, whose walking sticks had been discovered on the luggage rack above her dead body.

Tears leaked from Kate's eyes, trickled down her face and on to her lap. The ringing of her mobile brought her back to reality and she groped for it, relieved to be brought back from the horror of her hallucinations.

'DI Kate Young?' The voice was friendly, smooth and gentle.

'Who is this?'

'My name is Dan Corrance. I worked with Chris a while back on a story in Manchester about a paedophile ring.'

At the mention of her husband's name, icy tentacles wrapped themselves around her heart and squeezed. She caught her breath. 'You're the journalist from the other day. I've nothing to say to you.'

'Please don't hang up. I need to talk to you about Chris.'

She hesitated for a second. 'What about him?'

'Can we meet? I need to talk to you in person.'

'What about?'

'I'd rather not discuss it over the phone.'

'What's it about?' she repeated.

'I want to help you find out the truth about Chris.'

The invisible tentacles tightened their grip and grey spots appeared before her eyes. She struggled to gain control. Chris? What could Dan possibly know? This was some sort of ploy. The man was only going to pump her for information about the investigation. She pressed the 'end call' button.

The discomfort in her chest diminished, but she rubbed under her ribs all the same. A dull ache travelled from her cervical vertebrae into the top of her head, a result of taking far too many pills. Thank goodness she'd found strength to dump them, once and for all. She had to manage without them. She needed clarity of thought, and her over-reliance on them was threatening to derail her and the investigation. *The investigation.* That ought to be her primary focus.

She snapped off the set and checked her phone, looking once again at Emma's photograph of the three apples on Ian's kitchen wall. The pictures were likely to be no more than an ironic coincidence, yet the idea of the murderer choosing an apple to kill intrigued her.

She massaged her neck and browsed through information on the choke-pear, then flicked through endless websites but couldn't find any for sale. When she finally checked the time, it was 8.05 a.m., time to ring Fiona Corby.

Fiona sounded flat and groggy. 'Any news?' she asked without preamble.

'I need another chat with you. Is now convenient?'

'Can we do it over the phone? I have to take the boys to school in a few minutes.'

'They're going back to school already?' Kate tried to keep the surprise out of her voice. She'd assume they'd need more time to come to terms with their father's death.

Fiona's response was frosty. 'They miss their friends and school life. They'll be better off there than moping about here. Besides, we're under siege with journalists. We can't leave the house without being mobbed. At least at school there'll be some semblance of normality. How can I help you?'

'I need to start by asking about Rory. When did you last see him?'

'Saturday evening at his house.'

'What time did you leave?'

'Late. I can't be sure of the exact time, but I got home around half twelve. We had things to sort out,' she said, her voice dropping low.

'He told us you broke up with him.'

'I knew deep down I was always going to end it with him. It would never have worked out.'

Rory's alibi had held up, but there were more questions to ask. 'Do you know someone called Ian Wentworth?'

'No. I haven't heard of him.'

'He's an ENT surgeon.'

'None of us has visited an ENT surgeon.'

'Did Alex ever mention the name to you?'

'No. Should he have?'

'Possibly. Ian was one of his acquaintances. They met at Courchevel.'

'Oh, that was way before I came on the scene. He gave up skiing years ago. No, the name never cropped up.'

'What about Raymond Maddox? Did Alex ever mention him to you?'

'Definitely not.'

'Xavier Durand?'

'No. I've not heard of any of these people.' There was a heavy sigh and then, 'Have you any idea who killed my husband?'

'As soon as we know something, or arrest somebody, I'll be in contact. I'm sorry, Fiona. I understand how difficult this is for you.'

'I don't think you can possibly understand what it's like not to know how your husband died. I've only been told he was attacked. Nobody will give us any further details, and that's left me imagining the worst and wondering how much Alex suffered.' Her voice cracked.

Kate understood, but she couldn't divulge any details, not until they'd brought the killer to justice. She could only offer a crumb of comfort. 'Alex was probably not fully aware of what was happening. We believe he was drugged at the time.'

'Drugged,' Fiona repeated. 'Somebody put something in his food or drink?'

Unable to mention the injection, Kate remained silent as Fiona mulled it over. 'But he never ate lunch, so it must have been in a drink. You can't put drugs in a banana.'

'A banana?' Kate asked.

'Yes, Alex never ate meals during the day because he said they made him sluggish. He lived on bananas. The children nicknamed him Banana Man because he was always snacking on them.'

Kate heard the tears thickening the woman's voice, but a prickling in her scalp caused her to interrupt. 'Did Alex eat any other fruit? What about apples?'

There was a short pause. 'He didn't like apples. Or oranges.'

'Would there have been any apples in the house?'

'No. I'm not mad about apples either, and with going away to France, I didn't buy any for the children.'

The tingling sensation intensified. The apple must have belonged to the killer.

'Is this important?' Fiona sounded more alert.

'It might be. I have to talk to a colleague first, Fiona. I'll get back to you as soon as I can.'

'You will tell me what happened to him, won't you?'

'I will, once we've got all the facts straight.'

'Please. I *need* to know.'

Kate hung up. She was on to something. She swiped through the contacts list on her phone, selecting Ervin's name.

He picked up almost immediately. 'Morning, Kate. What can I do for you?'

'Hi, Ervin. It's about the apple at Ian's apartment. Have you discovered what variety it was yet?'

'Not yet. It's still being analysed. Have you any idea how many varieties of apple there are? Approximately 7,500 throughout the world!'

She could imagine the mock horror on his face as he spoke. Ervin thrived on factoids. 'More than I expected. Would you check it against the apple you retrieved from Alex's house?'

'Certainly. Do you think they're the same variety?'

'They might be. I've found out Alex never ate apples and there were none in the house, so it's likely the killer took it along with them.'

'Why specifically an apple?'

'I don't know yet, but the killer obviously attaches some importance to it.'

'I'll run checks straight away and see if they are the same variety. What if they are?'

'I can't think that far yet, but if so then the killer might have selected them for a reason, or both apples were purchased at the same time from the same batch.'

'I'm on my own at the moment so I'll handle this personally. We're extremely short-staffed and I've even lost Faith. I had to send her over to Ian's holiday cottage to lift fingerprints. I'll get back to you as soon as I can.'

'I'd appreciate it. Thanks, Ervin.'

Kate dropped her mobile into her bag, put her empty tea mug into the sink and headed for the station. Emma would have already left for Ian's cottage to join Faith, but Morgan might be in and she hoped he'd have news about Cooper.

She was halfway down the road when her mobile rang again.

It was William. 'Kate, can you meet me at The Lodge?'

The Lodge was a new-build residence in the affluent area of the Trentham Estate, situated in the south-west of Stoke-on-Trent, and a fifteen-minute drive from her own house. It was also where Superintendent Dickson lived.

'Everything okay, William?'

'No. John has received an unwelcome gift.'

CHAPTER THIRTY-SEVEN

TUESDAY, 8 JUNE – MORNING

Emma Donaldson was majorly pissed off. Morgan wasn't answering his phone and she could only assume it was because of the argument Kate had partially overheard as they'd entered the office the day before. Stupid prick! He'd gone off on one about Kate as they'd walked up the stairs together . . .

◆ ◆ ◆

'She's not right in the head. That fucking cake – all scrunched up in her bag, and then there's the pills. She's popping them like sweets.'

'Back off, you imbecile. She's okay. She's been through hell. Give her a fucking break.'

'William told us to keep an eye on her and you know as well as I do she's not up to this.'

'She's not gone wrong so far in this investigation, has she? She's following up all the leads we have, and she's not done anything out of the ordinary. I don't know what your problem is, but you can't go squealing to the DCI just cos you saw her take a couple of pills or because she's acting a bit weird. Whatever doubts you have about her, let them go

and don't tell the DCI or Super anything. Stick to working the inves-
tigation. Kate will sort herself out.'

'What if this investigation is compromised because of her mental
health? She's clearly not well. For fuck's sake, Emma. I'm going to say
something. We need to tackle her about it—'

She hoped Kate hadn't overheard any of it. She'd changed the conversation as soon as she'd spotted Kate in the office, making out
they were arguing about Cooper. She rang Morgan for the third
time, but again he didn't pick up.

She left another message. 'Morgan, you total shit. Answer your
phone!'

She stomped up the drive to Raven Cottage. Above her, sky-
larks sang brightly and the morning sun's rays warmed her back,
but nothing could put her in a good mood. The truth was, Kate
was behaving strangely, mumbling to herself, and Emma had also
noticed her boss's obvious reliance on medication. She had a huge
amount of respect for Kate and didn't want to see her unravel. She
hoped the investigation would retain her superior's focus and keep
her mind off the horror she'd witnessed in January.

Faith climbed out of the VW Polo and joined Emma outside Raven
Cottage.

'Hi. Sorry I'm late. The sat nav took me a circuitous route.
Ervin said you want to dust for prints, check for DNA, that sort
of thing.'

'Yeah. There's some kinky stuff inside. We'd like it tested.'
Emma led the way up the path to the house, where both pulled
on plastic overshoes and gloves before stepping over the threshold.

'Where first?'

'Upstairs,' said Emma.

Faith turned her head this way and that and wrinkled her nose
at the faded floral wallpaper as she climbed the stairs. 'This is nothing like his apartment.'

'I think this place served a different purpose and decor wasn't
his priority.' Emma reached the landing and made a sweeping
motion towards the bondage table. 'See what I mean?'

'Oh!'

'And there's some equipment in the travel chest.'

They crossed the room to the coffer and Faith peered inside.
'He certainly enjoyed experimenting. That's quite a haul.'

Emma grunted a response. She didn't want to look through it
all again, so when her phone rang she excused herself and pounded
down the stairs two at a time.

'Why didn't you call me?' she hissed at Morgan.

'I just have.'

'Fuckwit. I meant earlier.'

'I was busy. I've been trying to track down Cooper.'

'I thought you might have gone blabbing to DCI Chase.'

Morgan sounded affronted. 'We talked about that. I took your
advice. Kate knows what she's doing.'

'Glad to hear it.'

'Anyway, I had a stroke of luck. Turns out Cooper used to work
on the sly at another establishment – a private members' club in
Stafford.'

'You told Kate?'

'No, I rang you cos there were twenty missed calls from you,
and I thought you needed to talk to me urgently.'

'Twenty? You're exaggerating. Maybe three or four.'

'Or eight.'

'Okay, eight.'

'I thought you must be pining for me and I should ring you first before you fretted yourself to death,' he said.

'Don't flatter yourself. I only wanted to liaise with you. I'm over at Ian's cottage with Faith. She's testing a load of bondage stuff I found here.'

'I'll resist making a clever comeback.'

'Ha!'

'Look, I'll have to catch up with you back at the station. I'm monitoring something here in the hope it'll lead me to Cooper. I think I've worked out his Achilles heel – Sierra, his daughter. She's his universe, so he isn't going to go into hiding without trying to at least communicate with her and let her know he's okay.'

'Sound tactics, and they might work. Good luck.'

'Good luck with your toy box.' She heard him guffaw as he hung up.

Back inside the house, she looked around downstairs rather than go back up to the bondage room. There wasn't much lying about, but her eyes fell on a spiral notepad lying on the desk where the jar had been placed. Faith called down and she wandered upstairs with it in her hand.

'I wondered if you wanted the other bedroom checking as well,' said Faith.

'Yes, please, although I think we should focus on his "play room".' Emma flicked through the pages of the book. They were blank.

'Okay. Cool. What have you picked up?'

'Oh, nothing important. A notepad, but there's nothing written in it; no names of lovers or clues. Looks like a few of the pages have been ripped out.'

'Let me see.'

Emma handed it over and crossed the room to look outside so she didn't have to stare at the bondage table.

Faith examined it. 'Sometimes, depending on the pressure put on the pencil or pen, we can detect what was written. It passes through to the sheets below. Want me to see if there was anything important?'

Emma turned round. 'Go on then. We've nothing to lose.'

Faith opened her forensic case on the floor, fiddled with a plastic pot lid and sprinkled powder similar to photocopier toner into a flat plastic container.

'Let's try this,' she said, selecting a make-up brush from a bunch of brushes, which she rolled lightly across the powder and over the blank sheet of paper. Emma watched as she shook the residue into the container, giving the back of the book a gentle tap, dislodging the excess powder.

The message was clear to both women. It read:

Chris Young

Gazette

Wednesday 2 p.m.

Maddox Club

CHAPTER THIRTY-EIGHT

TUESDAY, 8 JUNE – LATE MORNING

The Lodge, Superintendent John Dickson's home, stood well back from a leafy road and was afforded a modicum of privacy thanks to a hawthorn hedge.

William was on the pavement beside his car, a phone clamped to his ear. Kate joined him and waited for him to hang up.

'Ervin's on his way,' he said, as soon as he'd terminated the call. He escorted her down the path and towards the wide-fronted house with a glass-fronted porch, where John Dickson was waiting. It seemed peculiar seeing him in civilian clothes: a pair of jeans and loose-fitting sweatshirt.

He scratched at the back of his neck. 'Thanks for coming over so quickly, Kate. William tells me Ian received something similar.'

She glanced at the glass object on the floor. 'Where did you find it?'

'Here.'

'The door was unlocked?'

'We always leave it unlocked for parcel deliveries. My wife shops online regularly, so it's easier to have goods deposited here if we're both out than left with neighbours. Obviously, the front door is locked and alarmed, so there's no danger of the place being broken into.'

'Neither of you have touched it?'

'No, my wife's in Kent, looking after her mother. I was at a conference yesterday and stayed over in London. I travelled back first thing this morning, and when I got here, this was waiting for me.'

'I see. Was the jar in a box?'

'No. It was exactly as you see it.'

Kate crouched down to study it more closely. The glass jar had a screw-on lid, and was the type used for pickling or for jams. It had been filled with a translucent liquid in which floated an eye, the iris the same shade of blue as Ian's. It was most likely in some sort of fixative, presumably formaldehyde or formalin. 'Are there any signs at all of a break-in?'

John shook his head. 'Everything appears to be as I left it.'

'I assume it's Ian's eye, isn't it?'

'It certainly matches his eye colour, sir.'

Dickson's breath was heavy as he exhaled. 'If it is his, I think we can logically assume I'm the killer's next intended victim.'

'What about your wife? Does she have any connection to either Alex or Ian?'

He shook his head. 'No. Elaine's never met either of them. You can't possibly imagine she's a target.'

'The jar was delivered here, but not addressed to you, sir. There's a chance it is intended for her.' Kate had to consider the possibility, regardless of the dumbfounded look on her superior's face.

He blinked repeatedly before shaking his head slowly. 'You're barking up the wrong tree. Elaine's been with her mother for over two weeks and is likely to be there at least another two, if not longer. If it had been intended for her, the killer would have deposited it in Kent.'

'Kent's a long way to travel,' Kate insisted, and earnt a scowl.

'Are you going to take this threat seriously?' he demanded.

'Indeed, I am, but I wouldn't be doing my job correctly if I didn't consider all options.'

Dickson pursed his lips, ready to disagree, but then lifted both hands in obeisance. 'You're right. I'll arrange for an officer to be stationed outside her mother's house. You'd better come inside. William said you wanted to ask me a few questions.'

Kate followed him into the house along a peach-carpeted corridor, past framed photographs hung along the length of the wall. Most were of Dickson with various individuals, some of whom Kate recognised immediately – the local MP, a couple of footballers, a well-known actor and the prime minister. There were others, taken at police balls or gala events, of Dickson in full dress uniform next to a pleasant-faced sandy-haired woman in a ball gown. A cabinet containing china figurines stood at one end of the corridor, where Dickson stopped, opened a door and ushered Kate and William inside.

The sitting room overlooked a garden, expertly designed to include a stone path that meandered between borders of pastel-coloured flowers to a lily-covered pond and then around to a summer house the colour of an insipid blue sky. Kate was offered a round leather chair rather than the cream settee filled with floral cushions positioned strategically to face a wall-mounted television.

'Fire away, Kate,' said Dickson, perching on a footstool he'd dragged across. The settee was obviously out of bounds to visitors and Dickson.

'What can you tell me about Raymond Maddox and Xavier Durand?'

He contemplated a response, rubbing the patchy stubble on his chin. She'd never seen him other than immaculately attired, with slicked-back hair, and clean-shaven. 'I met Raymond during a skiing holiday in Courcheval, back in 2000. I was with Alex and a couple of other chaps from my local pub at the time. We met both Raymond and Ian in the hotel bar. We got talking, discovered we were all from Staffordshire, and over the following days, skied the runs together and chatted at night. For a few years we kept in touch – even went on another trip back to Courcheval as a group and met up a few times afterwards, but I haven't seen Raymond for a long time. As for Xavier, he ran the hotel bar at the Ski Lodge hotel where we all stayed, so we knew him. Nowadays, he manages the Maddox Club.'

'What do you know about the Maddox Club?' Kate asked.

'It was Raymond's project. He set it up with help from a few of us – Alex and Ian both put up money for the venture. I'm not sure who else invested.'

'Did you?'

He shook his head. 'I didn't have any spare money to put into any venture.'

'Have you ever been to the club?'

'Several times. That was actually where I last saw Ian. Alex invited me along to join him and Ian for a meal there. Ian was celebrating getting an article published in a medical journal. It turned into a heavy drinking session and I ended up going to bed before the pair of them. I didn't see Ian the following morning.'

'You stayed over at the club, then?'

'We all did. They have a few rooms there. Alex, or Ian, sorted it out. I can't remember who.'

'When was this?'

'The first week of January. I'd need to check my diary.'

'Alex and Ian were both members of the club, weren't they?'

'Correct. Raymond granted them lifetime membership for helping him get it off the ground.'

'Sir, can you think of any reason a killer would target either man?'

He ran his hands over his chin again and Kate wondered why he hadn't shaved before he left London. 'No. I wish I could. It would help your enquiries if I could provide some clue or even a theory as to why both of them became victims. More importantly, it might throw some light on why the jar was left at my door.' He looked at William, who'd been sitting quietly for the duration. 'William, I think, given the circumstances, it would be prudent for me to move to a safe house while Kate's team continues to investigate. If Ian was murdered shortly after receiving Alex's eye, I can't ignore the fact the killer could have me in their sights.'

'I agree.'

Kate opened her mouth to ask why they weren't increasing the manpower on this investigation now that two high-profile victims had been killed, but Dickson was staring at her. 'How far along are you in this investigation, Kate?'

'We're still following up active leads,' she replied.

'I'm sure I don't need to tell you how imperative it is to identify the perpetrator quickly before they act again.'

'Indeed, and about that, sir, don't you think we should increase our manpower? If we're dealing with a serial killer, we ought to involve more officers.'

'I disagree. I believe you and your team are best suited to identifying the reasons behind these killings and unmasking the person or persons responsible.'

'That's quite a demand, sir. There's only three of us.'

'Three exceptional officers.'

Kate passed over the flattery. 'I still think it's a big ask for such a small unit.'

'We'll have to agree to differ on the matter. Upscaling the operation will only serve to suggest we can't cope.'

'Surely it would show we are taking the matter seriously—'

He lifted a hand, his voice crisp. 'Perceptions differ. The media will pounce on the fact we've increased manpower and reach all sorts of conclusions. I don't want this to turn into some sort of media circus and the public being panicked as a consequence. Moreover, they'll expect immediate results, ones that will have to be delivered promptly if a large operation is involved.'

'And probably will be if you second more officers—'

Once more, she was silenced. This time with a cold look. 'It's important we keep a lid on it as best we can. So far, we have two victims. And potentially, I could be the third. Why I have been targeted is a mystery to me and, although I feel it's prudent I retire from sight for the moment, I doubt this case has anything to do with a group of men who met on holiday.'

'Sir, with respect, we can't ignore the connection.'

He gave a weary sigh. 'I understand your unease, but I strongly suggest you don't focus on this line of enquiry. It will only result in misdirecting the entire investigation.'

She didn't follow his logic. Telling her to look elsewhere for the perpetrator only made sense if he wanted her to steer away from the holiday in Courchevel – if he was trying to cover up something or protect somebody. And why was he not more concerned about receiving his friend's eye? She'd have expected him to want to help them out, throw out ideas and potentially save his life. It didn't add up. The fact was, she couldn't trust Dickson and the best way to deal with this was to go along with him. 'Am I to understand you don't wish it to be known you have been targeted by the killer?'

'We have enough difficulty keeping morale high within the police force without something like this getting out, not to mention we would lose face with the public.'

'I don't see how, sir.'

He tapped his fingers again. 'Imagine the headlines, then: "Killer Mocks Staffordshire Police by Targeting Senior Officer" or "Senior Officer Goes Into Hiding". It's a matter of the public's perception. Do you really not comprehend?'

She gave in, even though she felt his reasoning was weak. This wasn't the time to argue. She had to back off before he lost his rag and chucked her off the case. 'I understand. Could you give me a list of names of the men who were in your ski party?'

'It was almost twenty years ago. Nothing sinister happened. It was a ski trip to *Courchevel*, Kate, an exclusive resort in the French Alps, not some orgy on a beach in Ibiza, and we were respectable men in our late thirties and forties, not drunken students on spring break.' Spittle flew from his lips in a light spray as he spoke.

'I'm not suggesting otherwise, but if I knew who else was on that trip, I might be able to connect some dots. I can't find any other connection between you, Ian and Alex, other than the ski trip.'

'Then you'd better look harder, Detective. I chose you to lead this investigation because you are astute and fastidious. It appears my life might now depend on you. Don't you think I'd tell you if I could think of any good reason as to why Alex, Ian and I appear to have been targeted by some lunatic?'

Kate concurred. If Dickson's life was in danger, she had an obligation to protect him and find the perpetrator quickly before they could act again. 'I'll have Ervin examine the eye. In the meantime, it'd be wise for you to go to a safe house.'

William shuffled forward on his seat. 'I'll sort that out. Are you okay to move out today, John?'

'I can be.'

'Then that's how we'll play it for the moment.' William got to his feet and Kate followed suit.

She returned to her car, where she phoned Ervin, told him of the latest development and made arrangements for the eye to be collected from Dickson's house. She hung up and gave a heavy sigh. Dickson might be the killer's next intended victim. If that was the case, why had he been targeted?

'Well, well, well! Dickson is playing a clever game. He's got you all running around protecting him, when we both know he's in no danger whatsoever. He arranged for Ian's eye to be delivered to his house while he was conveniently away at a conference and his wife was with her mother to throw you off the scent. He's extricating himself from all this by going into legitimate hiding, and he's got William wrapped around his finger. Either that, or William knows more than he's letting on,' said Chris.

'You're suggesting he was involved in Ian's death and probably Alex's, too. No, Chris. That's crazy.'

'Of course he's fucking involved. Come on, Kate. Use your wits, like I taught you to.'

'I'm not as good as you at flushing out the truth. You've got a keen journalistic instinct. I haven't. I can't see the full picture.'

'You've got instinct, Kate. Stacks of it. You'll soon see the bigger picture. Stick at this investigation.'

Morgan's incoming call halted their conversation. 'Boss, I've finally got some info on Cooper Monroe.'

'Go on.'

'Not only did he work as a security guard for Alex, he moon-lighted as a guard for a private members' club called the Maddox Club. Apparently, they sometimes needed a "heavy" to keep the clients in check.'

'I know the place you mean. I've been there. The club owner knew Alex and Ian.'

Morgan continued. 'Well, according to one of his workmates, Cooper told them the members sometimes got carried away by the entertainment laid on at the club and had to be kept in order, hence he was on hand to remove anyone who misbehaved. I pressed him, but that's all he knew.'

'I was told there isn't any entertainment at the club!'

'Not what I've heard.'

'Then somebody is lying. I'll investigate those claims myself. Any luck locating Cooper yet?'

'I'm still on the hunt for him.'

'What about his phone provider?'

'No joy. I'm following up some leads at the moment.'

'Has he been reported to MisPers yet?'

'Sierra says this isn't unusual behaviour. Her dad often goes off hill-walking and stays out of touch or can't get a signal.'

'You believe her?' Kate wondered if Sierra was covering up for her father.

'Yes. Both Bradley and the security guard, Jack, said exactly the same. Cooper suffers from depression and this is how he handles it,' said Morgan.

His words didn't sway Kate. 'Isn't Sierra worried her father has been missing for over forty-eight hours?'

'No. She's sure he'll be back in a few days' time.'

'She might know more than she's telling you. I can't believe she isn't the slightest bit concerned. Even I'm worried the killer might have Cooper in his sights, or have already struck. Talk to her again.'

Morgan said he would. She stared at the phone screen. Did the Maddox Club hold the answer to this investigation? It was somewhere that linked all the men. She wasted no more time. She ought to be able to catch Xavier at work. Maybe he could tell her about Dickson and enlighten her as to why the Maddox Club required a bouncer on its doors.

CHAPTER THIRTY-NINE

TUESDAY, 8 JUNE – LATE MORNING

Outside on the weed-strewn path to Raven Cottage, Emma shuffled from one foot to the other. The cool wind that had blown up whipped strands of hair across her face, but even with cheeks smarting, it was better being outside than in the grim cottage.

Kate picked up quickly.

'Hi, Kate. We've come across something you should be aware of.'

Kate's voice was guarded. 'What, Emma?'

'It's an impression on a notepad, a message suggesting Ian Wentworth arranged to meet Chris Young at the Maddox Club at 2 p.m., but we can't make out the date. I thought you ought to know about it.'

'There are lots of people called Chris Young. Why would it be my Chris?'

'He also wrote *Gazette* beside his name.'

Kate sucked in a deep breath. 'Okay. Leave it with me. I'll investigate it.'

'Kate, you realise if Chris is somehow involved, it compromises the investigation and you'll have to step down?'

Kate didn't miss a beat. 'I understand. Are you planning on sharing this information with anybody else?'

'No. I thought you should make that call.'

'Thank you. That's what I hoped you'd say. I'll handle this. If I think for a second I should let somebody else take over the investigation, then I shall. For the moment, let's keep this conversation between ourselves.'

'Deal.'

'Good. And Emma . . . thank you.'

Emma rang off. She was halfway back up the path when Faith came out of the house. Her mouth was a thin line in her face, her eyes flinty.

'What's up?'

'There are fingerprints on the table too small to belong to adults.'

'Children? He had sex with children?'

'For certain. I'll arrange for the table to be transported to the lab, but I'll take the travel trunk and its contents back with me for a more thorough examination. I've dusted upstairs for prints and taken some swabs of what looks like blood for analysis. I can't find any fingerprints matching Rory's anywhere. Are you going back to the station soon?'

'Yes. I'll lock up behind you once I've given you a hand to move the chest.'

'Did you mention the note to Kate?'

'I did. Look, would you keep it to yourself for the moment, until we work out how best to handle it or work out its significance?'

'I'm a forensic scientist. It's none of my business how you run your investigation. Mum's the word. Besides, I like Kate. I don't want to drop her in it.'

'Thanks. Any idea when the message might have been written?'

'Sorry. There's no evidence to suggest when Ian last used the notepad, but there's a layer of dust particles covering it, so I assume it was a while ago. I hope the note has no relevance to the investigation.' Faith glanced at her mobile. 'I have to go. I'll be in touch with any results.'

Emma helped her load her car, and once she'd pulled away, marched towards the cottage. Leaves, like the shaking of hundreds of maracas, rustled noisily, and were joined by the cawing of a huge crow above her, perched on a dead branch of an oak tree, beady eyes observing her movements. A second crow joined it, swooping low over her head before settling close to its companion, feathers lifting in the breeze. The door handle had to be pulled hard into the frame before the key would engage. It was as if the house were fighting her, and once locked, she returned to her car with quick steps, enveloped by a sense of hostility. Raven Cottage had left her discombobulated, and not purely because of what she'd discovered there.

◆ ◆ ◆

Kate rested her head against her steering wheel, allowing it to cool her forehead. Chris had arranged to see Ian Wentworth, but why? What had he stumbled across? He'd never mentioned Ian to her.

'Chris, what the fuck were you up to?'

'Research for an article.'

'What article?'

She was met with silence.

'Chris. Talk to me!'

No one replied.

She would divert to her house, halfway between Stafford and Stoke. Xavier could wait. She needed to check through Chris's gear.

Back home, she pushed open the door to his office and wrinkled her nose at the musty smell. There was no window to open to let in fresh air and she was forced to turn on the light to illuminate the little space. His computer keyboard was thick with dust, but she didn't glance at it, choosing instead to examine his 2021 diary. There were no entries for any meeting with Ian Wentworth.

She opened the filing cabinet and riffled through the manila files, her eyes grazing the names that meant little to her until she reached the letter 'M' and she read the name Maddox. Her heart thumped against her ribcage. What was Chris's involvement? Her hand hovered over the file. Should she?

The shrill ring of her mobile prevented her. William Chase was breathless, each word issued in a short gasp. 'Xavier . . . Durand is dead. He's . . . at the club.'

She slammed the drawer shut. She couldn't bring herself to look at the file and she had to get to the Maddox Club immediately.

CHAPTER FORTY

TUESDAY, 8 JUNE – AFTERNOON

Having spoken to Jack, the security guard, and another of Cooper's colleagues, Morgan was certain that in spite of all his SAS training, Cooper would still check on his daughter, even if he was in hiding. At present, they couldn't track his mobile; it was switched off and not emitting a signal. Morgan had involved the tech team and requested that Sierra's be monitored for unusual activity, especially calls from pay-as-you-go phones. Cooper could well have taken a burner phone with him, and if he tried to contact the girl with it, they'd be ready to trace it.

Morgan had been persistent and had tried talking to Sierra again, but she wasn't cooperating any more than Cooper's SAS friend Bradley, whom Morgan was currently watching. If Bradley suddenly took off, Morgan would be sure to follow him. The technical team was also monitoring calls made to and from both the man's mobile device and the house phone. Cooper would have to reach out to Bradley or his daughter at some stage.

At the moment, Bradley was currently outside his house, washing his car. Morgan had been watching through binoculars. He wasn't sure if he was going against protocol or not, but Kate had told him to find Cooper and that was exactly what he was doing.

They were working as a special team on this case, so he figured they'd have some dispensation to follow their own initiatives.

An alert pinged on his phone: a message to say an unknown number – a pay-as-you-go number – was attempting to contact Sierra Monroe. Morgan scanned the contents. The caller was in the Peak District, near Hartington. He slipped away unnoticed. He knew Hartington, a popular destination for tourists and walkers. There were numerous places for somebody to bed down there, including a campsite at a farm.

Morgan loped off in the direction of his car, parked some way down the road, abandoning his covert operation. He needed to be quick if he was to locate Cooper before the man moved off, maybe deeper into the Peak District. He launched himself into the driver's seat and, as he drove off down the lanes, rang Kate on the hands-free. She didn't pick up. He was alone in his quest to track this man down, a highly trained soldier who could well be dangerous. He might need support. He rang the person he knew would always have his back – Emma.

Like the other victims, Xavier Durand's hands and feet had been cable-tied and he'd been left dead in a chair. However, there was no sign of any apples and both eyes were undamaged.

Kate knelt beside the body of the young man, whose head was slumped against his chest.

'You can quite clearly see where he was injected with what I'm guessing was GHB, although I'll know more after I've examined him,' said Harvey, pointing at the angry red spot on Xavier's neck. 'He's been dead a good eleven hours and was probably murdered sometime late last night or the early hours of this morning.'

'What do you think was the cause of death?'

'Without a doubt, asphyxiation.'

'Caused by choking on an apple?'

Harvey shook his head and picked up a tube from his case containing a small object. 'Not on this occasion. The airway was occluded not by a piece of apple, but by this peanut.'

'Anything else you can tell me?' asked Kate.

'There are cuts on the insides of his cheeks and mouth.'

'Any leaf-shaped marks?'

'It's difficult to tell because the skin is shredded and covered by coagulated blood. I can't make out any distinct outlines. He clearly struggled and, as a consequence, there's a great deal of damage, masking any obvious markings.'

'You can't tell if the same implement was used?'

'Not without further examination in the lab. There are abrasions on both wrists and ankles caused by the bindings. He also has grazes, resembling friction or carpet burns, on the palms of his hands. Ervin has swabbed them for fibres. And finally, we found a sliver of what looked like white thread under one fingernail. I have no more for the moment.'

Harvey continued to amass his paraphernalia, ready for departure, and Kate left him to it. She crossed the room, avoiding the officers, to the bar in the corner where two empty whisky tumblers sat in evidence bags on the marble top and next to them, in another plastic bag, a ceramic bowl of salted peanuts. Ervin was nearby, crouched on his haunches, scraping at the table leg. She approached him and said, 'Can you spare some time and tell me what you've got so far?'

'A raging headache. I don't know how many people have visited this room but it's going to take forever to identify all the fingerprints in it,' he grumbled.

'Harvey says Xavier choked on a peanut and there's a bowl of them on the bar,' said Kate. She looked around. The furniture in the room seemed relatively undisturbed. There was no obvious sign of a fight. 'There's a forensic marker on the floor near the library table. Why's it there?'

'It's representing where we found a paperweight – a recumbent bronze Sphinx on a marble base – approximately seven inches high, three inches wide and five inches deep. It's one of a pair. The other one's still on the table.'

She spotted the object in question. 'Do you think it was knocked off by accident?'

Ervin got to his feet. 'Unlikely. We found Xavier's fingerprints on it, which wouldn't be the case if he accidentally knocked it over. I don't want to get your hopes up too high, but using luminol, we discovered microscopic traces of blood on it, *and* we've also found a droplet on the carpet close to the table. Xavier might have used the paperweight to attack his assailant.'

The whooshing in her ears was like a train passing through her head . . .

◆　◆　◆

The gunman's body lies face down in the aisle. Another body is covering his legs.

'One of the passengers prevented him from killing anyone else. They'd been shot but somehow still managed to attack him. They used this to hit him.'

The words won't come. Her lips are numb, her throat constricted.

The object is stained brown but is still in one piece. The heavy crystal award has a name engraved on it. She reads the inscription and her breath catches in her throat. She gasps for air, her eyes widening.

◆　◆　◆

Ervin hadn't noticed Kate's sudden lack of concentration and was still offering his theory of what had taken place. 'If the blood we found on the carpet isn't Xavier's, then we might have a clue to the killer's identity.'

Kate was focused once more. This could be the lucky break they needed. 'When will you know for certain?'

'Soon. Tom over by the window is running a few tests, including colorimetric assay.'

'What's that?'

'You want the short version or a lecture?'

'Brief as possible.'

'It's a biomarker. Men and women have slightly different levels of creatine kinase and alanine transaminase in their blood. By testing the sample against known colours, we can work out if it is male or female. This is a brand-new version we've got from the States. Normally we do this in the lab, but this is a version for use in the field. It's not as accurate as DNA testing, but it's pretty good.'

Kate was drawn to Xavier's body again. The killer had changed their MO. They'd not tortured him or removed an eye and Xavier had not been murdered at home. 'Why has the killer changed tack, Ervin?'

'Maybe they're becoming cocky, or they didn't have time to set up the whole apple and plate routine.'

Kate agreed it was possible, but she was sure there had to be another reason. It *felt* different this time. 'I take it that Faith hasn't returned from Raven Cottage yet?'

'I haven't heard from her so I expect she's still there or on her way back to the lab. This is bonkers. How many more victims are we going to stumble across? We've had three in a little over a week.'

'Only if it is one and the same person,' said Kate, absent-mindedly. 'Have you had a chance yet to find out if it was Ian's eye Dickson received?'

'It's still being processed. You should get results back soon. It was marked top priority.'

The gurney had arrived to transport Xavier. Tom called Ervin across to the window, and with their heads lowered they fell into deep discussion. Kate watched two paramedics lift Xavier on to the stretcher. Had the attacker changed MO out of frustration at not being able to reach Dickson, or was this the work of a different killer?

Ervin was back by her side. 'We've got a result for the blood on the carpet and the paperweight, and they're a match.'

'I sense a "but" coming,' said Kate.

'It's a sort of "but". The biomarkers point to an absence of the Y chromosome.'

'Are you certain?'

'As sure as we can be. Tom ran the tests three times. The results were the same each time.'

'Oh, crap! Either we've got a female murderer, or the blood isn't anything to do with this crime scene. Could be a visitor's, or it might even belong to one of the cleaners who cut herself on something sharp. I'll ask who might have been in here.'

William Chase appeared at the doorway and beckoned. She hastened across.

'The cleaner's outside by his van, waiting to be interviewed. He gave a statement to the first officers on the scene, but I asked him to hold on. You want to talk to him?'

'He?'

'Yes.'

'Then yes, definitely. Are you staying here for much longer?'

'No, I'm needed at the station. I'll leave this in your hands. Let me know if you need anything at all.'

'Have you spoken to Superintendent Dickson?'

'Naturally, I had to let him know about this development, and it goes without saying, we're keeping him well out of harm's way. Now, if you'll excuse me—'

She observed him as he took off at speed: long, purposeful strides across the lobby towards the main door without glancing back. Was it her imagination, or was he edgier than usual, and keen to depart once she mentioned Dickson?

The cleaner, in his late twenties or early thirties, thin and putty-faced, leant against the side of a van emblazoned with the name ABeClean. He spotted Kate approaching and dropped a half-smoked cigarette, grinding it into the gravel with the heel of his trainer.

'Hi. You feeling okay?'

'What do you think?' he said.

'I think it's been a pretty ghastly shock. I'm DI Kate Young.'

'I'm Mike. Mike Blythe.'

'Do you clean here regularly, Mike?'

'Ironically, I don't. ABeClean is my girlfriend, Tabitha Grant's, business. She usually cleans here along with another woman, but there's a gastroenteritis bug doing the rounds that's wiped out all of her team. Tabitha wasn't feeling too well this morning – probably caught it from them – so I volunteered to come in and do it for her. I've worked here a few times before.'

'Do you work for her?'

'Only when she needs a hand. I'm a musician – guitarist with a local band.'

'Did you know the man who was killed?'

'I've spoken to him a few times.'

'You didn't see anybody else about, did you?'

'No one, and there weren't any cars in the car park when I arrived at nine. The place doesn't usually open until about eleven thirty, so the front door was locked, as usual. Tabitha holds a set of keys so I let myself in via reception and cleaned downstairs, starting with the dining room, then along the corridor, doing each of the rooms in turn. The drawing room was the last on the ground floor.'

'You said you've worked here before. When was that?'

'When Tabitha first got the contract to clean here, she and I always did it. That was until she grew the business enough to hire other cleaners. We were short-staffed earlier this year, so I helped out then, too.'

'Do you know Alex Corby?'

'Should I?'

'He was a member here.'

'Name doesn't ring any bells.'

'How about Ian Wentworth?'

Mike pulled a face. 'I remember him – not the bloke, but certainly his name. He and a couple of other members stayed over at the club at the beginning of January. He stole a silk velvet bedspread. Tabitha told Xavier about it, but he said she was mistaken.'

'Does Tabitha supply all the bed linen?'

'Not provide it, no, but when she took on the cleaning contract it was with the proviso that she also dealt with guest rooms. All the towels, sheets and so on are sent to a local laundry service for washing and ironing.'

'Could the bedspread have been missed off a list?'

'No way. It was immediately after the Christmas and New Year break, the staff were still on holiday, so Tabitha and I cleaned and made up the all rooms together. The bed definitely had a bedspread on it – a deep maroon one. All the beds are prepared the exact same way with a matching bedspread and cushion set.'

'Did you confront Ian about it?'

'There was no point. The club owns the linen. If they want to let one of their members steal bedspreads, then it's their loss, not ours.'

'Tell me, how did you know Ian Wentworth stayed in that particular room?'

'Tabitha was sounding off about the theft to the kitchen staff and one of the waiters told her he knew who had stayed there. Ian ordered some brandy to be delivered to his room.'

'Do you know which waiter spoke to her?'

'No. Tabitha would have to tell you.'

'Do you know the boss, Raymond Maddox?'

'I've never met him. Xavier was generally the go-to person, but Tabitha might have spoken to Raymond.' He ended with a sigh and shoved his hands deep into his pockets.

'Would you prefer to go inside to talk, or maybe sit in my car?'

He raised his head. 'I'm better out here, thanks. In the open air.'

'I've only a couple more questions to ask. Are you okay to continue?'

'Yeah, sure.'

'Did anything strike you as odd when you arrived this morning?'

He shook his head. 'Nothing. Everything seemed the same as usual. I didn't notice . . . the body . . . until I walked into the drawing room.'

'Did you knock over or move anything inside the room?'

'Absolutely not. I ran straight outside and called the police.'

'And you didn't spot anything obviously out of place?'

'No. Oh, wait a second, there was an ornament on the floor near the door. I left it there.'

'You didn't knock into it?'

'No. It was definitely on the floor.'

'How many female cleaners work for Tabitha?'

'Six.'

'And do any of the others ever work here at the club?'

'No. It's usually only Tabitha and Poppy, unless they need an extra pair of hands or one of them is off for some reason.'

'Poppy?'

'Poppy Notts.'

'Have any of the other women worked here recently?'

He shrugged loosely. 'I don't think so.'

'I will need to talk to Poppy. Do you have her contact details?'

'I don't, but Tabitha will have them for certain. I know she lives near the railway station in Stoke, but I don't know her address or phone number.'

'Could you get them for me?'

'Yes, but why?'

Kate brushed away his concerns. 'It's for elimination purposes. There's a drop of blood in there that might have come from her or Tabitha. I'd also like to talk to Tabitha as soon as possible.'

'She was totally out of it this morning, but I'll see if I can get her to ring you.'

'If you think of anything else, here is my card. Call me.'

Mike pocketed the card she offered him and briefly looked away across the car park towards the white forensics van outside the large house. His words were cagey. 'I don't think I'll ever forget seeing him tied up like that. The image will fade eventually, won't it?'

A body, sprawled across the narrow aisle, lips contorted, silently condemning her for arriving too late to help.

She gave a strained half-smile and left it as if she thought it was a rhetorical question. She couldn't give him the reassurance he wanted. She had her own demons to battle.

CHAPTER FORTY-ONE

TUESDAY, 8 JUNE – LATE AFTERNOON

Chris wasn't in his den. Kate entered the room tentatively, pausing only to breathe in the lingering aroma of bergamot and oranges from his favourite aftershave, before opening the filing cabinet and removing the file marked 'Maddox'.

Once in the kitchen, she dropped it on to the table, poured a glass of water and drained it in one. Her head was beginning to thump again, a result of coming off the pills: *you're detoxing.* The water would help. She flopped on to a stool and opened up the file. It was subdivided into three sections. The first, entitled 'Private Members' Clubs', contained a series of articles about the origin of such associations. The second was named 'Traditions' and contained links to websites about what happened inside them, but the third, which Chris had named 'Gold Service', was the one she was drawn to. It comprised of a list of names and phone numbers, three of which she immediately recognised – Alex Corby, John Dickson and Ian Wentworth.

Why had Chris arranged to meet Ian? She lifted the phone to call him, then changed her mind and instead rang the first number on the sheet, but Raymond didn't pick up. She scanned the names in front of her, trying to work out which of them to ring next. She chose the second one, Stephen Brown, a vintner from Stafford. His phone also went straight to answerphone. She cursed aloud. The club was significant. She had a direct link to both it and to John Dickson. Thoughts, like washing in a machine, churned over and over. Why on earth had Chris written Dickson's name in the Gold Service file?

Her mobile rang and she snatched it from the table, hopeful it was Raymond.

Ervin was on the other end of the line. 'I've got some useful information for you, Kate. The eye left outside Superintendent Dickson's house definitely belonged to Ian Wentworth. Secondly, about your apple. I had to recruit an expert in apple varieties to help identify it. It transpires both of those left at the crime scenes were a variety known as Macoun, named after Canadian horticulturist T. W. Macoun, and mostly grown in the US. According to my specialist, it's a medium red apple with snow-white flesh.'

She'd never come across the name.

Ervin had more news. 'There are three sets of fingerprints on the peanut bowl you saw on the bar – one of which belongs to Xavier. The others are identical to those lifted from the whisky tumblers. My guess is two members had a drink, shared a bowl of nuts and left. If you can find who they were, we'll do the necessary to check the prints match. For what it's worth, I don't imagine either set belongs to the assailant.'

She could only agree. The killer had made no mistakes thus far. 'It would be too much to hope for. Thanks for the update.'

'I'll contact you as and when we get further information.' Ervin hung up, leaving Kate staring into space and pondering her next move.

She needed to bring her team up to speed and find out if the blood on the ornament and carpet had come from Poppy or

Tabitha. As far as she was aware, there were no other female members of staff at the club. If only she could get hold of Raymond and ask him. She rang Morgan, whose phone went immediately to voicemail. She had more luck with Emma.

'There's been a development,' Kate told her. 'Xavier Durand was killed at the Maddox Club, sometime late last night or early this morning.' She ran through what she knew.

'Do you suspect the blood belongs to the perp?' asked Emma.

'Given they've been uncannily clever, I think it's unlikely they'd have left any clue behind. The MO was different to the others, so we might even be dealing with two killers.'

Emma let out a low whistle. 'This gets weirder and weirder.'

'Are you at the station?'

'No. Morgan got a trace on Cooper's whereabouts and asked me for back-up. I'm not far from the rendezvous point. Do you want me to return?'

'No. Stay on Cooper's trail. I've a feeling he's pivotal to this investigation and we can't afford to let him slip away. I'll head to the station and meet you later. I have some tracking of my own to do.'

Call ended, Kate stared at the phone screen. 'Ian, Alex, Xavier and Cooper. They're all linked in some way to the Maddox Club.'

'And Dickson. Don't forget him,' said Chris.

'He spent a night at the club in January. I wonder if it was the same night the bedspread disappeared from Ian's room.'

'You need to find out if it was.'

'Yes, I know I do, but I don't know how to contact him. He's in a safe house.'

'And isn't that convenient? Out of the way so you can't speak to him.'

'Chris, why were you investigating the club?'

'Never mind that for the moment. It's more important you speak to Dickson.'

Chris was right. And there was only one way she could contact the superintendent: via William.

William blocked her request. 'We can't risk the killer uncovering his location.'

'He's the *only* person who can shed some light on what I'm dealing with here. Three men, linked to the club, have all been murdered within days of each other. This is unprecedented. What if the killer has a long list of intended victims, possibly all linked to the Maddox Club? We must stop them before they continue this killing spree. Tell me where to find Dickson, please.'

She took the silence at the other end of the phone to mean William was considering her argument. His response was little more than a grunt. 'Okay.'

'Where shall I meet you?'

'My house in fifteen minutes.'

William lived outside Stafford in what had once been a row of terraced cottages for farmworkers. They'd been converted into one long house but still retained an olde-worlde charm. William had retained many features, such as the black latches and ancient doors with gnarled knots in the grain, and old fireplaces in each of the rooms. A white long-haired cat with sapphire-blue eyes stretched languidly before climbing down from the kitchen chair.

'Hello, Wayan,' she said, stooping to scratch its head. William owned two Balinese cats, both with silky, flowing coats and full plume tails, and had named them according to Balinese custom.

Wayan wound himself around her legs. Kate stood up quickly at the sound of Dickson's voice.

'You wanted to talk to me again, Kate,' said Dickson, appearing at the kitchen door.

'Yes, sir. I can't get hold of Raymond Maddox and I'm desperate for some answers.'

William picked up the cat and stood beside the sink stroking his head while Kate spoke. 'What can you tell me about the Gold Service offered at the Maddox Club?'

The superintendent glanced at William. 'Could you leave us for a moment?'

William moved outside, disappearing into his lovely garden.

'This is to remain strictly between ourselves, understand?'

'Sir.'

'Let me make it perfectly clear, I wasn't aware of the service until the night I was invited to join Alex and Ian at the club.' The sigh that followed seemed to emanate from within his chest cavity. He shook his head at the memory. 'The Gold Service, if you must know, consisted of supplying members with prostitutes.'

'I see. And you had no idea this service existed before the second of January?'

'No.' His eyes narrowed. 'Can I remind you, I've divulged highly personal information that I expect you to keep to yourself?'

'Yes, sir. Understood. Could you tell me more about the evening, before you went to bed? How the subject came up?'

'It came out of the blue. I wasn't very good company. My wife and I had been going through a difficult patch and I had too much to drink and happened to mention our marital problems as we were eating. Ian then told me about the service, which he fully intended using after dinner, as did Alex. They both thought it would "cheer me up" and arranged for me to have somebody in my room, too. So yes, I was drunk and yes, I slept with a prostitute. However, it was a *one-off*.'

'Did you see either man in the morning?'

'I had breakfast with Alex, but apparently Ian took off before we got up. Xavier arranged a taxi to take him home.'

'Were you surprised he'd gone?'

'Yes. He hadn't mentioned anything the night before about leaving early. In fact, he'd said he'd see us at breakfast, but we assumed he was simply too hung over to appear.'

'Did you speak to him after that evening?'

'No. I was ashamed of my actions and I made no effort to contact him.'

'But you still saw Alex?'

'Only on a couple of occasions.'

'Do you happen to know if they still offer the Gold Service at the club?'

'Alex told me it stopped after that night.'

'Have you any idea why?'

'None whatsoever. I don't see where this line of questioning is leading us.'

'I apologise, sir, but there's nobody else I can speak to about this. Xavier is dead. Raymond isn't answering his phone. Would it be okay if I continue?'

He sighed again but gave his permission.

'Do you have any idea who arranged for the prostitutes to visit?'

'I assume it was Xavier. He arranged all the extras, and besides, he oversaw the entire running of the place. He was the manager. Nobody could have operated the service behind his back.'

'Raymond could have.'

'Unlikely. By all accounts, he wasn't often at the club.'

'Was he there on January the second?'

'I didn't see him, but I heard he'd dropped by for a while.'

Xavier had told her Maddox was away in the Maldives at the time – another lie.

'Kate, there's nothing more I can add. You know as much as I do. If you don't mind me saying so, I don't think delving into people's personal lives is the correct way of handling this. You need to look further afield.'

'Sir.'

He studied her carefully. 'I wanted you as lead on this investigation, but we now have three victims, Kate . . . three, and . . . well, I'm beginning to wonder if I haven't made an error of judgement. I'm not convinced you are on top of this.'

She kept her head lifted. 'We're working the case, chasing leads and doing it by the book, sir. As I recall, I asked if we shouldn't bring in more manpower, but you wanted it kept low key.'

He raised a finger of warning and pointed it in her direction. 'Don't get clever with me.'

'That's not my intention. We've worked flat out and pursued every avenue. We don't want to make mistakes, sir.'

He pursed his lips. 'I don't know. I wanted to give you the chance to get back on your feet and show us you still had what it takes to head a murder investigation. I wonder if I was wrong to throw you in at the deep end. Lighter duties might have been more appropriate.'

'I'm more than able to handle it, sir.'

'You say so, yet here you are asking about a service for club members that no longer exists, rather than rounding up suspects.' He waited a couple of heartbeats. 'Maybe it *was* too soon for you to return.'

'There's no reason for you to doubt my ability.'

He didn't reply. His silence was unnerving, but Kate maintained steady eye contact until he broke off with, 'I want results soon. I can't stay in hiding for much longer, and unless you can make rapid progress, I shall have to bring in a fresh team.'

'Sir.'

He turned on his heel, leaving her alone in the room. Damn the man! He'd just shown his true colours. Chris was right. Dickson was hiding something, and she was damn well going to find out exactly what it was.

CHAPTER FORTY-TWO

TUESDAY, 8 JUNE – LATE AFTERNOON

Hartington, a picturesque village in an area known as the White Peak, which formed the southern part of the Peak District National Park, was heaving with visitors. Emma parked behind a coach and hunted for sight of Morgan, spotting him beside the village pond. Cooper couldn't have found a better place to lose himself, she mused, as a crocodile of schoolchildren marched past her car, clipboards in their hands. She waved to Morgan and he ran towards her.

'Hi. I've not spotted him yet,' he said.

'No shit, Sherlock! Have you counted the number of tourists here? It's like the crowds at an FA Cup Final.'

He lifted his phone to show an image of Cooper: shaven head, wide eyes and a large flat nose. 'I've got his photo. All we can do is ask about.'

'Bluetooth it to my phone. We'll split up and ask around.'

Image received, Emma set off in the opposite direction to Morgan, stopping everyone to ask if they'd seen the man. She was about to try her luck at a quaint thatched cottage pub with colourful baskets hanging by the door when Morgan sprinted across to her and pointed towards the three-arched façade of the town hall.

'Woman over there saw him only minutes ago.'

'Where?'

'Outside Hartington Hall, sitting on a six-seater pub bench, staring at a map.'

Emma broke into a trot. 'Come on. He could take off from there along the Tissington Trail, and then we'll lose him for good.'

Morgan was hot on her heels as they jogged down the road with green hills and medieval stone walls as a backdrop. They raced on, past whitewashed pubs and tables of revellers, until, swerving around a group of hikers, the manor house came into sight. They slowed by the entrance, held up by couples and families out enjoying the warm afternoon.

'If he's not still in the grounds, we ought to head in the direction of Parsley Hays,' Emma said.

'What makes you think he'll go that way?'

'There's both a railway line and a cycle path there, which will give him more options. I'd head there if I wanted to gradually edge my way deeper into the Peak District.'

The manor house was an attraction in itself, built in local stone to an H-plan with three storeys and gabled bays. Nowadays a YHA, it offered affordable accommodation, a bar and a restaurant, and was also a popular wedding venue. They skirted around the crowds and Emma was the first to spot Cooper, folding up a map.

'He's still here. On the bench. Ten o'clock.'

They continued along the path, only metres from Cooper, who was eyeing them. Without warning, he stood up, shouldered his backpack and began to stride away.

'After him!' Morgan powered ahead, legs and arms pumping, but the ex-military man was quick and darted away, putting a greater distance between himself and his pursuers. Morgan rounded the bench and jumped over a small bush. Emma raced after them both, veering to the left to head Cooper off. Cooper sprinted behind the building, pursued by Morgan, who gained rapidly on the older man.

'Police! Mr Monroe, we need to talk.'

Cooper drew to a sudden halt and raised his hands. 'Police? Thank goodness.'

◆　◆　◆

Cooper was compliant and polite. Seated on another bench flanked by both officers, he apologised again. 'I'm sorry, I totally freaked out. I was sure you were hit men.'

'Why would hit men be after you?'

'It's a long story, and I'll tell you, but can I ask first, why have you been looking for me?'

'It's in connection with Bradley Chapman.'

'What's he done?'

'I don't know. What has he done?' said Emma, throwing him a hard look.

Cooper laughed. 'You're a tough nut, aren't you? I've met women like you before. Got fucking great chips on their shoulders and have to prove themselves. To my knowledge, Bradley hasn't done anything wrong, okay?'

Emma scowled, her dark eyebrows almost meeting. 'His alibi for Corby's murder doesn't stack up. Can you throw any light on it?'

'What do you need me to tell you?'

'Which day, or days, you saw him last week.'

'I saw him twice last week. The first time was after he dropped off my daughter, Sierra, from a driving lesson. Sierra left to catch the bus and Bradley was in his car on the phone when he spotted

319

me in the garden. He got out of his car and came to talk to me. He was with me for an hour or maybe just under, and then had to go. He had another lesson in the afternoon and he needed to grab some lunch. I saw him again a few days later – Saturday night. He came around for a chat.'

'What did you talk about?'

'About life and what a crock of shit it is.'

'Really?' Emma couldn't keep the incredulity out of her voice.

Cooper turned towards her. The capillaries in his eyes were bloodshot and his breath smelt sour. 'Look, you don't have to believe me, but you know nothing about me, or about my life, and you're in no position to judge me or make snide comments. I was having a particularly bad day. Bradley helped me through it. Okay?'

'Fair enough. I apologise,' she said.

He studied her again. 'Good. Thank you.'

'And, for the record, *I* don't have to prove myself to anyone,' she added.

He gave a half-hearted laugh. 'You've got spirit.'

Emma gave a tight smile. 'I understand you needed some time out, but I don't get why you took a burner phone with you to contact your daughter. Why all the cloak-and-dagger stuff, Mr Monroe? Why not ring her from your usual mobile?'

Cooper didn't answer at first, but when Emma opened her mouth again he held up a hand. 'I was . . . anxious. I've been getting gradually more paranoid the last few months. I thought somebody was following me and, more recently, I've had a couple of anonymous phone calls to the house – ones where the caller hung up when I answered. I left my mobile in my drawer at home so if anyone was tracking it, they wouldn't know where I was, and I used the burner phone simply to check in on Sierra.'

'Could just have been wrong numbers,' said Morgan.

'No. I'm pretty certain somebody has been watching me. I've been involved in enough covert ops in my time to develop instincts for that sort of thing.'

'So you came here to hide from them?'

'No, I came here to decide what to do about the mess I've got myself into.'

'What mess?'

'It's a long story.'

'We've got time.'

'I got involved in something that led to the deaths of several innocent people.'

'Can you be more specific?'

He pressed his fingers to his temples and inhaled. 'I think I'm partly responsible for the attack on the Euston train on January the sixteenth.'

Morgan sat back down and waited for the confession. As Cooper spoke, Emma's eyes grew as large as saucers.

CHAPTER FORTY-THREE

TUESDAY, 8 JUNE – EVENING

Ervin hadn't uncovered anything else at the Maddox Club. 'Look, why don't you swing by the lab and see Faith? She was working on some items removed from Ian Wentworth's place and she might have something on the white fibre Harvey found under Xavier's fingernail. She won't mind you disturbing her – in fact, she'll probably be glad of some company.'

'Yeah, okay. I'll drop in on her.'

'Good. I'll speak to you again tomorrow.'

Kate ended the call and stared again at the names Chris had written down: the men who'd used the Gold Service. She'd also spent a long time going through what information she could find on Dickson, only to discover what she already knew: he was a well-regarded officer with an unblemished record. A trip to the club and a night with a prostitute ought not to be ringing the alarm bells they were. Nobody she had contacted had been willing to discuss the Gold Service, saying they had done nothing wrong and committed no crime. Raymond was still not picking up his phone and, like Cooper, seemed to have disappeared.

The pencil she'd been holding at both ends snapped in two, and she threw both halves on the desk. The frustration had been building all day, and knowing Dickson could remove her from the investigation at any moment was making matters worse. She was getting closer to the answer, she knew she was. Faith might have something to enable her to piece it all together.

It was rush hour in Stoke-on-Trent, and although she didn't have far to travel, she snaked alongside other frustrated commuters on Queensway, attempting to circumnavigate the city centre. She'd pulled on to the A52 and was level with Hanley Park when her phone rang again.

This time it was the pathologist who spoke. 'I've been examining your latest victim, Xavier Durand. I recovered another white fibre suspiciously like the one I found under his nail from his nasal cavity. I'll have it couriered to Forensics as soon as I finish up. I thought you might also like to know there was a good handful of undigested peanuts in his stomach and digestive tract – twenty of them in total, but no apple. I've cleaned up inside his mouth, and although there is substantial damage to his tongue, inside of cheeks and soft palate, I believe there are one or two similar marks to those we found in the other victims. I can't say with a hundred per cent accuracy the same object was used to stretch open his mouth, but I'd say there's a strong likelihood. I'm not done yet, but I'll keep you up to date if I find anything else unusual.'

'I appreciate it, Harvey. Thanks.'

Although she couldn't be sure of it, Kate's instinct told her the killer had tipped the nuts down Xavier's throat using a choke-pear device. It was the same perpetrator, although they hadn't tortured this victim. Was it because they had insufficient time, or because they were getting sloppy?

She arrived at the university car park minutes later, entered the glass-fronted building and took the lift up to the top floor. She was met at the lab by a technician who was on his way out. He recognised her and held the door open for her, telling her Faith had just popped out for a minute. Kate wandered across to the window and stared out at the trees beyond, then strolled around the lab, taking it all in.

Although it had only been a few days since she'd last been here, it already felt like a lifetime. Her attention was drawn to a mobile phone on the bench that suddenly lit up. She let it ring out, and spotting a picture of Faith, she picked the device up for a closer look. It was a woman who looked a lot like Faith but with a plumper face. She had her arms around the waist of a handsome boy in his late teens, wearing shorts, T-shirt and a braided bracelet in green, gold, red, black and white – the colours of the Zimbabwe flag, if her memory served her correctly. Kate stared at the picture of contentment, the happiness of both woman and teenager. It was an arresting picture and reminded Kate of her father. Somewhere in her house was a strikingly similar photograph of them both, her father's arms wrapped her as she beamed for the camera.

'What are you doing?'

The sharp tone made Kate jump. 'Your phone rang. I think it was Ervin. I noticed the photo so I was just having a better look.'

Faith stretched out her hand for her phone.

Kate dropped it into her palm. 'Your sister? You look alike – the same smile, same eyes.'

'Yes. I suppose we do share certain features.'

'Is that her son?'

'It is.'

'So he's your nephew. I've got a nephew, too, although I've never actually met him. Daniel lives in Australia with my stepsister, Tilly. He's four. How old is he?'

'He was fourteen in the picture . . . He's no longer with us.' Faith's face closed.

'Oh, shit! I'm sorry. I didn't mean . . . I was only being . . .'

'I know. No harm done. I'd rather not talk about it, though, if you don't mind.'

'Sure.'

Faith slid the mobile into her lab coat pocket. 'I wasn't expecting you. What can I help you with?'

'Ervin suggested I visit in case you'd stumbled across anything useful on those items from Ian's house.'

'I'm sorry, I've not found anything, but I've still loads more tests to run.'

'He also sent across a white thread. Have you had a chance to analyse it yet?'

Faith nodded. 'I examined it as soon as I got it. That's partly why I haven't finished testing everything from Ian's cottage. It was a type of tissue paper, and matched identical threads from a leading brand of luxury toilet tissue.'

Xavier must have picked up the thread when he last visited the toilet; maybe he even blew his nose on a piece of toilet paper, which would account for the fibre in his nose. 'Damn!'

Faith steepled her fingertips; a small gesture of apology. 'I'm sorry I didn't have the news you hoped for. That's the trouble with forensic evidence. We collect loads, but not all of it is relevant to the investigation.'

'I was hoping the fibre would be a clue.'

'I have other news for you, regarding Ian Wentworth. I recovered fingerprints from Raven Cottage that clearly belong to children.'

'Oh, no!'

'I'm afraid so. I'm still working through the prints, but it's apparent what was going on there.'

Kate swallowed hard.

325

Faith seemed to study her for a moment. 'Is it . . . is this case more difficult than others you've headed?'

'In some ways it is. You know the saying, "Two steps forward and one step back"? Well, I seem to be taking several steps back and none forward.'

'I'm sure you must be making progress. You've all been working really hard on this. I've always wondered what it would be like to head an investigation.'

'Tough.'

'I can imagine it is.'

'Some days, we'd get nowhere without Forensics.'

'And some days, even with our help, you still get nowhere,' said Faith, eyebrows arching high.

The attempt at humour made Kate chuckle. 'Yes, pretty much.'

'Is the Maddox Club crime scene the same as the others?'

'There are similarities.'

Faith perched on a stool, her neat ankles together. 'What sort of similarities?'

'The victim was drugged and died of asphyxiation. He was found bound to a chair.'

'Exactly like the other victims, then?' Faith's zeal almost visibly bubbled, and Kate understood why Ervin appreciated her passion. It emulated his own. 'Did the perpetrator choke the victim with pieces of apple?'

'No, but as I said, there are similarities.'

'I'm sure you'll get a breakthrough.'

Kate shook her head. 'Unless something surfaces quickly, I'm in limbo. The assailant is like a ghost. Never leaves a trace.'

'What, no evidence at all? There must be something.'

'There are fingerprints, but I suspect they'll belong to club members or staff. There was a spot of blood on the carpet and on an ornament.'

Faith's eyebrows lifted slightly. 'Blood? Nobody sent it across for analysis.'

'Ervin tested out some new biomarker toy he got from the States and decided it was female. We ought to talk to the cleaning staff and obtain buccal swabs for comparison and elimination purposes. I'd have arranged it sooner, had we had time. I'll chase it up.'

'If you want to send those blood samples from the club across, I'll prioritise the tests for you.'

'Great.'

Faith's eyebrows puckered. 'I wouldn't hold too much store by the biomarker results. They aren't always truly accurate. Blood needs to be properly analysed and tested in laboratory conditions. We ought to run further tests on it to make sure.'

'I'm sure Ervin will arrange them.'

'You're right. He wouldn't trust the kit any more than I do. They've been known to screw up results. Still, if they're right and the killer is a woman, then who do you have in mind?'

Kate shrugged.

'Alex's wife?'

'Fiona was in France when Alex was killed.'

'Her mother?'

Kate threw her a look. Faith picked up on it, flushed gently and stood up, brushing imaginary dust from her lab coat. 'Oh, I'm sorry. I didn't mean to muscle in on your investigation. I'm just fascinated by all of this and sometimes I get carried away. A regular Nancy Drew, eh? I'll double-check the blood sample as soon it turns up and make sure it is missing a Y chromosome.'

Kate knew what it was like to be enthusiastic and want to succeed, and Faith was only battling to be the best. 'Thanks.'

Faith felt the side of her pocket. 'Someone's calling me.' She pulled out the mobile and glanced at the display. 'Ervin again.'

'I'll leave you to it.'

Faith made signs for her to remain, but Kate lifted a hand and slipped out of the lab. She ought to arrange for Tabitha Grant and Poppy Notts, the women who'd cleaned at the Maddox Club, to give swabs. She had been so busy searching for information on Dickson she'd forgotten to sort it out. It was unlike her. She clattered downstairs, annoyed with herself for such an oversight. They should have eliminated these women as quickly as possible. Maybe Dickson was right and she was losing her grip.

Back in her car, she took a call from the technician, Felicity Jolly.

'Kate, the encrypted file we located on Ian Wentworth's laptop was hiding something – his IPS. Your victim was searching on the dark web.'

'What was he hunting for?'

'He was investigating bodyguards and hired muscle.'

'He must have believed he was in danger.'

'I can't comment. I'm a mere technician. It's up to you clever bods in the crime unit to interpret those findings. 'I'll send over an email with all the websites he visited.'

'Thanks, you've been a massive help.'

'My pleasure. I hope you'll drop by again soon, even just to say hello.'

Cooper wetted his lips then began. 'I got the job at the Maddox Club thanks to Alex Corby. He told me late November 2020 they were looking for somebody discreet to work a few extra shifts at the club, and asked if I'd be interested. All I had to do was escort some girls and boys in and out of the premises. When I say girls and boys, that's exactly what they were, youngsters – some spoke no English, some were quite chatty. They were all immigrants sent over by a bloke called Farai. He and Xavier were mates. I think he was some sort of pimp.

'I'd pick the boys and girls up from a drop-off point near the big supermarket just outside Stafford, drive them to the club and escort them in via the back door. Xavier would meet them there and sort them out. I'd wait around in the kitchen usually, act as an unofficial doorman until all the members had left, and then take a nap in the drawing room until morning before taking the kids back to the drop-off zone. Xavier was worried they might try and steal from the members, so I was his insurance, if you like. With me acting as their minder, they weren't likely to take advantage of their clients, were they?'

Emma listened intently, her body rigid as she hung on to his every word.

'On Wednesday the second of January 2021, I picked up two girls and a boy and drove them to the Maddox Club. The girls were from Bulgaria and giggled the entire journey. The boy, on the other hand, was shy and looked so nervous I asked him if he was sure he wanted to go into the club. He gave me a look – can't describe it other than it was like a puppy who'd been kicked. "I have to," he said. "It's for my family." I didn't know what to say. Poor kid. He was a good-looking lad, African origin with hazel eyes. I'm still haunted by the look in them and I ask myself over and over again why I didn't just turn the car around and tell him to forget it?' Cooper balled his hands into fists and took a deep breath.

'You okay?' asked Morgan.

Cooper nodded. 'Yeah. Give me a second.'

He drew another breath then continued. 'It was about four in the morning when I was woken up. I'd dozed off in the drawing room. Xavier was stood over me, looking like shit. He needed my help. Something had gone seriously wrong upstairs and the lad had accidentally died – of an overdose or something. Xavier refused to report it to the police – the lad was an illegal immigrant and they didn't know anything about him or his family, and more importantly, they had to protect the member who'd been involved. I didn't want anything to do with it to start with, but Xavier said I was already involved, and if he went down, so would I; I was the one who collected the kids and I'd be implicated if it came out. I had to think of my daughter. She was all I had. I couldn't face charges or go to prison. Xavier offered me £20,000 to stay quiet. The member involved, Ian Wentworth, would pay me if I disposed of the body.

'God help me, I took the fucking money. Such a huge amount meant a lot to me. I was struggling to make ends meet after my bitch of a wife left me, and I could do so much with 20K. The kid was already dead. I didn't kill him. No one knew he was at the Maddox Club other than me, Xavier, Wentworth – and the Bulgarian girls, of course, but they wouldn't have any idea where he was, and would assume he'd gone home at a different time. I went upstairs with Xavier to Wentworth's room. The young man was naked on the bed, hog-tied, with a plastic bag over his head. He'd suffocated during some sexual game. It was fucking sick, I can tell you. His body was so bruised I could hardly look at it. Xavier and me untied him, wrapped him up inside the bedspread on the floor and carried him to my car. Xavier asked me to dispose of the kid's body. He couldn't face it. I headed home, picked up a shovel, then drove back to the club. I figured the lad wouldn't be discovered in the woods behind the place.'

'Could you show us where?'

'Yes.'

'What about the other club members? Did they know about this?'

'I don't think anyone else knew. It was pitch dark outside. The only other two members who were staying overnight were occupied with the Bulgarian girls.'

'And you felt bad about this afterwards?' Emma asked.

'Wouldn't you? I've seen all sorts of crap in my life, but the sight of that young boy sickened me more than anything I've come across. I mean it *really* burrowed into me. I couldn't sleep for days afterwards. Couldn't focus. I needed a few shots of whisky each night to get to sleep, and then two shots became several, and I'd race for the whisky bottle as soon as I got in from work.'

'And you told Bradley about this?'

'Like fuck I did! No way.'

Morgan's brow furrowed.

Cooper held up a hand. 'There's more. Hear me out. About a week later, Ian Wentworth phoned me to ask a favour. He wanted me to shut a journalist up. He reckoned, with my background, I'd be able to put the frighteners on the man, rough him up a bit and get him off his back. The guy was asking questions about the Gold Service. Heaven knows how he found out about it, but he'd talked to Wentworth and was beginning to ask probing questions. Wentworth was shit scared he'd find out about the lad. I told him I wasn't a hired thug. I don't beat up innocent people and I wasn't going to help him. I'd already done more than enough. Told him to find somebody else. I didn't think he would or could, but he did. He tracked down some loose cannon – a complete and utter fucking nut-job – from some dark website. Paid him in advance in Bitcoins. Wentworth rang me soon after he'd hired the bloke. He'd changed his mind and tried to call it off, but the guy told him to fuck off and was going ahead regardless. He wanted me to stop the motherfucker, but I told him to go to hell. I should have stepped in. I might have prevented what happened.

'The bastard turned it into a complete bloodbath. He didn't put the frighteners on or beat up the reporter – he murdered him, and not only him, but an entire train carriage of innocent people.'

◆ ◆ ◆

Cooper sat in the back of Morgan's car, eyes closed.

'Who's going to speak to her?' Emma asked.

'Fuck me, I don't know. Speak to William and let him tell her.'

'She'll go mental.'

'Which might be a good thing. She's been acting weirdly anyway. Maybe, this way, it'll shake her up or help give her closure, or whatever the shrinks say will help.'

'Okay. We'll ring William. This is . . . fucking awful.'

Morgan couldn't disagree with her.

Emma fumbled in her pocket, pulled out a coin and prepared to flick it in the air. 'Heads or tails?'

'Oh, for pity's sake. I'll speak to William, okay?' Morgan said.

'Good. I hoped you would. I'll drive Cooper back and get an official statement from him at the station. You can tell me what William says.'

'What if Kate gets wind Cooper's there?'

'Then you'd better hope William will have told her what happened to Chris before that happens, and come up with a plan, because I've no idea how she'll react.'

'Take your time going back to the station, then. I'll ring William en route.'

'Sure. I'll go the scenic route. And, Morgan—'

'What?'

'Thanks.'

CHAPTER
FORTY-FOUR

TUESDAY, 8 JUNE – LATE EVENING

Kate checked her messages and found one from Mike Blythe, the cleaner who'd found Xavier's body. He'd provided the address and phone number for Poppy Notts, who worked for ABeClean and regularly cleaned the Maddox Club.

She rang him back immediately. 'Hi, Mike. It's DI Young. How are you?'

'Still pretty shaken up. Did you get my message?'

'Yes, thank you. It's the reason for my call. I wondered if I could have a word with Tabitha?'

'She's asleep. The virus has totally wiped her out. Can it wait until the morning?'

'Okay. I'm going to arrange for somebody to drop by and take a DNA sample from her. It's just a simple swab test. Will you tell her?'

'Yes, I will.'

'Thanks.'

She was back on track. She rang Poppy, got the answerphone and left a message. Hopefully, she'd speak to both women in the morning and then they'd be able to find out if the blood on the carpet and ornament belonged to either of them. It was getting late and she hadn't taken a proper break all day. Her head was thumping badly – her body rebelling against the lack of medication and food. She needed to stop off home, grab a bite to eat, take some headache pills before pushing on.

She pulled on to her drive and hopped out of the car. The voice took her by surprise. It was the journalist who'd been plaguing her. She hadn't noticed his dark-coloured Volvo parked in the street. She hadn't the energy to scream at him for being outside her home.

'Oh, for goodness' sake. Just piss off and leave me alone, will you?'

Dan leapt forward, put a hand on her arm. 'Kate, please. Chris was a good mate.'

'*Was?* Did you fall out?'

He paused, mouth agape, then shook himself slightly and continued, voice now gentle. 'Of course we didn't fall out. We were mates. Kate, is everything okay? You seem . . . confused.'

Kate rubbed her forehead, but didn't reply.

'Okay. Listen. I have something *extremely* important for you. Chris shared some of his information with me – his suspicions regarding Ian Wentworth. He was on to something big and I owe it to him to follow it up through the proper channels. This is more than a scoop.'

She halted in her tracks. Why hadn't Chris shared this with her? 'What do you know about Ian Wentworth?'

'Chris and I were investigating a paedophile ring. Chris was sure Ian was involved in it, but you know what he was like – always played his cards close to his chest, and after . . . well . . . after what happened to him on the train, I had to let it drop through lack of information. He'd uncovered the bulk of it and I didn't have access to it. Besides, I had other assignments to handle. Anyway, I inherited Chris's desk, and a couple of weeks ago I had trouble with the bottom drawer, which wouldn't open. Maintenance fixed it last week and discovered this notebook taped to the underside. I was going to look into it myself, then a couple of days after I got my hands on it, Ian Wentworth was murdered. I owe it to Chris to pass this to you.'

She stared at the small black journal in his hand. Chris should have given it to her, or at least told her about it. She took it from Dan, opened it and recognised her husband's neat handwriting.

She began to speak, but Dan beat her to it. 'If you want to chat further about what we uncovered, I'll be happy to talk. I want to honour Chris's memory. He was a terrific guy – the best journalist I've ever met.' He withdrew to his car and opened the door.

She managed a soft 'Thank you' before he disappeared into its interior and started it up.

She didn't dally. This could well contain the clues Chris had wanted her to find when he warned her about her fellow colleagues, especially John Dickson. The small black book burned in her hand as she slammed the door shut and hurried into the sitting room, where she dropped on to the settee.

'Chris, I've got your journal.'

Silence.

'You hid it. Too bloody well. It's a good thing the drawer stuck or we'd never have found it. Why the hell didn't you leave it at home?'

'Because you never go into my den, Kate. You're too scared to face up to the truth of what happened. You've been blocking it out, relying on pills to befuddle your brain and keep you living in a bubble.'

The trembling began almost immediately. Something shifted inside her head, like somebody was raising a curtain. She wanted to tug it back down and retreat behind it once more, her pain obliterated by pills. Reality was coming into sharper focus, bringing the clarity she'd been avoiding for months. The urge to speak to Chris was overwhelming. She fumbled for her phone, thumbed her messages and pulled up the one she'd read by the fish van only a couple of days ago:

Sorry Babe

Shit signal here.

Speak soon.

Love you.

X

Her heart scorched a hole in her chest as she registered the date the message had actually been sent – 16 January – the day Chris had been killed.

The rush of memories emptied her lungs of breath and she rested her head in her hands. They paraded in front of her, leaving her powerless to ignore them . . .

◆ ◆ ◆

She's on her way home when the 'all units respond' call comes in, and given she's only two minutes from the railway station, she responds.

◆ ◆ ◆

She dropped her head into her arms. *Stop*, she begs, but they don't . . .

◆ ◆ ◆

The entire station has been cordoned off and officers have secured the area. Passengers have disembarked and been taken to a facility to be interviewed. The train is by platform 1, and glassy-eyed station staff stand in front of the coffee house there as she and other officers mount the steps on to the train and into the first-class carriage.

The smell is of death. Seats are stained crimson and the windows are splattered with blood like red paintballs. An elderly man is blocking the aisle and she must step over his lifeless body to continue, her eyes grazing the businessman slumped in the seat nearby, a hole in his forehead and jaw open. Two seats further on, a blonde-haired woman is face down on the table, her friend hunched in the corner of her seat. Ahead, on the floor, lies the body of the gunman, his weapon on the floor beside him. A body is spread-eagled on top of his legs, but Kate can't tear her eyes away from the auburn-haired woman who'd died trying to protect the child under her seat. Kate's heart shatters at the sight of the child's stockinged legs and the toy bear by her side. She barely hears the officers next to her talking in low voices.

'One of the passengers prevented the bastard from killing anyone else. He'd been shot but somehow still managed to attack him. He used this to hit him.'

She glances up. The words won't come. Her lips are anaesthetised, her throat constricted.

The object is stained brown but is still in one piece. The heavy crystal award has a name engraved on it. She reads the inscription and her breath catches in her throat. She gasps for air, her eyes widening.

Journalist of the Year

Chris Young

Why was Chris on this train? She was expecting him home much later, after the drinks party to celebrate this award. She stares at the crumpled *body of her brave husband, who'd tried to save his fellow passengers, and her knees buckle. William is by her side in a flash.*

'Kate, come on. Come away. Can I have some help here, please?'

◆ ◆ ◆

Her husband had died a hero, but the case, assigned first to the terrorism squad and then another crime unit, had not been resolved. Why the man had run amok was a mystery. She recalled the article in the local newspaper at the time. She knew every word off by heart . . .

Courageous Journalist Saves Passengers During Gun Siege

An attack on a busy train has left fellow commuters reeling. Passengers on the 4.30 p.m. train from Euston to Manchester Piccadilly two days ago, on Wednesday 16 January, suffered a horrendous ordeal when a lone gunman rampaged through the first-class carriage and killed its occupants.

Had it not been for the bravery of journalist Chris Young at the time, many more would certainly have been killed.

Quick-thinking Chris Young (38) from Stoke-on-Trent, who scooped the Journalist of the Year Award at a ceremony earlier in the day, had been returning from the event when the gunman, who has been named as Edward Blancher (51) opened fire in his carriage.

Shot in the chest by Blancher, Chris still managed to pursue the assailant and bring him down single-handedly, and in so doing, saved the lives of many others on the train.

The alarm was raised when the train stopped at Stoke-on-Trent station. DI Kate Young (34), wife to Chris, was one of the first officers to attend the scene of the crime, but was unavailable for comment.

Kate's senior officer, DCI William Chase, praised Chris for his bravery and quick thinking. 'Had it not been for his speedy actions, this would undoubtedly have escalated into an even more tragic event and a huge loss of life. We are of course all deeply saddened by the loss of Chris and our thoughts are with Kate at this time.'

Police have assured citizens this was a one-off attack. They do, however, urge all commuters to remain vigilant while travelling and report anything suspicious to either the train guard, or to the police.

A sob, like a seismic earthquake, began in the centre of her soul, shaking and vibrating as it travelled through her body. It rose steadily, passing through her chest and heart into her throat, and she threw back her head and wailed like a wounded animal until she was bereft of any energy.

CHAPTER FORTY-FIVE

WEDNESDAY, 9 JUNE – EARLY MORNING

Awakening with a start, and still in her clothes from the day before, Kate picked up her mobile from the coffee table to establish the time and saw she had several missed calls.

'Chris?' she whispered, even though she knew he wouldn't and couldn't answer her.

Silence enveloped her and she bit back tears. Self-pity was a luxury she couldn't afford. She listened to the messages: the first was from Emma to say they were holding Cooper in custody overnight. There were two further messages from her, and then another four from William Chase, wanting to know where Kate was and why she wasn't answering her phone.

The last was from Ervin: 'Hi, Kate. This is a mini update. I've just examined a second white fibre Harvey found in Xavier's nasal cavity and which I assumed would be the same as the one found under his fingernail. According to Faith's report, the first thread came from toilet paper, but this one doesn't, so I'm going to run further tests to establish where it has come from. That's all for the moment. Cheerio.'

Kate messaged Emma to say she was on her way to the station. William would have to wait. She had no idea what she'd tell him yet, but it certainly wouldn't be the truth. She didn't know whom she could trust to tell, and until she got the opportunity to read Chris's journal in private, she'd keep the meeting with Dan, the reporter, to herself. The book was in her handbag and she hunted for a safe place to leave it, settling on the empty box of cereal with the smiley face.

'You're not here, Chris, are you? My mind's been protecting me . . . shielding me from reality, and the pills, the bloody pills, have played their part. They helped keep me in a permanent fugue state. I've been living in a dream since January.' She blinked back more tears. She couldn't cry again. Not yet. Not while she had work to do.

'You were so brave. I don't know how many more innocents would have died if you hadn't acted.' She traced the grinning face with a fingertip. 'Oh, Chris! I can't live completely without you. I simply can't.'

'I can still be here when you need me to be,' came the reply.

Relief flooded through her. 'I'd like that.'

She shoved the book inside the box and rammed several plastic bags on top of it, replaced it on the kitchen top, where it would be hidden in full sight, then rushed away to shower and dress. She had to take up her role as lead detective again and not arouse any suspicions.

It was quarter past six by the time she reached the station. She'd spotted William's car in the car park so she wasn't surprised when the desk sergeant told her DCI Chase wished to see her as soon as she arrived.

She steeled herself for the inevitable dressing-down. After all, she'd been absent and out of contact during a crucial part of the investigation. She'd stupidly given Dickson the ammunition he required to have her booted off it, and she would have to fight to remain. She pulled at her blouse, squared her shoulders and knocked at his door.

'Come in.'

She strode in, head held high, prepared for battle, and was taken aback when William jumped to his feet and offered her a chair. 'Ah, Kate. Sit down.'

He waited until she was seated, then rested his hands together as if in prayer, fingers in front of his lips, before speaking. 'We might have a breakthrough on this case, but first there's something you should know. It concerns Chris.'

'Chris?'

'And Edward Blancher.'

'What about him?' She couldn't bring herself to say the name of the gunman who had destroyed her life and those of many others.

'Morgan and Emma have uncovered some vital new information and brought it to my attention.'

'New information?' she asked, wondering why Morgan and Emma hadn't told her directly.

'Blancher was hired to kill Chris.'

'And what about all those other people on the train?'

'It appears Ian Wentworth paid for Blancher's services. He instructed him to murder your husband.' He craned his neck, watching for any sign she would crack.

Kate inhaled deeply through her mouth, held her breath for a couple of seconds and released it through pursed lips, steadying her increased heart rate. 'I see.'

William continued, 'Blancher was only supposed to target Chris, but for some unknown reason he shot everyone in the carriage.'

'The London crime team who were investigating it never did establish why he went on the rampage, did they?'

William's face was long, dragged down by sorrow. 'They only established he'd undergone psychiatric treatment. I'm sorry, Kate.'

'We should have handled the investigation. The answer lay closer to home. It should never have been passed over,' she began.

William tried to interrupt, but she wasn't prepared to hold back. This was further proof Dickson was involved. He'd made sure the case had been taken away from her, from anyone on the patch who would have kept her informed. In light of what they'd established, that decision made perfect sense. He'd been protecting a friend.

'I want access to those files.'

'Kate—'

'I *want* access.'

'I don't think that's a wise move. It's a historical investigation; the perpetrator was established.'

'Yet you have fresh evidence indicating the gunman was acting for somebody else.'

'It doesn't alter the outcome! Blancher was responsible for the all the deaths.'

The look he gave was fatherly concern.

'Why was I denied access during the investigation?'

'Why do you think? You were fragile, Kate. We were concerned about you. You were fighting to maintain a front, determined to carry on as if nothing had happened. You came back to work almost immediately, against medical advice, and anyone could see you weren't yourself. Yes, you were courageous, resolute, professional, but very fragile. Superintendent Dickson discussed the matter with me and I backed you, told him it was better for you to be occupied at work. I know what this job means to you and it seemed cruel to part you from it when you most needed it. However, he agreed only on the understanding we kept an eye on you and monitored your behaviour, and we blocked any attempts you might make to extract information or become involved in the Euston investigation. It was for your own good. The decision about who led the enquiry wasn't ours to make. The command came from higher up, and believe me, we challenged it, but we were told Blancher had boarded the train in London so the investigation was to be carried out by a London team.' His voice was smooth, hands relaxed in his lap. There was no physical indication he was lying to her.

She lifted her gaze to his face once more, searched for empathy in his eyes and saw emptiness. She didn't believe him. She swallowed hard, and it was a few moments before she could speak again. 'Do we know why Ian hired this man to kill Chris?'

'We believe it was to silence him. Chris had stumbled across something that would have ruined Ian's reputation and led to the man's imprisonment. Something to do with the Maddox Club – a Gold Service there.'

'Who provided this information?'

'Cooper Monroe.'

William gave a résumé of what Cooper had told Emma and Morgan, and all the while, Kate absorbed the details, her eyes trained on William's mouth as the words tumbled out, and felt nothing. She'd simply run out of emotion.

'Do you intend removing me from the investigation?'

William made a helpless gesture with his hands. 'There's a conflict of interest here.'

'I don't see how knowing an assassin was hired by one of the victims to kill my husband is going to affect my judgement. Ian Wentworth is dead. I'm unlikely to go on some vendetta against him. William, I've worked hard to track down this murderer and my motivation remains the same. As it did from the off. I have to prove myself, not to you or Superintendent Dickson, but to myself. When I lost Chris, I lost everything, and I have to rebuild my life. This will help me find closure. You owe me, William. You can't leave me to flounder again at home with no focus or reason to exist. You said yourself, when you begged me to take on this investigation, you wanted the old Kate to resurface. You told me she was only temporarily out of sight. Well, she's here now, and she needs this.'

William began to shake his head, but she continued, calmly, voice level. 'We've come too far down this line to bring in somebody new. You put me on this case because you trusted me to track down Alex Corby's murderer – you and Superintendent Dickson both, and you still can trust me to bring the perpetrator to justice. My reputation depends on it.'

'I don't know, Kate. The super is worried you aren't up to the task.'

'And you, William, what do you think?'

'You disappeared yesterday evening, didn't answer your phone . . . I agree with him.'

'I was busy doing my job, tracking down potential suspects and clearing others. I arranged for Emma and Morgan to interview Cooper and I had other important leads to follow. If we had a full team, as we should on an investigation of this magnitude, I would not have to participate in active fieldwork and would be able to orchestrate the investigation as DI. Communication is not always possible when you are doing fieldwork. You know all of this, William. Remember what it was like when you and Dad used to work together? One or both of you would be out of contact for hours at a time. Policing hasn't changed hugely since then. The fact remains that we are close to catching this person, and if you remove me, you'll have to find a suitable replacement and start all over again. Another DI might not be so willing to operate as clandestinely.'

William bounced the tips of his fingers together silently. 'Okay, but no more disappearing off the radar, and if I suspect for one second you *are* on some sort of vendetta, I'll have you removed.'

'Fine.'

'Kate, you and I have history. Your dad wanted me to look out for you and I want you to know I have your best interests at heart.'

'Thank you.'

'I ask one thing . . . You keep me in the loop about everything.'

'I shall.'

He dismissed her and she left. She had no intention of keeping him fully informed. What she'd discovered about Ian only served to strengthen her resolve to uncover Dickson's role in it. Ian wouldn't have acted alone. Of that she was sure. First, she'd speak to Cooper, and later, she'd read the journal Dan had given her. A light was on in her office, and Emma and Morgan were both inside.

'Morning, both. There's not much time to do a full debrief, so I'll summarise as best I can. As you know, Xavier Durand, manager at the Maddox Club, was killed some time Monday night or early Tuesday morning. I've been unable to contact Raymond Maddox and I'd like MisPers involved and a trace put on his phone. I haven't had confirmation, but it would appear that Xavier was murdered using the same sort of device, which we believe to be a choke-pear.

'On this occasion, the killer changed their MO. They didn't remove any eyes and their victim choked to death on a peanut taken from a bowl in the bar. What might be significant is some blood, believed to be female blood, on a paperweight, and another drop of blood on the carpet. We need to talk to Tabitha Grant, the owner of ABeClean, and one of her cleaners, Poppy Notts, to find out if either of them cut themselves while cleaning a bronze paperweight of a Sphinx in the drawing room at the Maddox Club. I've arranged for a uniformed officer to take DNA swabs from both, but I'd still like speak to them. It'd be quicker than waiting for the results. Any questions so far?'

Her rapid-fire round-up had rendered Morgan and Emma speechless. She gave them a couple of seconds to respond, and when they didn't, she continued. 'And just so you are both fully aware, I know Ian Wentworth hired Edward Blancher to kill Chris. William's told me everything. I'd like to hear Cooper's version of what took place first-hand, so I'll be interviewing him.'

The tension fixing Emma's features in place drained from her face. 'Did he also tell you Chris had been investigating the Gold Service at the Maddox Club—?'

Kate silenced her with her hand. 'It's okay. He told me everything, and any blanks will be filled in when I speak to Cooper.'

Morgan shuffled uncomfortably and asked, 'Are you still lead officer on this investigation?'

'DCI Chase has agreed I can continue. We were tasked initially with unmasking Alex's killer, and although it has taken us down this path, we can't yet be sure if these deaths are linked to the atrocities that took place on the Euston train. Therefore, we carry on as we have been. I have confidence in our abilities as a team to uncover whoever killed Alex, Ian and Xavier. *That* is my primary goal in all of this. Right, I'd like to talk to Cooper. Morgan, will you sit in? Emma, are you happy to deal with the cleaning staff?'

Emma nodded.

'Good. Morgan, would you please escort Cooper to an interview room? I'll be down in a minute.'

As soon as he was out of earshot, Emma spoke to Kate. 'I was concerned about how you'd react.'

'To what?'

'To the news about Chris's death. You've been a little . . . odd, the last few days . . . the pills . . . the piece of cake for Chris in your bag.'

Kate cocked her head to one side. 'I've been off my game. The prescribed medication was messing with my head. I didn't grasp how badly it was affecting me until recently. I've ditched it and definitely won't be taking it again. I'm already feeling more like my old self – more focused.'

'You've had us worried for quite a while.'

'Really. I'm okay.'

'If you say so.' Emma gave her a serious look.

Kate gave a warm smile. 'I say so. Thanks for not mentioning the note at Ian's cottage.'

'I didn't want to rattle any cages and I was sure you'd handle it the right way. Besides, Faith noticed there was a fair amount of dust on the notepad so the meeting must have taken place several months ago. Knowing what we do now, it might even have been about the Gold Service.'

The meeting that caused Ian to panic and hire an assassin to murder her husband.

Emma glanced at the time and said, 'I'd better ring Tabitha.'

Kate left her to her work and hurried down the corridor towards the interview room to speak to Cooper. Chris was at her elbow.

'You're back already,' she said. Talking to him was unhealthy, yet it was the only comfort she had, and she craved it.

'You need support. Something about this doesn't sit right. I'm surprised Ian came up with such an extreme way to silence me. He could have kept me quiet in so many other ways: money, blackmail, threats, roughed me up . . . but a hit man!'

'I agree. I understand he panicked at the thought you'd find out about the dead boy, but to have come up with such an extreme

348

solution, and alone . . . I'd have thought he'd have spoken to Xavier or somebody else about it first. Maybe even confessed to his close friends – Alex and Dickson – and asked their advice.'

'Exactly. It would explain why Dickson wanted the case to be derailed.'

'You think he was involved?'

'Pretty certain. Aren't you?'

'He must have heard the screams coming from Ian's room and been suspicious. And why didn't he question Ian leaving early the following morning? He's claimed to know nothing, and we can't prove to the contrary because the only other people who knew what happened are dead. He knows more that he's let on. I'll get to the bottom of it.'

'I'm proud of you, Kate. You handled yourself well in William's office and back there in front of Morgan and Emma. They think they've got the old trustworthy Kate back. You hid your suspicions well. Keep them to yourself.' His voice dropped to a whisper. 'Someone convinced Ian to hire a hit man. He didn't come up with that idea himself. And whoever did that is going to let Ian take the fall for it.'

'I know, but I won't let that happen. I'm going to make sure those involved are held accountable.'

'That's my girl!'

'Are you coming into the interview room with me?'

'You bet.'

◆ ◆ ◆

Cooper Monroe was nursing a hot drink. Kate shut the door to the interview room and held out a hand in greeting. He accepted it and gave her a firm handshake, his calloused palm brushing against hers.

She sat down, Morgan next to her. 'Mr Monroe, I understand you were involved in an incident at the Maddox Club back on Wednesday the second of January.'

'I was party to a cover-up for which I accepted a hefty bribe, yes,' he replied.

'Did you know any of the men who ordered the Gold Service and stayed over at the club on the night of the second of January?'

'No.'

'A waiter told you Ian Wentworth was staying at the club?'

'He did.'

'Who was this waiter? Can he back up your story?'

'I only know his first name – Christophe. It was his last week there. He was returning to France the following week, so the answer is no, he can't back up my story. Raymond might have contact details for him.'

'Am I right in saying, then, you didn't know the names of the other members who stayed overnight?'

'Yes.'

'Would it surprise you to know Alex Corby also stayed that night?'

Cooper's face changed in an instant. 'Alex was there? Oh, shit! I know where you're going with this. Look, I didn't know who else was a guest there, okay? My job was to drive two young women and a young man to a drop-off zone at the club. Until that moment when Xavier woke me up and begged me for help, I had no interest in what went on inside the place. I did my job, earnt a little extra money for doing it, and asked no questions. That was it. I'd never even seen Alex around the club. He was my boss and my best mate's son-in-law. You can't honestly think I'd kill him?'

'To our knowledge, Bradley had very little love for his son-in-law. You could have been in cahoots,' said Kate.

Cooper slammed the mug on to the table, hands still clenched around it. 'I did not, repeat, *not*, kill anyone – not the young lad, not Alex and not Ian Wentworth.'

'Or Xavier Durand?'

'Xavier's dead?'

'He is.'

Cooper let out a lengthy groan and rubbed a tattooed hand across his balding head. 'Jesus! What a fuck-up.'

'We'll have to confirm your whereabouts for the days in question.'

'Yes . . . yes. Which days?'

'We'll discuss the matter in a moment.' She pushed forward a detailed sketch. 'This is a map of the club and its surrounding area. Are you able to tell me where the body of the young man you buried is hidden?'

He leant across the table and pointed out a spot in the middle of a copse. 'It was about there. I can show you more accurately if we go there. It's not something you easily forget.'

'Did you know the boy's name?'

'No. I didn't engage in any conversation with them.'

'Was there anything you remember about him? Any distinguishing features?'

'He was only a lad – younger than my daughter. Nice-looking boy with striking hazel eyes, and . . . resigned. He weighed next to nothing.' His face scrunched up as if it had been punched. 'I made a monumental error helping out that piece of shit.'

'Ian Wentworth?'

'Yes.'

'Did you feel anger towards Ian Wentworth at the time?'

'You bet I did, but mostly . . . mostly, I felt disgust.'

'Yet you still helped him cover up this crime?'

'I'm ashamed to say I did. I was stuck between a rock and a hard place. I was already involved. I knew what was going on in the club and I needed the money Wentworth was offering me for my silence. It paid for my daughter, Sierra, to go to college. She'd been through so much shit and I'd not been around when she'd needed me. Her mum and I had ruined her past, but the money meant I could give her a future. The boy was dead. He wasn't coming back, but Sierra was alive. Pretty messed up, eh?'

'You called the people you ferried to the club "boys and girls". Were they under age?'

'Maybe . . . Probably . . . but honestly, I don't know. You can't tell by looks, can you? I called them that cos they're all youngsters to me. Anyone who looks under twenty-one is a youngster in my book.'

Although instinct told her Cooper wasn't responsible for the deaths of Alex, Ian and Xavier, she still had to follow procedure and ask, 'Can you confirm your whereabouts last Thursday morning?'

'I was at home. I'd been on a bender since the night before. Sierra was out with Bradley on a driving lesson. When he dropped her off, he noticed me in the garden. I was in a crap state, weaving about outside, sobbing like a baby. He took me back in and got me a coffee. We talked.'

'By bender, I assume you mean drinking heavily?'

'Yes. I was still out of my skull when Bradley turned up.'

'Did you talk to Bradley about the boy you buried?'

'No.'

'Can you be sure you didn't? By your own admission, you'd drunk heavily and were depressed by what you'd done.'

'I don't blab when I'm drunk. Quite the opposite. I become tight-lipped.'

'But he is a very good friend. You might have opened up to him.'

'He and I fought side by side when we were in the SAS. I trust him with my life, but Bradley has a strict moral code, especially when it comes to children and family. He'd do absolutely anything for Fiona and the grandkids. If I'd confessed everything to him, he'd have insisted I turn myself in, or he'd have told you what had happened himself, so I only gave him a condensed version of events. I told him Ian Wentworth had asked me to rough up a troublesome reporter, and then begged me to stop the mercenary he'd hired to top the man, but I'd refused to assist and regretted the decision with all my heart. I said I wished I'd agreed because, with my training and circle of friends, I'd have stopped that lunatic with a gun before he could fire a single shot.'

'How did Bradley respond?'

'He was . . . understanding. Made me feel all the worse for holding out on him, because he kept repeating the train massacre wasn't my doing, I couldn't have foreseen what would happen and I should shake off the suffocating guilt. Maybe he suspected I wasn't giving him the whole picture because while he agreed I'd done the right thing to refuse to rough up the journalist, he insisted I give myself up to the police because Ian Wentworth had to be held accountable for his actions.' He lifted his head to the ceiling, his eyes damp with tears. 'I should have acted immediately, but I needed a little time to prepare myself for the fallout. Then, the same day, Alex was murdered, and when I found out Wentworth had been killed too, I got it in my head their murders were connected to that night at the club. I thought my own life was in danger, so I asked Bradley to keep an eye on Sierra for me while I disappeared for a while, and made him promise to keep quiet about what I'd told him. He agreed and didn't ask any questions.' He swallowed hard. 'The reporter was *your* husband, wasn't he?'

'He was.'

'For what it's worth, I'm truly sorry.'

'You didn't kill him, Mr Monroe. And I doubt, even with your many skills, you'd have succeeded in tracking down the man who did.'

He hung his head at her words. 'I could at least have tried.'

'Help us. Show us where you buried the boy.'

Kate pushed back her chair. Her heart was beating firmly. For the first time in a while she had clarity and focus. She was aware of Chris, watching over her shoulder. The faces of the dead from the carriage rose in front of her eyes. They weren't staring at her; they were urging her on.

CHAPTER FORTY-SIX

WEDNESDAY, 9 JUNE - MORNING

Emma rang Bradley. 'Sir, it's DS Donaldson from Stoke-on-Trent. Mr Monroe is at the station helping us with our enquiries, and we'd like to confirm some of the details with you.'

'Yes, I'll come by. Sergeant . . . Cooper's a good man at heart. Go easy on him.'

Emma's next call was to the cleaning company ABeClean to find out if any of the cleaners had injured themselves cleaning the paperweight, but Tabitha, who sounded groggy, was one hundred per cent certain neither she nor Poppy had sustained any injuries at any time.

No sooner had she finished the call than Kate and Morgan reappeared.

'We're going to the Maddox Club with Cooper,' Kate informed her. 'He's going to show us where he buried the boy. I'd like you to come with us. Did you get anywhere with that blood found at the club?'

'Negative. It didn't come from the cleaners. Should we request a list of personnel who work there, in case any female employees might have had contact with the object?'

'I'm sure they only employ men, but it might be worth asking the question. This does change the game, though, and beg the question – is our perp a woman?'

'Who the fuck could it be?' asked Morgan.

'Somebody with a grievance against Ian, Alex and Xavier . . . and maybe even the superintendent, too,' said Emma. 'What about the girls used by members – the prostitutes?'

Kate agreed. 'That's a strong possibility. We'll look into it further when we get back.'

◆ ◆ ◆

While Emma and Morgan took Cooper out to the car, Kate phoned Ervin.

'Hi, Ervin. It's Kate. Are you still at the Maddox Club?'

'No. I'm in the lab. I've been examining this fibre Harvey found in Xavier's nose. It appears to be plastic-protected paper, much like the stuff our forensic paper suits are made of. If it came from one of us, I can't understand how the contamination occurred. Only Harvey, you and I were close to the deceased, by which time he was, of course, incapable of inhaling.'

'Are you sure it's come from a paper suit?'

'Almost certain, although I'll test for other possibilities on the off-chance I'm wrong.'

Kate clicked her tongue. Ervin was never wrong. 'You can buy forensic suits online or even in specialist shops. If the killer wore protective clothing during the attacks, it would certainly explain why they left no evidence behind.'

'The same thought occurred to me. I'll keep working on this fibre and see if I can be more conclusive for you.'

'No, could you put somebody else on that? There's an unknown vic buried in the grounds of the Maddox Club and I'd appreciate it if you came along.'

'Another victim? I'll meet you there.'

◆ ◆ ◆

The temperature had risen and the day had become uncomfortably humid, but the thick canopy of leaves afforded shade; gooseflesh lifted on Kate's forearms in the cool of the copse as she and her team traipsed over fern-covered ground. Birds perched high above their heads, chattering warnings to one another as the group picked their way through the trees towards a clearing. Flickers of sunlight darted through the occasional gaps, transforming leaves from a universal dark green to a mixture of shades and hues: sage, olive, jade, sea-green and lime. Kate focused her attention on Cooper ahead of her, retracing steps he had last taken in January. Her fingers brushed lightly over wide tree trunks as she walked towards the light. Ten metres . . . five, and then Cooper stepped to the left of an oak tree and into the clearing.

He bowed his head. 'Here.'

Kate and her team gathered in a small group. Ervin issued instructions to his two forensic officers, who then headed towards the mound of earth and began digging. Cooper moved aside and stared at the sky rather than watch. Kate shoved her hands into her jacket pockets as the spades struck the shallow grave, and waited in silence.

Within minutes, one officer spoke to Ervin. 'We've got something.'

'Take it slowly and first clear away the dirt. We don't want to cause any damage.'

From where she stood, Kate spotted a piece of material. She knew the colour, even though it had been soiled. It was the edge of a silk velvet maroon bedspread. The deep brown earth was cleared away by hand, and the bedspread lifted and laid gently on the ground. The team approached Ervin as he unfolded the material to reveal the naked, unrecognisable face and torso hidden within.

A forensic anthropologist would be able to reconstruct his face, but the process of trying to identify him would take some time, especially if, as Cooper had suggested, the boy wasn't registered in the UK. Kate's eyes travelled the length of his body, some six foot in height, and came to light on his hands, where an object caught her attention.

'What's that?' she asked.

Ervin crouched down and examined it. 'It's a woven bracelet.'

Kate's synapses fizzed and spat. She rushed to Ervin's side, bent over the body and studied the interwoven strands. She'd seen this bracelet before. She counted the colours – five of them: green, gold, red, black and white. The realisation stole her breath.

'I think I know who this might be. Faith had a nephew. I saw a photo of him on her screensaver. He wore an identical bracelet.'

'Hold on a second, Kate. There could be hundreds of bracelets like this. You can't jump to outlandish conclusions,' said Ervin, getting to his feet.

Kate jumped up. She'd had an epiphany. 'Think about it. She has access to forensic paper suits. She knows enough about forensic science to leave little to no trace of her presence. She quizzed me about the crime scene at the Maddox Club *and* she was pushing to find out how much we already knew.'

Ervin shook his head. 'No, sorry, Kate. I won't have that. She's a bright and dedicated assistant. She isn't capable of any of the murders. It's one leap too far.'

Kate looked at Morgan. The creases in his forehead were enough of a giveaway. He didn't believe her. Emma was staring at the ground. They all thought she was wrong, probably imagined she was losing the plot, but she knew she was right.

'Where is Faith today?' Kate asked.

'She called in sick this morning. She's caught the stomach bug doing the rounds.'

'I need to talk to her.'

'Kate—'

'What about the fibres, Ervin? Those found on Xavier's body were surely identical. It makes no sense that one would come from toilet tissue and the other from a forensic suit. She lied. She lied to cover her tracks. Check both those fibres again and you'll see I'm right.'

Ervin scratched his chin. 'Well—'

'And the blood on the bronze ornament and the carpet? Your test kit revealed it was from a woman. It wasn't the cleaners' blood, and when I mentioned it to Faith, she was quick to tell me those testing kits were often faulty, and offered to re-examine it herself.' She shook her head. 'We should have seen this!'

Emma pursed her lips. 'We shouldn't jump to conclusions just yet.'

'She told me her nephew was dead and she doesn't talk to her sister, yet she has a photo of the two of them as a screensaver on her mobile. Why a screensaver?'

'It's probably important to her, especially if the boy is dead,' said Morgan.

Kate threw her hands up then with a sigh. 'All right. We'll do this step by step: find out who this boy is, check out Faith's story about her sister and nephew and establish when and where he died. There'll be records if he died in Zimbabwe. Ervin, please run those tests again on the fibres and see if I'm right. Find out what her blood type is and if it matches the droplet on the carpet. If this is her nephew, then she has all the motive she needed – revenge. She's been targeting people connected with this death.'

'Why would she kill Alex?' Emma said.

'He was at the club the night her nephew died. Him, Ian, Superintendent Dickson and Xavier. She's been after them all!'

Morgan nodded in Cooper's direction 'And what shall we do about him?'

'Caution him and take him back to the station. We'll sort out charges later.'

Morgan headed over to the trees, where Cooper had been standing lost in thought and not party to the hushed conversation taking place beside the grave.

'What now?' asked Cooper.

Morgan began, 'Cooper Monroe, you have the right to remain silent—'

'But I helped you!'

Kate marched over and pointed a finger at him. 'You could have *helped* a lot sooner if you hadn't assisted a murderer, concealed this body and kept quiet about it, or if you'd even told police about Ian Wentworth's intentions to hire a hitman. Then you would have helped – you'd have helped save several lives. Carry on, DS Meredith.'

She spun on her heel. She'd missed the fucking signs. She'd been so wrapped up in pinning something on John Dickson, she'd overlooked what had been right under her nose, and it rankled. Faith had been putting on an act. Every time Kate had shared confidences and talked to the woman, she'd been manipulated. Faith had been playing a game. She knew Kate was vulnerable and needed a friend, and had worked her like a puppet! She clenched her fists tightly. Shit!

A steady beat pulsated in her ears so loudly she didn't hear Ervin's quiet 'I'll finish here and then check the blood found at the club.' She gave a vague nod of acknowledgement and strode off purposefully, signalling for Emma to join her. The woman was not getting away with this. Nobody messed with Kate and got away with it.

CHAPTER FORTY-SEVEN

WEDNESDAY, 9 JUNE – AFTERNOON

The block of flats was a mishmash of red and grey bricks with windows of all sizes and shapes, as if a child had used odd-shaped giant Lego bricks and pushed them together haphazardly to create an L-shaped building, staggered in height so the first section contained six floors, the middle section four and the remainder three. Kate and Emma entered the tallest part and mounted the circular stone staircase to the third floor, where Faith's apartment was located.

'Faith, open up! It's Kate.' There was no response so she tried again, this time louder, and turned at a faint creaking. The door next to Faith's had inched open.

'Hi. I don't suppose you know where Faith is, do you?' asked Kate.

The door opened further and a scrawny young woman in a dressing gown with a towel wrapped around her head peered out, eyes wide. 'Faith?'

Emma held up her ID card. 'The woman who lives next to you.'

'Which one?'

Emma threw Kate a look before asking, 'How many women do you think live here?'

'Two. At first, only one lived there, then another one moved in.'

'Are you sure?'

'My bedroom wall backs on to the sitting room next door and the last couple of weeks or so I've definitely heard two women's voices. Walls are paper-thin in this building. You can hear people pee in their bathrooms.'

Kate had sidled up to the door. 'I don't suppose you caught either of their names, did you?'

'No.' The towel wobbled.

'Could you describe either women?'

'No. I've only seen one of them a couple of times. I think she might be a doctor. She wears a white coat like doctors in *Casualty* or *Holby City*. I saw her this morning when I came in from work, which was about six o'clock. She was on her way out of the block when I came in.'

'Did she speak to you?'

'She nodded a hello.'

'How did she seem?'

'Fine.'

'She didn't look ill?'

'No.'

'You haven't heard any movement or noises inside her apartment today, have you?'

'Not a thing. I think the other woman is out, too.'

'Did you ever hear what they were talking about?'

'No. Living here, you get used to blocking out all the noises, and I'm not interested in what goes on next door, or anywhere in the block.'

'And you're sure there are two women living in that apartment?'

'Positive.' She waited to see if there were any more questions, then excused herself and shut the door again.

Kate turned to Emma. 'We need to gain entry. Let's head back to the station and make the necessary arrangements.'

◆ ◆ ◆

Back at the station, Morgan had been gathering what he could on Faith, and read out what he had assimilated.

'I only managed to drum up some basic information. She came to the UK in September 2018 to complete a forensics course at UCL. She spent another year studying for an MSc, and then started work for forensic science services in Coventry in August 2020 until she got the appointment at Stoke-on-Trent in April this year.'

'Why did she move from Coventry after only eight months?' asked Emma.

'I haven't found out yet.'

'She said it was because she wanted to work with Ervin. Now I'm not so sure.' Kate chewed over the facts. Lisa Handsworth had been a pathological liar, but Faith was a master of deceit. She'd fooled them all: Ervin, her colleagues and Kate. Completely hoodwinked them. What angered Kate most was she had actually liked the woman. 'It might be an idea to check with her employers at Coventry and find out their version of events. I know Ervin said she repeatedly pestered him for a position, but now I think she had an ulterior motive.'

'Maybe she really did want to work with him,' said Morgan.

Emma grunted a response.

Morgan shrugged. 'It seems like a lot of this is guesswork. We don't have any real evidence yet to point to her guilt.'

Once the tests had been completed they'd have all the evidence they needed. 'Speak to her colleagues. What else can you tell us about her, Morgan?'

Morgan continued, 'UCL said she was a model student. Aced all her exams. I put a call in to the admin at the university at Harare where she studied, and I'm waiting for them to ring back. Her personal records show her as single, parents deceased and next of kin as Hope Masuku, aged thirty-five, listed as living in Harare. There's a contact number for her that I've tried ringing, but there's no answer.'

Kate spoke. 'Faith told me she was divorced.'

'Not according to her records.'

It had been yet another tale spun to earn Kate's trust. She balled her fist and tapped it against the table. 'All right, what about Hope? Do you have any info on her?'

'I've contacted the Zimbabwe embassy for further information.'

'She's got a head start on us.'

'We don't know she's gone,' said Morgan.

Kate ticked off each sentence on a finger. 'She phoned in sick but was seen leaving the building at 6 a.m. She didn't look ill. She hasn't been in her apartment all day. Her phone is switched off. On our way back, we rang it twice, and it goes directly through to a messaging service.'

'She could be playing hooky.'

'Morgan!' Emma turned on him. 'Stop being obstructive.'

'I'm being sensible. You're rushing into this without any facts or evidence to back you up.'

Kate held up both hands. 'Okay. Let's calm down. Can we trace her car?'

Morgan shook his head. 'I've tried already. She doesn't own one. She's been borrowing vehicles from the laboratory's car pool.'

'Contact her mobile provider and find out when and where the last call was made or received.'

Morgan leapt to it. Emma set to work hunting for a number for the forensic science services in Coventry. Kate paced the small room and replayed every conversation she'd had with Faith. She stopped to rest her head against the cool glass and inwardly groaned. It all made sense to her. It was her fault Faith had scarpered. She'd stupidly told her about the blood on the carpet being female. She'd unwittingly given away information that had sent Faith into hiding. The blood would place her at the scene of the crime. Kate knew it would. If only she had been focusing more on the case and not on Dickson!

Morgan had finished his conversation. 'The last call was made at three o'clock yesterday afternoon, to an unknown pay-as-you-go number. I'm waiting for full phone records, which should arrive soon.'

'How did she ring in sick today if she didn't use her phone?'

Morgan shrugged.

'She must have used *a* phone.' She chewed at her thumb for a moment. Outside, the traffic meandered non-stop past the building: vans, cars and lorries attached by an invisible cord. '*Shit!*'

She spun around again. 'We're stuck until Ervin comes through for us or we hear back from somebody. We've no option other than to search her apartment for clues to her whereabouts. Her neighbour said another woman has been living in the apartment with her, but couldn't give us any description. Morgan, I want you to go there, check with other residents in the block and see if anyone else saw or met either woman. Take the enforcer with you and meet me outside Faith's apartment in half an hour. I need to arrange a search warrant.'

'What about Cooper?' asked Morgan.

'Leave Cooper to stew. Our priority is Faith. Emma, carry on here and ring me if you need me or have any information. We must locate her.'

◆ ◆ ◆

With Morgan and Kate out searching Faith's apartment, Emma made swift progress and contacted the operations director at the forensics services in Coventry. Using Skype, she managed to link up with Oliver Bradshaw, a middle-aged man who'd retained a boyish full-cheeked face, set off by a large sprinkling of freckles and a thick crop of red hair.

'I remember Faith well – charming woman.'

'Can you tell me how you came to employ her?'

Oliver sat back in his chair and fiddled with a silver ballpoint pen. 'It was her who found us. She applied for three different jobs with us over a period of six months. We felt she was overqualified for all of them, so we turned down her applications. However, in July 2020 we offered a position working in digital forensics, and she not only applied for it but rang me personally to request an interview.'

'Did you think that was strange?'

'At first I did, but she was incredibly enthusiastic and the best candidate by a mile, so we snapped her hand off, so to speak, and hired her.' He flicked the top of his pen, a repetitive *click, click, click* as he spoke, before balancing it in the open hands of a miniature knight-in-armour pen holder on his desk. 'She came to us at the beginning of August.'

'And I assume she got on okay?'

'Oh yes, she was extremely good. So good, in fact, that when a position for head of department came up, I offered her the promotion, but she turned it down flat.'

'I expect her response came as a surprise.'

'It most certainly did. However, I was more surprised when she left us abruptly to take up an inferior position at Stoke. It seemed a bizarre choice when she could have been a head of department here.'

'Did she explain her actions?'

'Apparently she had friends in Stoke and wanted to be near them.'

'Did she make any friends in Coventry? If so, we'd like to talk to one or two of them.'

'She got along with everyone in the department, but to my knowledge didn't make any friends.'

'Did she mention any family?'

'Never.'

'Have you had any contact with her since she left?'

'None. This job is like any other. People move on, although maybe not as quickly as she did, and I'm still baffled as to why she didn't accept the promotion. She's an extremely intelligent woman and, I believed, career-oriented. I must have misjudged her.'

'You say she claimed to have friends in Stoke. Did she mention any names?'

'No, although I happen to know she went there most weekends or on her days off.'

'Did she drive here?'

'She didn't own a car. I imagine she took the train.'

'Is there anything else you can tell me about her?'

He lifted a fidget spinner and casually turned it over between his fingers. 'I can't think of anything else. She kept herself to herself.'

'If you think of anything, would you let me know?'

'I shall. Nice to talk to you.'

'And you.'

Emma ended her call. It was becoming increasingly clear to her that Faith had chosen to come to Stoke for a reason, had even been willing to take on a job beneath her abilities to get here.

Her inbox pinged: an incoming email. Faith's mobile provider had come good and sent across a list of all calls made and received, stretching back as far as September 2018, when the account had first been set up. She flicked through to 2019 and 2020. There were numerous ones to numbers with the Stoke-on-Trent prefix, even when Faith had been working in Coventry. Emma recognised Ervin's number and the laboratory's, but two stood out: a foreign number with a +263 prefix – no doubt the international dialling code for Zimbabwe – and a pay-as-you-go number that had only been rung a few times over the last two weeks and had been dialled the day before. She picked up the internal phone to speak to somebody in the technical department. If she could trace the owner of this number, they might just have found the lead they needed.

CHAPTER FORTY-EIGHT

WEDNESDAY, 9 JUNE – AFTERNOON

Kate cursed herself as she drove towards the apartment block she'd left only an hour earlier. She'd handled this investigation badly and wasted valuable time, but she'd pull it back. The traffic lights near the church turned to red as she approached, and she drummed the steering wheel impatiently. A bus had drawn up on the other side of the road and passengers crossed on the pedestrian crossing in front of her: a woman holding the hand of a five- or six-year-old boy. Behind them, shoppers, carrying bags for life emblazoned with slogans, and a group of teenagers who ambled across after the lights had changed, avoiding the gaze of irritated motorists. It had been a while since she'd been out shopping for pleasure. Then again, it had been some time since she'd acted as a fully functioning, normal human.

She pulled away, past the pub, whose cream facade was grey from traffic fumes, and was forced to stop again as a dark-skinned man darted across the road from Domino's Pizza with a cardboard box in his hands. He grinned his thanks, white teeth dazzling much like those of Faith's nephew in the photograph she'd seen. She searched the man's wrist for a sign of a woven bracelet, but spotted none, and then reasoned such bracelets were popular: she might be wrong to have made the association between the boy in the shallow grave and Faith's nephew.

Chris spoke out. 'No. You're on it. Faith is definitely involved in this somehow. Okay, maybe she's not responsible for the actual murders, but she's involved nonetheless. The boy you found at the Maddox Club is going to turn out to be her nephew. Of course, you don't know who the second woman is, do you? She might be an accomplice, or even the killer. It would help if you could identify her.'

'I need luck in that department, and some evidence or pointers wouldn't go amiss.'

'All in good time. Stick to procedure, keep digging and you'll get the results you're searching for, Kate. You've always worked that way, and it's always yielded results.'

'And I believed that was the right way to go, but . . . are they always the right results? I maintain Faith is involved or responsible for these murders, but what if I've overlooked somebody else who's managed to slip under the radar?'

'You're thinking of Dickson, aren't you?'

'Yes. He was at the club the night the boy was killed.'

'I'm sure he's mixed up in this, but you have to somehow prove it, and to do so you'll need to find Faith. You're doing fine. Don't beat yourself up. Remember, I believe in you.'

She waited for a car to manoeuvre into a parking space by the side of the road before continuing. 'I like you being here, talking things through with me, like we used to before—'

'I know you do.'

'Don't leave me alone.'

'I'm here as long as you want me to be.'

'Good.'

◆ ◆ ◆

Morgan stood in the stairwell with the enforcer, a small battering ram, in his hands. He spoke as soon as Kate appeared. 'No joy with identifying Faith's mystery guest. Some folk are still out at work. I'll try again later.'

Kate doubted he'd have much luck. The women, like the killer, were ghostlike, coming and going quietly and unnoticed. She hammered on Faith's door again. Nobody came out to find out what all the hullabaloo was about, further compounding her suspicions that it would be unlikely anyone had spotted the women. People in this building kept to themselves. It was probably one of the reasons Faith had chosen to reside here.

'Open it,' she said to Morgan, standing back while he pressed the battering ram against the door. It broke away without protest; only a sharp crack. He pushed it with his foot and it opened wide on to a sitting-cum-dining room: a white-topped Formica table with wooden legs and matching chairs to their right and a two-seater black fabric settee and wooden unit on which stood a small portable television at the far end of the room. Somebody had painted the walls off-white and hung gold leaf-patterned curtains on poles over the windows. Kate doubted it was Faith. This smacked of a furnished rental property with its flat-packed, easy-to-assemble cheap furniture.

Morgan's face scrunched up at the strong smell of bleach. 'Somebody's recently cleaned up.'

Floors, tops and every surface had undoubtedly been scrubbed. A door led into a corridor, at one end of which was a galley kitchen with white units, black worktops and a fridge-freezer. The paraphernalia associated with daily life was missing – no magazines left out, no slippers, cups or odds and ends to suggest that somebody lived here. Kate donned plastic gloves and peered inside the fridge. It was shiny-clean and empty. She spun on her heel and marched along the corridor, passing an open door. She peered into the room, spotted a shower cubicle and said, 'You take this one.' At the end of the corridor she found herself in a bedroom. The bed was stripped of sheets. Kate moved aside a peacock-blue curtain and uncovered a set of shelves over which was a rail for clothes. It was empty.

'There's nothing in the bathroom. Not even a toothbrush,' called Morgan.

'She's definitely cleared out.' They returned to the dingy hallway. Kate fell silent for a moment, questions exploding in her mind. Finally, she spoke. 'She can't have taken everything with her. She's been meticulous in cleaning this place and leaving no sign she was ever here. It was common knowledge she lived here, so she must have been getting rid of traces of something or somebody else.'

'The woman who was here with her?'

'Uh-huh. She didn't expect to leave today. Something triggered a sudden departure.' *You, Kate.* 'She's stripped the bed, taken the sheets, removed all her personal belongings, but she must have left some things behind she couldn't take with her – uneaten food, milk – consumables. If she's gone by train, she couldn't carry it all, and if she's got a lift or rented a car, she wouldn't want to take the chance of being spotted moving backward and forward carrying things. She'll have dumped it instead. There must be some communal bins to these apartments.'

The staircase rang with their footsteps as they clattered back downstairs and hunted for a back exit. A grubby door led to an area where two industrial-sized bins were placed side by side. Kate put a second pair of plastic gloves over her first, lifted the lid of the closest bin and recoiled at the smell. Holding her breath, she peered in again. 'There are about a dozen bags. We'll have to search them all.'

Morgan blew out his cheeks. 'Some days I hate this job.'

'Stop whingeing and grab one,' she said, tugging at the nearest black bag. It landed at her feet with a hefty thud and she set about opening it. The contents – half-eaten pizzas and other rubbish – spilled on to the ground. She picked through it gingerly. On coming across pots of baby food and nappy sacks, she shovelled up the waste and pushed it back into the plastic bag. This one had clearly belonged to a family. Morgan was hunting through another, face puckered in a grimace as he withdrew rotting banana skins and slimy peelings. She dragged out a third, lighter than the first, and tied up neatly and so tightly Kate couldn't undo the knot in it. Ripping a hole in the side, she saw what she expected: cheese still in its wrapper, a half-eaten pack of butter. 'Got it!'

Morgan abandoned his search. Kate pulled out an object and held it up.

Morgan eyed the red apple. 'Well, it's the same colour as the ones we found at the crime scenes.'

'I bet you'll find it's the same variety as the ones the killer used – Macoun. See if you can find any more.'

Morgan sighed and stretched his long arm into the industrial bin.

◆ ◆ ◆

Emma scratched at her cheek. She'd identified the majority of the phone numbers on the list and a picture was beginning to form. Faith had been hunting for somebody.

Morgan slammed the door open and stomped inside. 'Looks like Faith's our killer, or certainly involved in the murders.'

'What's happened?'

'She's cleared out of her apartment, but we found some apples like those left behind at the crime scenes. I want to check out something, so give me a second.'

'Where's Kate?'

'With Forensics. We had to drop a bin bag off with them. I'll tell you in a minute.' He concentrated over his keyboard for a minute, then mumbled, 'It's all pointing to Faith. Kate thinks the apples are a variety known as Macoun. They're grown in the USA, but according to this, there's a woman in Zimbabwe who grows them. She started up her own business growing apples in Juliasdale. She employs quite a few people. And Faith is also originally from Juliasdale.'

'Interesting. We've found a connection to the Macoun apples. We still don't know anything about the woman who stayed at Faith's apartment. She could be involved, too. I've got a theory.'

'Want to run it past me?'

'Since September 2018, she's religiously phoned this Zimbabwe number every week – it belongs to her sister, Hope. Two weeks ago, the calls to that number stopped. At the same time, this pay-as-you-go number appeared on her contact list and Faith made calls to and received calls from it on a daily basis, sometimes three or four times a day.'

'Have you rung her sister on the Zimbabwe number?'

'I did, but there was no answer. Nor from the mobile. Faith's neighbour was sure there were two women in Faith's apartment. I reckon Hope came to the UK, moved in with Faith and got the pay-as-you-go so they could keep in touch.'

'Why do you think the sister turned up?' asked Morgan.

'Come on, Morgan. Keep up. Faith has been hunting for somebody in the Stoke area since August last year. She rang various homeless charities, the library, churches, right up until mid-January this year. Then there were no more calls.'

He began to nod slowly. 'Because she found whoever she was looking for.'

'Then she ditched her job in Coventry in April and moved here.'

'It has to be her nephew, doesn't it? I'll get a trace on that pay-as-you-go and see if I can find out from the border police if Hope has entered or left the country.'

'Who's left the country?' Kate was at the door.

◆ ◆ ◆

As Kate came in, Emma launched into what she and Morgan had discovered about Faith and the apples.

Kate listened intently to their theories. 'I think we're on to something here. I can't see why else she'd move from Coventry to Stoke, especially with a promotion in the offing.'

Emma agreed. 'She told Oliver her friends all lived in the Stoke-on-Trent area.'

Kate had believed she and Faith were friends, or at least becoming friends. The thought rankled, but she pushed it from her mind. 'Well, we know she was lying. Ervin's been worried about her precisely because she has no friends here. Not one.'

'It doesn't add up, does it?' said Emma. 'She applied for three different positions at Coventry before wheedling her way into a job there, but then dropped it to take a lower-paid job in Stoke. It all points to her wanting to be in Stoke to find her nephew. I haven't had a chance to follow up on any of these Stoke numbers that Faith called. I'll do it straight away. Somebody might be able to corroborate our suspicions.'

'That's definitely the way to go,' said Kate. 'Check if a woman asked about a Zimbabwean boy. Do we know his name?'

'We've not heard back from the embassy yet,' said Morgan.

'Ring them again. Tell them it's a matter of urgency and might involve the death of one of their citizens.'

Morgan made for the internal phone, but Kate halted him with, 'Hang on a sec. If Faith, or Hope, or both of them, are behind these murders, we can assume they're out for revenge. They could hold others responsible for this boy's death – Raymond Maddox, Cooper Monroe and Superintendent Dickson. Somebody that hell-bent on seeking vengeance won't give up yet. They think they've outsmarted us, and they probably don't know we've uncovered his body so there's every chance they're sticking to their plan. It's just a question of who are they likely to go after next.'

'Raymond,' suggested Morgan. 'He owns the club. And besides, the other two are out of harm's way. Cooper is in custody and the superintendent is at a safe house.'

The thought of Dickson jogged her memory. It was almost 6 p.m., and Kate still hadn't read Chris's journal. She hadn't been able to bring herself to open it. Now was the time. There might be something in it that would help her bring Dickson into the heart of this investigation. He'd received Ian's eye for a reason. 'I'm going to request that Superintendent Dickson remains at the safe house for the time being, until we can locate Faith and maybe her sister. As for Raymond, we'll put out an alert for him. If we can't find him, the chances are, neither can the killer. We've got a lot riding on this, and if we're wrong—' Her words hung heavy for a moment, then everyone sprang into action.

Kate's phone buzzed. Ervin had news. She put him on speakerphone so they could all hear what he had to tell them. 'My apple expert says the apples you found in the bin are the same variety. We're testing for DNA, but as you know it takes time. Terry Wiggins is examining the body we found earlier today.' Terry was a forensic anthropologist who worked closely with Ervin in a laboratory further down from him in the same corridor. 'We've extracted DNA samples, but we can't identify him yet. There appear to be no dental records for him or anything to suggest who he was, other than a young African male aged about fifteen.'

'No distinguishing marks?'

'Nothing. I have a team sifting through the waste you brought across and we haven't yet found anything else of interest in there.'

'Can you look for evidence of a second person, other than Faith?'

'There's not a lot to give anyone away. There are no prints even on the butter wrapper or milk bottle. They were wiped clean with bleach.'

'Who cleans a milk bottle they're throwing away so thoroughly?' asked Morgan.

'Somebody who knows fingerprints and DNA can lead to identification. Faith didn't want whoever was staying in the apartment to be discovered,' Kate replied.

'I know I flagged the idea of Hope staying with her sister,' said Emma. 'But we've been speculating, and what if, actually, Faith has no idea what's going on? What if the person staying with her isn't Hope and is actually the murderer? They might have wiped her place clean and even kidnapped or harmed Faith.'

Kate paused for a heartbeat. Was it possible? If it was, it would blow her theory out of the water. She wasn't going to show any signs of doubt. 'No, we'll stick to our guns. We know Faith was searching for somebody in Stoke. Follow that up and we might have an answer. Is there anything else, Ervin?'

'Yes. The blood we found on the carpet and on the paperweight is definitely female and . . . you were right. The fibre Faith claimed came from toilet tissue did not. It is identical to the fibre we found in Xavier's nose. For what it's worth, I think you're on the right lines searching for Faith.'

Kate folded her arms. There had to be a way to establish the identity of the boy in the clearing. 'Ervin, can you run avuncular DNA tests against the blood and the victim we found today?'

'We could. Do you really think the boy is related to Faith?'

'I'd bet my life on it,' Kate replied.

'Then I'll see what I can do.'

Ervin rang off, and while Morgan and Emma fell to their tasks, Kate still had two unanswered questions. How was Dickson involved in all of this, and how could she prove he was? The answer might lie in the journal back in her house.

CHAPTER
FORTY-NINE

WEDNESDAY, 9 JUNE – LATE EVENING

Faith checked her watch. It was coming up to eleven thirty and she'd been in position in her car for over half an hour. She'd rung the house an hour ago using the pay-as-you-go phone, and nobody had answered. Cooper wasn't in, but she was patient and she knew his daughter would be back from her late shift at the cinema. The girl would know his whereabouts. Faith would make sure she got it out of her.

She leant her head against the padded headrest. She was tired – mentally and physically exhausted, but the fire that had burned inside her for months was still alight and wouldn't be extinguished until she had accomplished all she had set out to do. She could have done with more time, but Kate Young had a sixth sense when it came to murder investigations and was getting far too close for comfort. It was time to bail out. They'd soon identify the blood left at the Maddox Club. She'd been unaware of the injury, believing she'd only been bruised in the scuffle with Xavier, and cursed herself for her carelessness. Now, there was little time left to uncover what she needed to know. Kate was closing in. She was tenacious and irritatingly good at her job. Another officer might not have whisked Ian Wentworth's laptop away, preventing Faith from examining it first and erasing any clues. And another DI wouldn't have thought to ask about apple varieties. Macoun apples. It had been Faith's private joke – a variety that not only grew in Juliasdale but at the same orchard where her sister worked. Apples, a fruit linked to temptation . . .

◆ ◆ ◆

Alex Corby opens the door. 'How can I help?'

She lifts her ID. 'I'm one of a team investigating a delicate situation you might be able to help me with.'

A deep furrow appears between his eyes. 'I don't know how I can be of assistance.'

'It's regarding this young man.' She holds up a photograph of Joseph, and Alex studies his face. He shows no surprise, only puzzlement.

'I don't know him,' he says.

'Would you mind if I come inside for a minute?' She gives him a quiet smile and open eyes – the picture of innocence.

He hesitates. 'Well, I don't know how I can help you, but sure, come in.'

He leads her into a vast dining room, perfect for what she has in mind, and as he offers her a seat, she pulls out a syringe and sticks it into his neck. His eyes glaze and he tumbles to the floor.

◆ ◆ ◆

When Alex comes to, he is bound in the chair, groggy but alert enough to recognise he is in danger.

'What?' he slurs.

'Save your energy,' she says. 'I need answers, and quickly. Did you go to the Maddox Club in January?'

He blinks, tries to clear his head. 'I think . . . so.'

'Who did you go with?'

The drug is working. He is fuddled. 'Ian . . . and John. Dinner.'

'Ian who?'

'Wentworth. My friend, Ian.'

'And what is John's full name?'

'Dickson.'

'Who is John?'

'He's police. Super—' He loses consciousness briefly.

She is not surprised by this revelation. People from all professions have fetishes. She slaps his face and he comes round.

'What is the Gold Service?'

'How do you know?' His voice fades as he speaks.

'What is it?'

'Prostitute service for members.'

'You had sex with a prostitute in January, didn't you?'

'Yes – sorry, Fiona – mistake.' His head sags to one side. The drug, GHB, is confusing him, making him believe he is dreaming all this.

'Did you have sex with a boy as well?'

'No-oh.'

'Did John Dickson?'

'I . . . don't know.'

'Did you not talk about it?'

'No. Ian . . . gone in the morning.'

'Gone.'

'Breakfast with John. Ian gone.'

'Ian Wentworth disappeared overnight?'

'Yes.'

'Did he sleep with a prostitute?'

'Yes . . . boy . . . lots of noise . . . screams.'

'You heard somebody screaming in his room?'

'Screams, noise.'

'You didn't go and find out who was screaming?'

'No. With girl. Viagra. Couldn't stop. Sorry, Fiona. The girl meant nothing. I love you.'

She slaps his cheek and his eyes snap open and he mutters, 'Ian's an okay bloke . . . mistake. Paid. They got paid.'

'Ian hurt him.'

'I want to go to sleep.'

'What happened to the boy?'

'Don't know.'

'Did you see him?'

'No.'

'Did Ian talk about him?'

'Go away. It's none of my business what happened,' he mumbles before losing consciousness again.

His response irritates her. He's covering for his friend. Alex is as guilty as the bastard who made her nephew scream. Sweat prickles at the nape of her neck. Ian injured or killed her nephew, and this man did nothing about it. She reaches for the choke-pear, a tool she's had made for the purpose. It is a replica of an original but works as well as those it was modelled on. Originally used for heretics and liars, it is the most appropriate device she can think of for this task. She forces it into his slack mouth and, using the screw, unfolds it. His eyes fly open and he tries to speak.

'You had your chance to confess, to tell me what happened. Every time you lie, I'm going to drop a piece of apple down your throat, and you might or might not choke to death.'

He struggles weakly and Faith picks up the first piece of apple, formed into a minuscule cube. She dangles it in front of him.

'Is my nephew dead? One blink for no. Two blinks for yes.'

One blink.

She drops the apple and his eyes widen as it falls to the back of his throat and disappears. He gurgles and struggles. His eyes water but the piece frees itself and he is still alive. She reaches for a second piece.

'Is he dead?'

Alex blinks twice quickly.

'Good, now we're getting somewhere. Did Ian kill him?'

Two blinks.

'Do you know what he did with the body?'

One blink.

'Oh dear. Not helpful.'

She watches as he twitches at the sight of the apple. She lets the piece go. This time the noises are raw and panicked, but he survives.

'Did you help him bury Joseph?'

Two blinks.

'Did you bury him near Ian's apartment?'

Two blinks.

'In the park near his apartment?'

Two blinks.

'In the lake in the park?'

Two blinks.

She sighs. He's lying. She knows Joseph is nowhere near the apartment. Alex is lying to save his skin, but it is too late. She lifts a piece of apple, watches him blink over and over again, then drops it. She'll get nothing more out of Alex Corby.

There was no movement outside on the street. Faith didn't mind. She was patient. Patient beyond all expectations. She'd planned this perfectly and was going to see it through to the end. She wanted to know where Joseph had been buried and wouldn't leave until she did. As for the remaining two people who'd played their part in this . . . she might have to leave them alive. Even though it rankled, she had to consider her own self-preservation. She had to remain one step ahead. She permitted herself a small smile. She was always one step ahead.

CHAPTER FIFTY

WEDNESDAY, 9 JUNE – LATE EVENING

Morgan yawned and stretched, arms high above his head. 'We're unlikely to get anything from the Zimbabwe embassy until tomorrow. I've sent emails but, obviously, their phone lines are closed.'

Kate agreed they couldn't make further progress. She'd been assisting Emma by contacting all the charities and hostels and church wardens Faith had rung, to no avail. In many cases, personnel had changed, and those they spoke to had only been volunteering for a few months, well after the time Faith had rung them.

Emma was currently speaking to somebody at the church of St George's and St Martin, and Kate decided it was time to call it a day. They were all exhausted. She stood up, easing the tension from her back and neck. They had many pieces of the jigsaw, but no killer or killers yet. *Yet*. They would find them.

Emma caught her attention. 'The Reverend Father recalls Faith ringing him. She asked about two boys.'

'Two?'

'She was searching for two refugees who had made their way to the area and were living rough. They'd been spotted sleeping in his church. He says he spoke to them once, arranged places for them to shelter and didn't see them again. They told him their names were Abel and Joseph.'

'No surname?'

'No, but Faith said one of the boys, Joseph, was her nephew.'

'Then the body we discovered could belong to either Joseph or Abel,' said Morgan.

Kate frowned. This threw things out. 'If I'm going by the woven bracelet on the boy's wrist, then I'd say it was Joseph, but I suppose it could be Abel.'

'If the boy in the grave isn't her nephew, it will change the whole investigation,' said Emma.

Kate sat back down again. Everything pointed to Faith being the killer, but what if she wasn't? What if somebody else, related to Abel, was behind this? She needed to think, and she couldn't. Her head was jammed with conflicting arguments to the point where it threatened to explode. 'Call it a night. Maybe the morning will help us find focus, and Ervin might be able to turn up more evidence.' She reached for her bag. She was drained.

The internal phone rang and Morgan took the call. Kate, searching for car keys in the bottom of her bag, almost didn't pick up on the sudden energy in his voice. 'Right. Cheers, mate.'

'Who was that?' she asked.

'Tech boys. They got a ping on the pay-as-you-go mobile.'

'Where?'

'Abbots Bromley.'

Kate let go of her bag, which fell with a thud. 'Cooper lives in Abbots Bromley. She's after Cooper! She doesn't know he's in custody. When did they get the ping?'

'Two minutes ago.'

Kate rested her fingers on the edge of the table and lowered her head. They had to act. *Think!* A shiver raced across her shoulder blades. Cooper's daughter might be at home alone. 'Ring his house, immediately!'

'Sierra works at the Cinebowl Entertainment Centre in Uttoxeter,' said Emma, searching through her notebook for the girl's phone number. 'It shuts late. I doubt she'll be home yet.'

'What time does she get off shift?' asked Kate.

Emma glanced at her watch. 'Probably about now.'

'Shit! It'll take us half an hour at least to reach Abbots Bromley.'

'She'll have to catch a bus from Uttoxeter. We might have time,' said Emma. 'Found it.'

'Give it to Morgan. Morgan, ring and warn her not to go home, send a local officer to watch over her and then join us at the house. Come on, Emma.' Kate snatched up her bag again and was out of the door in a flash. She looked to the stars in the night sky and hoped they were aligned in her favour. If she'd called this correctly, the killer might be in the vicinity of the house, hoping to track down Cooper. If she'd called it wrong? She couldn't consider the possibility.

As Kate tore down the A50, blue light on, she rang William on the hands-free.

'What have you got?'

'At the moment, we don't know if we have one or two suspects. We're headed in the direction of Abbots Bromley, to Cooper Monroe's house.'

'Do you want back-up?'

'It might be too soon for that, and I don't want to alert a killer to our presence. Let us deal with it in the first instance.' She rang off.

Emma glanced at her from the passenger seat. 'You didn't tell him it was Faith we were after.'

Kate didn't answer. She had a gut feeling she shouldn't divulge everything to William. For some insane reason, she was sure he was relaying everything back to Dickson, and until she'd read Chris's journal, she didn't want him to be in the know. She was saved from saying anything further by an incoming call from Morgan.

'Sierra isn't answering her mobile. I rang the cinema, and she left fifteen minutes ago. By my reckoning, she'll be almost home.'

'Shit! Okay, we'll see you there. Make sure you turn off the blues and twos. I don't want to alert Faith, or whoever it might be, to our arrival. Park down the road and approach on foot. What's your ETA?'

'Eighteen minutes.' He wasn't far behind them.

'Let us know when you arrive.'

Faith's patience had been rewarded. Sierra was walking down the road, head lowered, unaware of Faith observing her from underneath the trees opposite the house. She waited while the girl unlocked the front door and for lights to come on. The curtains weren't drawn in the kitchen, and Faith watched Sierra remove her coat and cross the room several times, busying herself with a tin and a bowl. She heard the girl call, 'Crystal! Here, puss. Come on. Dinner!' The shouts were followed by clattering on a tin dish, followed by the bang of the back door as it shut again. The girl returned to the kitchen, traversed the room left to right and back again. It was time.

Faith rolled up the jumper she'd been holding and stuffed it under her skirt waistband and blouse, patting it to form a round lump, then snapped off the heel on her left shoe, pulled at her eyelids until the cool air made them run, then rubbed them hard, reddening them. She crossed the road and banged on the door.

The door opened a crack, held by a chain, and a white face appeared – Sierra's.

'Thank goodness,' wept Faith. 'Nobody else is in. My boyfriend and I had a terrible row and he threw me out of the car. I haven't got my bag or phone and I can't get home. Please could you ring me a taxi?'

Sierra studied Faith. 'Okay, but you'll have to wait outside while I do it.'

'Yes, of course. Thank you. Thank you so much. I've been walking for ages and I was scared stiff. I don't know this area at all.' She rested against the door frame and pulled off her shoe, looked at the heel and let out a sob. 'I hate him!' She put a hand to her swollen belly, drawing Sierra's attention to it.

'You're expecting?'

'I've only got one month to go,' said Faith.

'Come inside and sit down. I'll ring you a taxi.' Sierra unlocked the door.

No sooner was Faith inside than she rushed at the girl, bowling her over. Sitting astride her, she pulled out a syringe and plunged it into her neck.

The darkness was intense, and as the squad car's headlights fell on hedgerows and trees, they conjured menacing shadows, bogeymen and spectres that leapt up from nowhere and danced for a few seconds before shrinking and vanishing into the night. Black, shapeless houses, identifiable only by dully glowing windows, flashed past in a blur. The jet-black reservoir glittered menacingly as they crossed it. There was a rumour an entire village had been sunk under its waters when it was first built. Kate knew it was not true, but tonight a hundred ghosts seem to rise and beckon, urging her on as they tore up the bank and turned down Yeatsall Lane to a spot only a hundred metres from Cooper's house. She slid out of the car into the silence. A cow – a young calf, calling for its mother – mooed repetitively; its plaintive cries put Kate's teeth on edge. The sound stopped, and an eerie calm replaced it.

She and Emma padded up the road, pausing only at mournful honking in the distance before the geese on the waters settled once more. Emma tugged at Kate's sleeve.

'There!'

Parked in front of a gate to a field was a black Kia.

'Run a check on the number plate.'

Emma rang it through, mumbled quietly into her mouthpiece then joined Kate close to the front gate and whispered, 'Hire car.'

'Any idea who rented it?'

'They're checking now.'

A figure approached, large and wide, but light on his feet. Morgan had caught up with them.

'Scout around the rear, will you? Exercise extreme caution. Somebody is probably already here. There's a hire car parked opposite.'

Morgan slipped away. Curtains at one of the downstairs windows were not fully drawn and a sliver of light burst from between them, alighting on the grass outside like a shining sword. Kate dropped to her haunches below the line of the window frame and crabbed along the wall until she was directly under the ledge. She listened, and when she was sure there was no noise from inside, raised her head, glanced inside, into the kitchen. Squinting hard, she made out a table and a person. She adjusted her position to see better, imagining it might be the killer, but it wasn't. It was Sierra, who was tied to a chair, her head tilted backwards. They'd arrived too late. A movement and a raised voice kick-started her heart again. Sierra bucked in the chair and Kate let out the breath she'd been holding. The girl was still alive. But just as Kate felt a rush of relief, another icy hand cupped her heart. Faith appeared, wielding a kitchen knife. There was little time to act.

Her heart clattered wildly. *Think!* A vision of Chris . . .

◆ ◆ ◆

Stars explode in front of Chris Young's eyes and blood bubbles at his lips. He's dying. He knows he is. The gunman shot three people before Chris even registered what was happening, and now he is striding up the aisle, gun raised, killing everyone in the carriage. Chris has little time to act. The crystal award weighs heavily in his hand, more so in his weakened state. He recalls feeling the sheer weight of it when it was presented to him and when he proudly held it aloft. Best Journalist. *A fine award, but it will serve a greater purpose if only he can find the energy. He conjures up the apparition of his wife, brave Kate, who held his hand all those years ago when he was trapped in a car wreck and who has been by his side ever since. He draws strength from her exactly as he did the day of the car accident. She is the bravest person he has ever met. The image is strong, and he sees her serious face clearly before him.*

'Don't leave me,' he whispers.

'I won't . . . ever,' she replies.

He forces himself from his blood-soaked seat, stumbles down the aisle after the man. He is too late. There are bodies to his left and right, and ahead, a mother and child scream. He must save them. He gasps for breath but pushes forward, ignoring the excruciating agony ripping through his body. The man doesn't hear him until the last minute, and turns. Chris lifts the award, as he did during the ceremony, and brings it crashing down on the side of the man's head. He stares sightlessly at Chris before crumpling and falling to the floor.

The effort has drained him. Chris's knees buckle and he tumbles forward on to the dead man's body. He doesn't question why the gunman has acted. His last thoughts are of his wonderful wife, who stayed with him throughout.

◆　◆　◆

Thoughts of what Chris had endured during his final minutes on the train tugged at her. If Chris could do what he had done, then Kate could do this. She ran her hands along the wall and moved to a second window, shrouded in darkness. There was no sound from it. Keeping her head down, she scurried back to Emma. Morgan appeared from nowhere and regrouped with them.

He spoke quietly. 'The back door is unlocked. I suspect it leads into the kitchen or a utility room leading off it.'

Kate hissed, 'We have to act fast. Sierra's tied up to a chair in the middle of the kitchen and Faith's got a knife.'

'What about her sister?'

'I can't see or hear anybody else, but be mindful Hope might be there. Emma, when I give you the signal, bash on the door and yell Sierra's name as loudly as you can, which should give both of us enough time to enter the house from the rear and jump Faith. This is a hostage situation, so Morgan, I want your priority to be Sierra. Ensure she can't be harmed. Emma, once you've thumped on the door, scoot around the back and join us. All clear?'

'Clear.'

She and Morgan hugged the shadows and stole to the back door. The calf began calling again, but this time Kate ignored it, instead focusing on easing down the back-door handle and slipping inside, into a room that smelt of tropical flowers. They stood in what Morgan had correctly defined as a laundry room – only large enough to house a washing machine and a sink, but big enough for them both to wait for Emma to act.

Faith screamed, 'One last time. Where the fuck is he?'

Sierra sobbed a response. 'I don't know where he is. He said he'd be home soon.'

On cue, Emma pounded on the door, shouting Sierra's name. 'Sierra, it's the police. Open up!'

Faith rushed to the window by the sink to catch sight of who was there, and as she did so, Morgan and Kate burst into the kitchen. Morgan hurtled across the tiled floor towards Sierra, placing his bulky frame between her and Faith. Faith dropped the knife and reached for a frying pan hanging on the wall. She wielded it wildly, swinging it between the two as they approached. 'Stay back,' she hissed.

Kate spoke calmly. 'Put it down, Faith. It's over. We've got you surrounded.'

Morgan took a step closer and Faith swung hard and smashed the pan into his groin, doubling him over. Kate flew at the woman and pushed her into the sink with such force Faith released her grip on the weapon, which clattered to the floor. Arms and hands and legs intermingled as they fought each other. Faith kicked out, catching Kate's shin and causing pain to explode down her leg. Kate winced, eyes watering, but held fast, fingers digging into Faith's arm. Wild with anger, Faith shook herself free and shoved Kate away so hard she fell on to her back, knocking her head against a chair leg. The scene went black for a moment. When she opened her eyes, Faith was straddling her.

Kate twisted her body sharply to the left, then to the right, trying to shake off Faith and free her hands, to no avail. Bony knees dug into her ribs, making it impossible to move. Faith bared her teeth like a wild animal and flexed her long fingers. With immediate clarity, Kate understood what she was about to do. She was going to plunge her fingers into Kate's eyes. Every muscle strained as she bucked and writhed, destabilising Faith sufficiently so her nails raked the flesh of her cheeks, missing their mark. 'Bitch!' hissed Faith. Stinging blows rained down on Kate. This was not the woman with whom she'd shared a glass of wine.

Kate found focus, putting the pain behind her. Everything was happening too quickly, and she inhaled, slowed the events, became fully aware of the contempt flickering across Faith's face, spotted Morgan struggling to his feet. She'd freed her own hands, but kept them by her side for the moment. Time slowed further, and she locked eyes with Faith, gave a relaxed smile and waited for the woman to strike again. Faith snarled, curled her fingers and raised her hands, and only then did Kate react, with lightning reflexes, grabbing hold of the woman's wrists and yanking them backwards with as much strength as she could muster. Faith screamed.

Morgan appeared, wrapped strong arms around Faith's upper body and hauled her off Kate, threw her to the floor and dropped on to her legs. Within seconds, Emma had joined him. He cuffed Faith and sat on his knees, head back.

'Are you okay?' asked Emma.

'Bitch whacked me in the Crown Jewels, but I'll survive.'

Kate wiped away blood from her scratched cheeks with the back of her hand and looked across at Sierra. 'How many women? How many came in?'

The girl's face was ashen. 'Her. Just her.'

Morgan and Emma yanked a subdued Faith to her feet and frogmarched her outside while Kate cut the cable ties binding Sierra and helped her stand up.

'Are you all right?' asked Kate.

Sierra rubbed her tender wrists and nodded. 'She scared the shit out of me. She was going to kill me. She wanted to kill Dad, too. Do you know where he is?'

'He's safe. He's at the station. You can see him soon. Are you sure you're not injured?'

'I'm fine. I only let her in because she was pregnant and upset and her shoe was broken.'

'She wasn't pregnant.'

'Her belly was swollen.'

'She faked it.' Kate held up the jumper that had fallen out during the scuffle. 'She made it up so you'd let her in.'

The girl stared wide-eyed at the jumper.

'You've had a dreadful shock. We're going to take you with us, back to the station. Is there anybody we can ring to come with you? A relative, perhaps?'

'There's only my dad. He's all I have.' Sierra's voice cracked, and Kate's heart sank. The girl was about to lose the one person who meant everything to her. Cooper would most likely be imprisoned. Kate knew what it was like to lose those you cared most about, but life was like that. It dealt cruel blows and you had to learn to survive. Sierra would, like Kate, learn quickly enough.

'You'll be able to talk to your dad there,' she said, confident she could arrange for them to have some time together. She wished she could have had more real time with Chris, even if it was only five minutes.

CHAPTER
FIFTY-ONE

THURSDAY, 10 JUNE – EARLY MORNING

Faith could easily be mistaken for the inquisitor rather than the accused, her face searching Kate's eyes, scanning for signs of weakness. She sat upright, hands loosely folded in her lap. There was nothing in her body language to suggest she was a murderer. Kate found her attitude unnerving. She'd opened up to this woman, told her things about herself she'd told nobody before, and hadn't seen through her act. The pills and her fixation on Dickson had blurred all senses and almost cost her this investigation. While Kate was angry about Faith's deception, she was more furious with herself. Her head screamed at her to punish this woman, be as hard as she could on her, yet she needed to keep Faith on side because she could be instrumental in bringing down Dickson.

'We have sufficient proof to place you at the Maddox Club. The blood we found on the paperweight and the carpet is yours. We've uncovered vials of the drug GHB in one of the suitcases in the boot of a Kia rented in your name. Moreover, we have identified the body in the grounds of the Maddox Club as your nephew, Joseph Masuku. We know you murdered Alex Corby, Ian Wentworth and Xavier Durand. The tech department examined the sat nav in the

VW Polo you borrowed from the car pool and have been able to trace all your movements. You may have thought you'd erased the history, but as you know, our technical team have tremendous skills and have retrieved the information.

'Not only does it place you at the Maddox Club on Monday evening, but also at Alex's house last Thursday morning. You arrived at eleven-fifty and left two hours later. We also know you travelled to Lichfield and parked in the car park near Festival House twice on Saturday – once in the afternoon at one fifteen for half an hour, and then again in the evening at eight thirty until eleven twenty-four. Is there anything you wish to say?'

'No comment.'

Kate glanced over at the plain-faced young solicitor with a starchy attitude who'd been assigned the case. She didn't look much older than Sierra. Her face was as immobile as a china doll's and her eyes were fixed on her notepad. She clearly wasn't going to encourage her client to divulge any information. Kate would have to use the only weapon she had. She glanced at Morgan, next to her, who was aware of her intentions.

'Then you leave me no option. I'm sure Hope will be more accommodating, although I shall be obliged to charge her for aiding and abetting a criminal.'

Faith rose to the bait. 'Hope is in Zimbabwe.'

Morgan shook his head. 'Hope Masuku was detained earlier at Heathrow Airport and is currently in a police vehicle on her way here for questioning in connection with these murders.'

'No. You're bluffing,' Faith scoffed.

Kate spoke smoothly. 'I can assure you DS Meredith is telling the truth. He spoke to the officer who apprehended her at the gate.'

'She left first thing yesterday morning on a coach from Stoke station. I put her on it myself. Her flight left in the evening. She isn't here.'

Morgan turned over the printout of an email on the desk in front of him and read, 'Last evening, at seven minutes past ten, while waiting at Boarding Gate B38 for the eight forty Emirates flight to Harare, delayed by two hours, Mrs Hope Masuku was apprehended. She did not resist arrest and has been held by Metropolitan Police overnight.'

Faith remained silent, nostrils flaring.

'Right, then I suggest this interview is over. DS Meredith, if you wouldn't mind turning off the recorder, please, and then escorting Faith to the cells. We'll speak again later. And, DS Meredith, please call me when Hope Masuku arrives.' Kate pushed back her chair.

Before she reached the door, Faith spoke up. 'Hope had nothing to do with any of this.'

Kate turned around. 'With any of what?'

'The deaths. She only wanted me to find Joseph.'

Kate returned to her seat, pursed her lips in thought, then shook her head. 'No. Sorry. I find that difficult to believe. This is the only time Hope has visited you since you arrived in the UK, and it coincides with the death of three men. She stayed in your apartment with you. She will surely have had an inkling of what was going on. I'm afraid we shall be looking to charge her.'

'She doesn't know anything. She doesn't even know Joseph is dead. I couldn't tell her. Not until I'd found him.'

'I can't take your word for that.' Kate folded her arms, her head on one side. 'So, it's up to you, Faith. You tell me everything – every single detail, or we'll find plenty of reasons to charge your sister. What's it to be?'

Faith's lips curled. 'You hard-faced bitch!'

◆　◆　◆

Faith packs away her notes with a sense of purpose and satisfaction. The job at Coventry is not demanding, but her reputation is growing. If she continues to impress, she'll be promoted, and when the time is right, she'll return home and lecture in Harare, maybe give others the same opportunities she's had. Not bad for a poor girl from Juliasdale who, according to all the locals, had few prospects. She had showed them all. Only her sister believed in her. Hope encouraged her every step of the way, even sending her money she could ill afford to help her through her studies in Harare. Since she's been in the UK, Faith has managed to study and work part-time, washing up at a restaurant, so she is able to help her sister out.

She's closing her worn leather case when her phone rings. Her sister is in tears.

'Hope, what's the matter?'

Hope works in an orchard outside Juliasdale. It's a low-paid job but it is all she can get, given she fell pregnant at fifteen, didn't finish her education and was widowed three years ago.

'He's gone. Joseph has gone. He and Abel have run away.'

'They'll be back. You know what they're like. A week on their own and they'll return with their tails between their legs.' Although the words are meant to be reassuring, Faith's heart flutters like a butterfly trapped in a net. Fourteen-year-old Joseph is everything to Hope, and to her. He's a handsome and gentle lad. Abel, on the other hand, is a troublemaker – a likeable boy, but not averse to breaking the law. The pair are incredibly close and she fears Joseph has been tempted by his friend to get involved in something he ought not to be.

'Daniel says they paid somebody to take them abroad, to the UK.'

Daniel is another of Joseph and Abel's friends, but Faith finds the story incredible. 'Where would they find money to pay for anyone to transport them?'

'Abel . . . he's been involved again in drug-dealing. There were men in the town. I heard they were letting it be known they could get people out, away to Europe. I never thought for one minute—' Sobs render her speechless.

Faith freezes to the spot. She has heard of citizens attempting to make the ridiculously long journey to escape poverty, and even the political situation in their own country, but Joseph? 'Why would he do such a thing?'

'Elijah Falade.'

Elijah was held in esteem in Juliasdale. According to local myth, in 2000, at the age of seventeen, he made his way to the UK and started work in a restaurant, rising to manager within a few years, and moved to the USA, where he opened his own restaurant. His mother and cousin had disappeared one night and everyone believed they had gone to join Elijah. Faith had her own suspicions as to the truth of the story, but the youngsters in the town had believed it and Abel, for one, had often talked about becoming as successful as Elijah.

'What are we going to do?' asks Hope.

'Have you reported him missing?'

'Don't be stupid! Nobody is going to help me or my boy. They don't care. The police aren't going to waste time hunting for a potential refugee.'

It was true. Faith knew they would never trace him, and if the boys had reached the UK alive, the authorities there wouldn't hunt for them. 'What do Abel's parents think?'

'It's a good thing he's gone. They've five other mouths to feed and Abel was always getting into trouble – trouble they could do without. But you know that Joseph is everything to me,' says Hope. 'He's the only good thing in my life . . . so like his father. When I look into his eyes, I see Timothy.' The groan she emits lasts for an eternity. 'It's like losing my man all over again. I can't experience such pain a second time.'

Faith is heartbroken. Hope and Joseph are her flesh and blood. She loves them both with all her heart. 'What can I do, Hope?'

'You're in the UK. Find him, please. Please find my boy.'

◆ ◆ ◆

Faith spoke in a monotonous tone, as if each word were being plucked reluctantly from her lips. 'We had no option but to find him ourselves. We spoke to all their friends and eventually found out the boys were headed to Stoke-on-Trent to meet a man called Farai, who Abel knew via his drug-dealing contacts. Although I had the job in Coventry, I needed to be in Stoke to search for them, so I emailed Ervin. He said there were no positions available but he'd bear me in mind when he was looking for somebody to join the team. I was stuck in Coventry and travelled back and forth to Stoke in my free time. Several months passed, during which time we had no news of either boy. But finally, I got a lead.'

◆   ◆   ◆

Faith has travelled up and down to Stoke every weekend since the phone call from Hope, and tried every refugee centre, hostel, church, library and homeless charity she can locate. She's had little luck, other than a lead from a Reverend Father, but today she has heard where she might find Farai, the man the boys came in search of. It's cost her a hundred pounds of her salary and she now finds herself under a bridge on a dark January morning. It smells of urine and something else, the stale taint of unwashed humans. This is where many of the city's homeless end up at night when they can no long hide in the warmth of libraries or drop-in centres. She wraps her scarf more tightly around her neck. She is due in at work in an hour and she still has to travel back to Coventry. She'll be late, but if she gets news about Joseph and Abel, it will be worth it.

She turns at the sound of approaching feet. A tall, skinny figure is walking towards her, and next to him, a smaller ragamuffin whom she instantly recognises. It is Abel. She rushes towards the boy, eyes brimming. At last, she has found him. He stands rigid in her embrace, not the reaction she had expected, and she holds him at arm's length, stares into his cloudy eyes.

401

'Abel, it's me, Faith. Joseph's aunt. I came to find you and take you home.'

His hair is filthy, and he runs a grubby hand under his nose. 'I'm not going back.'

She looks at the skinny man, cheeks so sunken his face resembles a skull. 'What have you done to him?'

'Me? Nothing,' he booms in a deep voice. 'Kid don't want to go back, then I'm not gonna make him go back. You seen him, so you can leave.'

'Wait a minute. Where's Joseph?'

'I don't know no Joseph. I only hang with my brother Abel here. He's a good kid. He helps with the business.'

She catches the drift of his meaning. Abel is part of some drug ring, and judging by his appearance, partakes more than he ought to. She tries again, speaking directly to the boy. 'Your family miss you.'

The man laughs loudly. 'Sure they do. I seen them runnin' around, lookin' for him. She messin' with your head, baby boy. Your family don't give a fuck. Come on. We're going.' He begins to walk away, Abel trailing in his wake like an obedient puppy.

Faith shouts out, 'No! I'll pay you.'

The man turns. 'Two hundred.'

'I don't have two hundred.'

'What you got?'

She gets out her wallet. There's about one hundred and twenty pounds in it for food and travel. It's all she has until she next gets paid. 'Take it all, but tell me where I can find Joseph.'

She pulls out the notes, waves them at him, and his yellow eyes count them greedily. He holds out his palm.

'Tell me first.'

He licks his lips. 'Joseph was too pretty for this game. He was destined for another career path.'

'You're making no sense.'

402

Abel opened his mouth. 'He means a sex worker.'

Faith can barely catch her breath. 'Where? What?'

'You got your information. Hand over the payment,' says Farai.

She pleads with Abel. 'Where is he, Abel? He can't enjoy that work. Tell me where he is so I can at least talk to him. Please! His mamma is going out of her head with worry. I've spent months trying to find him. Help us.'

The tall man licks his lips again. 'You can't talk to him. He didn't come back from a job.'

'What do you mean?' The words splutter from her lips.

For the first time, Farai's face shows a glimpse of sadness, of humanity. 'I mean, sister, your boy, Joseph, went to some private members' club to pleasure a client and he never came back.'

'Which club?'

'It's called the Maddox Club.'

'Who did Joseph meet there?'

'A gentleman client. Joseph's pimp says they're not gentlemen. They've been offering a Gold Service and using his girls and boys for a while. He knows full well what they get up to in the club bedrooms. The day after Joseph went missin', the pimp is told the Gold Service is over and if ever he mentions a word about hirin' out boys and girls to the Maddox Club, he will get more than he bargained for. They have friends in high places.'

'When did this happen?'

'January the second.'

Faith's heart is jack-hammering in her chest. 'Is he . . . is Joseph dead?'

'He would never have left Abel. They were tight. Something bad happened to him to stop him coming home.'

'Abel?'

The boy shrugs. 'It's true.'

'Who can I speak to? I have to know exactly what happened. Please, Farai. You're the only one who can help me.'

403

He stares at her hard. She's sure he knows more.

'Please, Farai. For his mamma's sake.'

'Okay. There's someone. That night, one of the girls was with another client, in the room next to Joseph's. She heard screams. She asked the gentleman to go next door and make sure Joseph was okay, but he wouldn't. He was in the zone, if you catch my drift. Bastard is called Alex Corby.'

'Alex Corby. Can I speak to the girl?'

'No. I told you what she told her pimp. You find Alex Corby and ask him about the Gold Service.'

'Is that the only name she knew?'

'Isn't it enough?'

'Who was with Joseph? Please. Maybe the girl heard another name. Please, Farai. Joseph and his mamma are all I have in the world.'

'Maybe another name. Somebody called Ian. He's Alex's friend. You ask Alex about him. Pimp don't know no more.'

'Who's this pimp? I want to speak to him.'

'You just have, sister. That's everything he knows. Now, hand over the money.'

She does so, eyes once more on Abel. 'Abel, come back with me. You don't have to do this.'

Abel gives her a vague look. 'I'm happy here, Faith. I like Farai. He's good to me.'

'But I can look after you,' she says.

Farai places a hand on the boy's shoulder. 'Don't you worry 'bout Abel. I'll look after him. He's gonna be just fine.'

'Please. Please do look after him.' Her words are lost as both turn their backs and walk away. She is hollow. Every emotion has been extracted and she is left with only one thought – revenge.

◆ ◆ ◆

The room was warm and stuffy, and damp patches had formed under Kate's arms. The sadness of the tale was affecting her, and withdrawal from the medication was making her increasingly uncomfortable, but she didn't stop the interview. It was being video recorded, and next door, Emma and William would be watching how she handled everything. There could be no slip-ups.

Faith had unwittingly given her a clue. He'd mentioned a threat: 'friends in high places'. *Dickson?* She couldn't pursue that angle at the moment, not with William observing, but she hoped they'd be able to track down Farai to quiz him. Faith looked fatigued; dark patches under her eyes indicated lack of sleep. This quest had taken its toll on her. For a flicker of a second, Kate felt something akin to sympathy, but it vanished as quickly as it had appeared.

'Tell me what happened with Ian Wentworth. Why did you go back twice to his apartment?'

'I took the day off and planned to kill him, but no sooner had I drugged him than Ervin messaged me, asking me to go into work because they were so short-staffed. I gave Ian an extra-large shot of GHB to keep him unconscious and left him tied up, and returned to his apartment later the same day.'

'I spoke to you in the lab Saturday evening.'

'Yes. I'd intended leaving earlier but Ervin had to go out and asked me to stay behind to speak to you. It was a bit of a nuisance, but better to play the part than disappear and draw attention to myself. I left as soon as you'd gone and headed back to Lichfield.'

◆　◆　◆

Ian's fat cheek lolls to one side, his neck creased like an elephant's trunk. He's barely articulate, but another boost of the drug has rendered him compliant and he answers her questions.

'Do you know a boy called Joseph?'

'Beautiful boy. The best.'

'Did you have sex with him in the Maddox Club?'

'Poor boy. So perfect . . . so delicious . . . I broke him!' he wails.

'How did you break him?'

'No . . . no . . . no. Awful. Mistake. I should have taken the bag from his head in time but I was enjoying myself so much and . . .' Tears flow from his eyes. 'Broken,' he whispers.

'What happened to his body?'

'Xavier . . . Xavier fixed it. So sorry. So sorry.'

'Xavier who?'

'Manager.' Ian recedes to unconsciousness and she is sick to her stomach. This repulsive creature ruined the most precious human being, dehumanised him for self-gratification and perverted pleasure. She forces open his mouth, shoves in the choke-pear. She is going to kill him. This time she doesn't need to ask questions, just make him fully aware why she is torturing him. She waits. He'll soon come back round.

The walls in the interview room closed in on Kate. The urge to ask about John Dickson was strong, but she was afraid whatever Faith told her would reach her superintendent's ears before she got the chance to act on it. He might even be watching the interview, rammed in the room beside Emma and William. She had to tread carefully. 'Why did you leave Ian's eye on Superintendent Dickson's doorstep?'

Faith held her gaze, arms loose by her side, her whole face relaxed. 'Why do you think?'

'I'm asking you.'

'He was at the club the night Joseph died. He was in the room the other side of Ian's and would have heard the screams. If Alex

Corby heard them, then he did, too, and is as guilty as Alex. In fact, more so. He's a police officer. He ought to have acted like one.'

Although Kate agreed, and knew Dickson ought to have been suspicious, especially when Ian didn't show up at breakfast, she didn't want to pursue that line of enquiry. She had to behave as if she fully supported the man. 'Was he your next intended victim?'

'Yes, but he was moved into safe keeping. You lot like to look after your own, don't you?'

'What do you mean?'

'You gave him protection but you didn't offer any to Cooper or Xavier.'

'At that stage of the enquiry, we didn't know about their involvement.'

Faith lifted an eyebrow. 'Come off it! Superintendent Dickson knew who was at the club with him. He would have passed the information on to you.'

Kate maintained a poker face in spite of her inner voice agreeing with Faith. Dickson could and ought to have shared his fears, but he'd chosen not to, and that in itself was suspicious. She moved on, anxious to keep such thoughts to herself. Faith couldn't have known what had been shared and not shared. She believed Dickson would have told them.

'Did Xavier tell you about Cooper Monroe's involvement?'

'Yes. He blabbed and begged me not to kill him. He whimpered and fawned and swore he knew nothing about Joseph being at the club. According to him, the Gold Service was all Ian's idea, and the first he'd known about Joseph was when Ian rang him on the internal phone and asked for Cooper. I saw straight through him. Farai told me he had dealt with the club manager, not a member. Xavier arranged for sex workers to be delivered to the club.'

'Why didn't you didn't torture Xavier the same way as the others?'

Faith shrugged. 'I lost patience with him. I saw the peanuts in the bowl and used those instead of an apple. It was an interesting end to his life. I think he genuinely repented.'

The lawyer remained stony-faced, as she had done all interview, legs crossed neatly at the ankles, making notes in a tiny scrawl on her pad.

'That brings me to the device you used. What made you choose a choke-pear?'

'My ex-husband. I met him when I was studying at Harare. He taught European history and specialised in medieval history. He kept a small collection of torture devices in a glass cabinet in his office, among them a choke-pear. The marriage broke down, but I never forgot the choke-pear, and when I decided to torture my victims I decided it would suit my purpose. I couldn't simply buy one, so I had it made to order.'

'By whom?'

'A blacksmith from Derby called George Coombs. I emailed him my design and asked him to make it for me. I told him it was a present for my husband, who was a historian.'

'And he didn't think it was odd?'

'He didn't ask me any questions and was happy to take my money. He seemed to believe me. I can be convincing when I choose to be.'

Kate balled her hand tightly. Faith had certainly pulled the wool over her eyes. 'Tell me, Faith, why did you choose apples?'

'Is it not obvious to you? You're an intelligent woman.'

'It's a symbol of fertility and I understand its significance in the Bible, when Eve tempted Adam with an apple – the symbol of original sin. Is that why you chose it?'

'Partly. I was *enlightening* each of those men responsible for what happened to Joseph. The apple is a complex symbol. It can mean love, joy, wisdom, luxury or death, depending on the context in which you view it. But I prefer the idea of it as the biblical symbol of original sin. The sin that brought about the fall of men. Certainly, it brought about the fall of *these* men.'

There was no sense of regret or remorse. Faith had avenged a wrong and, in her mind, that was acceptable.

'Was there any reason you chose the Macoun variety? Was it because your sister works in an orchard where they grow the same variety?'

The woman put her hands together and applauded lightly. 'Well done.'

'What about the number of pieces? You cut them into thirteen pieces.'

Faith scoffed. 'I don't need to spell it out, do I?'

'I'd still like to hear your thoughts.'

She sighed. 'Thirteen is associated with bad luck. The superstition comes from the Bible again, when the thirteenth guest to sit at the table during the Last Supper was Judas Iscariot, who later betrayed Jesus. It seemed fitting. After all, I wanted them to betray their friends, and they were about to receive the worst sort of luck possible – death.'

'And removing the victims' eyes? Also related to the Bible – an eye for an eye?'

'In a fashion. It was more because I wanted to frighten them, let them know somebody had their eye on them, that somebody *knew* what they had done. It seemed a fitting message.'

'Which leaves us with Cooper. I suppose you wanted to kill him, too? You took the choke-pear with you. We found it in your car, although we couldn't find any apples. What did you intend to do to him?'

'You can't torture a man like him. He has had special training and would never confess to anything. Cooper is the only person who knows where Joseph is buried. He would have told me what I wanted to know, because I'd have held his daughter hostage and he wouldn't have wanted any harm to come to her.'

'You said you didn't tell Hope her son was dead.'

'Correct. I wanted undeniable proof. I promised I would find him, and I intended keeping my promise. Where did you find him?'

Kate looked down at the desk, pausing for a heartbeat before she told Faith what she'd been trying to find out for so long. 'A clearing in the woods in the grounds of the Maddox Club.'

'I suspected Cooper might have hidden him somewhere nearby. Can I see him?'

'Maybe we can arrange it. Tell me, Faith, why did Hope come to the UK?'

Faith's mouth twisted downwards. 'She'd been trying to get to the UK ever since Joseph went missing. She saved up all the money I sent her. She didn't tell me she'd finally been granted a visa and just turned up out of the blue. She almost messed up my plans.'

'I'm struggling to understand this. You killed three people while she stayed with you. You were out at all hours and throughout the time she stayed with you, yet she had no idea of what you were up to.'

'Luckily for me, she caught a stomach virus and was bed-bound for a great deal of the time. I told her I was part of an investigation, which explained my hours, and insisted she stay at home when I was out.'

'The virus only lasts a few days. She would have recovered within four days.'

'No. I made sure she didn't. I put small doses of laxative in her food. It was the only way to keep her out of all this. She had no idea. I swear she didn't.'

Kate was still not convinced. Hope and Faith were extremely close. There was every chance Hope knew exactly what her sister was up to and Faith was now protecting her. Kate would have to see how she reacted under interrogation.

Faith stared ahead, her perfect features unspoilt by sorrow, but her voice was heavy when she said, 'So, if the flight had been on time, she'd be on her way home as we speak.'

Kate still had an important question to ask. 'Why did you go to such extraordinary lengths to torture and murder these men? You could have gone to the police after you spoke to Farai, not taken matters into your own hands.'

'Gone to the police? Begged for help! Do you actually believe the police would have wasted precious resources searching for an illegal immigrant who'd turned to prostitution? Don't make me laugh. You're off your head if you believe that for one second.'

'His disappearance would have been investigated.'

'Do *you* think it's a fair system, DI Young? A *just* system where every citizen is treated equally?'

Kate held her gaze. 'I think we'll leave it there for the moment. You shouldn't have taken matters into your own hands, Faith. The police *would* have handled this for you.'

There was a pause and Kate thought they'd come to the end of the interview. But Faith didn't move, eyes locked on Kate's. She dropped her voice. 'You don't really believe that, do you? Open your eyes and look around you, Kate.'

Her cold stare was filled with hostility. Kate cursed herself for having been duped by this woman who'd only ever intended to use her for her own means. She swallowed the bitter taste rising in her mouth. Faith was cold, calculating and vengeful. In spite of all that, Kate couldn't disagree with her. Had she reported her suspicions to the police, it was almost certain they wouldn't have received the attention they warranted, especially given John Dickson's involvement with the Maddox Club and friendships with Alex and Ian.

Faith continued to hold her gaze. They might not be friends, but they shared common goals; a desire to uncover the truth and hold those responsible accountable for their actions. It was unlikely Faith would have got the justice she really wanted for her nephew any more than Kate would for Chris's death. Not unless she took matters into her own hands. Kate didn't flinch at Faith's words. She knew the woman was right, and she had a journal that would substantiate those claims.

CHAPTER FIFTY-TWO

THURSDAY, 10 JUNE – EARLY MORNING

Faith was charged at last. There was still her sister, Hope, to interview, but Kate allowed herself a breather. She stood outside the station. It was 3 a.m. and the only sound came from the odd car passing by on the main road. She sensed rather than heard William next to her.

'Great job, Kate.'

'I don't think so. It would have been a better outcome if we'd been on top of this before it got out of hand. She foxed us for a long while.'

'You were on her tail.'

Kate breathed out softly. 'And she's right. If she'd come to the station and told us about her nephew, he'd have only been marked down as a missing person. We wouldn't have spent the number of man hours searching for him that this case has forced us to.'

'Kate, listen to me. You saved Sierra and Cooper. You might even have saved Raymond Maddox, who, by the way, wasn't at the club the night Joseph died. I have been assured he only dropped by on the evening of January the second on his way to the airport, and left soon afterwards. His story checks out. You did an outstanding job. You're one of the best we have.'

'Then heaven help us all,' she replied, and without a further word, walked back inside.

◆ ◆ ◆

Three hours later, she drew up outside her own home. Blackbirds sang heartily as she unlocked her front door.

'I'm home,' she called.

There was, as she expected, no reply. Although he was dead, she simply couldn't break the habit of talking to him.

The journal was exactly where she'd left it in the cereal box. She extracted it from its hiding place and sat at the kitchen table, an invisible fog of sadness enveloping her as she felt the indentations on the exterior, knowing Chris's hands had touched it, and hoped by some process of osmosis that any left-over energy would be transmitted to her. She missed him with all her heart, soul and every atom of her being.

She turned to the first page, read the names and details Chris had written in fountain pen. These were people he suspected were part of a paedophile ring, presumably the one he and Dan had been investigating. How Chris had uncovered all this was a mystery, but he had interviewed victims and put together a comprehensive package pointing to a number of people, including names she recognised: celebrities, heads of institutions, others from educational establishments and even some clergy. If he'd written the article or articles, it would have blown careers, families and lives apart. The pages were documented with dates and websites and even meetings when victim and abuser had come together. She remained unaware of the time as she read on, and only when her eyes slid over and stopped on four words did she pause. Chris had written, 'Gold Service, Maddox Club'.

◆ ◆ ◆

'You knew,' she whispered.

'I suspected, but you uncovered the truth. I was close to exposing them.'

She read on. 'The prostitutes weren't of legal age.'

'Some were, but Xavier also requested children, especially boys.'

'Do you think Dickson slept with an underage girl?'

'I do, but you would need to prove it.'

'Faith mentioned a pimp called Farai. If I could track him down, he might be able to tell me who he sent on the second of January when Dickson, Corby and Wentworth were at the club. Joseph was under age. The Bulgarian girls might have been, too.'

◆ ◆ ◆

She stood up at once. She needed to search Chris's den. There might be even more information in there.

The door opened silently and she switched on the light, waiting for it to emit a soft glow before she entered. A crisp bluebottle lay on its back next to the dusty keyboard. Although the computer on the desk remained plugged in, it was password protected, so she'd not even attempted to turn it on. It would have been pointless. She didn't know his access code.

She had to track down and talk to Farai.

'What will you do if you find him and he confesses the girls were under age?'

'I'm not sure yet. One step at a time. It would be something to prove Dickson lied.'

'Think about this before you dive in. Who's going to believe the testimony of a pimp against a superintendent in the police force? He might have egg on his face about sleeping once with a prostitute, but he won't lose his position. It won't expose him,' said Chris.

'But he knew about Ian and Joseph. He ought to have stepped in that night, or at least helped direct the investigation in the right direction.'

'Ah, Kate. You're up against it. You'll be the one who will suffer in that battle. You'll need more ammunition than supposition and the word of a pimp.'

Her head fell back against Chris's leather chair and she groaned. Chris was right. She couldn't bring down her superior with such flimsy evidence. The overhead bulb was dimming, the glow flickering, as if about to go out. She reached forward to flick on the desk lamp and her hand brushed against the keyboard. The computer came to life with a tired wheeze, as if it had been dozing. There was no password as she thought. Chris must have removed it. Behind the dusty screen she saw their faces – her and Chris, laughing, happy, and her eyes filled once more. She pressed the home button and read the document file names, drawn to one entitled *Kate*.

She clicked on it and frowned at the heading, 'Potentially Corrupt – Sensitive Information'.

The photographs were of familiar faces, officers she knew and had worked with. How on earth had Chris come across these people, and what had made him suspect they were corrupt? There were so many – five, six, seven. She paused, cursor hovering over the person she had hoped to bring down – John Dickson. Her

416

pulse quickened. He might slip away this time, but she'd continue to pursue him until she could find something to lead to his downfall. There was another photograph under Dickson's. She scrolled, and as his face came into view, her mouth dropped open. No. He couldn't be.

Looking back at her from the screen was her father's best friend and her mentor, DCI William Chase.

ACKNOWLEDGMENTS

Although my name is on the front cover of this book, I can't take all the credit for it. I might have written it, but I'm hugely grateful to have such a first-rate team of professionals behind me who all played a part in bringing *An Eye for an Eye* to publication.

To everyone at Jane Rotrosen Agency, especially my agent, Amy Tannenbaum, sincere thanks for championing my script.

To my outstanding editor, Jack Butler, who recognised further potential in the script, guided me through the initial processes and teamed me up with the truly awesome Russel McLean. Russel brought masses of enthusiasm and insight to the editing process, transforming *An Eye for an Eye* from a good book into one that makes me ridiculously proud to call it my work. Thanks for the laughs along the way, Russel.

To my sharp-eyed copy-editor, Gill Harvey, and my amazing proofreader, Sarah Day, who are without doubt the best I've ever worked with.

To all the team at Thomas & Mercer involved in getting this book to publication, whose professionalism and expertise have been hugely appreciated.

To my street team and the numerous book bloggers and reviewers who generously help promote my work. Never underestimate how much your support means to us authors.

And to you for purchasing *An Eye for an Eye*. Thank you for your kind messages and emails telling me how much you've enjoyed my work. They mean more than words can convey.

Finally, to my other half, Mr Grumpy. Thank you for your patience and dependable support. You are my world.

ABOUT THE AUTHOR

Winner of The People's Book Prize Award, Carol Wyer is a bestselling author and stand-up comedian who writes feel-good comedies and gripping crime fiction. A move to the 'dark side' in 2017 saw the introduction of popular DI Robyn Carter in *Little Girl Lost*, the #2 bestselling book on Amazon, #9 bestselling audiobook on Audible and Top 150 *USA Today* bestseller. A second series, featuring DI Natalie Ward, quickly followed and to date her crime novels have sold over 750,000 copies and been translated for various overseas markets, including Norwegian, Italian, Turkish, Hungarian Slovak, Czech and Polish. Carol has been interviewed on numerous radio shows discussing 'Irritable Male Syndrome' and 'Ageing Disgracefully', and on *BBC Breakfast* television. She has written for *Woman's Weekly*, *Take A Break*, *Choice*, *Yours*, *Woman's Own* and *HuffPost*. She currently lives on a windy hill in rural Staffordshire with her husband, Mr Grumpy . . . who is very, very grumpy.

To learn more about Carol, go to www.carolwyer.co.uk or follow Carol on Twitter: @carolewyer. Carol also blogs at www.carolwyer.com